SUPERIOR POSITION

Evan McNamara

BERKLEY BOOKS, NEW YORK

THE BERKLEY PUBLISHING GROUP
Published by the Penguin Group
Penguin Group (USA) Inc.
375 Hudson Street, New York, New York 10014, USA
Penguin Group (Canada), 90 Eglinton Avenue East, Suite 700, Toronto, Ontario M4P 2Y3, Canada
(a division of Pearson Penguin Canada Inc.)
Penguin Books Ltd., 80 Strand, London WC2R 0RL, England
Penguin Group Ireland, 25 St. Stephen's Green, Dublin 2, Ireland (a division of Penguin Books Ltd.)
Penguin Group (Australia), 250 Camberwell Road, Camberwell, Victoria 3124, Australia
(a division of Pearson Australia Group Pty. Ltd.)
Penguin Books India Pvt. Ltd., 11 Community Centre, Panchsheel Park, New Delhi—110 017, India
Penguin Group (NZ), Cnr. Airborne and Rosedale Roads, Albany, Auckland 1310, New Zealand
(a division of Pearson New Zealand Ltd.)
Penguin Books (South Africa) (Pty.) Ltd., 24 Sturdee Avenue, Rosebank, Johannesburg 2196,
South Africa

Penguin Books Ltd., Registered Offices: 80 Strand, London WC2R 0RL, England

This is a work of fiction. Names, characters, places, and incidents either are the product of the author's imagination or are used fictitiously, and any resemblance to actual persons, living or dead, business establishments, events, or locales is entirely coincidental. The publisher does not have any control over and does not assume any responsibility for author or third-party websites or their content.

SUPERIOR POSITION

A Berkley Book / published by arrangement with the author

PRINTING HISTORY
Salvo Press / June 2004
Berkley edition / July 2005

Copyright © 2004 by Evan McNamara.
Cover design by Pyrographx.
Map by NH.
Interior text design by Stacy Irwin.

ISBN: 0-425-20390-5

BERKLEY®
Berkley Books are published by The Berkley Publishing Group,
a division of Penguin Group (USA) Inc.,
375 Hudson Street, New York, New York 10014.
BERKLEY is a registered trademark of Penguin Group (USA) Inc.
The "B" design is a trademark belonging to Penguin Group (USA) Inc.

PRINTED IN THE UNITED STATES OF AMERICA

10 9 8 7 6 5 4 3 2 1

To my wife

Acknowledgments

I would like to thank the people of Creede, Colorado, for their hospitality and for their wonderful town. Thanks to Steve Quiller, resident artist, and Kirby Self of the U.S. Forest Service for providing just the right color and species of tree and shrub in Mineral County. Thanks to N. S. Hayden for the perfect artwork.

Most of all, I thank my wife, my trusted reader, and my best friend.

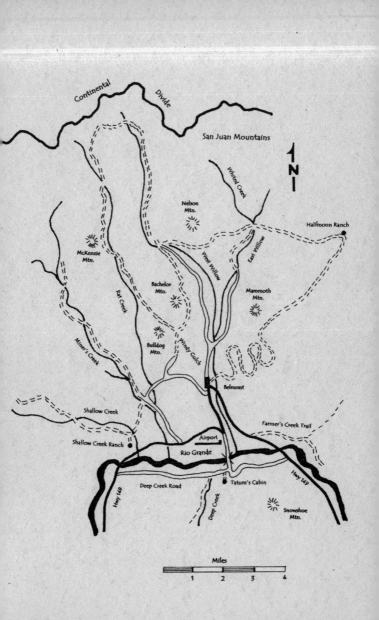

One

S ERGEANT RICHTER LEFT HIS BOOT IN MY ASS. Even after three years out of the Army, I still can't sleep past five in the morning. Waking up early suits my new job, though, so I don't mind much, really, and the San Juan Mountains at sunrise aren't so bad, either. Being a deputy sheriff of Mineral County, Colorado, isn't quite as glamorous as army sniper, but I get to ride a horse and wear a cool hat. Sergeant Richter makes me run, too, not that I have to chase down many purse snatchers in bustling downtown Belmont. Running keeps me in shape, though, and I don't make enough as deputy to afford bigger uniforms every year. The frigid predawn air chilled my lungs and cleared my head as I ran up Deep Creek Trail behind my cabin.

Deep Creek is a narrow, shallow creek fed mostly by runoff from Snowshoe Mountain, one thousand feet up. The creek tumbles north down a narrow valley for nine miles before passing my cabin and dumping into the Rio Grande River. The valley walls are steep—rising sharply in granite cliffs and wooded ridges. Deer and elk run those ridges, and I've hunted both along their trails. The creek dictates the topography of the valley floor, alternating between wide beaver ponds and dense, dark patches of evergreen. Deep Creek is a quiet stream, hardly making its voice heard even during the spring runoff, but I always hear its easy murmur around my cabin and up the trail.

I found the body at the second horse bridge. The beavers had dammed the stream, swelling the little creek into a pond. She was floating face-up near the outlet, sideways to the current; a submerged branch must have held her fast. The force of the current made her rock gently; the fingers of her left hand, pointing downstream, bobbed rhythmically. I saw her eyes first. She looked up at me from under the bridge, and even in the spare light of the new dawn, I could see the amber flecks in her corneas and the black, charred hole in her left temple.

I am a dedicated deputy, but I don't carry my radio when I run. I flew downhill to my cabin and called Marty Three Stones, our night dispatcher.

"Got a body here in Deep Creek, Marty." I was out of breath.

"Elk or deer?" she answered, as if her shift just started.

"Woman, white, approximately age thirty. Looks like a gunshot wound to the head."

"Holy shit, Bill. Did you hear the shot?"

I don't know why Dale, the Mineral County Sheriff, doesn't put Marty in the field. I hadn't even thought of the shot. The body was only two miles upstream from my cabin. In my sleep, I can hear an elk whistle halfway up the valley, but I hadn't heard any shots last night.

"No, Marty, didn't hear a thing. Would you please wake Sheriff Dale and ask him to meet me at my place? Have him bring Jerry, the horse trailer, and an evidence kit, too. I have the camera in my truck."

I have an evidence kit in my truck, too, but this was the first unnatural death in recent Belmont memory, so I figured we would need two. I put some feed in Pancho's trough and dressed while my horse ate. I wouldn't get the same luxury this day, but I did get a cup of coffee in the saddle. I had time to clear my head and observe as Pancho walked back up Deep Creek Trail. About one hundred feet downstream from the bridge and the dead woman, the trail entered a stand of blue spruce and juniper. I dismounted, tied my horse, and looked around.

I approached the bridge with my head down, inspecting the rocky path. I run this trail every day and know every inch of it, otherwise I'd turn my ankle. Walking was different though. I saw details only passed over while running. I saw nothing fresh—no new footprints, other than my own Asics running shoes, no horse tracks, nothing. To my right was a small open patch of turf between the trail and the opposite wall. Alpine meadows in the San Juans are fragile and unchanging—any intrusion leaves an indelible mark impossible to cover. I saw no scars of recent trampling. The woman did not die downstream.

I reached the far edge of the juniper stand. Beavers had dammed the creek near the bridge with an imposing structure of gnawed trees ranging from one to six inches in diameter—an amazing but routine feat for the industrious rodents. The trail ran along the west side of the creek uphill to the beaver dam. There it hopped the stream at the bridge and traversed the valley wall overlooking the large beaver-made pond to the right. This is where I found the body of the young woman.

She was dressed in day-hiker gear—khaki shorts, light-weight boots, long-sleeved shirt with the sleeves rolled up. Her Camelback water sack was still slung over her left arm, floating above her head. Her shoulder-length brown hair was pulled back in a ponytail—I knew that because it was floating, too, blown downstream by the liquid wind of Deep Creek. She looked like she was cooling off after a hot July hike, if it wasn't for the hole in her head.

I started working my way up the trail, looking for any recent sign of human activity. A steep alpine meadow climbed the valley wall to my left. Delicate purple lupine and white chickweed clung to the hillside low to the ground. To my right was a steep ten-foot embankment down to the pond. The beaver pond nearly filled the open area of the valley, tapering off on the uphill side at the inlet of Deep Creek, where the trail entered another dense stand of pine. The high cliffs on either side of the pond created a gorge more than a valley. I looked up the cliff wall to my left and couldn't see the top, only the imposing granite overhang one hundred feet above me. This part of the trail, like the approach to the bridge, was an evidence canvas—footprints, drag marks, or signs of a scuffle would've stood out like spray paint on Mount Rushmore. There just wasn't any sign.

I had just started snapping photos, wondering where her knapsack was, when I heard Sheriff Dale Boggett's voice on my radio.

"Where are you, Tatum?"

"Upstream two miles at the second bridge. Saddle up Pistol, and I hope Jerry brought his horse, too. Can't get a truck up here."

I could see Jerry Pitcher, the other deputy, wince all the way up the trail. Jerry grew up in Belmont but hates horses. He tried to convince Sheriff Dale to invest in all-terrain vehicles, but the sheriff would have nothing of it.

Sheriff Dale and Jerry walked up the trail thirty minutes later. I was glad Dale didn't come riding up on Pistol like a friggin' Mountie, but that's Dale.

"What've we got, Tatum?"

"Female, white, approximately thirty years old, average height and build, dead. Gunshot wound to the head, left temple. She's been here less than twenty-four hours, because I ran by here yesterday morning, and I would've seen her."

"What've you done so far?"

"Cursory inspection of the downstream side of the trail to the site of the body, from where I left Pancho. Found nothing. I took about twenty-four photos of the approach, the bridge, and the body. I walked a bit upstream, but didn't find anything."

"What are you going to do next?"

"Well, I was going to walk up the trail again. I didn't get a chance to go over it thoroughly, and I was hoping you and Jerry could work on the site at the bridge."

"What do you think, so far?"

"Well, sir, it didn't happen here at the bridge or down the trail. I don't even think it happened in Deep Creek at all—I would've heard the shot last night."

"Then how'd she get here?"

"Deep Creek isn't wide enough to float a dead rabbit nine miles downstream, let alone a human body, not with all the beaver dams and deadfall. If she didn't die here, she didn't shoot herself."

"You didn't answer my question, Tatum."

"I am speculating again, Sheriff, but this means whoever killed her had to haul her body nine miles down the trail from the Spar City trailhead, dump her in this pond, ride back to his vehicle, and drive away."

"Looks that way."

Jerry waited a little back down the trail, looking like a scared six-year-old standing behind his mother at the doctor's office. Jerry spent most of his early years in front of a computer or a Game Boy instead of out in the hills surrounding the small town, and his pear shape and sallow complexion showed it. Still, he was a fair administrator; neither Sheriff Boggett nor I enjoyed filing or office work, so Jerry picked up the slack and kept the office running while Sheriff Dale and I were on patrol. Jerry seemed to like the administration, and it meant we had someone to work dispatch when Marty Three Stones was off-shift. If I wasn't careful, though, Jerry would administrate himself right into the Mineral County Sheriff's office. His father owned the local repertory theater and two souvenir shops on Main Street. Thomas Pitcher was also the senior member on the town council, and his influence landed his son the position as the other deputy.

"Well, Tatum, unless you need to take any more photos, let's get her out of the water."

Sheriff Dale and I stepped into the pond and lifted her up to Jerry, who was standing on the bridge. She wasn't heavy, no more than one hundred twenty pounds with wet clothing and full Camelback. It wasn't until we turned her over and saw the gaping red hole in her back that I realized she'd been shot more than once.

The neat hole in her chest was obscured by her shirt. The bullet expanded after impact and blew most of her right lung out her back through a softball-sized hole.

"Oh my God, oh my God," Jerry stammered. He was losing it.

"Easy there, big fella," said Dale. "Just ease her up there, then do your business."

Jerry did both. Luckily, he did it on the downstream side of the bridge, leaving the crime scene unblemished. Who said Jerry didn't have an instinct for criminal investigation?

"Okay, Tatum," said Dale, after we got back up on the trail, "go ahead and continue your inspection upstream. Jerry and I will work here." Jerry didn't look too happy about this, but he knew better than to argue. His heart wasn't in it, anyway. I left them at the bridge and went upstream.

As I neared the south end of the beaver pond, I looked up from the trail and saw something in the spruce trees ahead—a swatch of color—red, not blood, but red, like a backpack, off the trail to the right, just inside the tree line. I took one step toward it, and the sharp crack of a rifle ripped through the gorge.

The shot came from behind me and to the left from the top of the cliff. I hit the ground and slid off the trail down the embankment, trying to put some terrain between the shooter and me. Sergeant Richter saves my ass again. When I heard the screaming, though, I realized I wasn't the target.

"Jerry's down," I heard Sheriff Dale on the radio. "Stay low and get over here. I need you."

"Roger," I called back. Dale knew I had combat medical and EMT training in the army and unfortunately had a chance to use it in Afghanistan.

The screaming continued, echoing off the rocks and drowning out the sound of falling water. At least he wasn't dead, but it sounded like he would be soon. I scrambled along the steep bank back to the bridge. There, I found Sheriff Dale in the water under the bridge, and Jerry writhing in pain next to the body of the dead woman. The left leg of his uniform trousers was soaked red to the ankle from the hole in his thigh. I could see his blood dripping through the slats in the bridge and into the water.

"He is going to die very soon unless I get a tourniquet on him," I said, hopping up on the bridge, undoing my service belt. "Call Marty and have the Lifeflight scramble out of Pueblo."

Sheriff Dale made the call from the creek, still scanning the eastern ridge for a muzzle flash. As I cinched the belt around Jerry's hefty upper thigh, I waited for another shot and a crushing impact. Jerry got very quiet all of a sudden and stopped thrashing.

"He's in shock, Sheriff Dale," I said. "We need to move him, now."

Dale and I were faced with a challenge. We had a crime scene to secure and a critical patient to evacuate. There was nowhere for the Lifeflight helicopter to land in the valley other than the municipal airport across the river. Luckily, the Deep Creek trailhead was only about a mile from the airfield, but we would have to leave the bridge temporarily to get Jerry back down the hill to the helicopter. In addition, I wasn't certain I wanted to hang around with a sniper in a superior position—not only was he above us on the ridge, the morning sun was behind him as well, making it impossible for me to see a muzzle flash. The tree line was only thirty feet away and our horses one hundred feet down the trail. My own rifle was tucked in its scabbard on Pancho's saddle, painfully out of reach.

The sheriff was big, broad shouldered and raw-boned. He took one last look up at the cliff, got out of the water, hoisted Jerry up in a fireman's carry, and started back down the trail toward the tree line. Just then, I heard an engine start from up on the ridge.

"Get the evidence and meet me at the station."

I assumed he meant the only evidence we'd collected so far—the body. I wasn't about to go back up the trail and reenter the field of fire to retrieve a backpack I may or may not have seen, so I picked up the dead woman and followed Sheriff Dale down the trail.

Jerry's horse was none too happy about the dead body lashed across his back, so Sheriff Dale was gone by the time I got back to the cabin. I heard the roar of an engine and the sputter of loose gravel at the end of my drive. Sheriff Dale didn't have time to unhook the horse trailer from his Bronco, so he took mine. He knew I kept the keys in the glove compartment. I secured the horses in the corral and took the body to the station.

As I crossed the bridge over the Rio Grande, I heard the Lifeflight helicopter coming up the valley from the east, over Wagon Wheel Gap. Jerry might make it, after all. I knew the medic on the Pueblo medevac—he was a real Army medic, learning his trade in Panama in 1989 with the special forces and in the Kansas City Knife and Gun Club after that. If Jerry were still alive when he got on Nick's chopper, he would make it. The big, red Kawasaki BK117 swooped into the valley and raced up the river toward the airport.

Two

THE BELMONT STRETCH OF THE RIO GRANDE Valley is a wide, twenty-mile caldera of flat, semi-arid plain surrounded by the ten-thousand-foot San Juan mountain range. The river meanders west to east from one side of the valley to the other, carving rocky gorges and hiding under soft cattle banks. Light green aspen forests cover the lower haunches of the mountains, while spruce and juniper line the damp draws and intermittent streams up to the tree line. Even in July, snow caps the upper summits of the peaks to the north along the Continental Divide.

Small communities of vacation homes and cabins dot the valley floor, clustering near the river and Highway 149, which generally follows the river's looping course. The most striking feature in the valley is a gaping crack in the north wall. The town of Belmont is tucked in this steep draw near the junction of two mountain streams, Willow and East Willow Creek. Tall cliffs and rocky ledges run right up against the homes and businesses of the town.

In 1887, Alfred Belmont discovered a river of silver in the cliffs above Willow Creek north of Belmont, and the term "Mother Lode" was born. Belmont is still a real-live boomtown—it even has a functional silver mine in hibernation, waiting for the price of silver to go up. Now, the town survives on tourism, art galleries, and the repertory theater. Like most mountain towns, the six hundred residents make their money from May through September, then hunker down for the winter and gut it out until the tourists come back.

I drove through downtown, past the false fronts of the galleries and shops, and pulled into the town hall parking lot by the coroner's office. The Belmont municipal building served as the town hall, sheriff's station, and county coroner's office. The building had a single cold storage unit for the recently dead. I unlocked the outside access door, lifted the body onto the roll-in roll-out gurney, and sealed it up again. Then I called Dr. Ed.

"Morning Dr. Ed, it's Bill Tatum."

"The morning's halfway over, Deputy Bill. Are you on banker's hours? I just saw you drive through town. Marty beat you to work by an hour."

I didn't realize it was already ten A.M. Four and a half hours had passed since I found the body on Deep Creek Trail.

"Got something here in the coroner's office you may want to take a look at."

"Well, I know it's not a fish, because you catch and release, unlike some of these Texas tourists invading our shores, pulling all the good trout out of the river. I'll be right over."

Sheriff Dale walked in just as I took the first sip of my second cup of coffee, waiting for Dr. Ed to come over.

"What did Nick say?" I asked.

"We got him out in time." Dale took off his battered Resistol and combed his fingers through gray hair. He looked old. "He lost a lot of blood, but that's about it. Nick said it missed the femoral artery, or he would've been dead before I got off the trail. Where's Marty?"

"Right here, Sheriff," Marty called from the dispatcher's room—a tiny cubbyhole lined with radios, a computer, and a TV with the Weather Channel on.

"Go home, darlin'. I need you fresh for tonight's shift." He turned to me. "Where's the body?"

"In the locker. Dr. Ed's on the way over," I said. "I think I better get back up there, Sheriff. The scene's getting pretty cold, and the shooter's had a chance to clean it up."

"I'll go with you," said Dale.

"Sounds good, but who's going to mind the store?"

"I'll relay the dispatcher's set to the sheriff's radio," said Marty, stepping out of the radio booth and stretching her back. Marty was about the same age as the dead woman, but that's where the similarities ended. She was five-ten, taller than I, with high Ute cheekbones and almond-shaped black eyes. No one would call Martha Three Stones petite, nor would they call her "Martha." She kept her long black hair in a single braid adorned with a strand of turquoise beads—no other jewelry or makeup.

"Sounds good, Marty, set it up and go home. Tatum, as soon as Dr. Ed gets here, we'll go back to your place."

We walked back to the coroner's office just as Dr. Ed was pulling out the drawer of the storage locker. Ed's office is also the examination room. We're just lucky to have a coroner.

"Holy smokes," said Dr. Ed, "that's a big hole."

"You should see the one in her back," I said, stepping around to the other side of the rollout. "Looks to me like a thirty caliber, probably a .308 or .300, judging from the damage. I doubt we'll find the bullet in her either, not with those exit wounds."

"Mmmhmm. Thank you, Deputy," said Dr. Ed, still looking at the body. "Now you run along back to your crime scene, and let me take care of this. I intend to wet a line at Oxbow Bend by three o'clock."

We drove across the river to Deep Creek. My cabin sat about two hundred meters back from Deep Creek Road. We both hustled out of our vehicles and into the cabin.

"What do you think, Tatum?" asked Sheriff Dale, leaning on my kitchen counter.

"I think we should go after him, Sheriff," I said. "I might walk into an ambush once, but not twice. I prefer to set one of my own—I've done it before."

"Okay. Let's do it."

I would take the lead on this one. Antisniper tactics are not something they teach mountain town sheriffs, but I had some experience with it. I retrieved the horses from the corral and led them into the barn. I kept my guns in a recessed cabinet between the studs. I pulled out my rifle, a single-shot Ruger Number One, and loaded a .30-06 shell in the chamber. I jammed it in the scabbard attached to the saddle, mounted Pancho, and rode out into the yard. Sheriff Dale had already laid his own rifle out on the hood of his Bronco and was searching the heights overlooking Deep Creek. I guided Pancho down the drive and turned right on Deep Creek Road.

We planned to leapfrog our way into position instead of traveling together. One of us would ride forward until out of sight, while the other rider pulled off the trail in a covered position and glassed the ridge, rifle at the ready, overwatching the point man. The forward rider would then stop and do the same for the rear guard coming up the trail. I volunteered to be the point man, and Sheriff Dale let me.

We worked our way up the east ridge along a jeep trail, approaching the sniper from the north. Unlike the path along the creek, this trail was wide and steep, full of boulders and washouts—an off-roader's dream. Pancho picked his way along the uneven track up the spur, while I kept my eyes on the ridge above. I felt alternately exposed and blinded as I moved from juniper thicket to open meadow. The trail climbed to the edge of a narrow draw, then plunged into a thick stand of aspen. Across the draw was the top of the high ridge overlooking Deep Creek that led to the sniper's position above the beaver pond. I stopped at the edge of the draw and called up Sheriff Dale.

Pancho and I continued down the trail into the aspen forest. The intermittent stream running down the deep draw was dry for the season, so the silence of the aspens pounded in my ears. The sides of the draw rose up around me. The trees were in high foliage, making the light and air seem tinged with green. The leaves and white-green trunks made it impossible for me to scan for a shooter, and I had to guide Pancho down the rugged slope to avoid stepping in a hole, taking my eyes off the ridge for the first time. I had been so preoccupied with looking for a muzzle flash or optic glare that I forgot to look down, until now. The fresh ATV tracks were obvious; even Jerry could have spotted them. It had rained the afternoon before, washing out the many tracks on this popular trail, leaving only one set. One set? I would have assumed two sets, uphill and downhill, ingress and egress, but there was only one set of tracks, going downhill, as evidenced by the uphill splatter of mud where the rear wheels dug into a small puddle where the stream should have been.

"ATV tracks, downhill only," I radioed the sheriff.

"Yup," he answered, "wondered when you were going

to see them." Sheriff Dale doesn't miss much, but I was a little miffed that I did.

"What do you want to do?" I asked him.

"Keep going," he said, without hesitation. "I already know what's behind me."

I agreed with him. I clicked at Pancho and got him moving up the opposite side of the draw toward the ridge.

I emerged from the aspens into a narrow meadow. The terrain was steep. We were on the shoulders of Snowshoe Mountain, and the slope launched out of the foothills to the summit—one thousand feet up to my left. I was close to Deep Creek valley, and the edge of the gorge was a careless step and tumble downslope from where I stood. The tilted meadow spread out into a wide oval covered with short grass and columbine. The trail carved a ledge into the side of the mountain and entered another stand of aspen. The sun filled the valley with dry heat and shadowless light.

I reached the aspen grove and checked my GPS—I didn't want to walk into another ambush. I was six hundred meters from the beaver pond below me in the gorge. I predicted the sniper had set up ahead of me at the edge of a juniper thicket. Sheriff Dale met me where I dismounted. He already had his rifle out and sighted down the trail. I grabbed my rifle and moved off the trail to the left, upslope. My plan was to climb the ridge and find an antisniper position above the shooter. Sheriff Dale would then approach on foot with me covering him. He was the sheriff, and I was a better shot.

I found my spot at the upper edge of the thicket, near the tree line. The terrain was rockier here, and a granite outcropping formed a perfect shooter's ledge, covered with spruce and juniper. I could see along the edge of the trees down to the sniper's ledge below me. I got down into the prone and put my scope on the spot. The unchanging alpine meadow was a perfect journal of his activities on the ridge. I could see clearly where he had pulled the ATV off the trail and walked to his overwatch. The sun, approaching noon, warmed the Rio Grande Valley. Sweat trickled between my shoulder blades.

"Okay, Sheriff, I'm set up. Here's how it looks," I said over the radio. "I'm about four hundred meters to your eleven o'clock, on a ledge near the edge of the trees. I can see the shooter's position below me by the cliff, a quarter mile down the trail in another open area. Looks like he's bugged out, but you never know. He picked a small mesa overlooking the beaver pond. I can see the trail on the approach through the trees. It's pretty thin from up top, so I can cover your movement most of the way. The open area is a postage stamp, only about forty meters long, so he'd have to be damn close to shoot you from up the trail. If it were me, I'd shoot from up here, and he's not here, but you never know. Whenever you're ready. Just keep the earpiece in, and I'll sing out if I see the sniper."

"If you see the sniper, shoot him," said the sheriff. Good point.

He wisely chose not to follow the trail, instead moving from juniper clump to boulder along the edge of the gorge. I had a little trouble following his movement, but I wasn't worried about him. I trained my rifle on the opposite stand of evergreens up the trail. We had been careless by the beaver pond, and Jerry had a big hole in his leg to pay for it. It wouldn't happen this time, or again.

A southern breeze picked up the distinctive scent of elk. They used this trail along with the mule deer and the ATV riders. I would definitely have to come up here in October.

"I can see his ledge, Tatum. No movement, nothing foreign. I think he's gone."

"I see you, Sheriff. No movement up the trail or across the valley. Everything's still as a photo. You are clear to inspect the area. I recommend my keeping this overwatch, though. This morning he let us get on scene and get comfortable before nailing Jerry."

"Yup," said Dale, "I'm pushing into the clearing. Keep your eyes open."

"You got it, Sheriff."

I ignored the sheriff and burned holes in the trees surrounding him, looking for a scope glare, a glint of metal, or a muzzle flash.

"Okay, Tatum. Why don't you come down here and take a shot at it? I've got a good spot to cover your movement and I'm in position."

I took one last sweep through my scope and backed out of the hide. I quickly shouldered my rifle and hustled down the slope. I had to use both hands to scramble down the steep, rocky terrain, grabbing on to the trunks of young aspen along the way. I realized I was in a hurry, so I stopped my downhill dash and forced myself to slow down and observe. I had to assume the whole valley was a crime scene, and it was imperative that I treated it as such and not act like a rookie.

I hit the trail a few hundred feet down from the shooter's clearing. I didn't walk on the trail this time as I approached the opening, but along the edge just inside the trees. I didn't find anything. This guy was clean and careful. I found Sheriff Dale on his belly near the edge of the gorge inside the tree line.

"I found the tire tracks we saw below," said Dale, as I knelt down beside him. "They pull off in the trees over there, but they come from uphill. You can see where he climbed the knoll and moved the rocks around on top to make a hide—nothing else. Looks like he cleaned up."

I looked out into the open area. It was nearly circular, with the downhill edge rising up in a small knoll crowned with rocks overlooking the gorge. What a perfect spot for an ambush. I guess the sniper thought the same. He had backed his ATV into the trees at the far edge of the clearing. I could see where the tire tracks dug into the dry turf as he left the trail. I crossed the clearing and started my inspection there.

He had nestled the vehicle in a clump of low spruce. Three of them growing together formed a small enclosure of evergreen. He dismounted to the left and walked through the tough, short grass to the bottom of the knoll. This was smart; the rain the night before had muddied the trail, and his boot prints would have shown up nicely. Even an ATV tire wouldn't obliterate every footprint. I could still see fresh deer and elk prints in the gray mud. I was not so lucky, however, as to find a single human track. So far, the scene was proving lean on evidence, but it gave me the obvious impression that the shooter was very, very careful, and he put a significant amount of planning into this operation, probably scouting out this area long before the actual shooting.

I climbed the small mesa. The knoll was about six feet up from the rest of the clearing. Low granite rocks like teeth jutted from the top at the edge of the cliff wall. The mesa was a parapet—the jagged granite provided natural loopholes that the sniper could shoot through without exposing himself above them.

I stood on top of the knoll and looked down into the valley of Deep Creek. The cliff wall plunged straight down two hundred feet into the gorge. The beaver pond and horse bridge where we found the body were roughly one hundred fifty meters upstream—an easy shot for a trained sniper or even a good hunter. I couldn't imagine a better spot than this small mesa to set up a sniper ambush—good standoff, relatively close range, 360 degrees of security, simple ingress and egress unimpeded by the target, overhead shot. The shooter even timed it right, having the rising sun behind him; besides having to look up into the bright morning light to see the shooter, his victim wouldn't be able to see any glare from the scope.

I mimicked the sniper's actions, trying to put together the sequence of events. He found a good loophole to shoot through—a two-foot-wide notch in the rocky crown of the knoll. He moved a few softball-size rocks from the spot, dug out a pin cushion cactus with his boot, and sighted in his rifle. I got down with my own rifle and placed it in the same notch. I looked through the scope, and the horse bridge immediately came into view. I could see Jerry's darkening bloodstains on the planks. Dead to rights, he had us the whole time.

I shifted my focus from the bridge to the far end of the beaver pond. As expected, he couldn't shoot at me along the trail—the bend to the left obstructed his line of sight. The steep bank where I dropped after the shot also provided cover. Luck, not mercy, had prevented the sniper from killing me. I adjusted my scope and looked for the red backpack or whatever it was I saw in the forest above the pond. I saw nothing but thick evergreens.

I looked up from the scope, ejected the live round from my rifle, and reloaded it. The Ruger Number One is a falling block, single-shot rifle; the shell casing simply ejects out the rear of the breach. The typical hunting or sniper rifle has a bolt action with a five round magazine below it. The shooter pulls back the bolt and ejects the shell, propelling it up and to the right. I imagined the arc of a casing as the sniper ejected it and loaded another in the chamber in preparation for another shot. Because the shooter had to fire up into the valley, his spent shell might launch up, over the rocks, and down the cliff wall.

The high July sun passed its noon apogee and worked its way west, pouring afternoon light into the valley. The bright rifle shell glittered like an amber jewel against the gray rocks and green lichen. The sniper left little or no evidence at the scene, but, in his haste to clear the area, it was impossible for him to retrieve his spent shell, twelve feet down on a tiny ledge. He would need a rope.

I called to the sheriff and told him what I found. Then I went back down to the horses to get a rope and climbing harness. I was a fairly experienced climber, so this wouldn't take long—a simple bounce climb. The sheriff would remain in position, covering my ass as I went backward down the cliff. The last time we got close to any evidence, the sniper rewarded us with a high-velocity rifle bullet. I hoped Sheriff Dale would see him first.

I slipped off my duty belt, took off my hat, and put on the climbing harness. I then anchored the rope to the largest spruce I could find. Once I was sure the anchor was bombproof, I tossed the rope over the edge, tied in, and backed up over the lip. I would only fall a short distance until the rope pulled tight. Such a fall and sudden stop would be shocking and uncomfortable, but it beat the alternative. I slowly worked my way down the cliff wall to the shell, not wanting to dislodge a rock and send our second bit of evidence into the gorge. When I was within reach, I pulled on my leather gloves, slipped the shell in a paper evidence bag, and put the bag back in my pocket. I climbed back up without incident.

I finished the sweep of the clearing and found nothing else. The rifle shell and tire tracks were all the killer had left. There was another crime scene we still had to find and investigate—the murder scene. That jewel still eluded us. We had no clue where the woman was killed.

"What do you think, Sheriff?" I asked. "I'd say we're done here."

"I want to go back to the ranger station and inspect the compound. Our ATV might've come from there."

The ranger station was a half-mile east of my cabin and unmanned. Doug and Wilma, the local rangers, usually worked out of their smaller station downtown during the tourist season. They stored their utility vehicles at the remote station and let some of the locals park their ATVs in the compound.

"You retrace his movement back down into the valley," the sheriff continued. "Then finish up what you started at the beaver pond."

Sheriff Dale's plan was a surprising deviation from our approach to the shooter's perch. I didn't think we were secure enough to split up and abandon our antisniper technique. The shooter could be watching us right now. I expressed my reservations to the sheriff.

"I think he's gone, Tatum," said Sheriff Dale, looking out across the valley. "By the looks of this site, he's cleared out. If he wanted to hit us again, he would've done so already. He had plenty of time to move to the opposite ridge over there and set up for another shot. You made a good target dangling over the edge, but here you are. I think he's gone."

"What about up the trail, sir?" I asked.

"Well, good point," said Sheriff Dale. "Consider a couple of things though. He did most of his work at night or early in the morning. He knows this valley will be crawling with tourists by now, especially in July, doing their hiking and fishing when the sun is high. He doesn't want to be around."

I thought about that. I trusted the sheriff's instincts and realized he was right. If the sniper wanted me dead, I'd be at the bottom of the gorge, but he lost the element of surprise and the initiative.

"Okay, Sheriff. I'll take Pancho back into the valley and let you know what I find."

"Got it. That'll give me a chance to swing by the station and call the hospital in Pueblo and see how Jerry's doing."

The sheriff was a good man. I, on the other hand, didn't even consider checking on Jerry. I guess that's why he's the sheriff and I'm the deputy.

We mounted and separated—the sheriff downhill to the ranger station, and I up the trail, retracing the ATV tracks. It was about 2:30 in the afternoon. We had lots of daylight left.

The jeep trail forked a couple miles up the ridge. The ATV tracks followed the lower trail into Deep Creek Valley.

"Come in, Tatum." I heard the sheriff's voice crackle over the radio.

"Roger, this is Tatum."

"ATV tracks come down the east ridge all the way to the parking lot of the ranger station," said the sheriff. "Tracks disappear at the gravel, but the lock on the gate's been popped with a bolt cutter. Someone pulled up with a trailer. Can't tell if they took one or put one back. We'll have to get an inventory from Ranger Doug."

"Got it. You want me to follow up?" I asked.

"Negative. I'll see Doug in town. I'll meet you back at the horse bridge. I'll head up there when I'm done downtown."

"Roger, Sheriff."

The condition of the compound seemed to indicate that the ATV was stolen and returned, or at least stolen then dumped somewhere. After shooting us from the ridge, the sniper drove down the hill and either left the ranger station lot in another vehicle or drove away on the ATV. Sheriff Dale would find that out in a hurry. We matched ATV tracks to tires all the time, chasing after poachers. If the ATV was back in the compound, the sheriff would identify it by suppertime.

I pieced together the shooter's movements based on the evidence. He had a busy night. He transported the body in another vehicle, towing the ATV up to the Spar City trail-head. Then he transferred the body to the ATV, traveled seven miles down the valley, and dumped the woman in the beaver pond. He then went back up the trail, traveled down the ridge, and set up his shooter's perch. He did this in the dark on a popular hiking trail, all before I hit the bridge around 5:30 A.M. He had timed each step down to the second.

He also knew a heck of a lot about my own backyard, which made me very nervous. He took a risk by setting up his ambush in a public area, but his sense of timing under-scored his knowledge of tourist traffic as well. As I thought about it, he knew a lot more than that. To have a successful ambush, he needed to understand not only my own patterns of behavior, but he had to predict the reactions of the local sheriff's department as well. Like any other small town, se-crets and privacy were about as rare as hen's teeth.

Based on the two crime scenes I investigated, I thought I had a pretty good idea of the person we were up against. He was obviously a good shot, probably a hunter. He knew the terrain and trail network like a local. He did his work at night or early morning and had the timing down perfectly, which meant he probably rehearsed it on site. He knew I ran every morning on the trail, and he knew the sheriff would be there in a flash. He did nothing careless up to this point; on the contrary, it was obvious he had planned this particular shooting to the last detail, which is why the pres-ence of the shell casing was such an anomaly. Why didn't he predict the arc of his ejected shell, so close to the edge of the gorge? I pulled the evidence bag out of my pocket and snapped on a pair of latex gloves.

The shell was a Winchester .270, a popular rifle for deer and antelope hunters in the Rio Grande Valley or any other big game hunter in North America. My larger bore .30-06 was better for elk or bear, but the .270 was effective on just about anything else, and very reliable. I had one of my own—a bolt action Remington 700 my father gave me when I was twelve. Marty Three Stones kept one in her Bronco. On closer inspection, I noticed the shell was a reload—the sniper loaded his own bullets. This didn't surprise me. Most avid shooters aren't satisfied with the performance of factory ammo. The shell had a high polish—reloaders tumble their brass before reloading it. The neck of the shell had a clean edge where he had trimmed it to seat a new bullet properly. He replaced the low-grade factory primer with a high quality one after the initial firing. He probably collected his brass at a shooting range. The fact that he was a reloader significantly narrowed the field of suspects. From a firearms perspective, the shooter left a signature up on the cliff. Our lucky break just got luckier.

I was burning daylight, as Sergeant Richter used to say, so I put the shell back in the bag and nudged Pancho down the trail. The sparse vegetation of the ridge thickened into deep forest as I descended into the valley. The soil was rich and water was plentiful along Deep Creek, and the trees were tall older brothers of the spruce and juniper on the ridge. Blue and Englemann spruce towered above me, blocking the sun's reach to the forest floor and taking the voice from the wind. Every footfall and creak of leather was a chorus of noise I had hardly noticed up on the ridge.

The trail continued through the forest for another mile before breaking out into the open at the beaver pond. I had no trouble staying alert, alone on a close-in trail with a sniper about. I dismounted just as I could see the thinning of trees up ahead. I tied off Pancho, took off my hat, and just stood, listening to the valley and the creek. We used to call this a "listening halt" on patrol. Once you became attuned to the normal sights and sounds of your surroundings, the differences leap out—a snapped twig, the brush of nylon against the bark of a tree, the smell of a cigarette butt.

I didn't expect to find the red backpack, but there it was, nestled on the trail side of a large boulder. I couldn't believe it. I hadn't seen it from the ridge, so I assumed the sniper returned to pick it up. Now, I knew better. He didn't have time to return to the scene after shooting Jerry—he was bugging out as fast as Dale and I. He either dropped the backpack in the dark or left it for me to find. It could also be completely unrelated. Only one way to find out.

I donned another pair of latex gloves and I picked up the backpack. It was a heavy day-hiker—small internal frame support with three compartments and a flat map pocket. I unzipped the top pocket and found a roll of toilet paper in a Ziploc, hand sanitizer, and insect repellant. The middle compartment held a Sony digital camera with a preview screen and slot for a floppy disk. There was a floppy in the camera and three more in a waterproof plastic case. I opened the large main pocket before I browsed the photos. It contained a Nalgene bottle of water, three Powerbars, a bag of trail mix, and an extra pair of wool socks in another Ziploc. The map pocket had enough room for a map and notebook. The map was a waterproof hikers' topographical, the kind you order online from National Geographic. Notes dotted the margin and large red circles marked places I recognized around Mineral County and the three surrounding counties to the north and west. The notebook was a little smaller than a standard sheet of paper, the words "Composition Book" on the black and white cover. I used the same kind of journal in junior high. The handwriting within was shorthand; I could read only a few regional place names and dates. It looked like a journalist's notebook, a woman's, judging from the loopy writing.

I wanted to look at the photos loaded on the digital camera, but I could do that later. I shouldered the pack and moved on. Checking the trail down to the edge of the trees, I was pleased to find that no one else had traveled it today.

I guess everyone was in town, getting ready for the Independence Day parade. I tentatively stepped out of the trees and into the open area of the beaver pond. The last time I was here the sniper took a shot at me, or at least I thought so at the time. Looking up the ridge to my right confirmed what I saw from the shooting position above—the sniper couldn't see me from where I stood here on the trail. The concave slope of the ridge curved just enough to block his line of fire. Lucky me.

I found the same nothing as I found this morning at the scene, not that I was complaining, though. Assuming I had the dead woman's backpack on my shoulder, lightning had struck twice. Finding both the rifle shell and the victim's pack with its trove of her recent behavior was more than I expected on the first day of my investigation. I radioed the sheriff.

"Sheriff Dale, this is Tatum."

"Go ahead," he came back immediately.

"Found some more evidence on the first site. I think you'll want to see it."

"Have you wrapped up your investigation there?"

"Roger."

"Take any photos up the trail?"

"Um, negative, Sheriff. I'll get right on that."

"I'll be there in ten minutes."

He was just down the trail. The man worked fast. I wondered what information he found in town.

I met Sheriff Dale at the bridge. Jerry's blood had dried quickly in the alpine air, but the stain soaked deep into the wood. We carefully stepped over it.

"I walked into the station and found Julie crying her eyes out in the waiting area." Julie was Jerry's wife. "I guess she didn't even know he left this morning. As crazy as things were, I plumb forgot to tell her about Jerry. The hospital called her around noon and let her know her husband had just come out of surgery. It must have been quite a shock."

"How is he?" I asked.

"Stable, but still in intensive care. He lost a lot of blood, but the bullet went clean through his thigh, missed the femur by two centimeters. They want to watch him for a couple days, but we can pick him up then. We'll need him on the radio."

The sheriff is a sympathetic man, but he knew we needed every able body for this investigation. Jerry liked it at the station, anyway. He could wheel around, sit in front of the computer all day, and be happy.

"Any progress on the ATV in the ranger station compound?" I asked.

"Funny thing, that. Julie told me Jerry was going to report his own ATV stolen this morning. Seems he went out yesterday afternoon on his day off and found it missing. He called around to see who might've borrowed it but came up short. Guess he was pretty steamed. Didn't mention it to me this morning, though."

"Jerry isn't much of a morning person. Did you match the tire tracks?"

"Sure did. His was the only Kawasaki Prairie 650 in the lot with Carlisle AT25 Turf Buster tires. We followed that tread all day up the ridge. It's back in the compound, but there's evidence of tampering with the starter."

I told him about the pack over my shoulder. He wanted to return to the station and go through it carefully. I retrieved my horse, and we went down the trail to my place at the bottom of the draw. I put up Pancho, and we headed into town.

Three

THE PARADE COMMITTEE HAD ALREADY STRUNG the large Independence Day banner across Main Street and was erecting the small grandstand below it when we drove by. They all stopped working and waved. Everyone waves at the sheriff. Even I get a few waves. One time, a tourist whose daughter was bitten by a local dog tried to wave down Jerry as he drove through town. Jerry just waved back and kept going. I was glad Jerry would be stuck in the station while we had a sniper around. Maybe Sheriff Dale would let Marty Three Stones out of the radio booth to help me with the investigation.

I saw Mayor Jeff standing over a crosscut saw. He wore a tool belt and was cutting planks for the decking of the grandstand. Jeff Lange was on his third term as Mayor of Belmont, Colorado. He also owned the Weminuche Wilderness Experience, the "WWE," the only sporting goods and equipment rental store in town. It happened to be holding up one end of the Independence Day banner, right across from the grandstand. Folks liked Mayor Jeff well enough, enough to elect him three times. He was the president of both the chamber of commerce and the Rotary club. The chamber of commerce was in charge of the Fourth of July festivities. The Fourth was the height of the tourist season in Belmont.

The Rotary club sponsored the Miner Ten-Miler and the Miner Olympics, held the weekend before the holiday. This year, the Fourth of July was on Sunday, so the race was in two days, on Saturday. Mayor Jeff won the Ten-Miler every year since he moved to Belmont, fifteen years ago. I came in second for the last three.

"You're not gonna catch me this year, Deputy Bill!" Mayor Jeff called out. I hated being called Deputy Bill. It felt so . . . Mayberry.

"Yes I am, Mayor. I've been training all summer—hills and intervals."

I knew I wasn't going to catch him, so did he. Mayor Jeff was only five-six and barely 145 pounds with his running shoes on, and he trained like a demon. Every day, I saw him running up and down the trails around the Rio Grande Valley. His energy was tireless in town, too. You couldn't walk around downtown without seeing him. He would first catch you with his sharp blue eyes, cross the street if he had to, then follow up with a smile and a handshake. I guess either one would make a sale or a vote.

Back at the station, I checked in on Dr. Ed and the body. I only found one of them and a note from Dr. Ed:

If you want to talk to me about this, I'll be at the first bend upriver from Marshall Park today and tomorrow. Otherwise, you may read my report and come by my office on Monday the 5th, as I am closed for the weekend and will be appearing in the parade.

True to his word, he was out on the river fishing by the

afternoon. I read his report. Dr. Ed was only a coroner, not a fully qualified medical examiner, so his assessment was brief. Death appeared to be caused by a gunshot wound to the left temple precipitated by a similar gunshot to the chest, penetrating the right lung and exiting through the back. Time of death based on core body-temperature tables was 1500, 30 June 2004—yesterday afternoon, give or take a few hours. No signs of struggle, other than small abrasions on the palms and knees when she crawled after the first shot tore through her rib cage. I walked back to the sheriff's office.

"Why don't you go out there and talk to him tomorrow morning?" suggested the sheriff. Sheriff Dale and Dr. Ed didn't get along. Dale doesn't fish, and Dr. Ed doesn't pay any attention to the parking ordinances downtown. Their relationship was adversarial at best. I, on the other hand, fished often with Dr. Ed on the Rio Grande and the other streams and lakes around Belmont. He knew all the best pools on the river and could match a hatch better than anyone in the valley. The flies I tied looked like tiny dead birds.

"Do you want me to go out there now, Sheriff?" The late afternoon stonefly hatch would just be starting by the time I made it out to Marshall Park.

"No, Deputy Tatum. You are going to process the pictures on that camera."

The sheriff wasn't a technical person—he still wound his watch—so I was in charge of capturing the evidence on the camera. This was right up Jerry's alley, but he was in intensive care, so I was the man.

Before I started browsing through the pictures like a tourist, I wanted to preserve what we had. The last thing we needed was to lose all the data because the battery was low or I hit the wrong button. First, I went online and down-

loaded the camera's instruction manual from the Sony
website.

One year ago, after much debate and sore feelings,
Jerry, Marty, and I convinced Sheriff Dale not only to upgrade the office computer from a double-disk-drive
clunker to a blazing fast Dell, but to install a satellite internet connection as well. Thinking it would keep us from going through with it, Sheriff Dale said we had no funding
for the high-speed connection. He didn't own a computer
and never would, and he got along fine, why did we need
an Internet connection? In response, all the deputies
chipped in for the steep monthly fee, and we got satellite
TV along with it. We were no longer isolated from the immense volume of criminal databases and collaborative
ventures with the other local, state, and federal law enforcement agencies. Marty Three Stones signed us up with
a new one almost every week. I also got to watch all the
Iowa State football games.

The sheriff took the backpack and its contents to his office to inventory, bag, and label.

I snapped on my third pair of latex gloves, put fresh batteries in the camera, and powered it up. I wanted to down-
load all the pictures on the camera to the floppy, save them
on the computer's hard drive, and then start printing. I
would have liked to dust the floppies and the camera first,
but I didn't think the dust would work too well on the com-
ponents. I could dust them later.

I dumped the digital pictures to the floppy disk in the
camera, pulled the disk out, and transferred the floppy to
the computer's disk drive. I saved every file on the disk to
the computer, and then did the same to the other three floppies in the waterproof plastic case. Only two had any data;
the third was blank. Not trusting the hard drive of the computer, I burned the digital images onto a CD as well. I then

sealed the camera and disks in evidence bags and set them aside.

There were sixty digital photos all together, each with a time and date stamp, ranging from 30 May to 28 June—two days before the woman's death. I quickly scanned the thumbnails, recognizing downtown Belmont, the airport, and other areas around town. She had taken over fifteen shots of the Elk Hollow RV Park. There were some landscape shots of San Luis Peak, North Clear Creek Falls, and a few valleys I did not recall. About halfway through the landscapes were a dozen people-shots, posed and candid, taken the weekend before, the 26th and 27th of June. These were the most interesting of the bunch, especially if you were the mayor's wife, Mandy.

Mayor Jeff's big grin filled the computer screen, followed by other pics of him posing at various trailheads and tourist overlooks around the valley. There were also a few of the dead woman, alive, and one particularly suggestive one of them together. The mayor had his arm around her and her earlobe between his teeth. I guess they spent a lot of time together.

I was taken aback by what I saw on the screen. Mayor Jeff had been married to Mandy for almost thirty years. They were both in their fifties, but Mandy barely looked forty, the envy of most middle-aged women in Belmont. They appeared very happy together, working side by side behind the counter at the WWE and on the grandstand at every Independence Day parade for the last fifteen years. I lived in Belmont for only the last three, but didn't expect a scandal like this—the dead woman was at least twenty years his junior, hardly older than the two daughters he raised in Belmont. I guess living outside of town kept me away from local gossip. I would have to pay a visit to Mayor Jeff.

The rest of the photos were clusters of houses and cab-

ins along the river. She took them from up ridges surrounding the valley. She alternated every shot of natural
wonder with one of the RV park or a group of cabins,
growing up a narrow draw like mushrooms. Next to the nature shots, they seemed to point out the encroachment of
man into the San Juan Mountains. This woman had a talent
for evoking a reaction with just a few photos. I wasn't an
environmentalist wacko, but I'd watched with disappoint-
ment the steady growth of Belmont, especially the seasonal
folks who built cabins and parked RVs. I loaded a stack of
photo paper into the color printer and started making hard-
copies of the images on the screen.

"What'd you find, Tatum?" I just about jumped out of
my skin. The sheriff was quiet. I wondered how long he'd
been standing behind me.

"Pretty juicy stuff, Sheriff. Mayor Jeff has some ex-
plaining to do." I showed him the shots of the mayor and
the dead woman.

"Woman's name is Gayle Whippany of Denver," said
the sheriff. "At least it says so on the inside cover of the
journal. Mandy's gonna be pissed if she finds out. When
are you going to talk to him?"

"I still hear his saw down at the grandstand. I could go
down there right now."

"Do it. Mandy will be at the WWE until seven, but don't
bring him back here. He likes to walk around town. Do
that, but don't spook him—treat him like the mayor, not a
suspect. Report the homicide and the name of the woman
and gauge his reaction."

The mayor and the sheriff were both elected officials, so
this investigation would be a little touchy for Sheriff Dale.
It was imperative for his conduct to remain impartial, or, at
least, to prevent the perception of political motive. I would
have to be his front man on this one. Good for me.

I wanted to review what else he found in the journal,

but when the sheriff says do something right now, he means get your ass up and do it. I grabbed my hat and left the station.

The sun was still high in the western sky, working its way toward the jagged slopes of the Weminuche Range. We would have light for another four hours.

Walking south through downtown, I passed the white clapboard front of the Belmont Hotel. Eunice was putting tablecloths on the outdoor tables in preparation for the dinner crowd. She served the best steak in town. Well, she served the only steak in town, but it's still outstanding. I rarely got a table there during the season. Patrons were already filling up the bar, waiting for the Eunice to reopen the kitchen for the evening. I smelled the fresh bread all the way across the street. She waved at me. I waved back and kept going.

Feeling a little like Wyatt Earp, I said hello and tipped my hat to everyone I passed. Most of the shoppers had already cleared out of town, but folks strolled on the sidewalk, ate ice cream from the Firehouse Bed and Breakfast, and window-shopped at the art galleries in town. Belmont is a big art town. We have six resident artists, two with their own galleries and the others sharing two more. Their medium was mostly landscape and watercolor, but we had one sculptor who did really cool statues that looked a lot like Frederic Remington. "Really cool" was the best I could do as an art critic, but I liked Emmett's sculptures, and so did many of the Texans who bought art every year by the truckload. Emmett was even commissioned to do a big sculpture of a grizzly for the atrium of some big oil company in Ft. Worth.

I heard Mayor Jeff's saw whine down as I approached the grandstand, the smell of freshly cut pine filling the air. I stepped over a pile of two-by-fours and found the mayor around the corner, measuring out his next cut. He spotted me and took off his protective glasses.

"Hi, Deputy Bill. What's up?" So cheerful.

"Got a minute, Mayor?"

"You bet." He dropped his tool belt and hopped over the neat stack of decking.

"Let's take a walk, Mayor Jeff."

Jeff took the curb side of the sidewalk, so he could wave at folks on both sides of Main Street.

"We found a body this morning up on Deep Creek Trail, two miles south of my place."

Jeff stopped smiling, but kept walking, looking over at me.

"Do you know who she is?"

I didn't say whether it was a man or a woman.

"Her name was Gayle Whippany. Not from around here."

"I know who she is, Bill." He looked forward again but kept walking, "She's a reporter from the *Rocky Mountain News*. She's been in town since Memorial Day, staying at the Belmont. She's doing a story on the rapid growth of small mountain towns in the state. She calls it 'mountain sprawl.'"

"Sounds like you know a lot about her."

He was stone-faced and took a few steps before answering. "She interviewed me as soon as she arrived in town. She briefed me on her project. I was uncertain whether I approved of her premise, but I certainly was attracted by the publicity we'd get." Always the salesman and politician.

"Did she give you any updates on her progress?"

"No, she didn't follow up with me officially. She'd come by the WWE once in a while to buy gear and ask directions, but she never did another interview."

"When was the last time you saw her?"

Another few steps. "About a week ago, Wednesday or Thursday. She said she wanted to spend the weekend in the mountains and was looking for some remote areas to hike in."

He was lying. The photos confirmed that he may have been the last, or second to last, person to see her alive. He was a very good liar. Go figure.

"Where did you tell her to go?"

"I recommended the Salt Peak Reservoir or the Wheeler Geologic Area. The regular tourists shy away from the long hikes in." I'd been to both.

"Do you know which one she chose?"

"No. She just bought a map and left."

"She was going alone?"

"That's what she said. She seemed competent enough, but I told her she should go with someone. Am I a suspect, Deputy Bill?"

I didn't expect that one out of the clear blue. It was my turn to lie.

"No, sir, I just came by to keep you in the loop on the investigation. Since you knew the woman, I had to ask. Did she do business with anyone in town besides you and Eunice?" I'd have to go by and talk to her, too.

"No idea. When I saw her, she was alone."

"You never saw her doing any other interviews?"

"Nope. She asked a lot of questions about the Elk Hollow RV Park. I gave her Dana Pratt's name."

Dana Pratt was a local developer who built the RV park across from the airport, and a few more like it around Mineral County. He had moved up from Ft. Worth, Texas, five years ago with a huge bankroll and dreams of low-cost land development dancing in his head. Upon arrival in Belmont, he immediately bought up large chunks of land along the river. Ignoring the protests of many in town, he built a series of RV and trailer parks—concrete slabs and sewage hookups were cheaper than extensive residential development. Elk Hollow was a source of mixed emotions in Belmont. On one hand, it brought in hundreds of retirees who spent the summer and lots of money in town. On the other, the place looked like a trailer park smack in the middle of the valley. You couldn't look down Main Street without seeing Elk Hollow with its scattering of Winnebagoes and Airstreams. Folks in town tore their hair and gnashed their teeth in public over Dana Pratt, but they quietly rang up the goods and took the money from the visitors of Dana's parks.

The mayor and I walked past the Rio Grande Grocery and turned back uptown. I saw that the Miner Olympic Committee had placed a new boulder in the arena, ready for the jackhammer competition on the Fourth. The sun touched the western side of the ridge overlooking town. We would have twilight soon.

"Can you tell me anything else about her?"

"Nope." No pause this time. "Like I said, she only came in a few times after the interview. Will you keep me informed on the investigation, Deputy Tatum?" Now I was Deputy Tatum. He didn't smile once this whole time, had to be some kind of personal record.

"Sure thing, Mayor Jeff. I might need to catch up with you again if I come up with more questions."

"Do I need to come by the station and make a statement?"

"Not right now. Just keep in touch."

"Will do." We were back at the grandstand. He shook my hand and returned to his decking.

I walked back toward the station. I wanted to drop in on Eunice at the Belmont Hotel and ask her a few questions about the dead woman, but Eunice was swamped with the dinner crowd. I would have to stop by tomorrow afternoon.

The sun disappeared behind the mountains, leaving streaks of orange and red, but taking the July heat with it. The warm southern breeze that had gently swayed the banner of Main Street was gone, too, and the still, high-desert air was sharp and cold. Temperatures would drop at least thirty degrees before sunrise.

I found the sheriff at his desk. The newly printed photos covered it. I included the time stamp on all of them, and he had arranged them in sequence.

"Mayor Jeff may have been the last person to see her. At least, before the shooter did," he said, not looking up.

"Yup, but that's not his story."

The sheriff looked up at me. "He lied, huh? Well, that doesn't surprise me. He doesn't know we have the photos. What else did he say?"

I filled him in on my conversation with the mayor. He said nothing, interrupted me not once, and then reflected for a full minute before saying anything.

"You need to go see Eunice and the hotel room, Tatum, right now," he said quietly.

Four

SOMETIMES I'M A DUMB SHIT. THIS TOWN HAS A way of adjusting your sense of urgency down a few notches—it's called "Belmont Time." Shopkeepers open up when they feel like it and close when the fishing is good; Eunice starts cooking dinner when she's good and ready; deputy sheriffs mosey around downtown when conducting a murder investigation.

The Belmont Hotel was only one block down and across the street from the station. I was there in two minutes.

The Belmont was the most beautiful building in town. Eunice and her husband Darryl had owned the place for over twenty years but just recently restored it to nineteenth century boomtown authenticity. It had a white clapboard front with a front porch on the first story and a balcony on the second, each extending the width of the building. Darryl hired talented carpenters to restore the false front, adding gables and fancy windowsills. He also repainted it every spring. The lot next to the hotel served as the outdoor dining area, paved with flagstone and surrounded by a low wrought-iron fence.

I walked through the swinging double-doors and took off my hat—Wyatt Earp again. The interior of the hotel was the real gem of the restoration. It was like walking into 1889. The bar area was a true saloon, from its solid wood floors and dark maple paneling, to its hanging fans turning lazily from the high ceiling. The mammoth bar faced the entrance, complete with a brass foot rail and a mirror almost as wide as the bar itself. Three bartenders in period outfits worked the taps and poured the whiskey. The stairs to the upper rooms climbed the wall to the left, and I expected to see prostitutes dressed in satin and velvet walking along the balcony overlooking the first floor. An out-of-tune upright piano completed the time travel. Instead of miners, gamblers, and hookers, however, I saw fishermen, Texans, and hikers.

The restaurant was to the right and led to the outside patio. Patrons jammed every table, eating, drinking, being merry. I walked back to the kitchen, straight down a narrow hallway. The smells of charred steak, french fries, grilled salmon, and fresh bread hit me like a train and got heavier as I approached the hot kitchen. I hadn't eaten all day. At least Pancho had.

I stood at the threshold of the kitchen, looking for Eunice, waitresses swooping around me like tree swallows, their arms laden with sizzling plates of Eunice's genius. I got four "Hi, Bill"'s before I finally found Eunice among the chaos. She stood over the new stainless-steel cooking range. Eunice had insisted on restoring the kitchen along with the rest of the hotel. She chose Twenty-first Century Modern, however, over Nineteenth Century Mining Town.

"You have to go around back for free leftovers, Deputy

Tatum!" Eunice called out when she saw me. I almost turned around and headed back into the alley—I was that hungry.

"Got a minute, Eunice?" I needed a new opening line.

"Nope." She wiped her hands and took off her apron, anyway. "Darryl, c'mere and watch the stove!" Darryl was running the grill outside and waved to me. He and Eunice switched positions. I followed her out back.

Eunice and I stood next to the big, hot grill and shut the back door, drowning out the sounds, but not the smells, of the kitchen. Things got quiet and dark. Darryl needed to add a light in the alley. Eunice lit a cigarette and took a long pull, then opened the grill to peek at the dozen or so rib eyes, T-bones, and salmon fillets. Mesquite smoke puffed out into the dry night air.

"Need to ask you a few questions about one of your guests, Eunice." She took another drag on her cigarette and waited, staring at me. Eunice was barely five feet tall and in her mid-sixties with the energy of a woman half her age and the crankiness of a national park grizzly. I just loved her.

"Woman's name was Gayle Whippany. She showed up in Belmont around Memorial Day."

"She's dead?"

Are people in Belmont just clairvoyant? "Uh, yes. How did you know?"

"You said *was*, Deputy Tatum, and she hasn't checked out of her room. I'm old, not stupid. Why else would you come bothering me at the dinner hour during the busiest week of the year?" Eunice raised a gray eyebrow, shifting the wrinkles that lined her face. She didn't bother with makeup anymore.

"Right, sorry. What can you tell me about her?"

"Nice girl, gone a lot during the day, kept her room neat. Usually ate breakfast early, had me make a sack lunch, didn't come back 'til after supper was over. I saved some stuff in the fridge for her." It was no surprise why the Belmont Hotel is booked for the season long before March. Eunice took care of you.

"Did she talk to you at all about why she was in town?"

"She mentioned that she worked for the *Rocky Mountain News*. I figured she was a photographer for the paper. She always had her camera with her and cranked away on her laptop down in the dining room every morning before breakfast."

"She ever do any interviews here?"

"Yup, one. Dana Pratt. Wouldn't call it a real success."

"When was the last time you saw her?"

"She left early Saturday morning. She asked for an extra early breakfast. I was up anyway, so we had pancakes and coffee together." Eunice paused, then the words came fast. "She's dead isn't she? She hasn't been back since. She told me she was coming back on Tuesday night. That was three days ago." Eunice was getting upset. She and the woman had become friends. This was hard. I never expected Eunice to be this way.

"She is dead, Eunice. We found her this morning. I can't go into it. I'm sorry."

"Just find the bastard who did it, Tatum," she said, the grizzly bear returning.

"Can you show me her room?"

"Sure, it's right upstairs." She put out her cigarette and told Darryl to watch the grill, too.

We walked up an outside staircase to the second floor. The front balcony wrapped around the side of the hotel. As we reached the top step, Eunice stopped.

"That's funny." she said. "The light's on. I know I turned it off when I checked the room this afternoon."

She went to the first door, pulled out a key, and let me in Gayle Whippany's room.

The place was torn apart. A tipped-over floor lamp threw crazy light around the room, its bare bulb burning my retinas. The mattress was thrown aside. Dresser drawers littered the floor, their contents spewing onto the nice rag carpet. In the bathroom, makeup, soap, shampoo, everything was dumped into the bathtub.

"Oh, Christ." I heard Eunice behind me.

"What time did you come up here?"

"I do the second floor during the afternoon break." Eunice closed her kitchen between lunch and dinner. "I checked her room at around three o'clock. It was just as she left it on Saturday."

"Neither you nor Darryl heard anything?"

"The place is quiet as a church from the end of lunch until five. We'd have heard something. Once six o'clock rolls around and the bar fills up, you could land a helicopter on the roof and we wouldn't hear it."

I picked through the room, finding nothing but clothes and toiletries—no computer, no books, no journals, no floppy disks, no photos—nothing I could call evidence. Where was a scribbled phone number on a matchbook when you needed it?

"How many keys do you have for this room, Eunice?"

"Three. Mine, and two extras. Well, only one extra, I guess. Back in the middle of June, Gayle said she lost hers, so I gave her the other. Haven't made a new one, yet."

I thought of the photos of the woman and Mayor Jeff. Did she give him the other key? Did he come up here after our conversation and ransack the room, looking for something? The camera, probably. He didn't have much time— our interview ended only an hour ago—he really hustled. I wondered if he took anything else.

"Do you see anything missing, Eunice?"

She scanned the overturned room, comparing it to the mental picture of the one she left a few hours earlier.

"Laptop's gone. She always left it on the table over there in the corner. She had a small day planner on the nightstand. It's gone, too." Sheriff Dale should hire Eunice as a crime scene investigator.

I poked around under the bed and behind the mattress, finding nothing. I sent Eunice back downstairs to tend to her guests. I had actually exhibited a bit of forethought and brought an evidence kit with me. Actually, Sheriff Dale reminded me before I left the station.

I found many prints around the room, as expected, at least three sets: Eunice's and the dead woman's, for sure, and the last I assumed were Mayor Jeff's. I doubt he carried a pair of latex gloves around with him in his pocket. He knew the clock was ticking. His panic was evident in the way things were tossed about the room. Not finding the camera immediately, he frantically turned the place upside down, more in frustration than anything. I sealed the room and went downstairs.

I found Eunice back at the stove. Her mouth was a thin, pale line. She looked every one of her sixty-three years.

"Eunice," I said quietly. "Please keep the room sealed. Sheriff Dale will want to come back and see it."

"No shit, Deputy."

"If you think of anything else, please let me know."

She nodded, and then waved a wrinkled hand toward the butcher block behind her.

"Made a couple plates for you and Dale. You probably haven't eaten all day and have a long night ahead of you."

Did I mention that I loved Eunice? I quickly thanked her and grabbed the hot heavy plates covered with foil.

Sheriff Dale was still at his desk, looking through the journal.

"Find anything in there?" I asked.

"Not much." He closed the journal. "I can't read shorthand. We'll have to find someone who does. Last five pages are ripped out, though."

We ate the steaks in his office while I told him about the room at the Belmont Hotel. My pocketknife sliced through the medium rare ribeye like butter. Sheriff Dale wasn't surprised about the condition of the room.

"Do you want me to go pick him up, Sheriff?"

"No, he's already spooked and panicky. Call him at the WWE. Tell him we have some new development he needs to know about ASAP. See if he'll come in on his own."

"My gut tells me he didn't do it, Sheriff," I told him.

"He's not a gun person, that's for sure," said Sheriff Dale. "I don't even think he owns one. He probably tossed the room to find the camera and save his reputation. If we lay it out like that, maybe he can shed some light on the rest of the case. I don't think he pulled the trigger, but that doesn't mean he wasn't involved."

"You think the shooter had help?"

"I know he did. Someone dropped him off at the Spar City Trailhead and picked him up at the ranger station. Mayor Jeff knows the area as well as anyone. He runs up there all the time."

Sheriff Dale had just vocalized the same suspicions that were running around in my own head. I was getting better at this. We were going to interrogate the Mayor of Belmont within the hour.

I made the call. It was already 9:30 P.M., but he picked up on the second ring.

"Sure thing, Deputy Bill, I'll be right up." His voice betrayed no hint of turmoil within.

He walked through the door ten minutes later. No smile this time. Not enough voters around.

I met him at the front counter. "Let's go into Sheriff Dale's office, Mayor." He led the way to the back corner office.

"Where's Sheriff Dale?" he asked when he saw the empty room.

"He's excused himself from any direct questioning of you, Mayor. He doesn't want any politics to get in the way of the investigation."

We both sat down around the small conference table in front of the sheriff's desk.

"I asked you earlier today if I was a suspect, Deputy." He dropped the "Bill."

"Well, sir, that's before I visited the dead woman's room at the Belmont Hotel."

He just sat there and stared at me. I think it was the first time Mayor Jeff was ever at a loss for words.

"Were you looking for these, Mayor?" I slid three photos in front of him. The earlobe shot was on top.

"You can't prove I was there." He was still staring at me, not acknowledging the incriminating pics in front of him.

"Well, Jeff." I dropped the "Mayor." Turnabout's fair play. "I lifted Gayle's and Eunice's prints out of the room tonight, but I found a third set, and I know about the other room key. I think they're both yours. Not only that, Darryl saw you going upstairs at around seven. He was on his way out to the grill to check on his steaks when he saw you back in the alley." I threw that one in for effect.

"You'll have to arrest me to get my fingerprints," he said, thrusting out his chin.

"Look, Jeff." I put my elbows on the table and leaned in. "We don't think you did it, but you may have been the second-to-last person to see Gayle Whippany. What you know could be material to the investigation. Now, your secret's safe with the sheriff and me, including the tossing of the hotel room, but you have to come clean on this. We have too many gaps in the investigation to fight with a material witness."

"I want a lawyer," he said quietly, looking down at the photos for the first time.

"Okay, well, you'll have to call ol' Buck Ishmael over in Del Norte. Course, it's too late for him to drive the sixty miles in, being seventy years old and all. He'll come out in the morning, but I'll have to hold you here until he shows up. What'll Mandy say then?"

"You are a son of a bitch." Gone was the beaming mayor of beautiful, alpine Belmont, replaced by a desperate adulterer weighing his options.

We said nothing for two whole minutes. I stood up and leaned back against the sheriff's desk. Mayor Jeff didn't move. I had an idea.

"Would you follow me, please?"

I led him back to the coroner's office. I think he was too stunned to keep up the belligerence. I opened the locker and pulled out the drawer.

"We need someone to identify her. You seem to know her pretty well, judging by the photos back there in the sheriff's office."

He said nothing. That was enough consent for me. I withdrew the sheet.

"Jesus," he said quietly. "Jesus." Then he turned away.

"Is this Gayle Whippany, Mayor?

"Yes, yes," he stammered. "Please, cover her back up."

We walked back to the sheriff's office. He sat down at the conference table, and I set a fresh cup of coffee in front of him, then I waited. It didn't take long.

"We started seeing each other the middle of June. She needed someone to show her around the valley. I volunteered my time, thinking I would get a lot of good press out of it. Frankly, when she started coming on to me, good press was still my motivation. Whatever I needed to do to get my face and this town in the paper."

"You were gone a lot, then."

"Yes, but Mandy can mind the store. She knew what I was doing. Well, not all I was doing, but she supported my working with Gayle. Mandy's a very ambitious woman. It was her idea that we move back here from San Francisco and start the WWE. She pushed me to run for mayor, too."

Mandy was a local who had moved to Berkeley as soon as she graduated from Belmont High. Some folks do come back home.

"When did you last see Gayle Whippany?"

"We spent the weekend in the mountains, leaving early Saturday morning. We hiked up into the Wheeler Geologic Area. The place is so remote, I knew we wouldn't see anyone, and we didn't. I know a lot of back trails tucked away in the canyons up there."

"When was the last time you saw her, Jeff?" I repeated.

"Right, okay, we took two vehicles up to the Equity Mine Trailhead on Saturday, the twenty-sixth. I had to be back at the store for the July Fourth preparations and customer surge at the WWE, but she wanted to stay at least through Monday. She hiked back to the trailhead with me on Sunday afternoon. I saw her last in my rearview mirror as I headed down the mountain. That was around three P.M. Sunday."

"What did she drive?"

"Red Jeep with a softtop. I think she rented it locally."

"Did she say where she was going?"

"She wanted to climb San Luis Peak. She'd already climbed ten Fourteeners and wanted to add San Luis to her list."

Fourteeners were peaks of fourteen thousand feet or more. Colorado has over fifty of them with varying degrees of difficulty. Many residents of Colorado make it their hobby to climb all of them, and July was a popular month for bagging Fourteeners. San Luis Peak is a relatively easy climb. You need no climbing gear, but it has a long approach to the base of the mountain—at least a six-mile hike from the Equity Mine Trailhead. Because of its remoteness, San Luis is one of the least popular Fourteeners on this list, which is why I climbed it once a year.

"Okay, so she was going to climb the peak?" I asked.

"That's what she said."

"Three o'clock in the afternoon is a little late to start a Fourteener."

"She didn't expect to finish, just camp somewhere on the trail and make the summit Monday morning."

"You didn't see anyone else up there, not even a vehicle at the trailhead?"

"I said we didn't see anyone in the Wheeler. We saw lots of folks on their way to the peak. We were hiking west on the Colorado Trail and met up with two other groups, I think. One couple, about my age, we saw just as we crossed the saddle where the trail splits to climb the slope of San Luis. The other was a group of Boy Scouts on the ridge right above the parking area. I don't think they were going to make it. It was late in the day and they still had six miles of tough hike in front of them."

"Did you remove anything from the room?"

"No. You obviously have the camera. That's what I was looking for."

I didn't get anything else out of the mayor. I think he was tired and frazzled more than resistant.

"Please stay around town, Mayor Jeff. I might have further questions for you in a couple of days."

"Yeah, no problem." He shrugged, slumped in the chair. "Like I'm going anywhere during the height of the season."

I didn't point out that he had maintained an illicit affair during "the height of the season," but there was no point in it.

I updated my notes and stepped out of Sheriff Dale's office at around eleven. Marty Three Stones was at her desk, reading over Dr. Ed's report and drinking a cup of fresh coffee. She just started her shift.

"Was that Mayor Jeff?" she asked.

"The one and only. Not very cheerful tonight, huh?"

"You all get comfy in there?" she asked, peeking into the sheriff's office.

"Where's the sheriff?" I was too tired to banter.

"He left a few minutes ago. He looked beat. You wanna fill me in on what all happened today?"

It was good to brief Marty. The day seemed a big jumble of actions and discovery, and talking it out allowed me to string together the events into a coherent report. I also threw in a lot of speculation that was bouncing around in my brain all day—Marty is good for that. She just sat there, listening intently without a word, her black eyes fixed on me.

"So you don't think the mayor did it?" she asked when I finished.

"Well, I didn't say that. I don't think he did the shooting, but he's capable of putting the whole plan together and assisting in the execution." Execution was not the best choice of words, but I was tired, too.

"Did you read the journal, yet?" she asked.

"Not even one look. The sheriff did and couldn't get anything out of it, except her name. It's mostly shorthand with a few place names."

"I could transcribe it for you tonight," said Marty. "I took shorthand down in San Juan State." This was the junior college in Del Norte.

I looked at Marty for a moment. "Isn't all shorthand personal, like handwriting?"

"Yes and no. You first learn the basic techniques, then make your own shortcuts as you use it." She picked up the journal and opened it to the first page. "It looks like Gregg Shorthand, Diamond Jubilee version. She's used it for a few years but stayed with the standard style. I think I can crack it."

"You never cease to amaze me, Marty Three Stones. Did Sheriff Dale mention your coming off the night shift and working with me on this?"

"Yup, after Jerry gets back from Pueblo. He's doing pretty well, I heard. Julie's with him. She said he'll be out of intensive care tomorrow or the next day."

I was glad to hear this. "As goofy as Jerry is, he doesn't have a mean bone in his body. I hope he pulls through."

"Why don't you go home and get some sleep, Bill? You look exhausted."

I was in bed within the hour, the rush of Deep Creek trying to tell me its secrets.

Five

D R. ED DOESN'T START FISHING UNTIL AN HOUR
after sunrise, so I swung the Bronco into the Marshall Park pull-off at six thirty. The sun was still just a soft
glow behind Snowshoe Mountain. I had to postpone my
run this morning, but at least I had a chance to drink some
coffee and watch the new dawn. Getting there early would
let me get my casting worked out before Ed showed up. I
didn't want to embarrass myself in front of my fly-fishing
mentor.

I started fly-fishing within the first month of moving to
Belmont and meeting Dr. Ed. With the patience of a high
school band director, he taught me to rig my line, cast, and
read the water. Once, I even hooked his ear on a back cast.
Without a word, he pushed the rest of the hook through his
earlobe, cut off the barb, and extracted it. That was three
years ago, and he doesn't give me lessons anymore, but we

still fish together at least once a week. Well, you really don't fly-fish with anyone, just near them.

I set up my line, put on my waders, and quietly shut the back of the Bronco. I took deep breaths of cool morning air as I walked to the river. Some folks do yoga. I fly-fish.

The Marshall Park campground was in a shallow gorge of the Rio Grande where the river made an s-curve around the wooded peaks of Seven Parks. Clusters of tall Englemann spruce lined each turn, holding the course in deep shadow until late in the day, but copper sunlight bathed the stretch upriver where we would fish. As I left the heights of the gorge, the approach was a gradual slope to the rocky banks. Here, the land opened up into a wide plain that stretched across the whole valley. The current slowed at each lazy bend of the river and dug deep pools filled with brown and rainbow trout.

I came within twenty feet of the first pool and stopped, not wanting to spook any trout with my clomping steps. The river made a wide turn, starting with a shallow riffle then slowing its pace, making pockets of slack water where trout would wait for food as it swirled around the exposed boulders of the pool. I stood motionless, carefully planning each set of casts to these pockets, where I would stand, how I would present the fly to the elusive rainbows and aggressive browns. I tied on two flies—one large grasshopper and a #18 green bead-head nymph. The hopper floated on the surface and acted as the strike indicator, while the tiny nymph bounced along the bottom, a foot and a half farther down the line. I loved this rig and caught fish on either fly, but the biggest ones usually nailed the hopper.

I gingerly stepped into the easy current at the downstream end of the pool. Even with thick felt soles on my wading shoes, the first few steps onto the slick submerged rocks were a dicey transition. The water was too cold to fill

up my waders this morning. I entered just above the narrow
rapid where the river choked down to a quick, short torrent
before hitting the s-curve of Marshall Park.

The water swirled like a living thing around my legs as
I stood looking at my first target—I guess snipers see
everything as targets—a large boulder where the water
flowed hard around it into a churning pool of slack water.
Trout would hang around in the easy current below the
stone and wait for living nymphs—mayfly or stonefly lar-
vae—to tumble down.

I started with few quick false casts to get my line out, not
letting the line touch the water, then I let it fly toward the
rock. The two-fly rig was a little awkward, but fly-casting is
about line control—you actually cast the line, not the fly.
My technique was to land the hopper on the upstream side
of the boulder, giving the trailing nymph a moment to sub-
merge, then let the current take the pair naturally into the
slack pool below. This is called presentation. The trout in
these waters were heavily fished, so any presentation less
than authentic would render my fishing day unproductive.

The hopper smacked the front of the rock and plopped
into the river on the downstream side. Not an ideal cast, but
adequate. I stripped the line back poorly with my cold fingers and ended up with a lot of slack as the hopper drifted
quickly downstream. It was good I didn't get a strike on
this cast; all the extra line out would prevent me from setting the hook. My second cast was perfect, landing in the
current where it split to flow on either side of the rock. I
kept my eyes on the hopper. The morning sun illuminated
the prickly yellow bug. At the end of the pool it stopped
moving, and I set the hook. The large brown hit the nymph
below the surface. I could see his bronze scales catch the
sunlight as he struggled in the pool. The nymph was a very
small hook, so I had to keep my rod high and line taut, left

hand slowly working in the line, bringing the fish closer to me. This was the best part of fly-fishing—the fight. It was one thing to entice a trout to take your hook, but fly-fishing takes on a whole new aspect when you play a fish well enough to get him into the net. The first year I lost more than I landed, mostly because I hooked so few fish I wasn't practiced enough in the fight. I was much better now.

I locked my right arm in an upraised position; tight lines were critical. Dr. Ed taught me to land the fish as quickly as possible, get the hook out, and release. This lessened the impact on the trout and increased his chances of survival. After a few crosscurrent moves, the brown shot upstream. I had to let him run, letting the line slip through the fingers of my left hand, rod still high. He jumped and shook—a flash of living gold and diamond water. I regripped the line. This was the moment of truth. He would either dislodge the hook, or I had him. He splashed back into the current, and my rod was still bent over like a reed—he was mine. I started working him in. He made it easy on me by swimming downstream, so I had to strip quickly. I reached behind me and unhooked the landing net from the clip on the back of my vest. The net was a rectangular-shaped ring of shallow netting. Deep nets were for keeping fish; shallow nets were for releasing them. I squatted, raised the rod high, and eased the fish toward the submerged net. While I was in this precarious position, the brown decided to make a quick run behind me. I tried to spin around with him and slipped on the slimy rocks. I was on my butt in the stream, but my rod was still high. I wasn't going to lose the first fish of the day. I lunged with the net and scooped up the wily brown, feeling an immense rush of excitement and relief. I sat there a moment, finally feeling the freezing water running down my crotch, but not caring, because that big boy was in my net. I stood up and quickly worked out the hook with my hemostat. I eased the trout back into the current. He never left the water during the whole procedure. This one would live. Maybe I would catch him again.

I looked up and saw Dr. Ed up on the bank, rod in hand, watching his student's antics. I guess I was pretty focused—he had walked right up on me.

"Nice landing, William," he said. "I don't think I taught you that technique, however."

"Thanks, Dr. Ed. I came up with that on my own." I emerged from the river, dripping my way up the bank.

"Don't take this the wrong way, William, but take off your pants. It's still chilly. You'll catch your death."

I did as I was told, shedding my shoes and waders and stripping off my soaked jeans. Fortunately for my humility, I was wearing polypropylene underwear. I wrung out my jeans and socks, shivering in the cool morning light. Warmth from the waking sun was still a few hours away.

"I thought I'd get a few warm-up casts before you got here, Dr. Ed. I hope I didn't spook the fish for a mile upstream."

"Looks like you got in two casts, and I think the fish are still there. That one was an early riser. I expect the masses to be up in a bit, waiting for me to fool them. Of course, I haven't been able to light into them like I used to."

Dr. Ed had complained about decreasing fish populations along the river for years. Most folks just thought he was losing his touch. I didn't.

We moved upriver to the next pool, neither of us saying anything. It would be unwise for me to bring up the dead woman before he had a chance to wet a line. That would come later. Dr. Ed fished the pool, while I worked a few hundred yards upstream at the end of a nice riffle. Ed released two fat browns before I got another strike. I managed to land the rainbow without getting wet this time.

After an hour or so, Dr. Ed stepped out of the Rio, sat

down on a big rock, and started filling his pipe. He was probably a little cold, but this was his signal that he was ready to talk about his findings. I let him get a few good puffs to ensure the tobacco was well lit, then I hauled in my line and joined him on shore.

"Nice rainbow, William, and your pants are still dry."

"Thanks Dr. Ed. What are you casting this morning?"

"Number twenty-two gold bead-head nymph."

"Geez, that's tiny. What are you using for a strike indicator?" I had to discuss fishing before I "opened up the warehouse doors," as Ed calls it when we discuss work while on the river. He knew it was coming, but rituals were rituals, and fly-fishing is full of them.

"I don't need a strike indicator. I know when there's a fish on." He did, too. He wasn't bragging, just stating a fact—I'd never seen him miss a strike. Dr. Ed was a Colorado native and had fly-fished these rivers for over forty years.

"I read your report on the dead woman," I eased into the subject. "Her name is Gayle Whippany, a reporter from the *Rocky Mountain News*."

Dr. Ed didn't respond to this, just sat there staring at the river, puffing his pipe. He was waiting for a question.

"What else can you tell me about her, Ed?"

He pulled out his pipe and kept watching the river. "I would guess she's around thirty-one, but looks younger. She obviously took very good care of herself. Her hair is her natural color and she had no dental work whatsoever. Not even a filling or a set of braces."

That fit the woman Gayle Whippany was shaping up to be, but I kept my mouth shut and let Dr. Ed continue.

"She had her left knee scoped a few years ago, but that didn't seem to slow her down," he said. "She has calluses on her feet and toes from lots of hiking."

"She liked to bag Fourteeners, I guess," I added.

"That would fit."

He said nothing for a minute, then said, "She had an active sex life. I found semen in her when I took swabs."

"Any evidence of rape or assault?" I asked.

"Nope, just plain old sex. Of course, I'm sixty-five, what do I know?"

"Can you tell me any more details about her death?" I didn't want to learn anything about the good doctor's sex life.

"The first shot penetrated her chest in the lower quadrant, so it missed her heart and all the major blood vessels. The bullet took most of her lung out the exit wound. She didn't die right away. There was a lot of bright red blood in her chest cavity."

There wasn't any blood at the scene, however, confirming my speculation that the sniper killed her somewhere other than Deep Creek.

"So the second shot killed her."

"Correct," he replied. "The bullet that entered her skull did not exit, but fragmented on the inside of her skull, sending small shards of lead and brass through her brain. I collected all the bullet fragments I could. They're back in my office."

This was huge. Even though the bullet was fragmented, we could still use the pieces to match the weapon, if we ever found it.

"I don't think it was the second shot, though, Deputy Tatum," he said quietly, waiting for me to absorb this.

"What do you mean? There were no other bullet wounds. Did I miss one?"

"No, you did fine, Bill. The woman was shot twice, but I think she was shot at three times."

"What did you find, Dr. Ed?"

"Rock fragments, buried in her left cheek and part of her left eye. They looked painful. I doubt she could see out of that eye."

"So you think the shooter took a shot and missed, hitting a rock and sending the pieces into her face?"

"You're the investigator, Deputy, but yes, that's what I think."

"Did you keep the fragments?"

"Of course, they're sitting next to what's left of the bullet I pulled out of her head."

If the rock was specific enough, we might be able to match it to an area in the valley and find the original scene of the murder, and I knew just the geologist who could help me.

"Is there anything else you can tell me, Dr. Ed?"

"That's not enough? What do you want from me, to solve the case for you?" He was smiling. "And I never said I finished my report, did I?"

"That's plenty, Ed, thank you. See you back at the station, and good luck with the rainbows. Tight lines." I got up to leave. I loved to fish, too, but duty called. Ed got up, too, but headed back toward the river. The sun was up and warm, and the morning fishing was just getting good. He would do well today.

After changing into my work clothes back at the cabin, I went into town. I wanted to collect the rock samples and take them to Ralph Munger, the owner of the Belmont Rock Shop and unofficial town geologist. I hoped to find him in his shop today and not hunting rocks somewhere in the valley. Ralph was on Belmont Time, too.

I found the sheriff at his desk, reading over Marty's transcript of the dead woman's journal. Marty was amazing—there had to be fifty pages of text in Sheriff Dale's hand. She must have worked on it all night. I warmed up his coffee from the fresh pot and sat down in front of him.

He dropped the transcript and locked his gaze on me, shifting gears. "Tell me about Mayor Jeff, Tatum."

I knew he had already read my report—I'd left it on his

desk last night—but he wanted to hear it from me in person. I laid everything out for him, from the first call to the mayor to his slouching departure from the station. When I finished, the sheriff said nothing for a minute.

"We have to be careful with Mayor Jeff, Tatum."

"Why's that, Sheriff Dale?"

"Well, I never told you this, but most folks know it already. I'm running for mayor myself in the fall."

This would explain his distance from the investigation of the mayor's activities. I figured it was political, but not that political. Campaigns in Belmont were blessedly short. Everyone knew everyone. Most folks made up their minds as soon as they found out who was running.

"Who's going to be sheriff, then?"

"Well, Deputy Tatum, who do you think would make a good sheriff?" he asked, smiling at me.

"Not me, Sheriff Dale. I'm only twenty-six. No one would vote for a kid like me."

"Look, Bill." He never called me Bill. "You've been my deputy for three years, and an outstanding one at that. Folks in town know you to be firm, effective, and accessible. That's all a small-town sheriff needs."

"What about Jerry and Marty Three Stones? They both have seniority on me."

"They can run if they wish, but I think they'd both rather follow you than try to lead."

"I don't think I have enough experience in law enforcement."

"You're right, you don't, but we're working on that right now, aren't we? Why do you think I made you the point man in this investigation? Do you think I like sitting on my ass in here all day, drinking coffee, and waiting for you to brief me on the latest interview? You're working on the only murder we've had in the last decade. Solve it, and no one in town will forget come this November."

I sat there mute, trying to absorb the longest string of words I'd ever heard the sheriff put together. When I moved to Belmont a few years ago, I felt lucky when the sheriff hired me with no law enforcement experience. I assumed I would be a deputy for many years and was happy with that. Never once had I even daydreamed about being the sheriff one day. I was very comfortable with my deputy badge. Change made me agitated, even if it was laced with opportunity.

"Are you still with me, Deputy?" asked the sheriff. I guess I spaced off.

"You bet, Sheriff Dale," I said, mentally shaking my head clear. "You just dumped a lot of stuff on me. Give me some time to think about it."

"I don't want you to think about it at all until you've solved this sniper case. Remain focused on that for now. What did you find out from the good doctor down by the river?"

Remain focused. How the hell was I supposed to do that?

I relayed the report from Dr. Ed. He agreed that I needed to see Ralph Munger right away about the rock fragments.

"What did you find out in the journal?" I asked.

"You can read it yourself when I'm through with it, Deputy Tatum," he said cryptically.

I grabbed my hat and scooted out of the sheriff's office, stopping by the evidence locker to pick up the rock fragments. Walking down Main Street, I tried to jam thoughts of running for sheriff way back in my skull. Images of shaking hands and making signs swirled around in my head.

The Belmont Rock Shop was about five blocks down from the heart of Belmont, technically on the outskirts of town, even though I could walk there in ten minutes. The shop was a stand-alone building, unlike some of the other businesses downtown. It even had its own little parking area. It looked like a general store from the late nineteenth century—wagon wheels hung from the eaves, bull and deer skulls looked down on the patrons as they stepped onto the creaking boards of the front porch. Mining paraphernalia—old jackhammers and rusted buckets—littered the front yard. Sanford and Son goes west. Instead of clapboard white, though, Ralph painted it olive drab. The words "Belmont Rock Shop" were nailed up in white letters that you buy at the hardware store. The "B" and the "K" were a little crooked, but that seemed to fit.

Ralph always left the front door open in the summer, and I could hear the high-pitched whine of a rock saw from deep within the bowels of the shop. I stepped over the threshold and it was cool inside, like a cave, light barely working its way through the display shelves and cabinets. I could smell the age of the earth, standing there in Ralph's front area, brimming with more geological specimens than a natural history museum. Ralph had installed two large glass display cabinets that also served as his counter for customers. He laid out his best specimens on black velvet under soft light. The counter was the only part of the shop dedicated to sales. Every other available space in all three dimensions was taken up by floor-to-ceiling shelving. The individual shelves were spaced only eight to ten inches high, crammed with samples of rock, fossils, geodes, and semiprecious stones, all taken from the Belmont Caldera. Ralph was never much for security—anyone could walk in and take a rare fossil off the shelf, and he would never know it. I don't think that bothered him, though, because he knew he could always go out and find a better one. He knew all the best sites in the valley and kept them to himself. No one had ever stolen from Ralph, anyway, in the five years since he'd opened for business.

Ralph wasn't a Belmont native. He was from Chapel Hill, North Carolina, where he'd been a professor at the UNC School of Dentistry. After twenty years of teaching and secure with tenure, Ralph decided that teaching wasn't what he really wanted to do. His first love was geology, and his pilgrimages to Belmont started long before tenure, while he was still in private practice. He had collected half of the samples in his shop before moving to Belmont. He took a few courses from the Colorado School of Mines and became resident geologist. Unmarried, he was out in the valley as often as he was in the shop, hunting for more rare specimens at his secret sites.

A narrow aisle cut its way through the center of the shop behind the display cases. I moved back there and called out, "Ralph!"

"Yeah!" I heard. The rock saw continued to whine.

I walked behind the counter, translating his "Yeah" as an invitation to come on back. The shelves towered above me, and I hoped Ralph had built them well. I envisioned a man-made avalanche and hurried down the aisle.

"Ralph!"

"Yeah!"

I don't know why I continued to yell. I could pinpoint his voice no better than I could identify the location of the rock saw, getting more deafening but not any more specific.

"Ralph!"

"Yeah!" He had to be somewhere in the back, so I kept going. The "Ralph's" and "Yeah's" continued for another two minutes, mostly for my own amusement. I found him at the bottom of a small staircase. His workshop was under the store. If the shop above ground felt like a cave, his workshop felt like the center of the earth. Waist-high benches lined the work area. Curled up on a tall, wheeled stool, hunched over the saw, was Ralph Munger, his feet tucked under the seat. He was carefully slicing a softball-sized geode, tapping the plain outer shell to expose the dazzling crystal within. Rock dust filled the air with a dry sediment mist, covering every surface. I tried not to cough. Ralph had a mask over his mouth and nose.

He turned off the rock saw and removed his prescription safety goggles, leaving a raccoon-mask of clean skin around his eyes. Every other inch of his body was covered in the fine dust that hung in the air, making him look like a survivor from the Mount St. Helens eruption. He got off the stool, unfurled his six-foot, three-inch frame, and shook the dust out of his hair. His head almost brushed the low ceiling of his workshop. I guess claustrophobia was not an issue with Ralph. He took off the mask, put on his wire-rims, and put out his hand. I shook it, sending up a small puff of dust.

"What's up, Deputy Tatum? Are you ready for the Ten-Miler tomorrow?" Ralph usually came in second behind Mayor Jeff until I showed up three years ago. I don't think it bothered him, though. He was fifty, and I think third place suited Ralph just fine.

"I just hope I can make it, Ralph. I'm working on some-thing pretty important, and I need your help." Ralph wasn't a hermit, exactly, but he had a low tolerance for small talk, so I got right to the point. I handed him the small vial of rock fragments.

"I'd like to know where these came from."

He took the vial and shook the fragments into his hand.

"Not much to go on." He squinted at them. "Why are some of them red?"

I guess Ralph had a low tolerance for gossip, too. "Dr. Ed pulled them out of a dead woman's cheek and eye, Ralph. We had a murder recently."

He looked up at me, but said nothing. He then turned back to his bench and carefully spread the fragments on a black rubber mat under a lighted magnifier.

"I'll need to keep them until tomorrow, and I'll probably end up destroying half the sample," he said, peering through the glass while pulling over the stool. He curled back up into the seat and was silent for a full minute.

"That's not a problem, Ralph."

"They're local, somewhere in the caldera, but that's all I can tell for now." He was quiet again. I think I'd been dismissed. I was not offended—this was just how Ralph worked. I had asked him for help, and he applied his superior focus on the task. I did not matter for the moment.

"Okay, Ralph. I'll come by tomorrow after the run. See you there."

"Good luck, Deputy Tatum. Stretch well tonight," he said, not looking up from the fragments.

I walked out of the center of the earth, through the cave, and into the light. I blinked at the high desert sun and felt the warm wind coming up from New Mexico, bringing the possibility of an afternoon shower to the valley. The crowd at Sam's Barbeque Trailer across the road was tapering off. I smelled the hickory and realized I hadn't eaten lunch yet. I walked over, hoping Sam hadn't run out of burnt ends.

"Sam, don't break my heart," I said, looking up at him through the service window. "Tell me you have some chow left."

Sam just turned around and came back with a hot burnt-end hoagie wrapped in foil.

"I'm your savior, Bill." Sam was still in college at Oklahoma State University. He funded his education by running his barbeque trailer around the tourist towns in Colorado during the summer.

"I just made a mesquite and hickory run back home," he said, leaning out the window. "I also picked up some extra beef brisket. Already sold about a quarter of it." He looked like a frat boy—short dark hair, clean complexion, hardly a whisker on his chin. I expected him to have a lacrosse stick leaning up in the corner of the trailer. He was also one of the shrewdest and most successful merchants in town, and he didn't even live here. He leased the lot where he parked the trailer and smoker from a local for free lunches and a catered Fourth of July picnic. Residents and tourists alike lined up every day to eat his barbequed chicken, ribs, and sliced meat. He also made the best baked potatoes known to man, so the women liked him, too, and not just for his college-boy looks.

"Whatcha up to, Bill?" He stepped out of the back door of the trailer and joined me on one of the picnic tables. He opened a Diet Coke and set one in front of me. "Is it the murder?"

I guess unlike Ralph Munger, Sam was a gossip king. This made sense, considering everyone ate lunch here and chatted with the amiable young man. Small towns have few secrets.

"What've you heard?" I asked him, neither wanting to answer the question nor stop eating the hot, dripping sandwich.

"Well, you found her yesterday. Don't know how she was killed, but I think I knew who she was."

"Really?"

"Yup, I think she was the reporter who's been poking around town for the last month and a half. Hard to miss her. She was a cutie. She stopped by at least once a week for a baked potato."

"Did she come alone?"

"Yup, every time. Came down here with only her note-book. Sat right where you are now."

"Did she ever mention what she was working on?"

"Well, I asked her, of course, that's how I found out she

was a reporter. Something about tourism and encroachment. She was pretty passionate about it. I really didn't
agree with her. Tourism and encroachment pays my tu-
ition," he said with a smile. "I start my MBA in the fall."

"Can you remember anything else about her?"

"Nope. That's about it. Like I said, she only came by
once in a while."

"Okay, well, stop by the station if you think of or hear
anything else. And, please, keep the rumors to a minimum."

"Are you kidding, Bill?" he said, laughing. "The last
thing I need is a murderer in town. Bad for business. I
know that's pretty heartless, but I can assure you, I'll keep
my mouth shut."

I left Sam at his smoker, pulling out a load of ribs and
inserting five whole chickens, getting ready for the dinner
crowd.

I walked back uptown to check in with Doug at the
ranger station. I wanted to find out about the Boy Scout
troop that Mayor Jeff and the dead woman ran into on the
way out Sunday afternoon. Doug was in, showing an older
couple a map of some of the nicer 4×4 trails in the area. I
waited until he was finished, looking at the colorful posters
of local flora and Smoky Bear telling me to prevent forest
fires. Together, Ranger Doug and his wife, Wilma, weighed
about 425, so the place was nice and neat. They never got
out much. Obviously, they were not law enforcement
rangers—the National Park Service counted on them to
minister to the tourists, and that was about it. Still, they
were nice enough folks. Doug knew the valley well. At
least, well enough from what he could see out the window
of his truck.

"Afternoon, Deputy Tatum!"

"Howdy, Ranger Doug. Got a question for you," I said,
setting my hat on the counter.

"Shoot."

"Does everyone who goes up into the back country fill out a permit and submit an itinerary?"

"Nope, but the bigger groups do, and parties going out for a long time. Whenever there's either liability or significant risk involved. Are you looking for someone?"

"Yup. Boy Scout troop. Left the Equity Mine Trailhead heading east on Sunday."

"This official?"

"Yessir."

He asked no more questions, but turned to his logbook and opened it, putting on his reading glasses. Skimming down the entries, he found what I was looking for.

"Here you go. Boy Scout Troop 117, eight boys, three adults. Their scoutmaster checked in here Saturday afternoon for a Sunday departure. He left his name—Maynard Eagleton, from Lamar. Their plan was to hike in Sunday to the base of San Luis Peak, summit on Monday, then hit four Thirteeners in six days—Organ Mountain, Baldy Alto, Stewart Peak, and Baldy Chato. After Chato on Saturday, they were going to hike back to the Equity Trailhead down the Cebolla Trail and come out Wednesday."

That meant they would finish their last peak in two days and start their return trip. I still had four days to link up with them after that. I would meet them on the trail Wednesday.

"Thanks, Doug. See you."

I stepped out of the ranger station just as an afternoon shower dumped its load on downtown Belmont, sending the tourists scurrying for cover into the welcoming arms of the shopkeepers. The chamber of commerce loves the rain. Luckily, the New Mexican wind was driving northward, pushing the rain against my back as I strode up to the town hall. The downpour stopped as soon as I crossed the threshold of the front door, but not before I had water pouring off the brim of my Resistol onto the entry rug of the station. Sheriff Dale froze me where I stood.

"You just turn right around and go on home, Deputy Tatum. I don't want you squishing around in my clean office."

"Got it, Sheriff Dale. You want me back, so I can read the journal? It's only fourteen hundred."

"No. Take it with you. I don't want to see you until after the run tomorrow." I guess that meant I was clear to run the Miner Ten-Miler in the morning. I'd been struggling with the decision for most of the day.

"May I take the photos as well? They probably complement the journal."

"Go ahead. I'll sign them out for you. And you're right, they match the journal entries. Read it over and let me know what you think tomorrow afternoon."

He packed everything up in a waterproof evidence folder while I stood there dripping and handed the package to me. I turned to leave.

"Good luck tomorrow, Bill. I'll see you at the starting line."

"Thank you, sir," I said, and walked out the door and over to my Bronco. The sun had returned and was trying to make up for its short absence, sending whiffs of steam up from the pavement and my soaked uniform. It almost felt humid.

A knot of anticipation tightened in my gut as I drove back to the cabin. I couldn't wait to get home and dig into the journal and the accompanying photos. Things went fast for the last thirty-six hours, and getting away from town would give me a chance to sort everything out and see where we stood in the investigation.

The previous owner of the cabin on Deep Creek was a local artist. He had some early success with his colorful landscapes and quickly spent his earnings on the cabin and a gallery in town. After a few years, however, the annual visiting art customers tired of his style. Unable to come up with something to spark any new business, he started picking up a bottle of Jack Daniels more often than his brushes. The town bank foreclosed on the gallery and the cabin six months before I arrived, but the artist was long gone. The place was a wreck when I bought it, but at least he left some nice paintings on the walls and two cords of wood stacked behind the kitchen.

I loved the log cabin almost as much as my horse. The artist built it himself, and by the craftsmanship, he might have been in the wrong line of work. The cabin was an A-frame, with a covered front porch, one main floor, and a loft where I slept. The front door led right into the living room; the kitchen and eating area were in the back. Rag rugs covered the hardwood floors, just like my grandmother's cabin in northern Wisconsin. He had installed an ingenious wood heating system that supplied warm air to the whole cabin during the freezing San Juan winters. The wood furnace was in the kitchen, underneath the floorboards. It burned six-foot logs using propane igniters that kept the wood burning steadily for hours. You simply carried the logs through the back door, dropped them into the furnace, and closed the lid. Fans and air ducts moved the warm air throughout the cabin, but the living room had a small stove for extra warmth. I had to wear socks and a nightcap to bed in the winter, though.

It was July, so I didn't burn any logs, even when the temperature dropped to below forty in the morning. I kept my windows open most of the summer, and my cabin stayed cool in the shadows of Deep Creek canyon. I added the horse barn myself the same year I bought the cabin and took the job as deputy sheriff. My carpentry didn't match the level of expertise that the former owner put into the main house, but Pancho liked it, and I set it far enough

back from the cabin so no one would compare the two. I
built a large corral that stretched up into the canyon pasture
for two acres. Pancho spent most of the day back there
when we weren't patrolling. I walked back to the barn and
brushed him off before I changed my own clothes. He got
caught out in the rain, too.

I put on jeans and a dry shirt and started a pot of coffee.
While the coffee brewed, I spread the photos out on my
kitchen table. There were sixty of them, so they covered
the entire surface. I arranged them in chronological order.
They were all black and white, like Ansel Adams, and
many of them had the same qualities of light and composition as the famous photographer. Whippany had shots of
Snowshoe Mountain, Bristol Head at sunset, the La Garita
Range, North Clear Creek Falls. She could have sold them
as postcards in downtown Belmont. There were many others I didn't recognize—alpine lakes and meadows, dry
canyons dotted with sage, high peaks covered with caps of
perpetual snow.

When I arranged them in the order that the dead woman
had them on the disk, the contrast with the developments
and RV parks in the valley leapt off the table. She juxta-
posed shots of human encroachment with scenes of untouched natural beauty. She was making a statement. A
statement that needed clarification. I put them back in
chronological order and opened Marty's text of the journal.

Her writing combined long soliloquies, interviews with
locals, and short descriptions of each picture. Coming up
with no other method, I poured myself a cup of coffee and
started at the beginning.

*I first came to Belmont when I was seven, the summer
between first and second grade. I remember it distinctly,
because I caught my first fish that year, on a yellow Mepps
spinner below the airport bridge. I still have the pictures*

*of my father and I—both of us beaming with excitement
and pride. You can see the fresh morning sun lighting up
the valley. If you stood in the same spot today, however,
you would see ten houses and cabins lined up along the
edge of the river. All thanks to Dana Pratt and his development dreams.*

The woman was already getting personal in the first
paragraph of her journal. It sounded like the opening lines
of her feature story.

> *Cabins now litter the valley of my childhood. I can still
> escape them by climbing San Luis Peak or hiking Ivy Creek
> Trail, letting the mountains and forests block out the en-
> croachment of the RV and the septic tank, but I still have to
> come back to the valley. How long will my sanctuaries hold
> back progress?*
>
> *The original period buildings of Belmont still stand as
> they did in summers past, the Belmont Hotel, the ice cream
> shop, and the local theater, but the town has crept out of
> the box canyon with trailer parks and row houses. The sil-
> ver thread of Highway 149 cannot avoid the blight of this
> mountain sprawl as it curves through town and overlooks
> Dana Pratt's latest vision—the Elk Hollow RV Park. The
> Winnebagoes and Airstreams huddle closely together like
> bedouin tents. Instead of camels, ATVs and Jeeps line up
> alongside, ready to penetrate my quiet valleys with engine
> noise and exhaust fumes. The narrow hiking trails of my
> youth are now reamed out wide by their knobby tires.*

This rhetoric continued for a few more pages, then she
did her first interview with the mayor on 27 May. The
opening questions covered the basics: personal history,
family, his multiple terms as mayor, most of which I already knew. She then hit the bigger issues.

Q: How will Belmont look ten years from now?

A: Much like it does now, actually. The City Council and I have a vision of Belmont, combining a need for progress with an eye on tradition.

Q: Do you support the further development of Belmont?

A: That depends on what you mean by development. If you mean progressive growth that preserves the historical ambience of the town, yes, I support that wholeheartedly.

Q: Do you think RV parks and trailer homes "preserve the ambience of the town," Mayor?

A: We ensure these developments are put together tastefully. I don't think they detract from the town or the valley itself.

Q: Then am I to assume you would support more projects like the Elk Hollow RV Park?

A: Certainly, as long as any development maintains the original historical and natural integrity of the Belmont Caldera.

Q: Isn't it really about the money, Mayor? I understand you give a nod to nature and the valley's rich mining history, but those RV parks bring in more tourists than ambience, right?

A: Tourism is the number one industry in Belmont. Without it, we'd be another ghost town. Ever been to Alta, Colorado? Sure, it's a tourist attraction, because the rotten timbers of the old saloons and flophouses are a novelty, but no one stays for the summer. Not much to support a family there, right?

Q: Don't you think people visit Belmont because of its remoteness, because of its lack of development?

A: I suppose, but people need to live somewhere. Will they stop their drive down the Silver Thread Highway if there's nowhere to park the Airstream? I don't think so.

Q: Do you find your impartiality challenged when faced with a decision about development in Belmont? I mean, you're a business owner and president of the two local business organizations. Do your private interests ever influence your public decisions?

A: *Careful there, Miss Whippany. Please take your implications elsewhere, or this interview is over.*

Q: *You didn't answer my question.*

A: *Look, Belmont has fewer than a thousand people living here year-round. Most of us who care about the community have personal as well as public interest in the success of the town. I think my decisions, both public and private, have been good for Belmont and its residents. I think the voters agree with me. They have in the last three elections, Gayle.*

Q: *So your vision of the Belmont Caldera is an endless carpet of seasonal cabins and RV parks, urbanizing the land from the valley floor to the tree line of the San Juan Mountains?*

A: *I never said that. We have to limit growth at times.*

Q: *When was the last time the city council denied a development?*

A: *I cannot recall.*

Q: *Come on, Mayor. You've been in office for almost eleven years. Certainly, you can come up with one project that your municipal government voted down.*

A: *I said I cannot recall.*

Q: *You cannot recall because there haven't been any denials. Most of the development in Belmont has happened in the last five years, when Dana Pratt rode into town. He's had the Belmont rubber stamp in his deep pocket ever since. Care to comment on that, Mayor?*

A: *No.*

I could feel the tension as Mayor Jeff's answers got shorter and more resistant. I wonder when the tension turned sexual. The relationship certainly started out an adversarial one. The woman sure could write fast, too. She must have taken dictation almost as quickly as the mayor spoke. The text of the interview was very detailed, capturing the aggressiveness of the interviewer and the belligerence of the mayor. Her reporting skills matched her talent as a photographer. I read on.

Q: Have you read the environmental impact statement for the Elk Hollow RV Park?

A: Of course. We pay very close attention to the environmental effects of any development in order to preserve the natural beauty of our valley.

Q: Funny, I couldn't seem to find the study in the town hall archives. Do you know where I can find a copy?

A: The only place I know it would be is with Shelly Duvall, the town secretary and archivist. Are you sure you were asking for the right document?

Q: Yes, Mayor, and I will go see her tomorrow and ask again. I heard Dana Pratt is planning another development. Even bigger than Elk Hollow. Can you tell me anything about it?

A: Yes. It's actually contiguous to the town, in the open meadow west of town overlooking the box canyon Belmont sits in. The National Forest Service is auctioning off the acreage.

Q: Won't this development become part of Belmont?

A: Most likely, yes.

Q: So you will support having RV or trailer parks on the hillsides surrounding Belmont?

A: Who said it was going to be a trailer park?

Q: I just assumed it would be. What are Dana's plans?

A: You'll have to ask him. He told me he planned to build a few large lots, but mostly small family start-up

*homes. You see, Gayle, not all development is bad. These
starter homes will get the folks out of the trailer parks in
town. He's even talking about a new school up there.*

*Q: I see. Have you seen the environmental study on the
new development?*

*A: I don't think Dana's filed it, yet. Why don't you go
ask him?*

The interview continued for another page or so, but the
reporter's questions got less adversarial and more stale, so
I moved on. I scanned a few of the descriptions of the photos. They revealed nothing I didn't already know. I looked
for another interview, finding her first entry when she tried
to approach Dana Pratt.

*7 June, 2004: I went out to interview Dana Pratt today
at his place. His sprawling ranch is west of town, just off
149 opposite the river. The Shallow Creek Ranch straddles
the stream of the same name and reaches back into the
wide canyon where the creek comes off the mountains. He
raises horses and sheep there. Well, he doesn't, but his
ranch hands do. He even has a few longhorn steers he
brought up from his home state. I wonder what kind of impact these animals have on Shallow Creek as it empties
into the Rio Grande. I doubt Dana wonders. He is a gentle-
man farmer, letting his men do most of the work while he
drives around the valley, looking for more untouched land
to develop.*

*I spoke with Mack, a surly young ranch hand with a
greasy black ponytail and a smirk on his face who couldn't
keep his eyes above my neck. He said the master was out
for today, but would be back at sundown, if I wanted to
come back after dark. I did not. When I asked him where he
thought Dana might be, he just shrugged. Obviously, Dana
doesn't hire on the basis of mental prowess.*

The woman really had it out for Dana Pratt. I had no love for the man, either, as I watched the Elk Hollow RV Park grow along the river below my cabin, but Gayle Whippany took Dana's work personally. I read on.

8 June, 2004: I talked with Eunice today about my troubles pinning down Dana Pratt. She told me he's been coming to the hotel every Thursday to have the steak special, without fail, for the last five years. I would have to set an ambush for him. I asked Eunice a few questions about Dana.

Q: So how long have you known Dana Pratt?

A: Ever since he started coming up here from Texas.

Q: You mean when he moved here five years ago?

A: No, he came up here for years, every summer. Stayed here at the hotel with his wife.

Q: I didn't know he was married.

A: He was. She died the year before he moved up here and built the Shallow Creek Ranch.

Q: I see. Does he see anyone in town, I mean, socially?

A: You mean does he have a girlfriend? [laughs out loud, raspy and genuine] No, Dana doesn't have any romantic interests here in town, dearheart. He loves his black Dodge Ram Duellie and his longhorns. I think he loves my steak, too.

Q: Okay, Eunice. I got it. So you think he'll want to talk to me on Thursday?

A: He will until you tell him what you're really after, girlie. Tell you what. You put on a nice summer dress. Wear a little makeup for once, and I'll get you to a seat at his table, but you're on your own from there. I hope you watch rodeo, because as soon as you start asking your questions, he'll be bucking like a bronco. The only thing that'll keep him in his chair is my steak, so I'll stall a little. He likes it well done, anyway.

Q: You're a gem, Eunice. A naughty one, though. I hope you don't lose his business.

A: [Raspy laugh again] He wouldn't dare. He'd have to fly back to Ft. Worth to find a steak as good as mine. Anyway, we girls have to stick together.

10 June, 2004: As directed, I dressed to the nines, at least, to the nines by Belmont standards. I actually had to buy a dress, lipstick, and eyeliner in town. I didn't expect to set a mantrap during this assignment, but here I was, hair back and nails painted. I didn't have any pumps, but I figured I'd get away with my Tevas. I'd be sitting down, anyway.

Eunice brought me over to Dana's table and introduced us. He was pleasant enough at first, but wary, liking the package, but uncertain of the product. Eunice only said I was a reporter from the Rocky Mountain News *and wanted to interview him. He accepted this with a grunt, but pulled my chair out for me.*

He is a lot shorter than I expected, barely taller than I at around 5'6". He's in his mid-fifties, but has all his hair, brown turning gray and straight, letting it grow long over his ears, neck, and forehead. Tiny black eyes that seem to squint all the time, even in the early dusk in the box canyon. Thin lips cover his small teeth, which I see very little of. They're stained yellow from the Camels he chain-smokes. Eunice lets him smoke at the outside tables. He has large hands with round knuckles, the right hand also yellowish from his cigarettes. He still wears his wedding band.

Like the interview with the mayor, she gathered background on Dana, then started in on the heart of her assignment.

Q: What did you do before you moved to Belmont?
A: Same thing I do now—land development.

Q: What projects did you work on in Ft. Worth?

A: You've been to Ft. Worth? How would you know any of my developments?

Q: I meant what kind of developments did you put together in Texas, and what scale?

A: I built just about everything down there—hotels, shopping areas, malls, residential.

Q: What was your vision in these developments?

A: Vision? I don't have any vision. I know what people want and I build it for them.

Q: How do you determine what people want?

A: Well, that's the kicker, isn't it? I don't take any polls or surveys, if that's what you mean. I make money in this business because I can project what an area needs, purchase the land, and build it. If the developer is a good one, people will come. If the developer doesn't know jack about human nature, he will fail. I am of the former group.

Q: So you've made a lot of money doing what you do?

A: You've been out at Shallow Creek, right? My ranch has more acreage than Orville James up in Halfmoon from the headwaters of Shallow Creek up on the divide to the Rio Grande Watershed. I own fifteen show-quality quarters and Arabians. Each longhorn steer munching my irrigated pasture is worth his weight in gold. I would say I've had my share of success.

Q: If you had so much success in Ft. Worth, why did you move to Belmont? Land development can't be nearly as profitable here. The population won't support it.

A: Well, that's why you're the reporter and I'm the developer, isn't it?

Q: Please answer the question, Mr. Pratt. Why did you decide to develop land here in Belmont?

A: Don't get your skirt in a jam, little lady. I'll get to your question. When Rhonda died, I had no reason to stay in Ft. Worth. She liked it there and only tolerated our visits

to Belmont. I prefer the mountains to the city, even though I
was making money down there like crazy.

Q: So, you sold your business in Ft. Worth and started
up here?

A: Nope. I hired out a management staff for my development firm in Texas. They keep me posted on projects via
e-mail, and I fly my Beechcraft Bonanza down there twice
a month to supervise.

Q: How will Belmont look ten years from now?

A: Belmont will double in size in the next five years,
then double again ten years after that. More and more
tourists come every year, and many of them stay the
whole summer. As the boomers start to retire, they'll buy
more RVs and summer cabins. Some will even move here.
Colorado is growing in population faster than India has
babies. These people will demand hookups, log cabins,
bigger grocery stores, more drugstores, restaurants, tav-
erns, and discount retail outlets. Belmont will have to
provide these for the town to survive, or folks will go elsewhere. People will need to work in these new establishments. These low-skilled workers will need places to live.

Q: And you will build it all for them?

A: If the mayor and the town council will let me, I will.
I assume the risk and take the profit. They get new jobs and
a stake in the survival of their fair valley.

Q: I think the valley will survive on its own. Why do you
think people visit Belmont?

A: How should I know? Some like to fish, I guess. Most
women who come up here like the art galleries downtown.
All I know is that they come here, and more are on the way.

Q: Don't you think many who live in or visit Belmont
like it just the way it is? I mean, you've been coming up
here for years, you know how much it's changed already.
Don't you think the valley loses a little of its charm with
each new development?

A: A ghost town is charming, but no one wants to live there, do they? Have my RV parks stopped anyone from visiting? I don't think so. Elk Hollow is maxed out from June until September.

Q: Do the mayor and the town council support your vision of Belmont?

A: They've approved every development of mine since I moved up here five years ago, so I guess they do.

Q: What about the people of Belmont? What do they think of your developments?

A: I really don't care what they think. The risk is mine, not theirs. They will only benefit from my success. Ask any shopkeeper in town. He'll tell you how business has improved in the last five years, much of it due to projects like Elk Hollow and the summer cabins down the valley. People answer with their wallets.

Q: Or their votes. What if you lose support of the municipal government after the election this November?

A: Belmont has elected the same mayor for the last three elections, and the last time a seat on the council changed over was ten years ago when one of them died. They're all pretty healthy, so I don't think we'll have any revolutions come Election Day.

Q: What makes you so sure?

A: That they aren't going to die on me, or that they'll all get reelected?

Q: Please answer the question.

A: I don't think I can.

Q: Do you support any of their campaigns?

A: This ain't Denver, sweetie. These folks don't campaign. They don't even put last names on their yard signs. Just "VOTE FOR DALE" or "JEFF FOR MAYOR." Most of them run unopposed.

Q: Has any of them ever voiced an opposition to your developing the valley? Not even a discussion?

A: Nope.

Q: How do you account for this unwavering support of the municipal government?

A: Beats me. I guess they feel the same way I do. Without me, their town dies.

Q: Belmont's been around a lot longer than you, Mr. Pratt.

A: Yeah, right. When was the last time anyone pulled silver out of the mountains here? The Equity Mine shut down twenty years ago when the price of silver dropped below six dollars an ounce. Not much of a chance it'll go back up any time soon.

Q: Hikers, fishermen, and families have been coming to Belmont for two generations, Mr. Pratt. They seemed to get along fine without Elk Hollow. You make it sound like tumbleweeds were rolling through town when you rode up in your Duellie.

A: You didn't ask a question, sweetie. You want me to make something up?

Q: No, thank you. How do you think your ongoing development and predicted surge in population will affect the valley's ecosystem?

A: I have no idea. I'm no biologist. You make it sound like I'm building a landfill. Read the environmental impact statement, if you'd like.

Q: I cannot seem to find it in the town archives. Maybe you can summarize some of the precautions you've taken to protect the Rio Grande Watershed.

A: I've taken all the precautions required by local, state, and federal law.

Q: I should hope. Then how do you explain the reduction in the trout population on the Rio Grande?

A: You have studies to back that up, or are you just pulling that out of your ass, Miss Whipper?

Q: It's Whippany, Mr. Pratt. This isn't the first time you've heard about those reports, is it? The Colorado Department of Wildlife has seen a steady decrease in the rainbow population for the last five years upstream and downstream from Elk Hollow. Certainly you've heard about it?

A: No.

Q: Then maybe you've heard about the unexplained algae bloom downriver? You know, where the Rio widens and slows down, just before it shoots through Wagon Wheel Gap?

A: No.

Q: Do you think the mayor or the town council know about these findings?

A: I don't know.

Q: How about the tourists or the residents? Might they know about it?

A: I don't know.

Q: I don't know how they'd find out. I read the last twelve months of the Belmont Chronicle, *but saw no mention of the DOW reports. The Department published them last fall. How do you explain the omission?*

A: I don't know.

Q: Doesn't Thomas Pitcher own the Belmont Chronicle?

A: Yes.

Q: Isn't Thomas Pitcher the senior member and chairman of the town council?

A: Yes.

Q: Don't you think that's just a little more than coincidental?

A: I don't know what you mean.

Q: I think you do, Mr. Pratt. I think you know exactly what I mean.

A: We're done here, Miss Whippany. I never invited you to my table, so just take your sweet ass out of here.

The text of the interview ended abruptly at her dismissal. I thought a moment on what the dead woman was driving at in her sessions with Dana Pratt and the mayor. Was she just fishing, or was there a connection between the Belmont municipal government and Dana's success? I doubt she had anything to back it up, but she had exposed a nerve with both men when she implied the collusion. I could sense it in the shortness of their answers and could almost hear their hostile tone when she touched on the subject.

I too had read the DOW reports about the trout numbers and algae bloom on the Rio Grande, but the report made no conclusions as to the cause. I still caught fish in those waters, just not as many rainbows in the last few years. Dr. Ed and I had discussed it a few times. He speculated that it was just a weather anomaly or a result of the ongoing drought. Neither of us made the connection to Elk Hollow that the dead woman had in her interview. I could see her point, though. The start of the decline of fishing stock in the local stretch of the Rio Grande did coincide with the construction and immediate success of the RV park. I decided to pay a visit to Dana Pratt myself the next afternoon, when I recovered from the Ten-Miler.

The journal provided a wealth of information about Whippany's activities in Belmont in the weeks preceding her death. We were very fortunate to recover this document, and even luckier that Marty Three Stones could translate the woman's shorthand, but I still didn't have a clue as to where she was killed. I thought I knew how and when, but the woman traveled all over the valley, it seemed, and I was no closer to finding the site of her killing than I was the day I found her floating in the beaver pond. I read on.

The Belmont Town Council has only three members who serve six-year terms. I guess the citizens of Belmont prefer as few elections as possible. The Mineral County Sheriff and the mayor are elected every four years, alternating every two. This year is Mayor Jeff's turn to run, and two of the council members are also running. Thomas Pitcher and Sheriff Dale Boggett both won their last elections two years ago. I spoke with Shelly Duvall, the town clerk, about the fall campaign. She is a small woman in her late fifties who's been the town clerk for all of her adult life.

Monday, 14 June, Interview with Shelly Duvall, town clerk and archivist

Q: So how does campaign season look in Belmont?

A: Oh, gosh, Miss Whippany, we really don't campaign here in Belmont. Sure, the candidates will put out a few signs, but that's just for show. None of them has had any opposition for years.

Q: Really? Why is that?

A: Oh, I just think most folks don't want to rock the boat or start any fuss. We're pretty happy with the way things are in Belmont.

Q: Who are the three members of the council?

A: Well there's Thomas Pitcher. He's the chairman. Been chairman for twenty years. Then there's Henry Earl Callahan. He owns the Gas'N Stop on 149 and the grocery store downtown. Becky Noonan is the junior member. She replaced old Sam Waterman when he passed on a while back. She runs the Horseshoe Ranch down by Marshall Park and the Willow Bend Bed & Breakfast here in town.

Q: Which of them are running in November?

A: Henry Earl and Becky. The mayor, too, of course. Sheriff Dale and Mr. Pitcher get to sit this one out.

Q: Anyone else on the ballot?

A: No, not yet. There's still time to sign up, but I don't think anyone else will run against them.

Q: Who was the mayor before Jeff Lange?

A: Sheriff Boggett. Back then he was both the mayor

and the sheriff. When Mandy James and Jeff moved back here, Jeff made a big stink about that. Said that was too much power and influence at one desk. Ran his campaign on it. I guess folks agreed with him. I think Sheriff Dale did, too, deep down. He was so busy doing both jobs. He seems happier just being sheriff.

Q: Mandy James?

A: Oh, I'm sorry. I knew her when she was little Mandy James, Orville's girl. She grew up in Belmont and went to California. That's where she met Mayor Jeff. Brought him back here and opened the Weminuche Wilderness Experience. She's such a sweet girl. I'm so glad she moved back here. So many young people from Belmont leave and never come back.

I was taken aback by the revelation about the sheriff. Dale never mentioned that he was the former mayor. I had no idea what to do with that one, so I kept reading.

Q: Shelly, did you have any luck finding that environmental impact statement for Elk Hollow? Mayor Jeff says he's sure it's here somewhere.

A: Now, how would he know? He hardly ever comes back here. Barely says boo to me, except in public.

Q: I see, so you haven't found it, yet?

A: No, I haven't. Do you have any other questions for me? I need to get back to work.

That interview sure ended on a sour note. I'd never seen Shelly short with anyone before. I started wondering about the impact statement myself.

I scanned through the journal to see if the reporter interviewed one of the council members. She had—Henry Earl. Henry Earl was a good ol' boy who'd lived in Belmont all

his life, pumping gas and selling groceries. She found him
at the Gas 'N Stop the day after she talked to Shelly.

Tuesday, 15 June, Interview with Henry Earl Callahan

*Q: Dana Pratt is proposing a new development west of
town. Will you lend your support to this project, Mr.
Callahan?*

*A: It's Henry Earl, Miss Whippany, and are you asking
me as a business owner or as a member of the town council?*

Q: First as a council member, and I'm Gayle.

*A: Well, officially, I think it's just fine what he's doin'.
Folks need to get out of them trailers down by the old
sluiceway from the mines, and his little houses up there
would be just the ticket for them, so yeah, I guess it's a fine
plan. I'll probably approve it.*

*Q: Now how about your answer as a business owner
and resident of Belmont?*

A: Well, I have to say my answer's still the same.

*Q: Do you subscribe to Dana Pratt's twenty-year vision
of Belmont?*

A: Do I what?

*Q: Do you agree that Belmont will double in five years,
then double again in ten?*

*A: Oh, I don't know, Miss Whippany. I just run the gas
station and the grocery store. I've seen this town go from
mining to art to tourism, and we seem to stay just about
the same.*

*Q: Don't you think a new development will blight the
hillsides overlooking the town? You know that won't be the
end of Dana Pratt's vision.*

*A: There's lots of hillsides around Belmont, Gayle.
What we don't have are nice houses young folks can afford.
That's why they all leave town. Maybe this'll keep 'em here.*

Q: Or they'll attract new residents, right, Henry Earl? That would be just fine with you, wouldn't it?

A: Now, mind your manners, Miss Whippany. Don't go insinuatin' in my own store.

Q: I wasn't insinuating anything, Henry Earl. You seem to have liked every one of Dana Pratt's projects, the whole council has. Have they all been good for business?

A: Now, Miss Whippany, there you go again. What are you driving at?

Q: I see a simple pattern when it comes to Dana Pratt's developments, Henry Earl—he submits them, then you and the council approve them, in record time, I might add. It seems you don't even seem to need an environmental impact statement from him. What do you need, just a nod and a wink?

A: That's just about enough, Miss Whippany. You got one more chance to be civil.

Q: Do you and the council even consider the impact these developments will have on the environment? Not just that, but on the integrity of Belmont itself?

A: I don't think I follow you, miss.

Q: Okay, Henry Earl, I'll spell it out for you. If you, the mayor, and the rest of the town council continue to blindly approve all of Dana Pratt's vision, this valley will lose all of its charm and become like any other urbanized mountain village. Is that what you want, Henry Earl?

A: I just want what's best for Belmont, Miss Whippany. I don't know about all that other stuff you're spoutin'. I think that's just about all I can stomach from you today.

This woman wasn't making any friends in town. She never let up on the theme that Dana Pratt was paving over the Belmont Valley. She was a little dramatic about the whole idea, I thought. Most of the county was National Forest and off-limits to development. Most of man's encroachment was limited to the valley itself.

Were they threatened by this woman? She had little in the way of solid evidence to back up her claims. From what I saw and read, she was stirring the pot to see what bubbled up. I don't think it was enough to want her dead. It was convenient for all of them that she was dead, however. No article in the *Rocky Mountain News* about "mountain sprawl" with Belmont as the centerpiece. No exposé linking the decline of the trout population with Dana's developments along the river. They could go back to building houses and selling stuff to the tourists.

> *Wednesday, 17 June: After my interview with Mr. Callahan, none of the other council members will even talk to me. I guess Henry Earl called ahead and warned them. Not even Shelly will give me the time of day, and she still hasn't found the impact statement. I doubt it even exists. I am convinced that Dana Pratt has the mayor and the town council in his pocket, but I just can't prove it. I'll have to dig deeper. Maybe I can pry it out of the mayor.*

So that's where it started. She was getting nowhere with the council, so she went back to Mayor Jeff and appealed to his more primitive side. I wonder if he agreed to guide her around just so he could keep an eye on her, to find out what she knew and what she was doing.

> *Sunday, 20 June: Jeff really levels out when he's out of town, in the mountains. I can see why Mandy married him. He doesn't have to be the good mayor or the helpful businessman, just Jeff. He's taken me to some fabulous places in the valley, views and trails only a local would know. The sights aren't relevant to my article, but I'm getting him to let his guard down. It won't be long until I'm inside his head.*

Friday, 25 June: Jeff came by the hotel early this morning while Eunice and I were having coffee. He said he wanted to do another interview, but not here in town. He suggested going up to the Colorado Trail for a couple days. He wanted to show me San Luis Peak and the Wheeler Geological Area. I'm packed and ready to go. We leave first thing in the morning. I wanted to leave today, but he had some things to wrap up in town. I wonder if Mandy suspects anything. I think it's highly unusual that she allows him to spend so much time with me. Our cover is pretty thin.

The journal ended with this final entry. Gayle Whippany was dead five days later. This woman wrote in her journal every day, so there was no way she would have omitted that much time from her writing, especially a potentially crucial interview with the mayor. Someone had removed the last few pages of the text, just like the last few days of photos on the camera. I had the original document with me and matched the final entry with Marty's translation. Sure enough, someone had carelessly torn five pages out of the thin volume, right after the 25 June entry. The ragged edges of the paper were still attached to the binding. Something happened up there in the mountains. She found out something that made her a target, but someone erased the record of it.

She'd been shot within a two-day hike from the Equity Mine Trailhead. Assuming the woman was in good shape and experienced on the trail, she could cover ten miles a day. Mayor Jeff said she intended to come out on Monday the 28th of June, but she was killed on Wednesday. She could have stayed in the mountains for a few extra days, expanding my search to twenty miles down any trail starting at the Equity Mine. I hoped Ralph would come through and narrow my options with his geological forensics. Hope, however, is not a method, so I would have to rely on my own skills to piece together the woman's final days. Great.

I would go back to Mayor Jeff. He had a secret to tell Gayle the last time he saw her, and whoever killed her removed that interview from her records. He was going to tell me his secret, if I had to put him in our tiny jail cell to get it out of him.

I put down the journal and leaned back in my dining room chair. I looked at the photos again, seeing nothing, then decided I needed to stretch. As I eased the tension out of my legs on the living room carpet, I thought about the race, the fast start and tough climbs, but my mind kept taking trails back to the journal. I gave up stretching and went to bed. I had a ten-mile run and a lot of investigation to do the next day.

I walked up to the start of the Miner Ten-Miler Saturday morning feeling like a truck ran over me the night before. I had slept poorly, a rarity in the cabin on Deep Creek, so I attributed it to either pre-race jitters or something else. I read somewhere that a good detective cannot sleep if he's missing something. Like the princess from the fairy tale, the subconscious tosses and turns on that tiny pea, the piece of information that doesn't fit or is overlooked. I was uncertain whether I was a good detective or a nervous runner.

The Miner Ten-Miler started on Main Street between Veteran's Park and the WWE. The park is just one-eighth of an acre plot of trees and grass with two small monuments—one to the hometown veterans of WWII and the other to those who fought in Vietnam. The park is always a busy place, because it has the only public bathrooms on Main Street, and the kids love to play on the old mine train with its yellow buckets. A large green and white elevated bandstand dominates the rest of the park. Bluegrass and jazz bands play there weekly, daily during the high tourist season. A Dixieland duet of banjo and tuba was warming up, plinking and oomping in the hard morning sunshine, there to see the runners on their way and meet them at the finish. The weather was perfect for a mountain run—sunny and windless. Cool enough to keep the runners comfortable, but not so cold as to demand extra clothing. Hopefully the frost would melt away before we hit the narrow, shaded spots of Willow Creek Canyon.

The start was in thirty minutes, which gave me time to stretch and jog around the block before dashing off uphill. Around fifty runners competed every year, and half of them were already milling about, checking in, pinning on their race numbers, warming up. I walked over to the check-in station to pick up my number from Mandy Lange, the mayor's wife. She's been the race director for the last ten years, but this morning she wasn't there. Her older daughter, Cynthia, was running things. She inherited her mother's talent for organization along with her ageless beauty and raven black hair, registering latecomers, handing out numbers, describing the course. When I made it to the front of the line, I asked her where her mother was.

"Mom had to make an emergency run to Pueblo. Something about hardware for the grandstand. She left early this morning."

"The grandstand looks pretty good to me," I said, nodding at the platform draped with banners and American flags.

"She was pretty vague, Deputy Bill. I think Dad forgot something and couldn't go because of the run." She looked impatiently over my shoulder. "She said she'd be back this afternoon. Come on, there are people waiting, and the race starts pretty soon. Why don't you go warm up?"

Moving over to the park, I sat down in the grass next to the bandstand with a cup of hot coffee—always a good pre-race warm-up drink—and stretched my cold legs on the damp grass. I wondered if Mayor Jeff came clean with his wife about the dead woman, triggering the absence of Mandy Lange.

I saw the mayor in a warm-up suit and knit cap, running easy laps around the block. He was already ahead of me. He'd finished his stretching and was getting ready for the start. I ignored him and the thoughts of the investigation banging on the front door of my sleep-deprived brain, forcing myself to forget all of that for now and concentrate on the race, my race, and how I would run it. Mayor Jeff and I had different strategies, and I intended for mine to succeed this year.

The Miner Ten-Miler was an out-and-back race up East Willow Creek for five miles, then back down the canyon to the finish line. The runners run up Main Street then out of town where the road turns to gravel, into the canyon where miners took silver out of the rocks during the boom times of Belmont, past the green tinted piles of tailings and rotting mining shacks and platforms along the canyon walls. At the half-mile point, the road forks where Willow Creek and East Willow creek merge. The runners take the eastern fork through North Belmont, which is the original location of Belmont itself. Only a few shacks and cabins remain of the first mining town. Fire gutted the hasty wooden buildings so often that the citizens of Belmont decided to move the town downstream to its present location.

Once through North Belmont, the runners zigzag through willow groves that lend the creek its name, following the one-lane gravel drive to its end at the East Willow Creek Trailhead. Here the race changes from a relatively flat road race to a mountain trail run, and the climb begins. The trail is narrow and rocky for three miles to the turn-around, and it's all uphill, winding along the steep western slope of the canyon, beneath towering Nelson Mountain and Inspiration Point.

I needed to be within two places of Mayor Jeff when we hit the trailhead. He would lead the pack through the fast start and blazing first two miles of the race. If I wasn't in striking distance by the time the trail narrowed to a footpath, I'd never catch him. I was much heavier than Mayor Jeff, and he was a rabbit going up hills—my weakest skill as a runner. I had worked the hills around the cabin all year in preparation for this race. I wanted to stay with him during his strong push uphill during the first half of the race, then let my heavier frame blow by him on the downhill side. I wasn't kidding when I told Mayor Jeff I'd been doing hills and intervals all year. If I could stay with him until we hit the turnaround, I had him.

Cynthia Lange called us to the starting line. I'd just finished my third lap around the block and was pulling off my sweat pants. Mayor Jeff was already at the front, doing sprint starts to get his legs ready for that first explosion. It looked like we had a record turnout this year—close to seventy runners slowly converged beneath the banner on Main Street. Some were the town regulars, but nearly half were tourists who heard about the race and wanted to give it a shot. I hoped they knew what they were in for. The race started at an elevation of 8,800 feet and rose 1,500 vertical feet before the turnaround. Acclimation to altitude running was critical, and many of the recent visitors to Belmont wouldn't have the time to get their systems adjusted to the thin air.

Cynthia called out the thirty-second mark. The tight knot of runners clustered at the starting line, and I could feel our collective tension, like a herd of buffalo ready to stampede. This was the worst part of any race—the buildup to the start. Once the gun went off and we exploded out of the starting chute, our tension would release in a rush of flailing arms and quickening steps. My heart already pounded away at race pace.

I looked up at the high box canyon surrounding Belmont and the run route, trying to relax and get ready at the same time. A stray thought hit me: Was I really going out into Willow Creek Canyon and run this race without even a cursory thought about the possibility of another shooting? I'd let myself fall into a false sense of security, thinking that the danger of another sniper attack had disappeared, or, worse yet, not thinking about the threat at all. Nothing had changed—I'd just removed myself from the line of fire, and, as a result, I let my guard down. I had spent most of the last twenty-four hours in the relative safety of town. Only deranged psychopaths shot into crowded areas with few avenues of escape. This shooter was not crazy. He killed with purpose and planning. I knew neither his purpose nor his planning. I had no idea who his next victim would be. I could be standing next to him.

I didn't intend to take myself out of the race. The chances were remote that the sniper would risk a shooting at such a public event, but it only took one shot. I imagined the run route and the high cliffs and ridges above it. The shooter would have at least three vantage points to shoot from and be able to get away cleanly with a little planning. I signaled to the sheriff, standing next to the bandstand, drinking coffee. I shouldered my way to the edge of the pack. I only had a few seconds before Cynthia fired the gun.

"We need to get somebody up there quick. At least to seal off any escape routes," I said to the sheriff, trying to keep my voice low enough not to panic anyone around me.

"You know something I don't, Deputy?"

"No, sir, just a bad feeling. Too many targets of opportunity."

He stared at me while this registered. "I'll get Marty up there as quick as I can," he said.

   Sheriff Dale walked quickly to the parking area behind Veteran's Park, pulling the radio off his belt and calling Marty, who was just getting off her shift. I assumed they were going to hop in their Broncos and storm out ahead of the runners, one on each side of the canyon. I kicked myself for not thinking of this sooner, but they knew the area well, and I was certain they could find good positions before any of us ran into a field of fire. They might not find him—the sniper would already be in place—but they might have a chance to spook him or catch him as he tried to escape over the Divide.

   Just as Sheriff Dale disappeared from view, the starting gun fired, and the pack erupted like a burst dam, pouring six dozen excited runners up Main Street. I could see Mayor Jeff already in the lead, his quick pace easily putting distance between himself and the rest of the crowd. I saw Ralph Munger among the top ten. My last-minute move toward the edge of the crowd placed me on the opposite side of the leaders and way back with the recreational joggers. Most of them were chatting happily or starting to puff. I was already behind. I worked my way past the non-competitors as we cleared town and hit the gravel, but there were still fifteen runners between Mayor Jeff and me. He was two hundred meters in front of me, nearing the first turn to East Willow Creek, his white turtleneck standing out against the gray rocks around us. I had time to catch him on the winding approach to the trailhead, but it would cost me. I could feel my heart rate churning well above my normal race pace, and it wouldn't have a break for another nine miles. The canyon walls narrowed and soared above us as we left the pavement, blocking the thin light and warmth of the morning sun. It felt ten degrees cooler, and patches of frost still hung in the dark corners of the rock.

   I made the right turn into North Belmont just as Mayor Jeff's white shirt disappeared into the willow groves at the far end of the canyon. I was gaining, but not much. There were still a few runners between us, and they all looked strong. I caught three of them, however, as we ran past the cabins in North Belmont. I only had one mile to get within two places of the mayor, then passing anyone would be nearly impossible on the rocky footpath up to the halfway point. I pushed harder.

As we left North Belmont, the gravel road became a one-lane jeep trail, still well-graded, but not meant for minivans or the family car. The dense, newly green willows hid East Willow Creek as it looped through the gorge. These were not the usual tall, weeping willows found near lazy pasture streams. They were ten-foot clusters of shrub-like alpine trees with no trunks to speak of. You couldn't really tell one tree from the next, just a wall of green. Willow flycatchers and violet-green swallows nested and flitted in the green refuge. The East Willow valley opened up slightly here, and the sun caught the tops of the trees as we scrambled through them.

This turn into the open area was the first field of fire I had pictured at the starting line. I momentarily broke focus on my mad pursuit of the mayor in White and looked up at the commanding heights on all three sides of the canyon. I spotted the perfect sniper hides among the rocks and stunted junipers on the east wall. Feeling exposed and helpless, I hoped Sheriff Dale and Marty Three Stones made it to their hasty positions in the twelve minutes it took the lead runners to reach this point. Realizing there was nothing I could do, I cut into the first sharp turn in the groves of East Willow Creek, waiting for the crack of a .270 Winchester.

My field of view closed to a dozen meters. The willows came right up to the edge of the jeep trail, which snaked right and left as if built by madmen, rather than the eager miners and CCC workers of the last two centuries. I guess

I could blame East Willow Creek for the meandering. Trying to ignore my inner turmoil, I leaned into every bend and curve of the road, feeling more like an indoor sprinter than a long-distance trail runner. The only sounds I heard were my shoes kicking up stones as I rounded each turn and the raspy heave of my lungs as I approached my aerobic limits. Willow branches scratched my face and pulled at my shirt as I cut off each corner, attempting in vain to straighten the route myself. The mayor's white turtleneck was lost to me, but I did catch Ralph Munger halfway through the maze of green. His long frame wasn't as agile as mine, and, unable to make the turns as quickly, this part of the run was his weakness.

"I thought I'd find you here, Bill," he said as I pulled up behind him. He didn't even sound winded. "What took you so long?"

"Uh huh," was all I could muster.

"Think you'll catch him?"

"Unnhh," I grunted.

"See you at the finish. Go on, now." He took the next turn wide, letting me cut by him on the inside. Ralph ran his own race.

Ralph runs the same race every year. As I pulled ahead of him, I knew I was nearing the leaders, even though I was still lost in the willow mass and had no sight of any other runner. I checked my watch, my only reliable reference on this part of the run. If I was running at the pace my lungs were screaming about, I was within a quarter mile of the trailhead. I had maybe two minutes to catch the mayor.

The road made a sharp left turn and leapt over the creek on a low, solid bridge, followed by a short straightaway to a quick upslope back to the right. This was my landmark indicating the end of the willows. I flew over the bridge and hit the right-hand bend as it climbed a steep rise to a level, open area of the valley. The trailhead was near. This was the second target area I'd envisioned back at the starting line. At the top of the short rise was a beaver dam and wide pond just downstream from the trailhead. The runners would slow down as they climbed the hill, facing north, and expose their heads and chests to the cliff walls. The angles were perfect for an easy sniper shot, and the higher elevation of the beaver pond made it closer to the divide and the many escape routes it provided on the backside of the ridge.

A small forest of aspens hid the trailhead on the west side of the beaver pond, and I saw Mayor Jeff's white jersey flash between the close, pale trunks as I topped the rise. I was within fifty meters. I'd made it and wanted to ease back a little, but I knew his quick feet would eat my lunch on the uphill footpath to the halfway point, so I kept up my breakneck pace and plunged into the aspen grove. To my surprise, there were no other runners between us, and I heard the first set of feet pounding over the bridge behind me. Probably Ralph pushing me along.

The jeep trail hugged the west side of the canyon, running through the aspens, and I labored a bit up the hill. The road flattened then ended as I shot through the parking area. A cluster of three tall aspens obscured the trailhead, and the visiting runners would miss it, if not for the large, blaze orange arrow marking the entrance. I blew through the aspen cluster, down a short drop-off, and stepped lightly down the footpath. The thick canopy of aspen leaves darkened the trail from the weak rays of the sun just clearing the eastern ridge. The darkness, however, was short-lived. The trail continued to race along the western edge of the steep valley walls, but the aspens stopped abruptly. I left the trees and entered the pale sunlight of the tilted meadow into the next sniper ambush area.

The packed trail of dirt and rocks muffled my footsteps, and the silence of the valley overwhelmed me. So quiet was the open area that I actually felt a pressure on my ears, and the morning sun shone directly in my eyes. I could imagine no better conditions for a shooter to take me out—I was blind and deaf, exposed and alone. Then I heard my heart pounding and realized that I'd been holding my breath. I gasped and blinked, breaking my helpless trance. I heard no shot, felt no explosion in my chest.

I remembered that the mayor was in front of me. I saw him drop behind a rise in the trail. He made it through before me. Was I imagining this threat? I reminded myself that the sniper wasn't a madman—he killed with precision and attention to detail. Maybe his target wasn't among the runners today. He had plenty of opportunity along this trail, and the town law enforcement was woefully unprepared for the contingency. He could have killed any of us by now, but didn't. All I could do was keep running and try to stay with the mayor. At least I was a moving target.

I finished my lung-bursting pursuit of the mayor. All I had to do was maintain his pace until we left the trailhead on the return trip. I would then break out in front of him and win in the last two miles of the race. That was the theory, at least. His strategy was to burst out ahead of the pack right at the start, bend the minds of anyone who tried to stay with him, then coast downhill to the finish with a comfortable lead at the halfway point. I'd never been this close to him before, so I doubt he knew I was with him. We had two steady uphill miles to the turnaround. I settled back into my familiar race pace. So did the mayor. I locked onto his white turtleneck and held on.

The trail ran up the western side of the valley, which widened toward the Continental Divide. Not only did the path climb vertically as it approached the five-mile point at ten thousand feet, it also rose and fell with the draws and spurs in the topography. My legs were hard lumps of clay after my mad scramble up the hill, and these dips and draws didn't give them a chance to loosen up and get ready for my downhill push. I'd trained for this part, however, knowing my weakness for hills. Mayor Jeff looked as fresh as he did at the start, stepping up the small hills and knolls like they were flats and straightaways. The man was a machine. I knew this was his part of the run, and my training, as painful as it was, centered on my overcoming this strength of his, or, at least, my keeping up with him. Once a week, I hammered the race route into submission, which is why I knew the trail by heart, including all the places for a good sniper ambush. East Willow Creek and Deep Creek trails were pounded flat by my running shoes for the last six months. I even snowshoed up and down the icy footpaths when snow blanketed the Belmont Caldera.

The halfway point of the Miner Ten-Miler was at the junction of two trails and three streams, surrounded on all sides by high cliffs and thick stands of juniper and spruce. Whited Creek approached from the northwest and emptied into East Willow, while another unnamed branch of East Willow Creek tumbled down the eastern ridge from Wason Park. The La Garita Pack Trail intersected the East Willow Creek Trail at the confluence of the three streams, passing just under Nelson Mountain from the west, then on into the plateau of the La Garita Mountains to the east. This plateau was a favorite elk and mule deer hunting area for the locals in town, and the Halfmoon Gun and Hunt Club owned most of it. If you followed the pack trail east for three miles, you would find the club's lodge at the base of La Garita Peak.

The small table and bright orange banner at the turn-around came into view. Each runner had to touch the trail marker at the junction of the La Garita and East Willow trails to avoid disqualification. Kind of hokey, but this was Belmont's race, and hokiness was part of the package. Chuck Dinnerstein and Max Toliver sat stoically at the offi-

cials' table, like they did every year. Chuck owned the local
Orvis shop and Max the Firehouse Bed & Breakfast next
door. I could even see their red coffee thermos from a quarter mile down the trail. Max made the best coffee in town.

The canyon opened up at this junction of trails and
streams, and the morning sun washed the valley with
warmth and light. The rays seemed almost white at the altitude, streaming out of the east over the Wason Park
Plateau. Chuck stood up with a clipboard as Jeff crossed
the bridge over Whited Creek and neared the marker, the
mayor's white jersey shining in the sun. I was forty meters
behind.

The white shirt exploded in red, and Mayor Jeff went
down. Then I heard the shot, high and behind me to my
right, from the ridge to the east on Wason Park. I tumbled
into the creek bed, diving for cover. Chuck and Max froze,
the clipboard still in Chuck's hands, staring at the motionless form of Jeff Lange, facedown, just short of the marker.
The red rose of blood on his white shirt grew and glistened
in the harsh light of the new morning.

Six

"GET DOWN!" I SHOUTED. I WAS SOAKING WET behind the shallow embankment of Whited Creek, looking back toward the eastern ridge for a scope glare or muzzle flash. All I saw was the brilliant sun.

The second shot jolted Max and Chuck into reality. They dove into the safety of the thick juniper grove next to the check station. I looked at Mayor Jeff. The back of his head was now a mass of red, shattered skull and hair. The shooter had just confirmed the termination of his target. The sniper was on his escape plan as I crouched there, helpless and wet, in the icy snowmelt of Whited Creek.

Then I remembered the radio. Chuck and Max always had one at their station tuned into the race frequency. I crawled up to Mayor Jeff and placed two fingers on his carotid—nothing. I wasn't expecting anything. What seemed to be most of his blood was pooling and soaking into the dirt. He was probably dead before he hit the ground. Trying to ignore the warm wetness on the bare skin of my knees and arms, I kept crawling over to the table. The red thermos was there, next to its lid filled with steaming coffee. You notice strange things during a crisis. I reached up, grabbed the radio off the table, and rolled into the junipers, joining Max and Chuck.

"Is he dead?" asked Max, flat on his belly behind a tree that would provide him no cover.

"Of course he's dead," said Chuck. "Did you see all the blood? Did you see what was left of his head?" Both men were on the young side of sixty and were like brothers, growing up and staying in Belmont all their lives. They were both pale and sweating. I hoped I didn't have to deal with two cases of shock as well.

"Yes, he's dead," I said, looking back through the trees at the eastern ridge, knowing I would see nothing. I tuned the radio to the sheriff's frequency. I heard Marty's voice immediately.

"I just made it to the Wason Park Plateau, Sheriff Dale, about one mile south of the La Garita Trail. I'm leaving the pack trail and going cross-country." Marty didn't reach the east ridge in time to stop the shooter, but she sounded like she might be in a position to intercept.

"Seen anyone up there?" Sheriff Dale asked.

"Negative."

"Do not expose yourself, Deputy. This guy could poke your eye out at three hundred yards. Ensure you see him first, then pursue."

"Roger, Sheriff."

"Sheriff, this is Tatum. I'm here at the marker."

"What's going on, Tatum? I thought you were in the race."

"The mayor's down. Two shots—just like the woman. Happened right in front of me."

"Shit. Chuck and Max okay?" Sheriff Dale knew they would be up there, like always.

"They're fine, Sheriff. It looks like he hit his target and bugged out."

"When?"

I checked my watch. "It was just before nine."

"Did you see where he fired from?"

"Negative. The sun was behind him. I just heard the shots from up on the ridge."

"Any need for medevac?"

"No, sir. He's graveyard dead. I'm gonna get Chuck and Max back to their truck and out of here before they go into shock."

"Roger. I want you to drive them down the mountain. Go home and get your work clothes on. Marty and I will remain here."

"Where are you?"

"Nelson Mountain, heading east." He was coming in on the La Garita Trail. A tight fit with a Bronco.

"Sir, You're not gonna make it here before the rest of the pack does. Ralph Munger's crossing the bridge right now. Someone needs to stay here and control the scene and turn the runners around. Otherwise, this crime scene will look like a herd of buffalo trampled through it."

A long pause on the radio, as Sheriff Dale understood his dilemma.

"Okay, Tatum, turn them around at the bridge, have Chuck and Max move their table if you have to."

"Got it, Sheriff." I turned to the old men still on their bellies in the pine needles. "Okay, gentlemen, here's what we're going to do. Chuck, go directly to the far side of the bridge and start checking in runners there. I'd do it, but they'd notice the mayor's blood all over me. I don't care what you have to tell them, just keep them on the other side of Whited Creek."

Chuck looked at Max, then back at me, not moving.

"Chuck! Now! Come on! Ralph is already over the bridge. He's gonna wonder why Mayor Jeff is blown away and whether he'll be next. The last thing we need is a bunch of oxygen-starved, panicky runners all over my crime scene. Go!"

Chuck got up without a word and wobbled past the body of the mayor, trying not to step on the bloody dirt and rocks.

"Max, you and I are going to move the table and chairs. We need to make it look like the turnaround is at the bridge."

"But we tell them to touch the marker . . . "

"Yes, I know, Max, but they won't care. They'll just want to get down the hill. Let's go."

I grabbed him by his jacket and pulled him out of the trees. Ralph Munger was already standing there, staring at the body of Jeff Lange.

"Ralph, I need you to go back down the hill, right now."

"The mayor's dead, Bill," he said, not taking his eyes off the bloody mess that was Jeff's head.

"Yes, Ralph, I know. I need to clear the crime scene. Please turn around and run down the hill."

"What?" He looked up at me in disbelief, blinking through his fogged wire-rims.

"Ralph, turn around and run down the hill," I repeated, pulling down the large race banner and covering the body. "I have seventy runners on their way here in minutes, and I don't want them trampling my scene." Chuck was already at the far side of the bridge, turning runners around. He even had his clipboard. Max was moving toward him with the chairs. A few of the runners looked in our direction as they reached the new halfway point, but none of them stopped or stared for very long. Chuck and Max had come through for me. I radioed the sheriff and let him know we were secure. Ralph was still standing there.

"Ralph, please, can you finish the run? We have everything in control here."

This really wasn't true. As far as I knew, I was wrong about the sniper, and he was lining me up for another shot.

"Bill, the mayor's dead. I saw him go down. He's lying there under the race banner. How the heck do you expect me to just pick up and run down the hill like nothing happened?"

"How far were you behind me?" I asked.

If he was a witness, I might as well treat him like one.

"About two hundred yards."

That meant he was a quarter mile back from the marker when the first bullet hit the mayor.

"What did you see from that distance?"

"I saw the mayor reach the marker, then he dropped. The sun was right on him. I saw the whole thing."

"Didn't you take cover?"

"I figured Jeff was the only target when the three of you were left alone. Max and Chuck just stood there like deer in the headlights. Not only that, I think I saw the guy, Bill."

I stopped trying to decide what to do next and looked at Ralph. He was coming around, sounding sharper every moment. He was a good witness, the incident was fresh in his head, and he might have seen the sniper. Standing there, bloody and freezing, I hoped my poor memory would recall this critical interview.

"Ralph, what exactly did you see up there?" I turned and looked up at the ridge. "That's pretty far."

"Well, I didn't see much. I heard the first shot and saw the mayor go down. That kind of kept me focused, but I didn't stop running. I think I actually sped up. When I heard the second shot, I stopped and looked up on the ridge."

"How did you see anything with your glasses on, and fogged up like that?"

"Bill, I'm farsighted. These glasses help me see the rocks in the trail. I have twenty-fifteen uncorrected distance vision, and they didn't fog up until I stopped."

"Okay. I have good vision, too, but the sun was in my eyes from here, Ralph."

"I was back down the trail. The sun was at three o'clock, just over my right shoulder. I could see the backside of that knoll at one o'clock. Someone was up there, moving off the ridge toward the trees, crouched and carrying something in his right hand."

"What did it look like, the thing he was carrying?

"Well, it looked like a rifle, of course, at least, that's how he was carrying it. I only saw him for a couple of seconds and two hundred yards away, so I really didn't get a good look at him."

"Where'd he go?"

"He scooted back across the ridge and into the Englemann spruce up there. He disappeared, so I kept on coming up the hill to see if Mayor Jeff was okay."

"Did you see a vehicle? An ATV or a jeep?"

"No. Once he hit the trees, that was it. He was gone."

"What was he wearing?"

"Shirt, pants, dark. That's all I could tell from down there."

"Did he have a hat, anything else remarkable?"

Ralph looked up at the ridge and reviewed the pictures in his memory. He was careful with his answer. I couldn't think of a better witness.

"He had long hair, Bill. Long, black hair tied in a ponytail."

"Could it have been a woman?"

"Yes, but it could have been Bob Marley, for all I know."

He was right. The hair wasn't much to go on, but it was

something. The shooter stepped out in the light and took a big risk on this one. He was exposed during the shot and the escape. He chose a public event for his assassination, even though few people were up this high cheering on the runners. Like the last ambush in Deep Creek, however, his planning and timing were impeccable. The sniper's edge was his acute knowledge of his target and operational area. He knew Mayor Jeff would be well in the lead, like he was every year. He knew Mayor Jeff would slow down to touch the marker at the trail intersection, making himself a nearly stationary target. He knew the small saddle jutting out into the valley overlooking the turnaround was an ideal vantage point. Finally, he knew the proximity to multiple backcountry trails and the Continental Divide gave him a variety of quick escape routes and an opportunity to disappear into the wilderness.

"Marty, this is Tatum," I said over the radio. "The subject is wearing dark clothing and has long, black hair. It might be in a ponytail."

"Did you see him, Bill?" she responded.

"Negative, but we had a witness this time. He was last seen moving east into the trees on the ridge. He might have a vehicle hidden back there. He did last time up on Deep Creek, an ATV."

"How long ago?"

"Fifteen minutes, twenty on the outside. He took off toward the trees after the second shot."

"Shit, Tatum. I think I missed him. I barely made it up here two minutes ago. I made a stop at Inspiration Point along the way, thinking he might shoot from there. Looks like it cost me."

"Just hold your position, Marty. It's a big valley. He's either heading north toward the Divide or east toward you. Maybe we'll get lucky. I hope you're concealed. You don't want him to see you first."

"I'm good."

Just then, I saw the sheriff coming down the La Garita Trail from the west, bouncing along the rocky path in his Bronco. By this time, the morning sun was up and doing its best to warm the high, open valley, but the wind was picking up, too. Straight out of the east, the stiff mountain breeze numbed my fingers and turned my toes to ice inside wet running shoes. I shivered through the entire interview with Ralph and hoped Sheriff Dale had some dry clothes in his truck. I walked up the trail to meet him; maybe the movement would generate a little warmth. He parked the Bronco outside the crime scene and tossed a duffel bag to me as I approached.

"Put some clothes on, Deputy Tatum. You'll catch your death."

As usual, the sheriff was prepared for anything. The clothes were three sizes too big—I am about as average as you can get, but I wasn't complaining. He even had a dry pair of wool socks and worn out hiking boots.

"Okay, Tatum. Give it to me."

I started with my own perspective of the shooting, then gave him Ralph's version. I was relieved to brief the sheriff, because he had a notebook and took everything down without a word. He walked over to Max and Chuck and pulled each of them aside. I stayed with him and listened, saying nothing, letting the process take over. I was slowly transforming from participant to observer, which is why the sheriff ran the show. I had to remove myself from the act in order to be objective. He talked with Ralph last, near the body. Ralph repeated his story, word for word.

"Can you think of anything else, Ralph? I really need you to clear out of here," said the sheriff. "You want Deputy Tatum to take you down? He needs to get out of my clothes."

Ralph looked up at the ridge again, then down at the

body of the mayor. "No, I can't recall any more right now, Sheriff Dale, but I'll run down the hill and finish. Maybe that will stir up some memories. Always does. By the way, Deputy Tatum, come by the shop when you're done up here. I have some preliminary results on your fragments." Then he turned and jogged stiffly back down the trail.

Sheriff Dale checked for runners down the hill and pulled the banner off the body.

"Same way as the woman," he said, mostly to himself. "You think it's the same shooter?"

"We'll have to check the ballistics, but it sure looks that way, Sheriff Dale."

"I agree. Why the mayor?"

This thought hadn't even crossed my mind. Why the mayor? I repeated in my head. Obviously, he had a relationship with the previous victim, but that was the only link.

The significance of the mayor's death began to sink in. Here we were, at the apex of the high tourist season—4th of July weekend—and we had a dead mayor. A dead mayor shot by a trained sniper during the kickoff event of the holiday festivities. Would we cancel the parade? Clear the town? Declare martial law?

"I don't know, Sheriff. There are ties, of course, between the mayor and the dead woman. You read the journal yourself, but there are a few pieces missing. Until we find them and put them together, we'll never know."

"I'll have to tell Mandy Lange her husband's dead. I didn't see her at the start of the race. Do you know where she is?"

"Cynthia said Mandy had to drive into Pueblo this morning on an errand. I expect she'll be back this afternoon."

"I'll have to tell Cynthia, too, and quick. She'll be wondering where her father is."

I'd forgotten about the race. Most of the runners would have finished by now, and the usual top three—the mayor, me, and Ralph—would not be among them. They would wonder what was going on. They would try to call Max and Chuck on the radio that was in my hand, tuned to the sheriff's frequency. I quickly snapped it back to the race channel.

"Max? Chuck? Come in, what's going on up there? Has my father checked in?"

It was Cynthia's voice, panicky and tense. I looked at the sheriff. He stared straight back at me. I followed the unspoken order.

"Cynthia, this is Deputy Tatum. I'm up here at the turnaround with your father. Ralph Munger is on the way down. All the other runners have checked in."

"Is my father all right? Why are you two out of the race? I'm coming up there." She would, too.

"Please stay in town. I'll be right there."

"What happened, Bill? Is my father okay?"

"Meet me at the station. I'll be there in thirty minutes." I switched the radio back to the sheriff's channel, cutting her off. I didn't want to answer her questions over the radio.

"You can take my Bronco. It'll take you forever through Windy Gulch. Go down through Wason Park on the east side," said Sheriff Dale.

"What about our sniper?"

"I think he's vanished again, Deputy Tatum. Marty should have intercepted him by now. He probably went north over the divide, staying in the tree line. He's probably halfway to Stewart Creek by now."

"We could track him."

"You ever track anyone up here, Deputy? Me neither. It's not in my sheriff's manual. The roads near the divide aren't like the nice muddy trail we followed down in Deep Creek. It's dry as a bone up here, and if he picks up one of the pack trails, we won't be able to tell his track from any of the other four-by-fours and ATVs out this weekend. Besides, I won't risk any more of my people walking into another ambush."

He was right, of course. We'd lost him and the initiative. We never had the initiative to begin with. The shooter could easily double back and set a trap for whomever pursued him. He was probably in his hide site right now, waiting for us to follow him blindly into the mountains. It wasn't worth the risk.

"When you get back to town, deal with Cynthia quickly, then seal off the trailhead from the south. I don't want any tourists up here. Marty and I can secure the site. Stay on our frequency. Get back as soon as you can."

The sheriff radioed Marty to inform her I was coming up while I hopped in the Bronco and took off up the trail, driving right under the sniper's knoll. I saw no sign of Marty's vehicle as I crested the ridge—she must have taken the sheriff's advice to heart and stayed out of sight. Not wanting to share the mayor's fate, I gunned the Bronco hard down the ridge and made it back to town in ten minutes, cutting across the open Wason Park Plateau and picking up the pack trail to the south. The switchbacks on the steep decent into the Belmont box canyon were particularly exciting as I sent gravel flying down the mountainside.

There were still a lot of people milling around, looking at the race results posted on the public bulletin board in Veteran's Park. A few volunteers were taking down the finish line chute and registration booth. I did not, however, see Cynthia Lange. She was either waiting for me in the station or on her way up the mountain to find her dead father.

I found her at the station pacing back and forth in the open office area near the radio room, probably listening to Marty and the sheriff. I hoped they'd thought of this and didn't mention the mayor's death.

"Goddammit, Bill, what the hell is going on?" She stormed over to me, blue eyes blazing with anger and fear.

"Come into the office and sit down, Cynthia. I'll tell you everything."

"I don't want to sit down, I want you to tell me what's happening up there. Where is my father?"

She wasn't giving me any chance to do it easily. "He's dead, Cynthia. Shot by someone at the halfway point. I saw it happen. I'm sorry."

Her beautiful eyes widened, not comprehending the blow I'd just dealt her heart. She was my age, but serious and focused—the older daughter. She was Daddy's Girl, and I'd just taken him away from her. She finally sat down at Jerry's desk and looked away, closing her eyes from the terrible truth of her father's death. Tears squeezed out and ran down her cheeks.

She looked back up at me. "Did you catch him? Did you catch the man who shot my father?"

"No, but we have a description. We'll find him, Cynthia." I hoped my words held more confidence than I felt.

"Take me up there, Tatum. I want to see him." She was getting back to her normal, demanding self. She wiped the tears out of her eyes and stood up. She was my height, 5'9", tall, like her mother. She stared right into my eyes, daring me to defy her. I did.

"I can't do that, Cynthia. It's still a crime scene. We've barely had enough time to work up there, and the sheriff would kill me if I brought you." I didn't sound convincing, but I didn't want to tell her that her father's killer could still be up there, setting up his next target.

Anger had completely replaced the fear and anguish in her eyes, and I stood in the full force of her fury. She did not yell this time.

"I don't care about your crime scene, Deputy Tatum. I

don't care about the sheriff. I want to see my father. I will go up there myself, and you can't stop me."

I'd had about enough of her petulance. "No, you will not, Miss Lange. You will remain in town and far away from East Willow Creek. I am tasked to seal off the trail from the public, and that's what I'm going to do. If you insist on disturbing the area, I will place you under arrest and lock you up, if I have to. I am very sorry for your loss, Miss Lange, but if you want us to find the person who killed your father, you will need to stay out of the way." I turned away from her piercing blue eyes and walked over to my spare uniform, hanging on the coat tree in the corner. When I turned back around, she was sitting again, eyes staring at the wall, at the midpoint of nowhere.

She was still there when I stepped out of the sheriff's office, back in uniform. I even had an extra Resistol and service belt. Sergeant Richter taught me well.

"Cynthia." Wyatt Earp was back, being nice to the ladies. "When your mother returns from Pueblo, I need you to tell her what happened. It'll be better coming from you."

"She's not in Pueblo, Bill," she said, not taking her eyes off the midpoint. "She left last night while Dad was still at the WWE. I think she's screwing around on him." Her voice was full of contempt. I wonder how she'd feel if she knew about her father's own transgressions.

"Do you know whom she was with?" I asked.

"No. She's been disappearing ever since I came home from school the first week of June. Sometimes in the middle of the week. Daddy's oblivious. He's so trusting, but I know better."

I didn't have time to interview Cynthia Lange—I had to get back up the mountain. She wasn't going anywhere.

"Please, Cynthia, just stay here in Belmont and sit your mother down when she gets back. I need to go."

She stood up, not looking at me, and left without a word. I followed her out the door, hopped in the Bronco, and headed back up into the canyon, following the run route. I placed a barricade and police tape at the trailhead, feeling stupid. Ten feet of yellow tape and an orange barricade were only a passing thought in the expansive San Juan Mountains.

Not wanting to bounce up the rocky three miles to the crime scene, I backtracked to town and took the stock driveway back up the mountain. Marty and I had both driven this way, so I assumed the route was safe. Trying to minimize the impact of driving back and forth across the killer's potential ingress or escape routes, I followed my own tire tracks across the plateau. I had to go a little slower, but I still made it back to the top of the ridge above the crime scene in fifteen minutes. I radioed the sheriff.

"Tatum, proceed to the gun club and find out if Orville saw anyone moving up or down the trail this morning. Marty's checking out the shooter's firing position and approach. We have the scene under control."

I turned the Bronco east down the La Garita Trail and headed for Halfmoon Gun Club, two miles away.

Seven

THE JAMES FAMILY HAD OWNED THE HALFMOON
Ranch and Gun Club since silver was king of the valley. Orville's grandfather, Wilbur James, bought the entire
four thousand acres of the Wason Park Plateau in 1890, including La Garita Peak and five miles of the Continental
Divide on its northern border. The miners in Belmont
thought he was a fool—no one ever took silver out of the
wide-open meadows and lush draws of the high plateau.
Wilbur was not after silver, however; he was after the
money it attracted. Railroad men, mining executives, and
other capitalists came to Belmont to supervise their various
activities, but they didn't want to stay in the dirty squalor
of the mining town. Wilbur James brought them to the rustic hunting lodge of the Halfmoon Ranch, fed them five-
star meals cooked by a Paris-trained chef, and introduced
them to other pursuits of the valley—fly-fishing and big
game hunting. Soon, men came to the Halfmoon Ranch

just to catch rainbows or shoot elk, and they kept coming long after the Mother Lode yielded no more silver. Wilbur taught his sons to guide, track, and manage bull elk and mule deer bucks, so their visitors were guaranteed trophy animals year after year.

Orville James and his older brothers, Bernard and Walter, were just learning the trade when the Japanese bombed Pearl Harbor, and they all went off to war. Orville was just 17. The Army pulled Orville out of France in 1944 when Walter was killed at Leyte Gulf in the Philippines. Bernard was already under Iron Bottom Sound in Guadalcanal.

Orville returned to the mountains to help his father and bachelor uncles with the ranch. Business had dropped off during the Depression, and fewer and fewer visitors came to the ranch in the years after the war until the end of the next. Orville's father almost closed the hunting lodge until Orville suggested that they open the ranch to the locals. The James family had always looked down, literally and figuratively, on the rabble in Belmont, but Orville convinced his father that dues paid by the locals would keep the lights on and the lodge warm. Orville began adding members to the Halfmoon Gun Club right after Truman fired MacArthur. Every male who could shoot a rifle or cast a fly had been dying to set foot in the hunting paradise of the Halfmoon Ranch for years. At his father's demand, however, Orville limited the rolls to one hundred members and kept the dues high. Even so, he filled his roster and started a waiting list within a year, and the ranch survived. Orville built a trap range near the lodge and began raising chukkars and blue grouse, expanding the diversity of his hunts and clientele.

The success of the Halfmoon Ranch outpaced Orville's skills in keeping the books, and the lodge nearly went bankrupt in the late eighties. Knowing her father was too proud to ask, Mandy returned to Belmont from California with her new husband in tow. Mandy had a shiny, new accounting degree and immediately cleaned up the Half-moon's teetering financial situation. She also opened the Weminuche Wilderness Experience Sporting Goods Store in downtown Belmont. The WWE was the public face of the otherwise remote Halfmoon Ranch, and the two businesses succeeded in tandem.

By 1995, the Halfmoon Ranch had surpassed silver mining as the most successful industry in Belmont. Orville added stables and groomed nordic skiing trails at Mandy's suggestion to bridge through the off-season slump and attract wives and children to the ranch. Mandy rented mountain bikes and skis at the WWE and offered the private trails of the Halfmoon as a complete package. The ranch became a year-round attraction, offering fishing in the spring and summer, hunting in the fall, cross-country skiing in the winter, and horseback riding and mountain-biking any time.

Orville was now eighty, but he still guided elk hunts and showed his clients where the biggest trout lay. Having only one daughter and no sons, however, Orville had to hire a staff to keep the complex operation running. He had a full-time game manager, similar to the *jaegermeisters* of German hunting grounds, who maintained the bird pens and monitored the growth and harvest of the elk and mule deer herds. Knowing very little about dogs and upland game, Orville hired a seasonal bird guide who brought his own shorthairs and spaniels in the fall. Like his grandfather, Orville had a Paris-trained chef in the massive lodge kitchen. Philippe could lay out a spread to feed fifty lumberjacks or cook dainty meals and finger food for the ladies' art workshops the ranch hosted.

Orville still believed that the gun club memberships were the foundation of his success, and he gave the local hunters from Belmont the same opportunity to hunt trophy bulls and bucks as his best clients. In turn, the locals recommended the Halfmoon Ranch to their customers and business contacts. Orville was very strict on bull and buck management. If you killed a bull elk before maturity, you were out of the club, no questions asked. No one ever broke the rules, and the huge animals from the Halfmoon Ranch were legendary.

I drove through three miles of ranch property to get to the hunting lodge, high rolling meadows and deep draws lined with thick stands of ponderosa pine. I tried to focus on the task at hand and the body of the mayor in East Willow Valley, but I still kept my eyes open for big mulies or elk. This fall would be my first official hunting season as a full member of the Halfmoon Hunt Club. I was allowed to join the club at the end of last year, after Orville personally attended one of my elk hunts on the ranch. I didn't kill one on that hunt, but he approved of my skills and patience. He saw me shoot three nickel-size groups at three hundred meters with both my .30-06 Ruger No. 1 and .270 Winchester Model 700 on the club rifle range, so my shooting was not a concern. As a new member, I would have to go on at least three hunts with veteran members before I could go off on my own. This was a fifty-year tradition, so I didn't mind. The old guys knew the ranch better than Orville's guides, anyway. Only Darren Schmidt, the ranch biologist and wildlife manager, knew the terrain and game herds better than the club members, but he was still second to Orville.

I crested the ridge above the lodge and looked down on the ranch complex, sitting on the northern bank of Lake Madeline, named after Orville's grandmother. Family lore said that naming the lake after her was the only way Wilbur convinced his new, St. Louis–born wife to accompany him to the top of the mountain. A forest of Douglas fir and Englemann spruce flanked the ranch and both sides of the lake, but the land was open to the south, offering a commanding view of the entire Rio Grande Valley. The lodge was an A-frame, like my own cabin, but massive. Each generation of the James family added to the original structure, but stayed loyal to the late-nineteenth-century rustic style. Constructed entirely of local timber, the main lodge was three stories tall. Two-story wings extended back from the lodge, giving the whole building a chevron shape. Mandy's addition didn't add more square feet to the place, it added light. She had windows cut out of the old timber walls along the south side on all three floors of the main lodge, pouring light into the dark main hall. The view from the ground floor was stunning.

From my vantage point, I could see the other outbuildings of the ranch. The horse stables stretched east and west directly behind the lodge. A couple of guests and the stable master were getting ready for a late morning ride. The tall nets of the bird pens were up the hill behind the stables, next to the empty bird dog runs. A few blue grouse flapped about, but most of the raised birds stayed on the ground. The trap range was on the northwest corner of the complex. I could barely see the firing positions of the rifle range on the opposite side of the meadow. The ranges were quiet now, waiting for hunting season. In late August, as the tourists began to dwindle and the days got colder, the gun club members would climb the mountain and begin the annual rituals. They would fire up the trap throwers and break a few clay targets. Later, they'd open the rifle range and fine-tune their optics out to four hundred meters. They would sit in the main hall of the lodge, talk to Darren about the strength of the herd, and try to coax out his secrets. Darren gave them the usual report and other vague references to concentrations of elk and mule deer, but they would have to go out and scout for themselves. Every serious big game hunter in Belmont was a club member or on the waiting list. The rolls included Chuck Dinnerstein, Max Toliver, Sheriff

Dale, Henry Earl Callahan, and Thomas Pitcher—but not Jerry. Mayor Jeff, Orville's son-in-law, never wanted to be a member, and now he never would be. Dana Pratt had been denied membership for five straight years. He was pissed when Orville let me in after being on the waiting list for only three years. Orville was an Army sniper during the war, so I think that helped my case.

Just before I entered the forest on the western shoulder of the ranch, I noticed two figures down by the banks of Lake Madeline. One was casting into the mirrored surface of the cobalt blue water, and the other was observing. Probably Orville coaching a guest on the fine art of fly-casting. No one in Belmont could read trout water like Dr. Ed, but Orville James was the better caster.

Not wanting to drive right up on Orville with a client, regardless of the urgency of my visit, I pulled into the small gravel lot on the north side of the lodge. It was nearly full of SUVs with empty bike racks. I passed through the tall lodge doors and into the slate-tiled foyer. The interior of the lodge was made entirely of roughed-out logs. The building had been restored a few times over the last hundred years, but the original timbers, three feet in diameter, still held up the ceiling. In the entrance I was greeted by the largest bull elk I'd ever seen. Well, I'd seen it here before, but I never ceased to be amazed by the huge head mounted on the north fireplace, greeting each visitor with its six-by-six rack. The central feature of the lodge was its massive hearths and chimneys. There were three of them in the main hall, freestanding to the vaulted timber ceiling, like pillars in a cathedral. One on the north end, where the huge elk head was mounted, and one in each southern corner. All of them displayed the finest trophy animals taken out of the Halfmoon Ranch. Most of them were recent, a result of the fine game management by Orville and Darren. I walked through the main hall and out onto the southern deck. I still had the chill from the freezing wet morning in my running clothes, but the climbing alpine sun was all I needed.

I jumped off the deck and clomped down the gravel path to the lake, stopping a dozen meters or so from Orville and his guest, far enough back to keep from getting caught in the back cast. He already knew I was there. Orville told his guest to keep casting, and walked up to meet me.

He was dressed in jeans, scuffed ropers, a long-sleeved twill shirt, and a beat-up old cowboy hat. This was his summer uniform. I rarely saw him wear anything but. In the winter, he added a leather sheepskin coat and Sorel boots. He was about two inches shorter than me, and thirty pounds lighter. He passed on the old man's gut by personally running the ranch. He preferred to walk or ride a horse to keep his operation going, and he extended that requirement to anyone who set foot on his ranch. He allowed mountain bikers at Mandy's insistence, but no ATVs. At eighty, he moved like a man of half his age. The only indicator of his true number of years was his wrinkled face and full head of white hair.

"Morning, Deputy," he said, squinting up at me in the bright sunshine. "What brings you up here? You don't look like you're here to sight in your rifle."

"Morning Orville, sorry to interrupt you, but it's urgent."

"No problem. Why don't we go inside?" He turned to his guest, a tall, awkward man with brand new gear. "Mr. Davis, I must go inside and chat with the deputy. You keep workin' it. Remember, it's all in the wrist. Don't arm it."

We walked back through the glass patio door and into Orville's office in the western wing of the lodge, just off the main hall. His workspace was spartan but comfortable—a few worn leather chairs around his grandfather's old desk. The only mount in the room hung behind the desk, a beautiful typical mule deer buck. A large, glass-topped map table dominated the center of the room. On it, a 1/24,000-scale map of the ranch was carefully pieced together out of multiple USGS topographicals. There were no doors in any of the common rooms in the lodge, so we just hung up our hats and leaned on the map table. I'd never seen Orville sit during the day, unless it was on a horse or in a tree stand.

"Out with it, Deputy Tatum."

"Well, sir, I have some bad news. Your son-in-law was killed this morning. Shot on the trail during the Ten-Miler."

"Holy Christ." He turned away from me and stared at the map, not seeing it. "Who did it?"

"We don't know. He fired from the eastern ridge above the marker at East Willow Creek. I'm sorry, Orville."

"Does Mandy know?"

"No, sir. Cynthia told me she went into Pueblo this morning and won't be back for a few hours still. She's going to wait in town and tell her herself."

"So Cynthia knows. How did she take it? Well, I know Cynthia. She's probably madder than hell. Wanted to storm up the mountain and find the guy, didn't she?"

I nodded. He knew his granddaughter.

"Son of a bitch. Who would do this? Jeff was the nicest guy in town. Always treated everyone fair and equal. Took care of Mandy and the girls. Didn't flinch when she wanted to leave California and move back here."

I hated to interrupt his eulogy. "Orville, did you see anyone up here this morning, maybe out on the northwest quadrant? The crime scene was just down the trail a few miles to the west. He may have passed through the ranch on the way up or back."

Orville looked at the map in front of him. "Show me where it happened."

I scanned the left side of the map table and found East Willow Valley. The large-scale map was very detailed, showing each contour line and intermittent stream with great accuracy. The sheriff's department used similar maps, just a smaller scale. I had pieced together multiple 1/50,000 maps to form one giant map of Mineral, Hinsdale, and Saguache Counties and mounted it on the wall at the station.

"Here's the turnaround," I said, showing him with the tip of my pocketknife, "right where the three streams and two trails intersect."

"He waited until Jeff slowed down to touch the marker," he said, studying the terrain. "I know this area. He probably fired right from this knoll to the east. It's only a three hundred yard shot, and the draw behind him gave him a covered route to reposition."

He was right, of course. I said nothing. Orville continued to stare at the map, thinking like a sniper.

"Did Max and Chuck see him?" He knew the traditions, too.

"No. Sun was in their eyes, like me. I was just approaching the bridge after the first shot."

"He was only after Jeff, then. Otherwise you, Chuck, and Max wouldn't be breathing."

"That's what it looks like. Did you see anyone this morning, Orville, between seven and nine?"

"No. No one. Darren and I were on the opposite side of the ranch, in the southeast quadrant, though, checking on the bird cover in Bellows Creek. We left at dawn."

"Maybe some of your guests were out that way."

"I'll have to check. Jacob had some new riders out this morning. They may have been out on the west side." Jacob Stackhouse was the stable master. Orville pulled the radio off his belt and called him in. "He'll be here directly."

We looked back at the map table and stared silently at the killing zone. The fine brown contours and blue stream lines detailed every rise and cut in the valley, but said nothing of the violence and death that happened there this morning.

"That's just how I would have done it," he said quietly. "From that high ground he could shoot, confirm, and disappear into the wilderness. Jeff never had a chance."

Just then, Jacob walked in the office. He was a head taller than I and half a head again taller than Orville. It didn't help much when he took off his cowboy hat. His blonde hair was plastered to his head like mine probably was. He was thin and rangy, not yet twenty-five, but he grew up riding horses like most kids grew up riding bicycles. His family owned a dude ranch up the valley.

"Jacob, Deputy Bill has some questions for you. I'll step outside for a moment."

I knew Orville needed a smoke more than he wanted to give us some privacy. Marlboros hadn't killed this cowboy.

"What can I do for you, Deputy?" asked Jacob.

"Jacob, I understand you had a few guests out on horseback this morning on the western side of the ranch. Can you show me where you took them?"

"Sure." Jacob walked over to the map table and oriented himself. He poked a bony finger at the ranch complex.

"We started here at the stable, that's this long rectangle behind the lodge. Left at seven, right after breakfast." He traced the route. "Then we followed the La Garita west for a mile or so. We were moving slow. The guests I was with never rode before, so I was taking it easy.

"At the edge of the woods on the western side of our valley, we turned north. See the trail? It runs right along the edge of the forest and up toward the divide. View is real pretty up there. We stopped a lot to take pictures."

"Are your guests still here at the ranch?" I asked him.

"Sure, they're probably eating lunch in the dining hall right now. Philippe's makin' rib-eye sandwiches." He pronounced the chef's name "Fillip."

"How far did you ride with them?"

"Well, we hit the tree line up around eleven thousand feet and then turned west again," said Jacob, pointing back at the map. "We went another couple of miles or so off ranch land into national forest then back into the trees above the falls on East Willow."

The falls were only a mile and a half upstream from the marker where Jeff was killed.

"Can you remember what time you arrived at the falls?"

"The trail is pretty narrow and rocky, turns a lot. The folks I was with had a hard time getting through it. I'd say we made it to the falls by eight or so."

"Did you see anyone on the ride out? On foot, ATV, or in a vehicle?"

"No sir, no one. Tourists up from town usually don't make it up this high until really late in the morning."

"How long did you spend at the falls?"

"Not very long. The woman was getting sore and wanted to go back. I don't think she liked riding much. We headed back up the trail then south as we left the trees."

"Which way did you circle back toward the ranch?"

"We hit the La Garita trail around nine o'clock and headed east. That's where we saw Marty coming up the trail."

"Marty Three Stones, the deputy?"

"Yup. She was coming up out of the East Willow Valley in her Bronco. She drove up to us on the plateau and asked if we'd seen anyone, just like you, then told us to clear out back to the ranch. We were already moving that way, anyway."

I wondered why Marty never reported seeing them.

"Did you see anyone else on the trail?"

"Nope. We made it back to the ranch by nine thirty."

"Thanks, Jacob. That's it for now. Would you please tell Orville to come back in?

Jacob put on his hat and walked through the door. Tired of staring at the map, I moved over to the huge stone fireplace. The broad mantel held dozens of photos. A few frames of celebrity pictures adorned the mantle, even one of Charleton Heston squatting over a big bull elk, but most were family shots and pictures of club members after successful hunts. A yellowed image of young Orville was hidden behind the newer rows. I picked it up, knocking over another. I caught the frame before it shattered on the rough stone of the hearth.

Heart pounding from the narrow escape from embarrassment, I looked at the photos, one in each hand. In my left was the one I'd reached for—Orville and his spotter. They wore the baggy pants and jump boots of the 82nd Airborne's 505th Parachute Infantry Brigade. Orville made the jumps into North Africa, Normandy, and the Netherlands before he was sent home as the last living son of the James family. He cradled his scoped M1903A4 .30-06 Springfield sniper rifle in one arm; the left arm dangled at his side, the ever-present cigarette between his fingers. His observer looked as cocky and relaxed as Orville, a large pair of binoculars hanging from his neck. Deliverers of long-range death at the top of their game. A game if you ran, you just died tired.

The photo in my right hand was taken more recently, but it was still old—snapped in the late sixties. It was similar in composition to the war photo, Orville standing, cradling a rifle. In this shot, however, the person standing next to him was an eighteen-year-old Amanda James. She cradled a scoped, bolt-action rifle in her left arm. I squinted and recognized the rifle as a Remington Model 700 ADL, just like the one my father gave me. At their feet lay a pair of mule deer bucks, one of which was on the wall in the office. Mandy's was bigger. She had a huge smile on her face—the smile of an only child who knew she'd made her father proud. Her beauty still radiated out of the old picture, dark eyes shining and cheeks flush with excitement. Mandy's black ponytail tumbled out of her cowboy hat over her left shoulder. Her hair was longer then, almost down to her waist, but the color was the same.

Connections flared in my head—black ponytail. Mandy was the daughter of a combat Army sniper. She grew up on a big game ranch, learning to stalk and shoot elk and mule deer from a man trained to kill other men. She probably knew the terrain as well as Orville, who taught his daughter everything he'd learned from three generations of hunters on the Halfmoon Ranch.

There was motive. Small towns have few secrets, and Jeff wasn't very secretive of his activities with Gayle Whippany. The digital photos confirmed that. Had Mandy found out about their fooling around, then killed them both in the controlled rage of a woman scorned? Motive and opportunity—Mandy Lange had plenty of both.

Eight

"WHATCHA LOOKIN' AT?" I JUMPED OUT OF MY skin and nearly dropped both pictures. I turned around and there was Orville, standing right behind me. The man was a cat.

"What was your spotter's name?"

"Wendell Dawson, from Philadelphia. They put us together before the jumps into North Africa, and we stayed a team all the way through Market Garden."

"Do you still keep in touch?"

His eyes became clouded and distant. "He was killed right after they pulled me out and sent me home."

I changed the subject. "Mandy was quite a hunter in her youth." I nodded at the photo in my right hand. "Her buck is bigger than yours."

His eyes came back to the present. "She still is a good hunter. Shoots better'n me. 'Course, I'm eighty, now. Even you shoot better than I do."

I put both frames carefully back on the mantel. "Tell me, Orville, who shoots a two-seventy in the club?"

"Who doesn't? Well, I take that back. A lot of the younger guys do. Us older and wiser members prefer something with a little more power—seven millimeter Mags and thirty-aught sixes. Can't shoot an elk with one, either."

You could if you were good enough. "I see. Do a lot of the members reload, too?"

"No, maybe a dozen of the hundred. We all reload for the rest of the members. They put their orders in after the season—specifying muzzle velocity and bullet weight. The club buys the powder, bullets, and empty cases in bulk to save on cost. We usually get them all loaded by August. Already finished this year's batch. Now I'm just loading for the guests. Some of our regular clients place orders, too."

"Would you recognize a reload of the club just by the shell?"

"Maybe." He eyed me. "What are you drivin' at, Tatum?"

I handed him the shell. "Can you tell me if this was one of the club's reloads?" I pulled the paper bag with the empty casing out of my pocket and handed it to Orville. He took it and peered at the case.

"I'll need to take it out."

"Sure, no problem." I handed him a pair of latex gloves. He stared up at me for a moment like I was asking him to put on lipstick, then he awkwardly pulled them over his knobby fingers. He held the shell by the ends between his thumb and index finger.

"Might be. Tough to say. All the boys who reload have their own benches at home. Let's go down."

He turned and led me out of the office and into the grand foyer, carrying the shell. The split-timber staircase ended at the ground floor, but the flagstones continued downstairs to the basement. The stairs spiraled once and stopped at a heavy, locked steel door. Orville opened it, and we went inside.

Where the upper floors were rustic and old, the underground level of the lodge was practical and modern. Orville had refinished the original basement with off-white asphalt tile and fluorescent lighting. A long heavy worktable dominated the center of the room, probably used for cleaning guns. Gray equipment lockers lined one wall, followed by cold rolled steel gun cabinets along the next. There were at least two-dozen of them, probably filled with rifles and shotguns.

"Are these all yours?" I asked, sweeping my arm along the wall of steel.

"Nope, just the first few have my guns. The others all belong to the members. Most of them store their gear up here."

We passed through another door and into Orville's workshop. Benches lined the walls, each with its own function—gunsmithing, woodworking, tack repair. A drill press and table saw sat in the middle of the floor next to a saddle rack.

"Nice saddle," I said.

"Yup, that's one of my guest's. She needed a little work done on it. It's pretty old, and she doesn't ride that much. Hate to have her go off on a ride and the thing falls apart."

We walked over to the reloading bench. On it lay the various tools and machines used for reloading rifle and shotgun shells—a tumbler, powder measure, scales, case trimmer. Two presses were bolted to the edge of the table: one rifle press, and a larger press for shotgun shells. Below the table were cardboard boxes of empty shotgun shells and rifle brass.

"Now, I don't load much two-seventy. The guys who reload tend to specialize. That way we get it done quicker. I do the thirty aught-six and three hundreds mostly. I have some two-seventy here, though."

He set the shell on the bench and opened the cabinet above it, pulling out a plastic box the size of a shoebox. Inside were about six dozen loaded rifle shells, standing neatly in their individual foam holders. He drew one out and leaned in under the light attached to the bottom of the cabinet, comparing it to the shell I found in Deep Creek.

"Well, it might be one of ours. Same brand of brass. Neck looks trimmed about the same. Pretty common, though. It's not like we put our logo on every shell, Deputy Tatum."

"Who loads your two-seventy shells?"

"Denver Petry. Where'd you get this shell, Deputy?"

"Sorry, Orville, can't say right now."

"Is this the bullet that killed Jeff?" He locked his hawk eyes on me, lower jaw jutting out in anger and defiance.

"Orville, you know I can't go into this with you. Sheriff's business."

"Looks like it's my business, too, Tatum. Jeff was family, the father of my grandchildren, killed just down the trail from my home. This is my business as much as yours."

"I understand, Orville, I really do, but I'm sorry. I cannot go into the details of the case with you at this time."

He stared at me for a second, then released me from his glare and turned back to the bench.

"You going to visit Denver Petry?"

"Probably."

"Well, step lightly around him. He spooks easy. Doesn't care much for government."

"Got it. I'll be careful."

He swung around and faced me again, balled fists on his hips. "You do something else for me, Tatum. When you find this prick, I want you to take him out. You know there'll be no justice for my daughter and grandchildren. You just take him out the same way he killed Jeff."

His vehemence surprised me, but I recovered quickly. "Orville, I am a deputy sheriff, not a vigilante. I will do everything I can to bring Mayor Jeff's killer to justice, but I will not hunt the man down."

He crossed his arms and twisted up his mouth. "Are we done here, Deputy? I have guests to attend to."

"Yes, Orville. If you remember anything else, please let me know."

"I'll do that, Deputy." His words were icy. He didn't show me out.

I left him in his shop, brooding. As I walked through the cathedral entryway and into the light of the afternoon, I spotted Jacob near the stables, just finishing mucking them out. The smell of freshly turned bedding and horse leather filled my nose as I approached the stable master.

"Hey, Jacob, I thought of something else."

"Okay." He hung up his scoop shovel. He must've mucked out the stables in record time—he was sweating profusely and breathing rapidly. The veins in his bony arms stood out like tree roots.

"Do you think I can talk to the guests you took out to East Willow Falls this morning? I need to confirm a few things."

"Like what? I told you everything." His eyes darted from me to the lodge then off to his left. He seemed agitated. He was cool as a cucumber in the first interview.

"Just being thorough. You know, they might've seen something you didn't."

"Well, I doubt that. They spent most of their time just trying to stay in the saddle. They didn't look around that much unless we stopped." His eyes darted as quickly as his fingers, which were busy curling the brim of his Stetson. He couldn't keep still.

"Anyway, I'd like to ask them a few questions. Can you hook—"

"No," he interrupted me, speaking rapidly and a bit too loud for our proximity. "They checked out right after the ride around eleven. That's check-out time, you know."

"They checked out on a Saturday? Right before the 4th of July?"

"Yup." He must have been terrible poker player. He could've saved himself the time and written "LIAR" in big bold letters on his forehead.

"Did they say where they were going?"

"Nope."

"Did they leave a home address, a phone number?"

"Maybe. I don't handle that stuff."

"Do you remember their names?" My left brain was tiring of the vagueness, but my right brain was prickly with suspicion.

Jacob stared off over my shoulder. "Andy and Heather. Don't know the last name. Didn't tip me a dime."

"Do you know how I can find their last names?"

"You could ask Orville."

"Does he check people in and out?"

"No, Wendy takes care of that."

"Who's Wendy?"

"She's like the concierge of the place. Not really certain what that means, but she'll know."

"Where can I find her?"

"Wendy? She's probably in the kitchen, helping Philippe."

I left Jacob and his vague and agitated self at the stables and headed back toward the lodge. The ranch kitchen was on the east side of the main hall. I'd heard the sounds of lunch preparation from there when I left Orville, and the clatter was even louder when I entered the long kitchen, just off the foyer. Very much like Eunice's kitchen at the Belmont Hotel it was—the lodge's rustic charm ended at the kitchen door. Stainless steel and copper cookware lined both aisles. Philippe had built a cooking facility to rival any of his peers' in Denver, San Francisco, or New York. No one had on chef's white, however. The staff was dressed casually in jeans and matching green twill shirts with the Halfmoon logo embroidered above the left breast pocket—a bold, white "HR." Instead of white hats or hair-nets, they wore baseball caps, turned backward, with the same logo stitched above the bill. They hustled like it was lunch hour at the Broadmoor in Colorado Springs. The only noise was the clanging of pots and the slamming of oven doors. I ambled over to the nearest cook, turning rib eyes on the indoor grill.

"Hi there, do you know where I can find Philippe?"

"You found him." He glanced at me for one second, then turned his attention back to the steaks. There were twenty of them. He was a few inches shorter than me, and ten years older. Thin and compact, the man was a ball of energy, checking and flipping the nearly two dozen steaks. His knotted forearms rippled below the rolled up sleeves of his shirt. He wasn't even sweating over the hot flames of the grill.

"I'm Deputy Bill Tatum. Would it be all right if I asked Wendy a few questions?"

"She's right over there." He pointed with his long fork at the wide backside of one of his helpers, tossing salad in the opposite aisle. He didn't look up. I walked around the center counter.

Wendy was the only one in the kitchen with her green Halfmoon shirt untucked and baseball cap turned the right way around, soft blond curls peeking out from underneath. Unlike her boss, she was perspiring like the salad was on fire.

"Miss Wendy? My name is Deputy Tatum with the Mineral County Sheriff."

The girl nearly dropped her salad forks. I'd startled her. She quickly regained her composure and turned her pretty face toward me. I thought the term "cherubic" was invented for this girl.

"Deputy Tatum, you scared the dickens out of me!" She held her hand to her ample chest, but kept smiling. Wide-set hazel eyes glinted at me over a freckled nose.

"I understand you're the concierge of the ranch. I have a few questions about some guests of yours."

"Concierge? I guess you could call it that." She had a schoolgirl voice and dancing laugh. She must have been great with her guests. "Can we talk here? Philippe needs all the help he can get. We have a full house, and one of his summer boys didn't show up. I think he got drunk last night and can't take the altitude, the little shit."

"Pretty late for lunch, isn't it? It's almost two."

"Our guests set their own meal times, kind of like a cruise ship. Some leave real early in the morning to ride or cycle and just grab a muffin and a cup of coffee. They come back for lunch early. Our fishermen eat a late breakfast and go out when the sun is higher and the trout more active. They fish through the regular lunch hour. That's who we're feeding now. They'll go back out for the evening hatch, then we cook a late dinner. We pretty much cook nonstop." She talked fast and loud, a little too loud, even with all the commotion of the kitchen.

"A couple went for a ride with Jacob this morning and checked out at eleven. Names were Andy and Heather. I hoped you would have their last names and maybe a number or forwarding address."

"No one checks out on Saturday. Lunch is included even on the day you check out, and no one misses Philippe's ribeye."

"Are you sure? Maybe they slipped out while you were in here."

She placed her hands on generous hips. "Deputy Tatum, none of my guests slip by me. Nothing happens around here without my knowing it. That's what Orville pays me for. Andy and Heather Amundsen checked out yesterday. They were driving home to Minnesota and wanted to make it back by Sunday."

Okay. Someone was lying.

"Would you have their return address or phone number?"

"Uh huh, but I'll have to make it quick. The dining room is full." She sidestepped around me, barely squeezing between me and the steel counter, and headed for the kitchen door.

"Be right back, Philippe." The chef said nothing, still poking furiously at the steaks.

She carried her weight smartly on tiny feet, passing quickly down the east hall to her office. I had to move out to keep up with her. She swung around an immaculate desk and plopped down heavily in her office chair, the springs crying out in agony. She snapped on her computer monitor and unlocked the screensaver with her password.

"Here we go. Andy and Heather Amundsen of St. Cloud, Minnesota. Stayed for two weeks to celebrate their fifth wedding anniversary. Checked out yesterday at ten A.M., right after the breakfast bar closed. Didn't stay for lunch. Never rode once their whole stay."

She scribbled the Amundsens' address and phone number on a Post-it note and handed it to me. She even wrote their vehicle description and license plate number—red Nissan Xterra with Minnesota plates. She stood up again and aimed her bulk at the door behind me. I got out of her way.

"I hope that's it, Deputy Tatum. I really need to get back

to the kitchen," she said as she scooted by, little feet doing their quick time again.

"That's it. Thanks, Wendy," I said to her jiggling rear as she moved off down the corridor.

"Tatum, where the hell are you?" I heard the sheriff's voice over my radio. I pulled it off my belt.

"I'm wrapping things up here at the Halfmoon, Sheriff Dale."

"Well, wrap it up now and get your ass down here. We have another situation in town."

"Roger, I'm on my way."

Our little department was getting a workout today.

Nine

I T WAS MID-AFTERNOON WHEN I DROVE INTO TOWN
and heard the helicopter. I kept right on going to the airport. As I left Highway 149 and picked up Airport Drive, I
saw Nick's red BK-117 Lifeflight chopper landing next to
the little shack with the windsock that constituted Mineral
County Airport. Two sheriff's department Broncos were
parked nearby. Sheriff Dale must have taken mine again.
He probably didn't like sharing with Marty.

I saw them both dash out from behind one of the trucks,
carrying a loaded gurney between them. Sheriff Dale
shoved the gurney into the rear bay doors, said a few words
to Nick over the headset, then backed away. The Lifeflight
roared off over my head, heading east.

"Who was that?" I asked. The helicopter was already
cresting Wagon Wheel Gap and passing out of sight.

Sheriff Dale reached into my Bronco, pulled out his Resistol, and jammed it on his head. "Some kid, high-school

age. Just collapsed in front of his friends in the middle of Veteran's Park."

Marty leaned against the truck and closed her eyes. She looked exhausted. She just pulled a double shift.

"Pupils dilated, heart rate through the roof, hotter than hell," she said. "It looked like he was having a heart attack, then, sure enough, his heart stopped when we got here. Dale had to pump his chest while we waited for Nick."

"Any sign of his parents?" I asked.

"They ain't here. He's working a summer job," said Sheriff Dale.

I thought of the missing cook in Philippe's kitchen. "Did he work up at the Halfmoon? They were missing someone this morning. The concierge said a boy from town didn't show up."

"Hadn't even gotten that far," said Dale, "We just got the call and hustled down the street. He was lying in the grass, convulsing, scaring the tourists to death."

Marty was silent and motionless against the truck.

"Sounds like he OD'd on something. Crystal meth, maybe?" I offered.

"Won't know until we hear back from Nick, but it looks that way," Sheriff Dale said reluctantly.

Crystal methamphetamine had been a huge problem all over rural America since the mid-1990s, especially in the West, where manufacturers found cheap supplies and remote production sites. The scourge spread as far as Alamosa but never made it over the mountains to Mineral County. Until now.

"Marty, go on home. You look tired." Sheriff Dale made the understatement of the day.

"Roger, Sheriff. See ya, Deputy Tatum." She slowly got in her truck.

"Hey Marty, one second. I just need to confirm something." I hated to stop her. "Did you see a group of three riders around nine o'clock up on the La Garita Trail?"

"Yup. They were from the ranch, moving west, toward the marker. Just before nine, actually."

"Was one of them Jacob Stackhouse, the stable master?"

"Correct. Mandy Lange and Orville were riding with him. They said they were heading toward the halfway point to cheer on Mayor Jeff. I turned them around."

Now I knew Jacob was lying.

Worse yet, so was Orville.

"Did they have any rifles with them?"

"Come on, Bill. Give me a little credit." Marty was tired and a little irritable. "No, they were unarmed, and not very happy about turning back to the ranch."

"Did you tell them about Mayor Jeff?"

"No. We didn't know the mayor was dead until you called it in," the sheriff interrupted.

Marty not only placed the mayor's wife near the scene, but her combat sniper father as well. I quickly relayed the conflicting stories from the ranch.

"Now there's a wrinkle," said Sheriff Dale. "You have anything else for Marty, otherwise we need to let her go. I can fill you in on the rest."

"You want me to drive you home, Marty?" I asked.

"No, I can make it. Rush hour's still a few hours away." Even after eighteen hours on duty, Marty kept her dry sense of humor.

"All right, Tatum. Let's go back to the station. We have a lot to talk about." We exchanged keys and drove back to the station.

I got a little surprise when I walked in the door—Jerry Pitcher was sitting at his desk, in uniform, as if he didn't have a hole in his leg.

"Hi Deputy Bill!" He reached around for a pair of crutches leaning against his chair and hobbled over to me.

He looked a little pale and maybe even a few pounds lighter, but was still the same soft-palmed, pear-shaped Deputy Jerry we all knew and loved.

"Hey Jerry. How's the leg?" I asked.

"Hurts like a mother, but I'll live."

"I found him here when we brought back the mayor," said Sheriff Dale, "Why don't we all go in my office and get up to speed."

"What about the dead woman's body?" I asked. "There's only room for one in the coroner's locker."

"Dr. Ed released her this morning. Family sent a funeral director all the way from Denver, so we had room at the inn."

It was strange to have the mayor in cold storage at his own town hall. I buried the ill feelings and sat down in the sheriff's office. Jerry ambled in on three legs and eased into a chair, waving off my attempt to give him a hand.

"It's all therapy, Bill. Got to get around on my own." Jerry seemed to have a new lease on life. He must have left his sullen self back with his pint of blood in Deep Creek. I guess a bullet through the thigh and a brush with death has an effect on you. Sheriff Dale opened the briefing.

"We found nothing at the shooter's position up in East Willow, not even a shell casing this time. No tire tracks, nothing. Well, we found lots of tracks—that was the problem. Nothing evident. Marty checked it out herself."

"I'd still like to go up there and take a look," I said.

"That's fine, Tatum, but this sniper case is getting out of control. The murder today was remote enough to keep the tourists from fleeing the valley, but I'm not certain that's a good thing. Most of the residents already know the mayor's dead, killed up on the mountain, but they're not spreading the rumors to our tourist population." He paused. "We need to protect the folks in our town. We cannot have another shooting. The parade is tomorrow, and we need to cover it."

"We should cancel the parade, Sheriff Dale," I said.

"I already tried." The sheriff's face darkened. "Chairman Pitcher would have nothing of it."

Jerry squirmed a little at the mention of his father, but said nothing.

"What authority does he have?" I asked.

"All that he needs," said Dale. "He's acting mayor until this fall's election, and he said the show must go on. Something about 'That's what Jeff would have wanted' or some crap like that. He's the boss. I'm just the sheriff."

"Can't we call in the cavalry, the state police or FBI?" Jerry asked.

"I called them right after my nice talk with your dad. They have their hands full with the convention and the film festival."

The Republican Party was holding their national convention in Denver this year, prompting the need for every available law enforcement agent in the state to protect the president and the delegates.

Alec Baldwin was hosting the Telluride Film Festival at the same time, sort of a counter-convention of Hollywood liberals. Both events were prime targets for every terrorist and weirdo militia group in the world. Dale was right—neither the state police nor the FBI would have the resources to commit to our little parade.

"So it's up to us, then," I said gravely.

"Yup. A woman, a gimp, an old man, and a hayseed from Iowa." Sheriff Dale did his Ronald Reagan impression, breaking the tension. "What a lethal force. How are your antisniper techniques, Tatum?"

"A little rusty, but this job's not complicated. We'll need to be in place before dawn, though."

"We'll meet back here at eight and go over your plan. I'm taking Marty off the night shift. She'll be your other shooter." He looked at Jerry. "You, my boy, are going on night dispatch, but you'll be back in the radio room by ten to cover the parade. We need a hair trigger on the Life-flight, just in case."

"You got it, Sheriff Dale." Jerry straightened up, happy to be included, but even happier to not be in the field.

"Where will you be, Sheriff?" I asked.

"In the crowd, calming the herd. Protection through presence."

"What about the investigation?" I asked. "There's a lot of lying going on up there on the mountain, and the mayor's wife is nowhere to be found. She may even be hiding out at the ranch."

"You have until tonight to wrap whatever loose ends you can, Deputy, then put the investigation on hold until after the parade," said the sheriff. "Go back up the mountain and get your hands on every two-seventy Orville has in the basement. Pin down Jacob and squeeze him a little about his story. Bring him in if you have to."

"What about Orville?" I didn't want to confront the old man. Orville was my mentor, but he had lied to me. I was having a hard time with that.

"Just work on Jacob for now. I think Orville will sign the consent form. If he makes a stink about a search warrant, tell him we already called the judge in Alamosa, and the request is on his desk."

"Is it?" I asked.

"No, but it will be." The sheriff leaned back in his chair. "I'm not worried about Orville. He's eighty. Not really a flight risk. He hasn't come off that mountain in thirty years. An avalanche wouldn't knock him out of his lodge."

"Anything else?" I looked at my watch. It was already three o'clock. I had five hours to get up the mountain, get the rifles, interrogate Jacob, and draw up a plan for the parade.

"Nope. That's it. Jerry, go home and get some rest. Be

back by eight. I'll get Dr. Ed's report when he's done with the mayor. Any questions?"

We had none. We had our marching orders.

At 3:30, I stepped out of the truck at the Halfmoon Ranch. An afternoon storm was building over the divide to the northwest, shutting off the sun, and making the ever-present wind at altitude cold and biting. The gray, empty surface of Lake Madeline rippled and shivered with each gust. The stables were locked. No sign of their stable master. A hard rain chased me into the lodge.

Orville was in the main hall of the lodge, alone, staring out the huge windows at the storm, brooding. The only warmth in the room came from the fires in each pillared hearth. I wasn't looking forward to my task.

"You're back, Deputy. Have you found Jeff's killer?" he asked without turning around. How did he do that?

"No, sir, but that's what I'm here for." I was turning my Resistol around by the brim. "I need to take all the two-seventy rifles back to the station and have another talk with Jacob."

"You got a warrant?" he asked, still staring out the window. The darkening clouds raced across the sky, erasing whatever blue was there this morning. Faint hints of lightning flickered in the west.

"No, but the sheriff will soon. He was hoping you'd co-operate."

He spun around and fixed me with his icy blue eyes, rimmed with red. "You think one of the members did this? Killed Jeff like some animal and ran away?"

"We're just gathering evidence, Orville. If you want me to come back with the warrant . . . "

"Shut the hell up, Deputy," he said quietly, pulling the keys off his belt and holding them out. "Take whatever fucking guns you want. You won't find it here. I have nothing to hide. You're wasting your time."

I took the key ring. "Have you seen Jacob? I need to ask him a few more questions."

"He ain't here. Cleaned out the stables and left. No one's riding this afternoon."

"Doesn't he live here?"

"That doesn't mean he has to stay here. I had nothing for him."

"Any sign of your daughter?" I asked.

"No. I haven't heard from her," he said.

"Okay, Orville. I'll just be a few minutes."

He said nothing, but I could feel his eyes boring into my back as my boot heels echoed through the cavernous hall. Thunder followed me down the stairs to the locked steel door.

I walked inside the equipment room and went straight for the gun cabinets. Upon closer inspection, they were all neatly stenciled with the names of whomever owned the guns inside. Most had two names where members shared a cabinet. Forty-eight names in all—almost half the membership of the club. I recognized a few of them. They were the old-timers—Thomas Pitcher, Henry Earl Callahan, Chuck and Max. I guess with rank and seniority came access to the club's storage facilities. I preferred to keep my guns at home where I could get to them quickly.

I started opening cabinets and searching for the right caliber. I found a .270 in the fourth one—an old Sako bolt action with a peep sight belonging to Max Toliver. Doubtful of its use in the recent crime, I laid it on the long table in the middle of the room and moved on.

I found four more .270 rifles in the heavy steel lockers—one Ruger Number One like mine, a lever-action Winchester with a cheap Bushnell scope, another 700 ADL, and a new Remington model 700 BDL SS DM with a composite stock, brushed stainless steel, and Nikon Titanium scope. It was a beautiful gun with a heavy barrel—

similar in design to the sniper rifle I carried in Afghanistan with the 82nd. This last one was Thomas Pitcher's.

I opened Orville's lockers last. I kept my eyes open for the rifle I saw in the picture—the vintage Remington Model 700 ADL cradled in Mandy's arm, but didn't find it. Orville had only .30 caliber rifles or larger, true to his word. I relocked the cabinets and turned back to the center table. Orville was standing at the other end, staring at me, hands on his hips.

"You done?"

Trying to push my hammering heart out of my throat, I managed a "Yes."

"You better not take those pieces out in the rain. You'll find cases on top of the lockers where you got them."

"Is this all of them? The two-seventies, I mean."

"You mean, where's Amanda's, right? I know you saw it in the picture today." He was really pissed, but his voice was deadly quiet. I was trapped with him standing in front of the steel door, my only way out of the basement of an isolated hunting lodge on the top of a mountain, miles from town. Thunder rumbled in the distance, a feeling more than a sound.

"Yes, that's what I mean, Orville." I met his gaze.

"She doesn't keep it here. I don't know where it is." He crossed his arms, not moving from my path of escape.

Reaching up on top of the gun cabinets, I pulled down three soft and two hard cases. Matching the cases to the rifles, I packed them up, tucked four weapons under my arms, and slung one over my shoulder. Orville slowly stepped out of my way. I left the keys on the table and went up the stairs in the heavy silence.

I was soaked by the time I raced out to my truck. The cold rain slashed down from over the divide, aided by a strong northwest wind. The brim of my Resistol took a beating. Not wanting to fool with the back hatch, I filled the back seat with the gun cases and jumped in behind the steering wheel. The rain drummed on the metal roof of the Bronco and clouded my windshield with sheets of water. This was no summer cloudburst. Even with the wipers going at full crazy speed, I could barely see the road through the hammering water.

Sunset was hours away, but the darkened skies paid no heed to time. I switched on the headlights, merely illuminating the torrent all around me. Still, the light was comforting. In retrospect, I should have stayed on the mountain and rode out the storm in front of one of the massive, warm fireplace columns in the main hall. Orville, however, was pretty ornery, and I thought I'd rather face the nasty storm than the old man. Not only that, if he had any part in the shootings, which my gut told me otherwise, the lodge wouldn't be the safest place for a little old sheriff's deputy.

Ten

I FINALLY GOT THE BRONCO POINTED IN THE RIGHT direction after groping my way out of the gravel parking lot. The intensity of the storm was unabated. I knew I was going in the right direction more by feel than any other sense. The jeep trail was going uphill, and I was headed straight into the driving rain. Once I entered the protection of the evergreen forest west of the ranch, I could see the road more clearly. This was a good thing—the narrow road twisted through the trees, offering plenty of opportunities for me to depart from it.

The dark sky replaced the dark evergreens as I cleared the alpine forest, and the storm greeted my return with a sheet of water against the windshield. Rain gushed down the single lane road in a torrent. I felt like I was pushing upriver in a paddleboat. I really should have stopped, but I pressed on. I had a mission, and I wasn't going to fail voluntarily. The pack trail turned due west then worked its way south on top of the Wason Plateau, and each gust of wind rocked the truck as I turned broadside to the storm. I eased my death grip on the steering wheel, wiping each damp palm on my damper field pants, and tried to unlock the tension in my neck and shoulders. The toughest part of the drive was still ahead of me—downhill.

When I hit the first switchback on the descent into the Belmont box canyon, the rain had turned the soft, fine dust on the jeep trail to a slippery layer of gumbo. I was thankful I had locked down the hubs on the Bronco before I left the station. Not that four-wheel drive would help when all four wheels were sliding down the mountain, but it made me feel better anyway. I crawled around the hairpin turn of the switchback. At least my tail was toward the rain, so the whipping wipers did some good. Not that I could actually see the road. The rain had washed most of the shoulder away, obscuring what was pack trail and what was mountainside. Memory and traction kept me on the right course. Neither was very reliable.

The storm followed me down the mountain and sat like a buffalo in the valley, pelting the caldera with wind and rain. I could see the rooftops of Belmont intermittently through the sheeting water and blurry windshield, so I knew I was on the right path, for the most part. Below me was a nice two-hundred-foot drop-off—not a cliff, but steep enough to want to stay on the trail.

I started a controlled right slide into the last switchback overlooking town when I heard a crack and the Bronco lurched to the left. At first, I thought it was thunder or a rock smacking the undercarriage, but then my already mushy steering wheel went completely soft. I never made the turn. My left rear tire lost whatever meager traction it had, and I was going over the edge, ass first, down the steep side of the canyon. Nothing but prairie grass and sagebrush to stop me.

The first part of the slide was agonizing. My mind

slowed everything to a crawl, exquisitely capturing my terror and helplessness when I realized I was merely a passenger in a two-ton teacup ride. Things sped up, eventually, as the initial rotation of the vehicle swung around the heavy front end, and I found myself with a front-row view of my plight as the Bronco plummeted toward the bottom of the canyon. All I could do was keep the wheels straight to prevent any more rotation. I knew rotation might lead to spinning, then rolling, and I was not interested in adding that to my already desperate situation. I was heading right for Joe Bender's cabin and quickly gaining speed.

I tried to maintain the illusion that I was still in control of the truck and could turn away from the impending collision when I hit Joe's backyard. I got it half-right. I didn't just hit Joe's backyard, I slammed into it. The Bronco was too old to have airbags and my seatbelt strained against my chest, but held most of me in the seat. All but my head, which I managed to smash against the steering wheel. This impact, however, only made me a little foggy. The real pain shot up my hands, still gripping the wheel. Joe's backyard failed to halt my slide completely, and his back deck and bay windows grew bigger through the haze. I stood on the brake, slid easily through Jody Bender's vegetable garden, and bumped into the deck, shaking the entire structure. Then all was quiet.

Joe stepped out onto his now-rickety deck and gingerly walked over to the Bronco. He was wearing overalls, a red shirt, and no shoes. He pushed the flop of hair back over his bald spot and squinted down his long nose, peering at me through the windshield.

"You all right, Deputy Tatum?"

"I don't know, Joe," I answered. "How do I look?"

"Well, your head's split open and blood's drippin' off your nose, but otherwise you look okay."

Joe hopped off the deck, opened the driver's side door, and helped me out. I half-fell, half-slid out of the truck and sank down in the mud, still groggy from the smack against the steering wheel. Joe pulled out a blue handkerchief.

"Here, wipe your forehead," he said, holding out the hanky. "Does your head hurt?"

"Yeah, a little, but my wrists hurt more," I said, gingerly dabbing at the bloody gash.

"Are they broken?"

I gently rotated my hands. They hurt like hell, but everything seemed to work without too much pain. No bone-on-bone grinding, at least. Joe bent over and examined the laceration.

"Yeah, I think you're gonna need a coupla stitches, Deputy Bill."

The rain had slowed to a soft drizzle. Small pockets of sunlight peaked through where the clouds were breaking up off to the west.

"Hey, Joe, I'm sorry about your yard," I said, "and your deck, and your wife's garden."

"Oh, don't worry about it." Joe waved it off. "Jody's been getting on me about tearing this one out and building a new one. Just hadn't gotten around to it. And she hasn't weeded that garden in three months. She's been pretty busy in the shop selling beads and stuff."

Jody Bender sold beads and other jewelry out of a little shop off Main Street. She and Joe collected local amethyst, rose quartz, and other crystalline minerals from the caldera. Joe made the beads, and Jody peddled them.

Joe was also the town groundskeeper, cleaning the town hall, caring for the grass in Veteran's park and the softball field, cleaning the streets with his little motorized sweeper. He was up long before sunrise and got most of his work done before the shops opened, giving the town a daily polish to achieve its pristine alpine look. He spent his afternoons at home, grinding beads for Jody.

"Well, let's get you inside." Joe lifted me up by the elbow and led me into his cabin. He plopped me down in his tattered green easy chair and plodded into the tiny kitchen.

"I'm soaking wet, Joe," I said. "Isn't this your chair?"

"Now don't fret, Deputy Bill," he called out from the kitchen. "Jody says I spend too much time in that chair, anyway." He emerged with a cup of steaming coffee in a chipped blue mug. I grabbed it in both hands and sipped, thanking him profusely. While I was distracted by the coffee, he pressed a piece of gauze against my forehead and fixed it in place with first aid tape.

"What were you doin', drivin' around down the mountain in a thunderstorm, anyway?"

"I was up there and had to get down. Sheriff Dale needs me here in town."

"Sheriff Dale needs you alive, too, don't he?" I guess he was right. I said nothing.

"You hear about the mayor?" asked Joe.

"I was there. Saw it happen."

"No shit," he said softly. "Damn shame. Jeff Lange was a good man. I'd a voted for him again this fall. You know who got him?"

"No, sure don't."

"Is that what you were up there on the mountain for, investigating?"

"Can't say, Joe, sorry."

"Yeah, I suppose you can't." He looked out the back window. "Well, the rain's stopped. You're gonna need to get that forehead stitched up. Why don't we get you outta here?"

"I don't want to leave my Bronco in your yard, Joe. I have some evidence in there I need to get to the sheriff."

"Okay." He reached over and pulled on a pair of Wellingtons. "I'll go change the tire. You stay right there."

"No, I'm feeling better, I'll help."

I wasn't much help, other than handing him tools and keeping the lug nuts out of the mud. The left rear tire took a shredding on my slide down the mountain. I helped him lift it into the back.

"Damn, Deputy Bill," said Joe, inspecting the tire, "What'd you hit?"

"I don't know. It just blew out when I made the turn into that last switchback."

"That's a hell of a turn to miss, Bill," he said, looking up at the muddy tracks of my descent into his backyard.

"I know it."

"Pete and Zooey should be able to fix that blowout," said Joe. "They stay open through the holiday with all the tourists in town. You shouldn't drive anywhere without a spare in this county."

"I'll go by and see them tomorrow."

He was talking about the McClaren brothers. Pete rented jeeps and ATVs to the tourists. Dashle, "Zooey," fixed their tires. Their place was west of town down 149, not far from Dana Pratt's ranch.

I thanked Joe for the coffee, bandage, tire change, and emergency barricade and did my best not to sideswipe his house as I worked my way back to the pavement. Joe's cabin was only a few blocks from the town hall. Well, everyone's cabin in Belmont was only a few blocks from town hall, so I was back at the station quickly, regardless of the snail's pace at which I drove the truck.

The sun returned to the valley when I pulled into the gravel parking lot of the town hall. Belmont seemed normal; tourists wandered up and down Main Street, either unaware or unfazed by the violent death of the mayor and his mistress.

I gathered the five rifles in my arms again. I hoped to find Dr. Ed in his coroner's office, so he could stitch up my forehead, but first I wanted to drop the guns off with Sheriff Dale. The front office was empty. Marty and Jerry were both at home resting up, but I saw a light on in the sheriff's office. Dale was sitting at his desk, staring intently into the screen of a laptop computer. He didn't hear me come in.

"Hi, Sheriff."

He smacked the lid of the laptop closed and looked up at me like I was Marley from *A Christmas Carol*. I probably looked the part, loaded down with the gun cases, covered in mud, a bloody bandage on my forehead.

"What the hell happened to you, Deputy Tatum?" He quickly recovered from the start I gave him. "And why are you tracking mud in my office?"

"Well, Sheriff, I had a little excitement on the way down the hill."

"Uh huh."

"Tire blew out right above town. Made a new shortcut into Joe Bender's backyard."

"The truck okay?"

We had a limited vehicle fleet. I could understand his concern about my Bronco.

"Think so. It got me back here just fine. I'm fine, too," I added sarcastically. "Is Dr. Ed around? I need some thread for my forehead."

"Yeah, yeah, he's here. Did Orville give you any trouble?"

"He's mad as hell, but he cooperated. Did you get the warrant?"

"It's right here." He laid a hand on a piece of paper next to the computer. "Get yourself cleaned up. You still have a couple hours to put together the security plan for the Independence Day parade."

"Yes, sir." I went to find Dr. Ed.

The county coroner was sitting at his desk. Thankfully, he was finished with his examination of Mayor Jeff's body and had him sealed up in the locker. The only light in the office came from a small green desk lamp. No windows for the coroner. No one really wanted to look in at what went on in here anyway.

"You look like twelve miles of bad road, Deputy," said Dr. Ed, setting down his pen. "Nice laceration in your forehead, too. You put that bandage on yourself?"

"Joe Bender gave me that in exchange for some nice tire tracks in his backyard." I told him what happened.

"Some day, William, you will realize that you are not invincible, no matter how many perfectly good airplanes you jumped from in the Army," he lectured, flicking on the bright exam room lights and coming around the desk to look at my wound. He ripped off the tape and gauze, and I tried not to wince. Dr. Ed had the bedside manner of a large animal veterinarian. After cleaning the cut, he applied an anesthetic and closed the wound with five stitches. He was rough, but quick. No wonder he could tie flies faster than Danny Boyle, who supplied flies to Chuck Dinnerstein's Orvis shop. At least he didn't seal the wound with epoxy.

"I received the toxicology report on the dead woman in the mail this morning," he said while inspecting his work. "Vitamins and birth control—that's all she had on board."

"What about the mayor? Are you going to do a tox screen on him?"

"Certainly, though I doubt he has anything foreign in his system. He didn't drink or smoke. He even refused pain medication for the sprained ankle he sustained while trail running last year. Jeff Lange was healthier than you, and twice your age."

"When do you think you'll get the results?"

"I would guess by Wednesday or Thursday. The holiday slows things down a bit." He pulled a penlight out of his breast pocket and began a full neuro exam. "How does your head feel?"

"Okay, I guess. Smacked it pretty hard on the steering wheel," I said.

He checked the light reaction of my pupils then did a manual examination of my head and neck.

"Did you lose consciousness?"

"Things were a little foggy for a minute or so, but that was it. I feel fine, now. My wrists really hurt."

"You were holding the wheel on impact, right? I'm surprised they're not both broken." He pulled two Ace bandages out of a drawer and started wrapping my wrists, like a boxer's. "They're probably both lightly sprained. Leave these on for a few days."

I held up my hands and wiggled my fingers. "I need to be able to hold a rifle tomorrow, Dr. Ed. We're covering the parade."

"You think the sniper will risk it? Broad daylight, lots of people?"

"The guy's good, Doc, a very careful planner." I let out a breath and shook my head. "If he's going to kill someone tomorrow, he's already rehearsed it and timed his escape. Probably been working on the details for weeks. I have one night to come up with a plan to beat him."

"Maybe your mere presence at the parade will discourage him, throw a wrench in his scheme."

"Maybe, but I think he's already worked us in. He has to expect that we'd try to counter him tomorrow. I would. You always plan for the worst possible contingency."

"Well, if it adds to your confidence, I intend to make my

usual appearance at the parade." Dr. Ed was a clown in the parade. Orange fuzzy hair ringing his bald spot, big shoes, riding a tiny bicycle—the whole package. The kids loved him, except that he handed out pocket first-aid kits instead of candy.

"Well, William, you're done. You seem none the worse for wear, really, aside from a few minor complications. Why don't you get your bedraggled self home?"

"I'll do just that, but I'm back here at eight." I stood up. "Thanks, Dr. Ed."

"My pleasure, Deputy." He turned off the overhead fluorescent and returned to his desk.

Eleven

I‍T WAS SIX O'CLOCK WHEN I PULLED INTO THE
drive at my cabin. I stopped by the corral to feed Pancho
and put him up for the night. He was happy to see me. It
may have been the carrots in my pocket, though. After taking a shower and putting on my last clean uniform, I
cleared my kitchen table, except for the coffeepot and my
topo map of Mineral County.

Belmont was only a few blocks wide, jammed inside
the box canyon where Willow Creek tumbles off the
mountain. Main Street ran through the center of town,
north and south, and continued up into the canyon to the
old mines. The narrow canyon allowed for only two other
north-south streets on either side of Main, and the cross
streets lay out the town in a simple, rectangular grid. A
sniper could sit anywhere along the canyon wall and have
a perfect shot down to Main Street—the avenue was in full
view and well within range. Eliminating his target didn't

pose a challenge, but getting away did. Only two jeep trails ran away from the canyon on either side. The sniper would have to climb out on foot along a concealed route to make his escape.

Staring at the contours on the map and trying to recall the downtown area in my head, I realized that the west side of town would be his position of choice. The slope of the canyon was more gradual, compared to the nearly clifflike sides of the east wall. I could attest to that, having driven down the east side in my Bronco recently. The western slope had more escape routes as well. No jeep trails, but three shallow draws ran up the mountain and intersected with the dirt road at the crest of the ridge. The shooter could fire, drop into one of the draws, and move up the hill out of sight. He could hop on his ATV at the top and disappear unseen. The western approach was his most likely course of action, so that's where I would be. If the sniper got off a shot and started maneuvering back up the hill, I didn't want Marty to be the one to intercept him.

The goal of the counter-sniper is to place himself in a position where he can see the sniper, but not be in the target area himself. It was not essential that Marty and I be in range of Main Street, but we would form an outer ring, behind the shooter, allowing us not only to detect him before he pulled the trigger, but also to seal off his escape route as well. I picked a spot on the east ridge for Marty. Only one draw extended from the canyon. The sniper could use it to move away from the area and pick up the trail to Wason Park, but that was his only option.

For myself, I chose the last visible contour line above town. Any farther back, and the terrain would block my view of Main Street. The ridge was four hundred yards from town, a long shot even for a good hunter, so I was confident I would be outside his shooting position. The next ridge below me was within three hundred yards of the

parade route, perfect for our shooter. From my chosen
counter-sniper location, I would have a commanding view
of the entire Belmont town proper and still retain the ability to move laterally along the ridge to block any avenues
of egress.

I was wasting time. I had an hour to confirm my map reconnaissance and get back to the station.

I dragged an Army duffel out from under the bed and
withdrew two sets of my old desert camouflage battle dress
uniforms—BDUs—from my days with the 82nd Airborne.
Marty was taller than me, so I didn't think she'd have a
problem fitting into my old BDUs. The Army gave me some
great stuff to fight in Afghanistan, and I kept most of it. I
still had a couple pairs of desert boots, sage-colored nomex
flight gloves, floppy boony hats, and a few other items as
well. They went into two tough, green nylon backpacks—
assault packs. My rifle and binoculars were already in the
truck, as were Marty's. I opened my gun cabinet and chose
a box of premium .30-06 shells I had loaded myself. Last to
go into the duffel was my Camelback Mule and a few
Powerbars. We would be up on the ridge for more than eight
hours, and baking like roof tiles in the hot July sun. I filled
a travel mug with the last of the coffee, threw the packs in
the Bronco, and drove back into town.

I left the highway just before passing the softball field
and took Bachelor's Loop up the west side of the canyon.
This newly paved road led to my overlook where I would
spend most of Sunday. I took the left-hand turn at the fork
on top of the ridge past the old miner's cemetery, then
looped back to the south along the dirt road running parallel to the line of the canyon. I would set up just below this
dirt road, and as I eased my Bronco along the ridge, I confirmed my map recon. The terrain dropped off on the
downhill side of the road then leveled out in a step. There
were no cabins up this high, though there would be soon if

Dana Pratt convinced the town council to approve his plan. He no longer had to worry about the mayor.

Below my step was another, wider flattening of the terrain, one hundred to one hundred fifty meters down the ridge. On it were cabins and small homes owned mostly by the residents of Belmont and occupied year-round. This is where I expected the sniper to set up. Even if he chose a lower part of the ridge, he would still be in my range of vision. From my vantage point, I could even see the three dry gulches that ran up to the top of the ridge, although they were choked with juniper and sage. Without stopping, I picked a lip in the slope, just a rise of rock in the contour, but enough to hide a prone shooter from eyes below. I captured the waypoint on my GPS and drove back down Bachelor's Loop to scout Marty's position on the eastern ridge.

Marty's side of the canyon was much steeper than mine, and less likely to be the sniper's point of attack. The eastern ridge, however, had a better view of downtown, pressing against the easternmost block of cabins. The close terrain could bring the shooter one hundred meters nearer to the parade route. This proximity would give him an easier shot, but his egress was limited, and he would be exposed to everyone at the parade while trying to scurry up the mountain and get away. On the northeast spur of the ridge, I found a concealed spot for Marty, below the pack trail in an outcropping of rock. She could look down on the parade route from an oblique angle, rather than the broadside view I would have on the western side. She could also see the entire face of the eastern ridge, including the muddy tire tracks from my decent into Joe Bender's backyard. I didn't stop the Bronco, but tossed a twelve-hour chemlite into the site and marked the waypoint on my GPS. The lightstick would still glow softly and guide her when she moved into position in the darkness before dawn.

I carefully drove back down the hill, passing the spot

where I'd left the trail in the rainstorm. Facing north, I stopped the Bronco and looked at our only uncovered avenue of approach. The north side of the canyon was the most extreme of the three sides. Unlike the east and west ridges, the north was a rocky cliff wall. The shooter would have to scale this cliff to get to any realistic vantage point, then he would be trapped, unable to climb up or down with any efficiency after hitting his target. Only Windy Gulch on my side of the canyon might give him a covered and concealed escape, but the sides were very steep, and the intermittent stream at the bottom was swollen with the recent rains. I could be there in minutes with my truck before he had a chance to climb out of the gorge. I chose to risk leaving this northern option uncovered. I really had no choice. I was out of bodies.

It was getting dark when my tires crunched into the gravel parking lot of the sheriff's station. Marty Three Stones, Jerry, and the sheriff were already there. I was rarely the last to arrive for any operation or daily patrol briefing—Jerry usually had that honor. Maybe the guy was turning over a new leaf. He picked a good time to do it. We had to rely on everyone for this mission to succeed. I pulled my gear out of the back and went inside.

The three of them were sitting on desks in the front area, drinking coffee. They all looked relaxed and ready, even eager. Three empty plates from Eunice's kitchen littered one desk, but one plate remained covered.

"Evenin', Deputy Bill," Jerry called out, his new enthusiastic self brimming with excitement. "We got you a plate, if you're hungry."

"Eat it before it gets cold, Tatum," said the sheriff, "then proceed with your briefing."

"Thanks, that's great." I tried to remember if I'd eaten anything since lunch. Hell, I couldn't even remember lunch. I laid out the topographical map of Belmont on the center conference table and tore into Eunice's baked chicken and mashed potatoes. They all leaned into the map, trying to decipher the circles and arrows I had drawn on its acetated surface.

"Got a call from Nick, the medic in Pueblo." The sheriff turned to me. "The kid's heart stopped twice on the flight to the hospital. Nick couldn't get it started again the second time."

"What was it?" I asked through a mouthful of mashed potatoes.

"You were right," he said. "Crystal meth overdose."

"Son of a bitch." I stopped chewing. "That's the first one we've had out here."

"Yup, our little town is growing up." He turned back to the map. "When this operation is over, Marty, I'm assigning you to the meth case. Corral his friends and find out where they got the stuff."

"You got it, Sheriff." Marty was finally getting out of the office.

My food was gone in ten minutes. I tossed away all the plates and moved over to the conference table. They moved aside, including the sheriff, and I had the floor. Our success or failure would depend upon my ability to deliver a simple but critical counter-sniper plan to three untrained local law enforcement officers. It felt like ranger school all over again, only I was warm and dry with a nice cup of coffee.

"Okay, folks, here is our mission. At twelve hundred hours, four July, we are to prevent the Belmont sniper from killing or injuring another civilian during the Independence Day parade, in order to preserve the safety and peace of the citizens and visitors of Belmont, Colorado. We will accomplish this by conducting a counter-sniper operation, consisting of two marksmen, one target-area security officer, and a command and control operator. Secondary, but not critical, to our mission, is the capture and prosecution of the shooter. Sheriff Dale, do you approve of this mission statement?"

"Yes."

"Good. I'll continue, then. Please understand, you may know most of this already, but I must be thorough. Our area of operations is the Belmont box canyon, bordered on the north by Bachelor Mountain, the east by the southern spur of Mammoth Mountain, the west by the foothills of Bulldog and Bachelor mountains, and the south by the Rio Grande Valley. Belmont itself is a small urban area, three blocks wide by eight blocks deep, consisting of storefronts in the downtown area and cabins and houses on the periphery. Willow Creek runs through the middle of town, north to south, and continues until it dumps into the Rio Grande River, two and a half kilometers away.

"We expect the weather tomorrow to be clear and sunny, highs in the low eighties in the early afternoon. Low temperature will happen around sunrise, high thirties to low forties. We will experience this forty degree temperature change firsthand, requiring not only cold-weather gear, but plenty of water as well. Sunrise is at zero-four-fifty, with nautical twilight starting thirty minutes prior to that. We will need to be in position by zero-three-twenty. We will have a full moon tonight; it rises in less than an hour and sets after the sun is up. This should allow us to move into position without much trouble or artificial light. Marty, I marked your spot with a chemlite. I'll give you the coordinates. Winds are generally from the south at ten miles per hour, up the canyon, but the rock formations and extreme terrain will cause eddies and side currents in the air flow.

"The terrain in our area of operations is varied and critical, from a built-up urban area full of civilians to high cliff walls. Observation from our vantage points, which I will review in a moment, is unobstructed into the target area. There are many mounted and dismounted avenues of approach into the area. Highway 149 loops through the south part of town. Main Street runs north out of town into the canyon before forking at North Belmont. The eastern fork terminates at the East Willow Trailhead, the western at the Equity Mine. Bachelor Loop is a half-paved, half-dirt road on the western foothills and intersects with Highway 149 at the southwest corner of town. The only approach from the east is the Wason Park Pack Trail. Dismounted avenues include the three draws and Windy Gulch on the west and two draws on the eastern slope. Windy Gulch is the only draw of the six with a stream, and it is running with the current summer runoff. Key terrain features are the suspected target area of the parade route along Main Street and the top of each ridge on the east and west side of the canyon. We will possess this key terrain during the early stages of the operation. Obstacles to movement include Willow Creek and the cliff walls on the north side of town. I do not think they will have a significant impact on the operation. Cover and concealment is prevalent throughout the area."

"What's the difference between cover and concealment?" asked Jerry, interrupting. It was actually a good question.

"Cover protects you from bullets," I told him. "Concealment doesn't."

"Oh." I think he was glad he'd be in the radio room.

"Residential and commercial buildings provide significant cover, but everyone participating in and watching the parade will be exposed. Concealment in the form of natural vegetation lines the draws and grows sporadically around the canyon. Juniper, spruce, sage, and bitterbrush are most prevalent. I believe the sniper will take advantage of this concealment during his egress plan. Any questions on terrain? Anything to add?" Nothing from the floor, so I went on.

"Our enemy is a single marksman, a sniper, equipped with what we believe is a two-seventy Winchester rifle and scope, capable of extremely accurate fire out to four hundred meters, eight hundred if the shooter is a professional. He has killed or injured three people in the last five days, including one killing today in broad daylight at a public event. He's used a stolen ATV, and we are certain some form of motorized vehicle will be part of his escape plan. We believe the sniper is a careful planner. He knows the movements and actions of his targets in great detail, as well as the reactions and capabilities of local law enforcement. He has a local's understanding of the terrain in the valley, and uses the terrain to his advantage in choosing his target areas, shooting position, and avenues of egress. He is a master of timing, forcing us to conclude that he rehearses his executions on the actual terrain. He is comfortable moving around at night, but is not afraid of daylight operations. I suspect he's predicted our counter-sniper operation and has already worked us into his plan. He may already be in position and have noticed that all of us are here after hours."

"Do we have any physical description?" Jerry again.

"An eyewitness in today's shooting saw a person running from the area where the shots originated, possibly carrying a rifle. This person was wearing dark clothing and had long black hair. We suspect this individual was the shooter, but that's all we have for a description."

"So, it could be a woman?" asked Marty.

"I don't think we should rule anyone out." I continued with the brief. "I believe he will choose one of three courses of action tomorrow. His least likely course of action will be from the northeast, on the cliff wall overlooking town. The vantage point is a good one, allowing him to view the whole parade route in a single line of fire. Disadvantages include a difficult and dangerous ingress and egress up and down the cliff, and that he will be exposed on the rocky face without concealment.

"His second option is a shooting position from the eastern ridge. This ridge is closer to the downtown area than the western ridge, and it also has two vegetated draws for escape. I think this course of action is also unlikely because of its limited mounted avenues of egress. His only option is to take the pack trail up to the plateau, or he must go through town to get back to Highway 149 to the south. The terrain is still pretty steep on the eastern side as well, making his foot movement more of a challenge, which is why the western side will be his most likely course of action.

"The western slope provides multiple mounted and dismounted avenues of approach and egress. It has a significantly more gradual slope into the foothills to the west, making foot movement much easier than the other two areas. In addition, Bachelor Loop and the multiple side roads into the foothills provide many options for the shooter to escape by vehicle, either north to the Divide, or south to Highway 149. Three draws and Windy Gulch extend from his vantage point to the Bachelor Loop trail complex above. Minimal lateral movement along the ridge will lead him to any of these draws, allowing him to escape from the target area along a covered route, out of sight by most. The easier slope of the western ridge allows for more vegetation to take hold, especially in the draws where water washes down intermittently. Cabins and houses climb the ridge above town, offering lots of cover and concealment for his shooting position within three hundred meters of the parade route. It will be impossible for us to search all the homes, sheds, and other outbuildings on the ridge and provide a feasible counter-sniper plan.

"I believe his most likely course of action will be to occupy the step with the topmost row of cabins on the western side of the canyon, probably near the northern draw. He will chose a vantage point in a cluster of buildings. After acquiring his target, he will fire twice into the crowd, and, in the ensuing panic, escape into the foothills behind him. I think he will move up Windy Gulch on foot to get out of the immediate area. This draw provides the most cover and concealment of any on the west side, and any good sniper will shift laterally after shooting. Lots of people will look up to where the shots came from. He probably has an ATV or Jeep stashed two hundred meters or so up Windy Gulch. On it, he will quickly move away from the canyon and escape into the wilderness or down to the highway."

"Why don't we just back off, set up road blocks, and nab this guy?" asked Jerry. "Sounds like we could catch him on the way out."

"Yes, Jerry, you're right. We could set up an effective outer ring or cordon, seal off all the mounted avenues of escape, and intercept the sniper," I said. "Unfortunately, this would not help whomever his target is tomorrow. He or she will be dead and bleeding in the street while we sit and wait safely at your roadblocks. Will we sacrifice this person in order to catch the sniper? With a full complement of state patrol or FBI, we could do both, but we must focus on preventing another shooting and leave his capture as a secondary goal. Remember the mission statement for tomorrow's operation. I worded it specifically for this confusion in priorities. If we try to defend everywhere, we will defend nowhere. We will catch this guy, but we may not catch him tomorrow. Our intent is to stop him from killing anyone in the parade. Are we all clear on this?" Nods all around. I could not stress this point more forcefully. If we lost focus and started thinking about arrest and prosecution, someone would die. I read back the mission statement verbatim and ensured the sheriff still approved.

"Okay, here's how we're going to do it. This operation will have three phases—insertion, surveillance, and interdiction. During the insertion phase, Marty and I will move on foot into the target area early tomorrow morning and be in place no later than zero three twenty, one hour before nautical twilight—the time it starts getting light out. Marty, you have the east ridge here, at the spur. I will get you the GPS coordinates after the briefing. I take the west side, four hundred meters south of Windy Gulch. We will then settle into our positions and wait for light. I considered moving in immediately following the briefing, but we'll need to be sharp for the parade, so we'll rest here tonight. Once we've occupied our sites, we will begin our surveillance of the area. Marty and I will be the eyes. Sheriff, you'll be the feet of the operation, confirming or denying anything we identify as a threat. We are all familiar with daily activities in town, starting with Joe Bender's street sweeping at dawn, so we must key on anything out of the ordinary. If we can interdict or interfere with the sniper's own infiltration of the area, we will succeed.

"The real interdiction phase begins when folks start showing up for the parade, usually around zero nine hundred, when the shops open. The parade moves north to south down Main Street, and all the participants set up in an assembly area just north of town, across from the underground fire station. Sheriff, Marty and I can't see into that area from our positions, so I need you to be in the vicinity as everyone starts to gather up there. We can't have you there the whole time, just have it on your beat as you move through town.

"Marty, you and I will have our rifles, loaded and ready,

but they are not our primary tools in this operation—our binoculars are. We will only use our rifles as a last resort, to protect life. Our rules of engagement must be very clear. First, if we identify the shooter, we observe and report. Sheriff Dale will move to his location, and we will cover him, rifles up, bad guy in the crosshairs. He will probably have his own binoculars up, so it should be easy to see him make a move to fire. Should he take up his rifle and look through the scope as the sheriff approaches him, we must assume that he is preparing to fire, and we must engage. Target a non-life-threatening area, shoulder or thigh."

"What if the first time we see him he has his gun up?" Marty asked.

I'd thought about that one during my recon. I knew what the right answer was—shoot him on sight. That's what Sergeant Richter and I would have done.

"If you see him with a shouldered rifle, take him out, Deputy," Sheriff Dale answered for me. "We can't take the risk. If he chooses to observe the parade through a rifle scope, that's his problem. It's all the lethal intent I need." As always, the sheriff was very clear in his guidance.

"Jerry, you are command and control," I continued. "You are our link to the outside world, especially any emergency response we need. Place a call to the Lifeflight boys in Pueblo tomorrow morning and let them know we might need them. Do not go into a lot of detail, just enough so they take a look at a map and file an initial flight plan. In the event any of us lose radio contact or get out of range for some reason, you will relay and ensure communications between everyone on the ground."

"Got it." Jerry was ready, happy to be included.

"Great. The time is now eight-thirty. Wake up is at two A.M. Are there any questions? Did I miss anything?"

"If the shooter's already in position, then we're sitting

right in the middle of the target area right now, aren't we?"
asked Marty. "And if he knows us as well as you think he
does, he probably knows we're all here."

She was right. The sniper knew our movements and predicted our reactions. One of his primary objectives would
be to know the exact location of local law enforcement at
all times. There were four Broncos parked in the lot. We all
entered the station in broad daylight and did not leave. He
had us right under his thumb.

"Do you think we're in any danger?" asked Jerry. I
could understand his concern. His last encounter with the
sniper was a painful one.

"No, Jerry, I don't think any of us is his next target," I
told him. "Marty's right, though, this does pose a challenge. If he's already in place, we'll need to get out of the
target area and into position without his knowledge."

"Won't that be a long night for him, though?" asked
Marty. "I mean, he'll have to be in his hide site for at least
eighteen hours before hitting his target, assuming he does
have a target in the parade. He'll need to be sharp, too,
right?"

"He may have help," said Sheriff Dale. "Deputy Tatum
forgot to mention that in his brief. We suspect he had assistance in the staging of the body in Deep Creek. Whoever is helping him can be his eyes during the day while
he rests."

"Either way, we have to prepare for the worst possible
contingency," I said. "We have to assume he knows where
we are and will have eyes on us until he plans to egress. His
observer could even keep us in sight during the shooter's
escape plan, allowing him to adjust to our response. We
have to assume he's in position right now. I should've
briefed you all somewhere else off-site."

"There was no time to set that up, Bill," said the sheriff.

"Don't beat yourself up. Here's the deal. He saw us all go in the station. The key is to maintain that perception, make him think he's got us nailed down."

"But how do we get out?" I asked. "The building's right out in the open, surrounded by streets or parking. There are only three doors—ours, city hall, and the coroner's. You can see all of them from either side of the canyon. There's no way." We sat quietly for a moment, then Jerry spoke up.

"There is one other way in," said Jerry. We all just looked at him.

"Jesus," said Marty, looking down at the floor, shaking her head. Then I knew what Jerry meant.

"The body locker," I said.

"Yup," said Jerry, crossing his arms, "The locker opens on the northwest side of the building and faces the western cliff wall. The L-shape of the town hall blocks any view from the south, so our only risk is if the shooter is set up on the west side. If his observer is across the street, he'll be out of the picture. The sheriff can pull his Bronco right up to the building, open the hatch, and make like we're moving the mayor's body. The raised door will obscure any movement behind the truck, and you and Marty can crawl into the back. There's no light back there, either. It's creepy. Sheriff Dale will have to stop at least twice on the way out of town. You all can roll out and move into position. He can drive around a bit like he's making a quick patrol. The shooter focuses on the truck, drawing his attention away from you two while you move into position. The sheriff then makes like he's driving to Alamosa or something to drop off the body, but he really parks somewhere up the valley and returns a couple hours later, and we're set."

We all wondered where he came up with it, but, unpleasant as his plan seemed, it was a good one. It was the only plan.

"Okay, Jerry, that's what we'll do," said the sheriff. "Now, unless there's anything else, folks, I suggest we pull out the cots and get some sleep."

Twelve

SHERIFF DALE FLICKED ON THE LIGHTS IN THE main office promptly at two A.M. The fluorescents burned a hole in my retinas. My guts churned, and nausea spread over me like a warm, wet blanket. My insides rebelled against the early hour.

"We move in twenty minutes," said the sheriff.

I sat up and placed my feet on the cold floor. This helped clear the grogginess out of my head, somewhat. I unwrapped the Ace bandages and wriggled my fingers. At least I could pull a trigger. I looked over at Marty Three Stones. She already had her boots on and was moving toward the coffeepot. She and I had slept in the desert BDUs I brought from home. I heard a creaking behind me—Jerry's crutches. I ignored the coffee for the moment and moved over to my desk, desert boots in hand. I laced them up, and the soft, broken-in suede felt good against my bare feet. Sergeant Richter taught me to break in my boots barefoot for hot-weather operations, and I never broke the habit. I'd freeze my toes before the sun came up, but once the heat came on, I'd be a lizard.

I stood up and took a quick inventory of my gear laid out on the desk, then moved over to Marty's and did the same.

"Are you inspecting me, Bill?" Marty walked up and handed me a steaming cup of Sheriff Dale Special.

"Yes I am, Marty, and I want you to do the same for me. Am I missing anything?"

She stepped over to my equipment and lightly touched each piece of gear, matching it with her own.

"You're straight. I love your Ruger, but don't you want something with a few more rounds in the chamber?" She picked up the Number One and opened the single-shot breach. "I mean, while you're fumbling to load a second shot, he'll be long gone."

"I won't need a second shot."

"Ah, okay." She lay the rifle back down. "I'll go top off our Camelbacks while you pack everything."

I loaded our gear into each assault pack. They were light and only half full. This was good. Soldiers have a tendency to fill every inch of the cargo space given them, hauling around more than necessary.

"What about our belts and service pistols?" Marty handed me the full bladders and I slid them in the special pockets stitched into the assault packs.

"We can still use them, but you're going to be on your belly most of the time, so I made some adjustments. Put yours on." She did. "You see? I moved all the equipment to the sides and back, so you don't have to lie on your pepper spray all morning. Your Smith goes in this." I held out a shoulder harness, also courtesy of the 82nd Airborne.

She shouldered the pack, picked up her rifle, and bounced on her toes. "Weight's not bad," she said. "I could run in this."

"If you have to move quickly, drop the assault pack. You won't need it. All the essentials are strapped to your body."

Sheriff Dale poked his head in from the hallway leading to the coroner's office. "Are you girls done playing dress-up? We need to move, now."

"Let's roll." I grabbed my own rifle and followed the sheriff down the hall.

This was the gruesome part. Sheriff Dale opened the locker and rolled out the drawer holding Mayor Jeff's body. Thankfully, Dr. Ed had zipped him back up in the pale body bag.

"Roll that exam table over here and lock down the wheels," directed the sheriff. "We'll put him there for now." Marty wheeled it over.

"How're you going to get him back in? Jerry sure can't help you," I asked.

"I will have the good doctor come by and assist. Let's go, on three." Sheriff Dale was moving with a sense of urgency. He wanted to get this over with as quickly as possible.

Marty Three Stones steadied the stainless-steel table while the sheriff and I lifted the body out of the drawer. When the mayor was solidly on the table, Marty strapped him down and wheeled him into a corner. She didn't even blink an eye. The woman was a rock.

"I'll drive the truck around. Push your gear through first, then crawl through," said the sheriff. "Be sure you shut the lights off in here before I open the outside door. No talking until you're in position." Marty and I looked at each other for a moment, then, without a word, loaded our rifles and packs onto the drawer recently occupied by the former mayor of Belmont. I turned off the lights and waited in the dark for the sheriff, trying not to look at the strapped-down body in the corner.

Not two minutes later, we heard the outer door open.

Marty and I both pushed the drawer shut. Sheriff Dale un-
loaded our gear into the back of his Bronco and returned
the drawer to us. Marty went first. She took a deep breath,
stepped up on Dr. Ed's desk, and, without hesitation, lay
down on the stainless-steel tray, head toward the outside. I
leaned into the drawer with both hands and slid it home,
sending her into the cold refrigerator space meant for dead
bodies. Quiet shuffling from the other side, and the long
tray returned empty, ready for the next passenger.

I repeated Marty's mounting of the drawer, lying down
face first on my stomach, trying not to think about the bodies of Gayle Whippany and Jeff Lange spending a few days
in this same space. With no one to push me in, I had to
reach up into the cold locker and pull myself in far enough
for the sheriff to grab my outstretched hand.

Closed spaces don't bother me much, but the cold, narrow cavity, smelling of death and chemicals, did little to
prevent an early onset of phobia. I was thankful to feel the
strong grip of Sheriff Dale's hand on mine, and he jerked
me into the cold night air. I took a deep breath of it and
scrambled into the back of his truck. Marty was already
huddled there, crouched below the back seat. Sheriff Dale
had turned off the dome light; only the taillights provided
an eerie red glow. This, too, disappeared when the sheriff
lightly closed the back hatch, leaving it ajar for our immi-
nent exit.

Sheriff Dale turned on the headlights and slowly pulled
away from the building, heading south toward Highway
149. There were two stop signs on this stretch through
town. I was to exit at the first one, and Marty the second.

We were at the first intersection in two minutes. The
sheriff said nothing, just slowed to a stop long enough for
me to crack open the hatch. I slipped out and squatted
down by the bumper. Marty shoved my assault pack out
and handed me my Ruger Number One. As soon as my

hands gripped the stock of the rifle, Sheriff Dale moved through the intersection. The whole maneuver took less than six seconds.

I scurried low into the shallow, grassy ditch on the right side of the road. Only one row of little cabins backed into the ridge to my right, up against the west side of the canyon. To my left was Sam's Barbeque Trailer and the softball field. I waited motionless until I barely heard Sheriff Dale's Bronco a few blocks away. I was left with the cold night air, the thin hum of the wind, and the quiet shush of Willow Creek running through town. We had no street lights in Belmont, so on clear nights we could see more stars than city folks see their whole lives. Tonight was no exception. Even with the intense light of the full moon, I could see so many stars, the constellations were obscured by them. The mountains were black masses against the galaxy backdrop.

The moon was a cold cousin of the sun. Once I'd sat still in the dark for a few minutes in my listening halt, my eyes adjusted to what little dark remained. Pale, silver light flooded the valley, illuminating the softball field for a ghostly night game. Platinum ripples shimmered downstream on the Rio a mile away. Light without heat, or even light that brought chill to the air.

Hearing nothing but the ambient noise of my beloved mountain town at the nadir of human activity, I sought out the route to my hide site. The moon shadows were black and sharp as the light, and the row of tiny cabins offered me interlocking darkness for me to disappear. I was near the southern outskirts of town, close to the fork in the road where Bachelor Loop climbed the canyon wall on the west side of town. I was still somewhat exposed at the outer rim of the shooter's target area, and I was anxious to remove myself from it. It was doubtful he had a night vision device, but tonight he might not even need it for a close-in shot with a good light-gathering scope, so I wasn't taking any chances. I had to assume he had some form of light-intensifying equipment, so I would need to move slowly. The key to observation is noticing movement, not changes in scenery, trusting your peripheral vision as closely as your binocular vision. At night, the good observer would rely on his peripheral vision, where the rods of the eye dominate the black-and-white world of low light and shadow. A well-trained sniper at night will scan his target area, never looking directly at anything, trusting his rods to see things more clearly than the weakened cones in the center of his vision.

My goal was to stay out of the shooter's periphery and move as slowly as the full moon across the sky. I had a full hour to move less than a mile, and I would use every minute of it. My route would take me smack against the canyon wall, slipping from shadow to shadow behind the cabins. I would then slide into the draw that held Bachelor Loop. I would be exposed crossing over the road, but only for a moment. From there, I would follow the contour of the spur to the next draw to the south—this was my avenue up the hill, covered, concealed, and out of range. Once in this draw, I could move quickly and out of sight. Achieving this draw was the decisive point of my movement into position. I'd be out of the target area and on a path to get behind the shooter, should he be on the west side of the canyon.

I'd waited long enough. Shouldering my pack and strapping the long rifle across my back, I took a breath of frigid air and crawled out of the ditch into a narrow alley between two cabins. I knew none of the residents in this row, so I hoped none of them owned a big dog, or even a little dog. I wondered what one of them would think if he were wakened by a deputy sheriff, sneaking around his garbage cans with a rifle at two in the morning. I didn't want to find out, so I picked my way very carefully down the row, staying as close to the canyon wall as possible and keeping my eyes and ears open for Lassie.

I reached the intersection of Bachelor Loop without incident. I spent no time reveling in my success, slipping across the new pavement and into the opposite ditch. My boots made no scuff against the road. Sergeant Richter had me replace all the hard rubber soles with soft, grippy vibram. They wore out quicker, but were infinitely more comfortable on foot marches and allowed me to feel every rock and twig in my path. I was reasonably covered crossing over; the walls of the draw that cradled Bachelor Loop at the base of the canyon were steep and blocked most observation from above. At least, that was my theory.

I rose up out of the ditch and did a three-point crawl around the spur on the south side of the draw. The leather palms of the tight-fitting nomex flight gloves protected my hands from the sharp rocks, but I managed to stick my hand with a stumpy cactus needle. I winced but drove on into the second, deeper draw that would lead me to my hide site. I huddled in the bottom, took off the glove, and extracted the spine. I sat still for a moment, listening for movement—a tumble of pebbles or the scrape of a boot, but heard nothing. The sides of the draw were steeper than the last, offering more protection and allowing rapid movement up the slope. I was a little uncomfortable with the limited range of observation, the walls blocked out all but a narrow corridor of stars above me, but observation was not my priority in this part of the operation. I checked my watch. I still had forty minutes to get into position, then another hour before the glow of the morning sun started creeping up behind the La Garita Range to the east. I started up the draw, doubling my speed from the first part of the approach.

The draw led me north and west, toward the top of the

foothills above Belmont. Using both hands to scramble up the loose rock and sand, I made it up the draw with alacrity, one of Sergeant Richter's favorite words. The dark sky opened up and offered a thousand stars. The moon was behind me, casting its light across the top of the hill. I crouched in the draw, looking out over the round, moon-washed plateau. I wasn't winded from the climb, but the effort warmed me, fighting off the bone-dry cold of the alpine desert night. I wore no thermals in anticipation of the movement, just the BDUs and a Coolmax T-shirt. I would freeze in my hide site until the sun came up, but at least I wouldn't have to fight off a sweat-soaked chill. "Travel light; freeze at night," as Sergeant Richter would say.

Although I was out of the shooter's area of observation, or so I thought, I would have to move carefully across the open area of the hilltop. Clumps of bitterbrush and little groves of juniper would provide concealment for me as I leapfrogged across the ridge, but I still had to move slowly. Quick movement made noise and drew attention. Nothing moved fast at this time of night. I plotted my route and emerged from the draw in a half-crouch. An upright-man silhouette was a dead giveaway in any light, so I kept my steps wide and body low, creeping across the hilltop. The maneuver was agonizingly slow as I toe-heeled my way to a big stand of bitterbrush. I felt exposed and vulnerable in the half-day of the full moon, but I kept my self-discipline and resisted the urge to run. I hoped Marty Three Stones listened to me as I explained the technique back at the station.

"Yeah, I got it, Bill." she'd said. "Just like a still hunt. I've done it before. My grandfather taught me to move like that when I was a little girl back at the res. Don't worry, I got it."

I hoped she was right. She probably was. Women have more patience for this.

I finally reached the pile of bitterbrush. I squatted behind it, keeping the dense thicket between the canyon and me. I paused again, listening to the night.

I remained below the topographical crest of the hill as I moved across the open area, staying on the "military crest"—high enough to control the terrain below, but downslope from the top. Profiles make easy targets on hilltops. My desert BDUs had the same tan and brown hues as the dry hillside, and I hoped they reflected the moonlight the same way.

I dropped into another draw and halted for a moment, out of sight. I waited five minutes and listened for anything outside the ambient noise of the valley, the breath in my lungs, and my heart beating in my ears. Silence dominated. I was close to my goal, now, within three hundred meters. I would have to move more slowly during this phase of the movement. If my predictions were correct, the shooter was within four hundred meters, but down the hill. I was out of his primary field of fire, but his ears worked 360 degrees. I checked my GPS and took a bearing to the exact location of my overwatch position, then lightly stepped out of the draw.

As I moved up the slope, I noticed geometric shapes to my front, shining a dull gray in the moonlight. I got closer and remembered where I was—the cemetery, where last century's miners buried their dead. Mining accidents, drinking, fires, and freezing to death led to a capacity crowd on the hilltop. I was somewhat creeped out, but after my method of extraction through the coroner's locker, nothing could really vex me now. I used the larger tombstones as concealment, moving right through the center of the graveyard. The dead would have to forgive me.

Bachelor Loop had a network of roads and gravel trails on this part of the ridge, and I used the shallow ditches while moving toward my hide site, listening for any indication that my approach was compromised. One hundred more meters of careful movement and I was in position, tucked within a cluster of tangled juniper and sage. The canyon wall fell away rapidly to the front, giving me a perfect perch to watch the parade route and, more important, any activity on the step below me. I crawled into the hide site and felt instantly secure, hidden from the cold rays of the moon. I lay in the prone, motionless, eyes closed, leaving the pack and rifle strapped to my back. I relaxed and let my heart rate leave my inner ear and return to normal. My breathing deepened, and the thrill of the night movement dissipated, replaced with a wary caution.

After ten minutes of stillness, detecting nothing out of the ordinary, I opened my eyes and scanned what I could. The moon was to my left, north-northeast, hanging above Mammoth Mountain and illuminating the valley below. A few lights were on in town—a blue glow from a television left on, a driveway lamp shedding yellow light between two trailers, one or two lights from cabins on the opposite ridge. Farther down the canyon ran the dark ribbon of Willow Creek, into the valley where it merged with the wider band of the Rio Grande. No man-made sound, no screen door slamming or dull thud of a shutting window. The wind cooled my right cheek and the thin line of sweat on my hairline.

I shrugged off the assault pack and laid it to my left, then carefully slipped the rifle from across my back. I had attached a bipod with spring-loaded legs to the front of the stock while getting ready down at the station, and I now extended the legs and set the rifle down to my right, careful not to let the barrel emerge from the confines of the sage and juniper to my front. I quickly loaded the Ruger with a shell from the leather case on my belt and quietly shut the breach. Nothing penetrates a quiet night like the metallic click of a rifle mechanism—the safety releasing or the bolt driving home. After all this movement, I stopped again for another five minutes, waiting to be compromised. Still nothing. Not even a dog barking.

Sweat between my shoulder blades chilled my back as it evaporated, and my bare feet inside my suede desert boots started to wooden, so I eased open the top zipper on my assault pack and pulled out three necessary items. First came a black wool watch cap—I was losing heat rapidly from the top of my head. I felt instantly warmer as soon as I had it on. Next came my favorite night-surveillance item—the desert parka. Developed in the early nineties just before the first desert war in Iraq, the parka was designed to combat the huge temperature swings in the desert. It was a mottled olive drab and dark green—matching the desert night. It was roomy, too, with big pockets and deep shoulder wells, capturing body heat and keeping it warm against the wearer. The length dropped below the waist, so I wouldn't have to press my crotch against the cold sand all night, and it even had a hood. Marty had one, too, and I hoped she was wearing it.

The last thing I pulled out was my poncho liner. This camouflaged, quilted nylon blanket was essential to all infantry soldiers. I never went anywhere without it when I was in the 82nd. Thin and extremely packable, the liner kept me warm many a cold night on surveillance. I wrapped it around my legs and feet. Now no part of my body touched the cold earth, which would suck the heat out of you in minutes. The only challenge was to stay awake.

Properly attired for night surveillance, I reached into the pack for my binoculars. It was too dark to use them, but I wanted to have them out in order to reduce any movement during the day. My hand bumped something hard and smooth while digging around for the rubberized Bausch & Lombs—a small thermos. Marty must have slipped some coffee in my pack while I was slithering through the coroner's locker. She was awesome. I would wait until I got really cold or sleepy before I opened it, which would probably come sooner than later. It was risky, though—the smell of coffee or any other man-made aroma leaps out in the wilderness, overcoming the faint wisps of sage, elk, and evergreen. I'd have to check my discipline when the coldest hour arrived. Maybe someone down in the valley would make coffee and cover the scent of my own.

I settled in to my new position, hidden in the juniper. I checked my watch—3:30 A.M. I called in to Jerry and reported that I was in place.

"How you doin', Marty?" I asked, looking over at the shadowy patch of canyon where she would be.

"Just fine. What took you so long?"

"My pack was pretty heavy. Did you put a rock in it?"

"Nope, check again."

"I did. Thanks, Marty. Did you get some for yourself?"

"Roger."

"That's enough, children. Maintain radio silence." It was the sheriff.

I put down the radio. The sheriff, as usual, was right. Unless we stopped now, we'd be on it all night. Whispers could carry a lot farther than expected in the wilderness, especially at night.

I had a few hours to kill and nothing to look at but moonlight and shadow, so I took the time to revisit my theories surrounding the Belmont sniper.

The most obvious theory was the jealous wife. Amanda Lange seemed to be the most likely suspect. Her motive was clear—jealous rage took the lives of many husbands, wives, girlfriends, and boyfriends every year. Gayle Whippany may not have been Mayor Jeff's first dalliance, either. Mandy might have suspected his adultery, even tolerated some of it, to a point. Maybe the young reporter was the last straw, breaking the fragile restraint of an angry wife, boiling over from one tryst too many.

   Mandy certainly had the ability to carry out the sniper
attacks. Although I'd never seen her fire a gun, and her
only trips to the ranch were for business, it was clear she
possessed the required skills. She knew the terrain well
enough—it was literally her backyard. She was a skilled rifleman—the photo of her trophy buck attested to that. She
would have plenty of expert assistance, if her father or Jacob conspired along with her.

   Marty placed all three of them near the scene of Jeff's
murder. "Near" was a relative term, of course. If this were
Denver or Kansas City, being within three miles of a murder was not considered "near," but out here, it was darn
close. Spatial relationships were a little different in the
mountains. Mandy was close enough to draw attention, at
least. Of course, her long black hair matched Ralph
Munger's description of the person he saw up on the knoll.
Her daughter's story, however, conflicted with Marty's report, but it was unlikely that Cynthia was involved in
killing her own father. I suppose it was possible for Marty
to mistake one person for another at a distance, but I
thought she said she spoke with Jacob directly. I would
have to follow up with her later. Once we found Mandy
Lange, we would get her version as well, if she ever turned
up again.

   These shootings, however, seemed too clean for an act
of passion. Murders for love were usually messy and spon-
taneous—a husband arriving home early to find his wife
warming the sheets with another man, a wife meeting her
man at the door with someone else's panties in one hand
and a gun in the other. The violence explodes in one sudden bloodletting and that's it—conflict resolved. Our murders were stretched out over days and miles of
mountainous territory. Why not just kill the mayor and the
reporter together? They were attached at the hip, pun intended, for most of the month of June. Mandy Lange

would've had many opportunities to catch them in the act.
She must have known their secret early on in order to plan
both murders to the point of detail displayed by the evidence. These cold, meticulous assassinations in Belmont
did not fit with a jealous rage. The shooter was careful,
well rehearsed, and disciplined—attributes usually not associated with crimes of passion. I thought these murders
had a higher purpose than simple rage or jealous revenge,
which led me to my next theory.

Dana Pratt had a lot to benefit from the death of Gayle
Whippany. If I read the journal correctly, she was on to
something, and it all led back to Dana Pratt's existing and
future land developments in the Rio Grande Valley. What if
Gayle Whippany was on the verge of uncovering a political
scheme between Dana and the municipal government? If
Dana Pratt were cozy with the Belmont mayor and town
council, he could do just about anything he wanted and get
away with it. What if she stumbled on an ecological night-
mare just downstream from Belmont that was killing off
fishing stock and turning the Belmont Caldera into an EPA
cleanup site? What if it were both? Was it severe enough to
warrant the killing of an innocent woman whose only
crime, besides adultery, was to shed light on corruption
and pollution? I needed to know more about Dana Pratt and
the Shallow Creek Ranch.

I had planned on interviewing Pratt after the race but
was overcome by events. All I really knew about the man
came from what I heard in town and the dead woman's
journal. I passed him on Main Street once in a while, but he
usually blew right by without a word, boot heels clicking
rapidly on the sidewalk, cigarette burning between lips or
fingers. He always dressed in black—black jeans, black
twill shirt, black cowboy hat—even in the middle of a hot
July afternoon. I saw his black Duellie pickup truck, the
white "SCR" and longhorn symbol branded on the door,

parked in front of town hall more often than I saw the man himself. He met with one town official or another at least once a week. Every other month or so, I heard his Beechcraft take off from the airport across the river from my cabin, confirming the journal report that he traveled to Ft. Worth to manage his holdings down south.

Did Dana Pratt have the means to carry out these sniper attacks? Possibly. He was a big game hunter, so he claimed, although I'd never seen his skills as a rifleman first hand. The shootings were not terribly difficult, ambushes really, with the sniper having all the advantages. Dana knew the terrain well enough, having visited Belmont for many years, hunting and touring, as well as living here for the last five. He was his own boss, with no real schedule to keep or behavioral patterns to maintain, which allowed him freedom of movement and a cloak of unpredictability. He had a full staff at the Shallow Creek Ranch as well as in Ft. Worth, giving him a bucketful of loyal employees to provide alibis for him.

Unlike their boss, I had lots of opportunities to encounter the boys from the Shallow Creek Ranch. There were five of them, all hired on from the dusty, backward towns of hardpan-flat eastern Colorado, living year round at the Ranch, like a boys' club. There wasn't much real ranch work at Shallow Creek, so Dana used them to run labor crews on his projects and provide security at his RV parks and summer cabin developments in the valley. They all thought they were modern-day cowboys, riding into town in their pickup trucks—they each had their own and never rode together—stirring up the locals. They liked to drink and fight and drive, usually in that order. I don't know how many times I'd arrested them for drunk and disorderly at one bar or another, giving me a chance to play Wyatt Earp, cleaning up Tombstone. Dana Pratt bailed them out every time. Their ringleader was Mack, a big ornery unshaven creature. Gayle Whippany bumped into the pony-tailed ape when she tried to interview Dana at the ranch.

Mack and I had a real come-to-Jesus encounter my first month on duty. He responded very well to my thumb-lock, folding like a six-foot cot, while his two compadres lay crumpled on the sidewalk outside the San Juan Tavern. They didn't just teach me to carry a rucksack at ranger school.

Ponytail—that got me thinking. Mack had a black ponytail. I didn't envision Dana Pratt getting his hands dirty with the actual killing. Dana ran his operation from a distance, why would he run a series of shootings any differently? He had plenty of help, and I doubted that any of his goons would hesitate to pull the trigger on anyone their master wanted. I could see him directing the operation from his ranch, and the boys carrying out the grim tasks. One hole in my theory, however, was the dead mayor. Two holes, actually. I couldn't see why Dana Pratt would want Jeff Lange dead. The good mayor did nothing but support Dana's projects, stamping every one with his approval. The motive would have to reveal itself in time.

I had no clue where to begin following up Gayle Whippany's investigation of Dana Pratt. I would interview the man as soon as I got a chance. It would be nice to find Mandy Lange first. Her husband was dead, and the last time anyone saw her was on a horse down the trail from where he lay dead and bleeding. I was still shaken by Orville's possible involvement in the conspiracy. The man seemed genuinely enraged by the death of his son-in-law and mortally offended when I suggested that his only daughter, his only child, might be involved. My gut told me something different, but who was I to trust my gut—a green sheriff's deputy on his first murder case?

I opened my mind to other possibilities, other suspects,

other victims. A nagging question from day one was the staging of the dead woman's body in Deep Creek. Why would the killer do that? Why not just dump the body somewhere else, off the beaten path? There were miles and miles of unbeaten paths in the San Juan Mountains. Better to make the journalist simply disappear, another missing hiker lost in the vast Colorado wilderness.

A missing hiker, however, would prompt a massive search, involving not only local law enforcement, but also volunteers from town, tourists and locals alike. We would scour the hills and valleys, walk down every path and jeep trail, and peek down every abandoned mine. Maybe the shooter wanted to prevent this dragnet, maybe he was hiding something in the hills, and Gayle Whippany stumbled upon it, leading to her demise. He had to take her out, get her away from the original crime scene, and focus the sheriff's office on another, secondary scene—Deep Creek Valley. This original crime scene still eluded me, the woman's final days lost to the mountains and a boy scout troop from Lamar, Colorado.

The sniper failed to remove one bit of residue, however, from the target area—the rock fragments Dr. Ed pulled out of her face. Ralph Munger mentioned that he wanted me to come by soon. Did he match the samples to a known geological area in the valley? I was dying to find out. Every day, every hour that went by, my chances of catching the sniper diminished exponentially. Unless, of course, he kept on killing. The clock had reset itself yesterday when he shot Mayor Jeff, a grim second-chance for the bumbling efforts of the town sheriff and his merry band of fools.

The motive for Jerry's shooting was still a mystery, too. The wounding was intentional, of course. This sniper was deadly accurate, immensely capable of putting a bullet right through Jerry's heart, but he chose the meaty part of his thigh instead—the million-dollar wound. This proved he was no madman, killing for his own enjoyment. Murdering Jerry simply was not part of his plan. His killings had a purpose, but what was the purpose of shooting a sheriff's deputy? Why did he take the risk? His staging of the body succeeded in drawing the sheriff away from the original kill zone, so what end did another ambush serve? His intent was not to draw us away from Deep Creek so he could sterilize the scene. The shooter left immediately after putting a bullet into Jerry. He could have shot me just as easily when I first found the body, but he didn't. He waited until I reported the dead woman and brought out the boys. He wanted a BOGSAT—Bunch of Guys Standing Around Talking—on the bridge.

Maybe I was over-thinking the motive. Maybe he was going after simple numbers—take out a deputy, and the sheriff had less manpower to investigate. Why not shoot the sheriff, then, the most competent man in the department? We would be lost and leaderless without Sheriff Dale.

The shooter was manipulating us with his actions, pushing us into making certain decisions. Maybe he knew Sheriff Dale very well, enough to want him to stay in charge, knowing how the sheriff would proceed. The three attacks taken together, along with the Thomas Pitcher's foolish decision to have the parade, forced Sheriff Dale to focus away from the investigation and concentrate his dwindling resources on protection, keeping his deputies close to town. Maybe Belmont was exactly where the shooter wanted us, fixing his only adversary in the valley.

The sniper mastered the clock and the calendar as well. The Republican Convention and the Telluride Film Festival drew additional law enforcement away from Belmont, giving him the perfect opportunity to carry out his plan. The sheriff said it himself—a woman, a gimp, an old man, and a hayseed from Iowa were all we could muster to counter the sniper.

We were catching up to him, though. So far, we'd executed the parade operation with as much care and precision as the sniper planned his own shootings. The shooter may know we'd plan something for the parade, but I doubt he knew we were already in position, and behind him. He probably expected us to deploy only a few hours before the start of the parade, in full view of himself and the rest of the town. If our deception plan was successful, he thought we were still holed up in the sheriff's office.

Thirteen

I MANAGED TO BURN A COUPLE HOURS WITH MY thoughts. The sun sent its red messengers to the eastern sky, illuminating the thin rows of cirrus clouds above the La Garita Mountains. This was the coldest part of the day, moments before sunrise, when the earth has gone the longest without the sun's rays. Shades of gray and dusky color drove away the silver light of the moon, and scattered the ghosts of miners to their daylight hiding places in the shafts and shacks where they used to pry wealth from the earth.

I heard an engine crank in the street below me. Joe Bender emerged from the machine shed in his street sweeper, dusting the night off the town and getting her ready for the show. I smelled the exhaust fumes of the diesel two-stroke, but in them was a wisp of something else—coffee. Amazing what you can smell in the wilderness, even if the wilderness runs right up against your town. Joe had a plastic coffee mug with a lid in his hand, steering the sweeper with the other. This was my cue to break open my own thermos, courtesy of Marty Three Stones, but I resisted. I wanted to let my eyes adjust to the new light as it crept into the canyon. Once my cones took over from my rods, I'd pour myself a cup. I needed one, too. The cold ground had leeched away most of my body heat. I could barely repress a bout of violent shivers, allowing only a steady vibration to ripple through my aching muscles. I wiggled my toes constantly to keep them from turning to wood. A few ounces of hot liquid would drive away the chill, but I did my best to concentrate on the changing features of the scene below me. My job was surveillance, and I wasn't about to let a little cold distract me from my duty.

The sun pushed up from behind Wagon Wheel Gap, its brilliant brass light pouring into the Rio Grande Valley, illuminating the snowy crests of the mountains behind me. I felt its warmth on my face as I shut my eyes and welcomed our life-giving star. We used to worship the sun in ranger school. I went in the winter and was never so cold in my life. One would think Florida, Georgia, and Texas would be nice to visit during the coldest months of the year, but when you're wet, numb, and up all night with a ruck on your back, they don't seem like good vacation spots. Comparing any discomfort to ranger school always helped my morale. Even huddled in a hide site in the bitter cold mountains of eastern Afghanistan, Sergeant Richter and I told each other ranger school stories to keep ourselves warm.

I opened my eyes, set my binoculars in front of them, and watched Belmont wake up. I'd chosen my position well. I had a perfect view of the whole village, from the north end where the cliffs thrust up against the first few cabins to the softball field and welcome sign on Highway 149. The town was still in shadow, sunlight wouldn't overcome the high cliff walls for another half hour or so, but the natives were stirring. Independence Day was the biggest day of the year for Belmont, coming at the peak of the tourist season, so it was like Christmas in Whoville. I saw Eunice sweeping the front porch of the Belmont Hotel. Joe had already finished with the streets and was hanging red, white, and blue banners along Main. The bell on the door of the Mountain Grown Coffee Shop jingled as Marjorie Dunwater stepped out with her newly chalked sign of daily specials. A healthy column of smoke rose straight up from Sam's smoker. He stood in front of it, loading the racks with ribs, chicken, and brisket for the throngs of hungry mountain pilgrims that would flock to his trailer at lunchtime. The boys at the fire station at the north end were washing the trucks for the parade. Dedicated firemen—I bet their hands were frozen in the icy buckets of water.

I noticed Sheriff Dale's Bronco coming up the valley on Highway 149. I wondered where he'd spent the night. He had good timing, carrying out the perception that he'd moved Mayor Jeff's body, and returning when he could be easily identified. I trained my binoculars on the opposite spur, looking for the barrel of Marty's rifle or a shiver in the bushes concealing her hiding place. I couldn't find her, which was good. She'd hidden herself well and wasn't fidgeting. I was proud of our little department. We were making this work.

A puffed-up mountain bluebird sat in a juniper off to my right, waiting for the sun to warm it. His dull-colored mate joined him in the tree, bouncing him gently as she landed on the same branch. They would hunt as a pair, flitting from tree to bush as the morning heat roused insects from their nocturnal dormancy. A black-masked chickadee lit on the ground in front of me. He hopped about, then turned his head and looked right at me, curious. He took two fearless hops toward me and looked again, cocking his tiny head left and right. A flutter of little wings, and he was inside the hide site, standing on my barrel. I heard the beat of his wings and the soft click of his nails on the gunmetal. I guess I sat pretty still, if this little character was unfrightened of me. He hopped around, then he got bored with me, departing through the rear entrance of the hide.

The rest of the morning passed without event. I lay in the hide, drank some coffee, and ate a couple Powerbars to break the monotony. Eventually, the cold night air yielded to the sun, and the dry earth warmed quickly in the summer heat. My shivering ceased, and I carefully removed my parka, hat, and poncho liner, stuffing them in my pack. Most of my activity was restricted to scanning the canyon, keeping my eyes moving, alternating between binoculars and naked eye. Nothing moved on the east and west ridges—either the sniper was already in position and chose not to reveal himself, or we were the only hired guns in town. I hoped it was the latter. Although we were prepared to interdict the shooter, I preferred to capture him when his rifle was in its case.

Around mid-morning the parade preparations shifted into high gear. A steady stream of trucks, floats, tractors, and vintage cars rolled through town all morning, heading for the assembly area across from the fire station. Traveling vendors, artists, and local shopkeepers set up tents and tables on the side streets intersecting Main. The Rotary club and the chamber of commerce joined forces in erecting a beer tent in the side street across from the grandstand, making it the most popular place in town. Four black pickups from the Shallow Creek Ranch were parked illegally in the post office lot next to the beer tent. Dana Pratt's boys were already drunk, I imagined, but not all of them, unless they car-pooled. One truck was missing. Dana Pratt's Duellie was also nowhere to be found. I figured he'd be greasing palms at the grandstand with the other nobs.

The parking lot next to Henry Earl's grocery was already full—cars and SUVs lined the back streets and alleys, and more were coming. The place was an American Mecca. I heard the bouncy rhythm of the Dixieland tuba-and-banjo combo from yesterday as they alternated between Bourbon Street jazz and blue grass. It sounded like a fiddle had joined them for the occasion. The hot dog stand on Main Street was blazing away with three extra grills, and the smells of hot beef franks and polish sausage made their way to my well-tuned nose, making my mouth water. Independence Day in Belmont wasn't just a parade, it was a carnival. The day was perfect for the event. The sky was the same color as the mountain bluebird from earlier that morning, and not one cloud marred its expanse. The sun warmed the valley floor, and with little wind to carry the heat away, the little canyon that cradled Belmont baked in the sun. Only the altitude saved the village from becoming a kiln. The hot dog stand would sell as many snow cones as wieners today.

I drank water steadily from my Camelback. All memory of freezing feet and shivering shoulders burned away in the hot July sun. The coffee did not come out again. I was a lizard. Lucky for me, the juniper and sage of my hide protected me from the direct rays. Marty and I had spelled each other in ninety-minute shifts since sunrise, allowing each time to sleep and rest weary eyes. We both needed to be sharp for the parade. Our superior positions allowed a single shooter to cover the majority of the town, but four eyes were better than two. An hour before the parade kicked off, we were both up and on high alert. Sheriff Dale was on his beat, tipping his hat, sampling the wares, and walking an irregular pattern through the streets of Belmont. Our mission shifted from surveillance to interdiction. Marty and I tried to ignore the activity below and focus on the ridges above town. We zoomed in on every lip of terrain and potential hiding place in the canyon, searching for any sign of activity—a rifle barrel, a glint of optics, or a shift of camouflaged clothing. We saw nothing. This guy was good, I told myself. Maybe the shooter wasn't going to show. Maybe we'd done our job, and he pulled off, balking at the risk. Maybe he was just too good to be identified.

"I found Jacob Stackhouse," Sheriff Dale called in over the radio. "He's down here in the assembly area. Looks like he's leading a cowboy act of hands from his daddy's ranch."

This would explain his absence from Orville's place yesterday. Sometimes the simplest explanations are overlooked for more sinister reasons. At least we found him.

"Maybe we can question him afterward," I suggested.

"In due time, Deputy," said the sheriff. "Let's focus on our current task."

"Roger, Sheriff."

A yellow school bus turned off the highway and worked its way uptown on the east side, stopping in the school parking lot. A high school marching band streamed out of the front and rear exits; the teenagers gathered in little knots of like-instruments and started warming up. Soon they formed ranks and files, and a drumbeat marched them up the street to the assembly area. I watched them and remembered my days in the band, playing trombone. I didn't share that with many people. Sergeant Richter never found out, or he would have hounded me to no end for being a band geek. Their ranks were pretty straight, I noted.

"Sheriff Dale, this is Jerry, come in."

"Go ahead, Jerry," said the sheriff.

"Ranger Doug just called. Said there was another break-in last night at the compound."

"Anything missing?"

"He thinks so," said Jerry, "There was only one motorcycle stored there. Kawasaki 250 dirt bike. It's gone."

"Maybe the owner just came and picked it up for the weekend."

"He doesn't think so. The lock was snipped again."

"Okay. Have him come in and file a report. See if he can dig up the owner."

"You got it, Sheriff."

We all knew what this meant. It was highly likely that the sniper had something planned for today and stole the dirt bike to use as a method of escape from the target area. The 250cc dirt bike would fly down any goat path or foot trail, giving the shooter increased flexibility in choosing his escape route.

Spectators started lining the parade route at eleven o'clock, marking their claims with folding chairs and older children. Only foot traffic moved on Main Street. Sheriff Dale set up the roadblocks himself earlier that morning, diverting traffic away from the parade route and the immediate blocks along it. The murder of the town mayor didn't dissuade folks from coming. Rumors would fly through the crowd, of course, but I didn't think they'd all flee for the outskirts of town once they found out. Nothing like a little mystery to spice up a public event.

"This is Marty. I think I got something," Marty's calm voice came over my radio headset.

"Where?" Sheriff Dale asked.

"West ridge, down in that draw with the Amethyst Trail. I think I saw a glare," she said.

I swung the binoculars to my lower left, but the top of the draw blocked my line of sight.

"I cannot confirm," I said. "The trail's in defilade for me."

"I'm close," said Sheriff Dale. "Be there in ten. Shift to your scope."

"Already there," Marty came back. She made the switch to her rifle before making the call. Good girl. The crosshairs of her scope now lay on the potential target. Sheriff Dale moved under her overwatch.

"I have your sector, Marty," I said over the radio as I

widened my scanning range to encompass Marty's area. We couldn't leave the rest of the canyon uncovered.

"Okay. I'm at the trailhead. Guide me in," said the sheriff.

"Seventy-five meters up the trail, halfway up the south wall. Pile of rocks at the top of a scree field," Marty identified her target.

"I see the area. Don't see the glare," Sheriff Dale called back.

"It only flashed twice a bit ago. Nothing since," Marty said. "Walk up the trail. You're covered."

"Moving."

I could only picture the sheriff as he moved into the draw. If the sniper was there, Dale was walking right down his gun barrel.

"Okay, Sheriff, you're just about even," Marty's voice had a touch of excitement, now. "Keep going and get behind him. Walk right by about thirty meters and don't look over until I tell you."

"Got it."

I scanned the rest of the canyon as best I could, trying not to be drawn over to the sheriff. I couldn't see him anyway. I could only wait. The happy sounds below me grew louder as I waited for the crack of a rifle—Marty's or the shooter's. The people enjoying the day on Main Street were oblivious to the deadly conflict above them. I heard the marching band tuning their instruments, the clop of horseshoes on pavement, the noisy start of a Model-T Ford.

"Okay, Sheriff. Nice and easy, turn around and tell me what you see. Should be up and to your right," came Marty's voice over the radio.

"Nothing. Just the pile of boulders. I'm going up there. Got me?"

"Got you, go ahead."

The seconds crept by as if they were climbing uphill toward noon. I kept up my surveillance, needing something to do, helpless to assist in the dangerous task to my left. I thought about the location along Amethyst Trail. Not a bad spot to shoot from—covered and concealed, nice escape route, just like I'd briefed. Limited sector to the objective area. The draw was high and tight and hugged close to downtown, giving the sniper a narrow corridor to fire. The sniper would eliminate his target and flee up the Amethyst Trail.

"You're just about on him, Sheriff," said Marty, tension bleeding out through my headset.

"Yeah, I'm here," the sheriff sounded disappointed. "I found your glare, Marty. Glass pop bottle. Someone must've tossed it up the slope. Kind of teetering on a rock. Wind is pretty stiff through here."

"Roger Sheriff, sorry." Marty was embarrassed by her false alarm.

"Now, Marty, don't you go sounding down in the mouth," the sheriff encouraged her. "You did exactly the right thing. This is just what we talked about last night. Good work. Pick up your sector from Tatum. The parade will start in thirty minutes."

"Roger Sheriff."

"Sheriff, this is Jerry," the other deputy's breathless voice came over the radio. "We got a problem."

"Okay, son, take it easy. Whatcha got?"

"Some kid is in here freaking out. Says his buddy collapsed and won't wake up."

"Where is he?"

"Over by the school." Belmont had only one school, K through 12.

"I'm on my way."

We'd been on the hillsides for eight hours, and now things just started happening. At least I wasn't having any trouble staying awake.

The school lay on the east side of town, so I had a good view from my vantage point. I swung my binoculars over to the school and saw what Jerry was talking about. Sure enough, a teenage boy was sprawled on his back beneath the elementary school playground equipment. He was a bit too old to be climbing around on the brightly colored jungle gym, so I wondered what the hell happened. Even if he'd fallen, the drop was nothing a six-year-old couldn't handle.

"I see him, Sheriff," I reported. "Male, white. He's twitching a little, so I don't think he's dead. He's lying right under the purple slide."

"Roger, Tatum, thank you," said the sheriff. "I'll take it from here. Pick up your scan."

"You want me to call the Lifeflight, Sheriff?" Jerry asked.

"Negative, Jerry. I'll take the Bronco and his friend and see what's what. He may just have a bump on the head." We were all a little eager. Five minutes later, I saw the Bronco pull up in front of the school, and the sheriff's voice was back on the radio.

"Jerry, call the Lifeflight. This boy looks just like the one we sent up yesterday. Pupils dilated, hot to the touch. His heart rate is around 180." Another meth overdose.

"You need any help, Sheriff?" asked Jerry.

"What can you do, son? Stay on the radio. I still have his little buddy here. I'm certain he'll love to help me. We can have a nice chat in the truck about crystal meth while his friend's heart is exploding. You all will just have to keep things under control while I'm gone. I need to get out of here before the parade starts." It was almost noon.

I watched the sheriff's truck crawl through town toward the airport and wondered how the heck we were going to carry out this counter-sniper operation without anyone on the ground. With Sheriff Dale pulling medevac duty, we had no one to confirm or deny our observations from above. The rules of engagement just got more complicated. We would have to take action with the only tool at our disposal—a high-powered rifle. The only way to prevent the sniper from killing would be to fire first, not quietly arrest him on the ground. We had no choice, really; the kid under the slide would die without Nick's expert trauma care. Dr. Ed was dressed in a clown suit somewhere in the assembly area. This was the reality in mountain towns—urgent medical attention was hours away. I wondered when the other shoe would drop.

Like an avalanche or an alpine glacier, the parade would not be denied. Thomas Pitcher, the acting mayor and new parade marshal, had gathered the town council and business leaders on the grandstand and was giving a little speech. I only caught little snippets; the speakers were pointing the other way. It sounded like a eulogy for the newly departed mayor followed by a rousing effort to get the spirit back into the event. Spirit wasn't in short supply, however, considering the beer tent was overflowing with revelers right across from the grandstand. Their happy hoots and cheers got the rest of the crowd going. The speech was blissfully short. Pitcher reached over, pulled the lanyard on the old steam whistle borrowed from the Belmont Historical Society, and, as the howl of the whistle echoed through the canyon, the parade was on.

The high school band led the way. I was impressed by their well-dressed ranks and smooth marching. They had tuned their instruments well, and the canyon walls amplified their rendition of Sousa's "Stars and Stripes Forever," turning the little marching band into a powerhouse of sound. Band geek to the last.

The rest of the parade was what you'd expect—fire trucks, clowns, old cars, and a few covered wagons and mucker's buckets thrown in to maintain the town's western character. Once the marching band passed by, I had no difficulty keeping my attention above the din. The eastern ridge was quiet as ever. All movement was on Main Street.

Just then, an explosion rippled through the canyon. I looked frantically about for a muzzle flash or a dead body, but found neither.

"What was that?" Marty's voice was frantic over the radio. "Was that a shot?"

"I don't think so," I said. "Anyone go down?"

"Negative. What's going on?"

Some of the tourists had their faces turned upward in all directions, the source of the blast still unknown to everyone in the canyon. The parade continued, and most of the locals paid no attention to the explosion. Then another thunderous roar rocked Belmont, followed by howls and cheering.

"I think it's behind me," I called in, "in the next draw to the west."

As soon as I clicked off, a third explosion rolled out of the foothills west of town, accompanied by more hoots of approval.

"Take it easy, folks," Sheriff Dale's voice came in over the radio. "It's just the Belmont Cannon. I can see them from down here at the airport."

"I knew that." I was embarrassed, and I hoped Marty was, too. The Belmont Cannon was a real cannon brought out every 4th of July, or whenever the cannon committee felt like it. They launched everything from pumpkins to softballs, usually accompanied by an iced-down keg of Coors.

We settled back down into our surveillance. I was a little frustrated that we hadn't found the sniper, yet. We did everything right, but he still had the advantage, and the stolen dirt bike was out there, probably hidden near his perch, ready for him to hop on and disappear again.

Jacob Stackhouse and the rest of the hands from the Stackhouse Ranch came in behind the fire trucks, riding beautiful mounts and dressed in full cowboy regalia. They were talented riders and ropers, twirling lassos and guiding their horses, it seemed, by thought alone. As they made their way down Main Street, I noticed a calf in the middle of the cowboys. They took turns roping it and keeping it in their tight formation. Impressive. Jacob stood out in his salmon-colored twill shirt and yellow bandana. He'd traded in his beat up, sweat-stained brown Stetson for a well-shaped gray Resistol. He was in the lead of the formation, whirling his bay 180 degrees to control the calf, his well-trained pony walking backward without missing a beat. I couldn't help but watch the performance. I'd never seen anyone do that on a horse before.

I had my binoculars trained on him when his head exploded in a red mist of blood and bone. He toppled off his horse like a wet bag of cement, his living rope dying with him. Then I heard the crack of a rifle, off to my left, down in Windy Gulch.

Fourteen

"SHOT FIRED, SHOT FIRED!" MARTY'S VOICE screamed over the radio. "I saw the muzzle flash in Windy Gulch! Who's down? Who's down? Tatum? You see anything?"

My pounding heart shook me out of my trance from watching a second man die violently in as many days.

"It's Jacob Stackhouse, he's down," I said. "Right behind the fire trucks. Can you see the shooter?"

"Negative, negative. I'm scanning. I can't see him at all."

The crowd was in an uproar, peeling away from the body. The other cowboys jumped off their horses and crowded around Jacob. The sniper didn't take another shot. He didn't need to.

"I'm relocating," I said. "I can't see down in Windy Gulch from here, but I can be there in two minutes."

"You're covered. He moves, he's dead." Marty's voice

was icy calm. We'd already failed, but maybe we could catch the shooter.

There was another crack of a rifle, and chaos reigned in Belmont; spectators and participants scattered like prairie dogs. I tried to ignore the pandemonium down on Main Street. There was nothing I could do for Jacob Stackhouse, now, nor could I control the chaotic scene from my position on the ridge. Our only on-site lawman was sitting at the airport babysitting a meth OD. I looked for another victim lying in the street, but saw no one. Then I heard the unmistakable whine of a small-block motorcycle engine—the missing Kawasaki 250. The sniper was moving, becoming a ghost again, and all I had to catch him were my leather-bound feet.

"He's moving, Marty! I hear the engine! Can you see him?" Marty did not come back. I didn't have time to wait. She said I was covered, and that was good enough for me. I was on my feet, sprinting across the ridge toward the deep draw of Windy Gulch. I could still hear the dirt bike, winding up and down as it negotiated the rugged path up the draw. I was in a desperate race and well overpowered. It was about four hundred meters to the edge of the gulch, and I covered the distance in two minutes. I threw myself down on the dusty earth and crawled the last ten feet. I didn't offer my big head to the sniper by popping up over the ridge. Peeking over the lip of the draw, I saw movement to my left, two hundred meters up the slope. The sniper was standing up on the dirt bike, working his way up the trail, this time wearing a white helmet and dark clothing. I didn't see any long black hair. I brought up my rifle, snapping the bipod legs into position. Finding him quickly in my scope, I wanted to squeeze off a round, but my racing heart and heaving chest from my dash across the ridge prevented any chance of getting off a decent shot. I struggled to control my breathing and slow my heart rate as I watched the shooter get farther and farther out of range. He disappeared into the thick pine and aspen mix in the upper reaches of the draw, three hundred meters away. I had one more chance to tag him. The trail left the trees and jogged to the right at the top of the draw. I had only twenty meters of open area to acquire and shoot before he disappeared behind Bachelor Mountain and into the wilderness.

I lay the cross hairs in the middle of the open space and waited for the killer to enter my field of fire. I would have to squeeze off just before he hit the center of my scope. It was a long poke, 450 meters, but I'd made hits like this many times, although none on a moving target. My .30-06 would have no trouble covering the distance in a hurry. I tried to pinpoint the location of the fleeing sniper in the trees, hoping to predict when he would burst out into the open. I heard the engine gear down and idle. My finger brushed the checkered metal of the trigger. I took a deep breath and exhaled, waiting for the moment of stillness before my next breath. Then I realized my mistake.

I barely had time to roll before hearing the snap of a bullet passing over my head as it broke the sound barrier and nicked one of the bipod legs in my desperate flaying to get out of the way. I heard the crack of the shooter's rifle as I slid five feet down the sandy, eroded wall of the draw. I had foolishly forgotten whom I was chasing—a cold-blooded killer who planned everything down to the last measure, including a quick ambush on any deputy sheriff stupid enough to lie out in the open.

I stopped sliding, righted myself in a crouch, and stumbled forward into a vertical cleft in the wall, using it as cover. I heard the motorcycle engine increase its rpm's. The sniper was breaking for it. I threw up my rifle in a desperate attempt to sling a bullet his way, but even this was impeded by a scope-full of sand. I lowered the rifle and watched him streak across the open area and up the trail. Then he was gone.

Another, bigger engine roared on the ridge above me, and I stuck my head up to see my own Bronco bouncing over the terrain toward me, roof lights blazing. Who the hell was driving my truck? I took one more look up the slope then struggled out of the draw. Jerry was driving. What the hell? I waved at him. He zoomed up to me and hit the brakes hard in a cloud of dust, opening the passenger door to my dumbfounded self. His crutches lay across the seat.

"Get in!" he shouted. "Sheriff wants us to pursue!" I obeyed and slid in next to him.

"What the hell happened?" he asked, hitting the gas and skidding up the ridge toward the trail, "You just disappeared on the radio."

I reached down to my belt for my radio and found the pouch empty. "I must've dropped it somewhere. He went that way." We intersected the trail out of Windy Gulch and turned north. I didn't see the shooter. Our bumpy ride smoothed out as we left open terrain and hit jeep trail. I was still a little stunned by the odd turn of events.

"What are you doing driving, Jerry?" I saw a spot of blood on his left thigh where the wound was seeping through his uniform trousers. "Your leg is bleeding, buddy."

"I know, but what else could we do?" he asked, "When the sheriff lost both you and Marty on the radio, he freaked. He left the meth OD and his friend at the airport waiting for the Lifeflight and took off to look for Marty on the east ridge. I jumped in your Bronco and came up looking for you. Well, I didn't really jump, I sort of hobbled. Sheriff didn't stop me."

"What about Jacob?"

"He's dead. Not much we can do for him, now," Jerry

said flatly. "Dr. Ed was a few blocks ahead of him when it happened. He and Joe Bender moved Jacob to the coroner's office and got everybody quieted down. Most folks just got in their cars and left. Nice little traffic jam. Lights and sirens work great."

I tried not to envision the bizarre, macabre scene of a parade clown moving the lifeless body of a cowboy off the street. "There was a second shot. Was anyone else hit?"

"Don't know, that's right about when we lost Marty. Then we heard the third shot, and you didn't respond either."

I picked up the handset on the truck radio. "Sheriff Dale, this is Tatum. I am with Jerry and in pursuit of the shooter. He's on a dirt bike, moving north, wearing a white helmet."

"You okay, Tatum? Thought we lost you," said Sheriff Dale.

"I'm fine, sir. Do you have Marty?"

"Roger. I picked her up from her hide. Bastard took a shot at her."

"Is she injured?"

"Negative. Just a little shook up. Bullet went right through her hat. We're moving north up the main road below you. We're the anvil; you're the hammer. Let's get this prick."

"Careful, Sheriff," I warned. "He already took a shot at me, too. Set up a nice, quick ambush."

"Yeah, well, that's why they pay us the big bucks. Keep me informed of your position. Out."

I hung up the radio and turned off the rooftop lights. "I don't think we'll run into too many traffic jams up here, Jerry," I said.

We reached the flat top of Bachelor Mountain, and the trail split off into multiple side trails and goat paths, most leading to old mining claims, others leading nowhere. There was no sign of the shooter. I had Jerry stop and turn off the engine, so we might hear the distinctive sound of the motorcycle engine above quiet mountain stillness. We both stuck our heads out the windows.

"I hear it!" said Jerry. "Moving north. You hear it?"

"Yup, let's roll." We tore off across the top of the mountain, following the main trail toward the divide. As we sped north, the number of trails reduced to one or two, giving the shooter fewer opportunities to mislead us. The jeep trail eased off the top of the ridge into the gradual slope above West Willow Creek, eventually running parallel to it. We left the alpine meadows of the southern face and entered thick forests of Douglas fir and and Englemann spruce. The trail improved to a gravel road with shoulders and reflectors at the tight turns, but I cringed at every blind curve, waiting for the impact of a rifle bullet through the windshield.

We took a sharp turn to the east down a steep hill and emerged on an open area with West Willow Creek running through the center.

"Whoa, stop!" I shouted. Jerry stood on the brakes, and we skidded to a halt before we were completely exposed.

"Back up, now."

Jerry threw the truck in reverse and swerved up the hill.

"What's going on?" he asked.

"The last thing we need to do is burst out into the open. This guy could be waiting for us in the trees right over there." I pointed to the forest on the other side of the meadow, thick and deep with shadow.

"What do you want to do?" asked Jerry. "We need to go after this guy. Sheriff's on his way up."

"I don't want to get shot at again. I don't like being on the wrong end of a two-way rifle range without my gun up. You wait here and don't move until I tell you. Stay below the dashboard." I grabbed my spare handset out of the charger base and slipped out the door with my Ruger, rolling over the shoulder and into the woods on my right.

I ran through the trees and reached the edge of the alpine meadow, staying within the evergreens' protective concealment. I found a nice little hide and got down on my belly, scanning the area. My desert BDUs didn't match the surrounding green and olive drab, but I had little choice. I relaxed and listened. Only the quiet idle of the Bronco to my left and the easy tumble of Willow Creek broke the silence here at eleven thousand feet. That's what worried me. We weren't that far behind the sniper, and we heard his engine during the entire pursuit. We would hear it for miles up here in the wilderness, so where was it?

I scanned carefully, not hurrying across the scene, looking for the one thing out of place, a flash of white helmet, a freshly broken tree limb, a glint of metal in the natural background. Then I saw it—a scarring of the grass where the dirt bike veered off into the trees on the far side of the meadow. I brought up my scope, which I'd taken the time to clean on the way up, and zoomed in on the area where the shooter had entered the trees. My heart slammed my chest as I tried to acquire a target before I became one.

Gradually, things began to appear in my scope—the rear-view mirror of the dirt bike sticking up at an odd angle, a hint of white mud guard, a black knobby tire tread—nothing was black in the woods except a burn. The shooter carelessly dumped the bike in the trees; his hurrying was evident. Maybe he didn't expect us to pursue so quickly. Maybe he posed the bike to divert our attention from his shooting position. I kept scanning. From the quick glimpse I'd had in Windy Gulch, the sniper had on dark clothing, which would blend in to these surroundings quite well. I lowered my scope and took in the whole scene. Where would I set up a sniper ambush? He was only about five minutes ahead of us, not much time to move away from his bike and get in position. He was probably within two hundred meters of the motorcycle. He would want to cover both avenues of approach. Three trails passed through this area—our own from Windy Gulch on the southwest side, the main road from the south, and the jeep trail north to the Equity Mine. A small but sturdy bridge crossed over West Willow Creek running down the center, merging the Windy Gulch road with the main road. I looked for movement, but the clearing was as still as an Albert Bierstadt landscape. The sun was high and behind me in the southern sky, but the trees protected me from it and the wind as well. Only the creek moved, but that motion was perceived, not observed, my brain connecting the sound of rushing water with its tumble down the mountain.

"Tatum, this is the sheriff," Dale's voice wedged into the silence. "What's your status?"

"This is Tatum," I said as quietly as I could into my handset. "We're at the bridge over West Willow. The shooter dumped the bike in the trees, but it might be another ambush. I advise you hold your position until we clear the open area."

"Negative. We're on the main road, about half a mile south. We'll approach on foot."

"Why don't you move up another hundred meters or so and drop Marty. Have her set up on the south side."

"Wilco. I'll come too. No point sitting here in the truck. You two can cover me while I circle around the clearing."

"I don't think that's wise, Sheriff."

"I wasn't asking for your opinion, Deputy. Marty will cover from the south and you from the west. I will circle around through the trees on the east side of the clearing. We all just can't sit here, hoping he'll give himself up. We're moving."

I didn't argue. If the sheriff wanted to try to stalk a trained sniper on foot, he could do so, and I would do my best to keep him from getting his ass shot off.

He was obviously frustrated by our failure to prevent

another killing, and now he was taking risks to make up for it. Maybe that's what we needed to catch this guy. I stopped thinking and picked up my scan, this time with the rifle scope, carefully working my way out from the motorcycle. I thought the best position to cover the clearing was from the northeast. The terrain was steeper there, and the shooter could observe and fire down both southern approaches to the clearing. His enemy—us—would come from one of those trails, and he would want to protect his escape route to the north. That gave me an idea. As soon as Marty and the sheriff got into position, I would move north and attempt to cut him off from his northern egress. I had the burden of failure on my shoulders, too, and I wanted to get this guy. Twenty minutes later, Marty called in.

"This is Marty. I'm in position. Just inside the tree line on the south end, west side of the main road."

"Roger, Marty," I whispered back. "I'm up and to the left, about eight o'clock if you're six."

"Got it," she replied. "Where's the dirt bike?"

"Northeast end of the open area, about two o'clock. If you follow the southwest road, you'll see his tire tracks disappear into the trees. It looks like he came down this trail, crossed the bridge, and kept going straight into the woods."

"Roger. I see them."

"You two just sit and cover," Sheriff Dale came in. "I'm moving up the east side."

"Sheriff, if I may," I said. "Move up about one hundred meters and find a position, then I'll leapfrog up this side. Just like in Deep Creek." Ten seconds went by.

"Okay, Tatum. Let's do it," the sheriff agreed with my plan.

"Marty, your sector is nine to three; I'll take twelve to six. Sheriff—you have six to twelve when you get set up."

"Roger. Moving," was his reply.

The clearing was only 250 meters long and half that wide. It wouldn't take the sheriff long to move up the east side. I found him in my scope—not the safest method of finding friendlies—and scanned the forest ahead of him. The afternoon light penetrated the first few meters into the thick Englemann spruce, but there was only darkness and shadow behind it. I moved my field of view slowly to the left, staying in front of the sheriff and working my way toward the abandoned motorcycle. Nothing but trees and sparse undergrowth entered my scope.

"Okay, Tatum, I'm at three. You're covered," said the sheriff.

Too many snipers get their heads blown off by their enemy peers. Instead of popping up and presenting my skull as a target, I simply rotated in the hide and cleared my own path, looking for likely places for the shooter to take me out. I saw nothing. I lowered my scope and blinked my eyes back to distance focus and scanned again. Only then did I slowly rise up out of my hide.

I toe-heeled my way through the trees, familiar with the movement after years of hunting, but uncertain whether I was predator or prey. I doubted the sniper chose this side of the clearing to set up his ambush, but that thought wasn't very reassuring. I was conscious of my mismatched desert camo, feeling naked in the green shadows of the forest. I was far enough from the tree line to escape the direct sunlight, which would expose me as a fraud. I didn't even match the gray exposed granite around me.

I eased up to the road where Jerry dropped me off. This would be the most dangerous part of the movement, crossing over. If I were the sniper, one of my fields of fire would go right down this jeep trail, and, if he'd acquired me through the trees, he already had his scope centered on the lane, waiting for me to jump out into the open.

"Okay, folks," I whispered into my handset, "I'm at the gravel road. Keep your eyes open and shoot the bastard if he takes me out. Then come get me."

"Don't be so dramatic, Tatum," said the sheriff. "Just get your ass across the road." Sheriff Dale was blunt as usual. I bolted across the open space and into the safety of the trees on the other side. No shot fired. No holes in my uniform. I moved on.

The terrain on the northwest side of the clearing sloped upward toward the divide, rising above the level of the clearing. I found a small ledge twenty meters back from the tree line and called in my position.

Sheriff Dale moved swiftly through the trees on the opposite side, emboldened by our luck so far or simply tired of dicking around. Probably the latter.

"I'm up to the bike," he called in a few minutes later. "I want both of you to focus on the north end, the high ground, ten to two. If he's still here, that's where he'll be."

I'd become familiar with the ground at the north end of the clearing, and familiarity leads to carelessness, so I cleared my head and scanned the sector as though it was the first time. The different angle from my new perch helped with this effort, and I gave the area a fresh look. I found all the likely vantage points and some new ones—a rock, a clump of gnarled juniper, a cut in the hillside. I strained to see through the vegetation into the shadows, looking for the soft satin reflection of a rifle barrel or the fleshy curve of an ear. I lost time, immersed in the effort of finding the sniper before he pulled the trigger.

"Okay, folks, I'm at the north road." The sheriff's voice jarred my focus. "Tatum, close the loop."

I doubted the sniper was between me and the sheriff, but I didn't let that thought cloud my judgment, taking careful steps to complete the sweep without getting tagged for my laziness. I did not. I stopped at the road at the north end of the clearing and waved at the sheriff across the way. We met on the road.

"Well, what do you think?" he asked.

"I think the bike was a decoy, a stalling tactic to keep us occupied while he escaped."

"I agree. Don't see we had any choice, though."

"Nope. Not after the way he set us up in Deep Creek and Windy Gulch."

"I'm going to leave Marty in place to cover us while we search the area. She can watch our backs while we've got our heads down."

"Good idea. Let's start at the dirt bike." I strapped the Ruger across my back, and we walked over to the bridge where the shooter left the road. The tire tracks proved my original thought—the sniper crossed the bridge and didn't take the turn on the main road. Instead, he drove straight up the easy slope through the short mountain grass and into the woods. It didn't even look like he slowed down until he hit the tree line. The bike was pitched on its left side a few meters into the trees.

The inspection of the motorcycle yielded nothing, just a Kawasaki 250, matching the description of the one reported stolen. The sheriff took down the license plate while I started working the immediate area of the clearing.

I walked slowly around the bike, looking for any indication of the shooter's flight from the abandoned motorcycle. My circles widened, spiraling outward deeper into the woods, then I found my first sign—the bark of a tall spruce had been torn off as he brushed past it. I drew a mental line through the trees and followed it to another sign, this time a crushed deadfall, so rotten and buried in pine straw that it looked like a rock, but a clearly-defined toe print stood out in its soft surface. The toe pointed south, back toward Belmont.

"That's strange. The track leads south, not north. Why

would he go south?" I asked no one. The sheriff continued
to examine the dirt bike.

"You sure it's not mine from before?" asked Dale.

"Yes, sir," I said, not looking up. "I just found a toe
print—definitely south."

"Hmmph. Well, drive on," he said.

I wasn't a tracker, not by a long shot, but the shooter
made the job easy for me, crashing through virgin alpine
forest. I stepped carefully to the left of the track, not wanting to mar any sign. Lining up the scrape in the tree and the
toe print in the rotten log, I found the next track ten meters
away—a broken branch. The sniper must've grabbed it and
snapped it off to keep it away from his face. I kept going,
finding sign every five meters or so, steadily working my
way south.

"Marty, this is Tatum." I figured I better tell her where I
was, to keep her from plugging me. "I'm following a track
south of the bike."

"Roger, I see you." I felt a little queasy, knowing she'd
just lined me up in her scope to confirm my location, but
I'd done it before, and I trusted Marty. She wasn't some
redneck or scared rookie who shot anything that moved. I
was glad it was she and not Jerry.

I got lucky about fifty meters south of the motorcycle. A
bed of green moss captured two prints—a toe and a heel.
The subject was running, I thought, making an amateur assessment. The toe dug deep into the moss and kicked up
the soft dirt below as it left the earth, followed by a hard
heel strike in the next track. Looked like running to me.

I followed the line, but it petered out. The vegetation
thinned along the track, and no sign was evident anywhere.
I started making ever-widening circles from the bed of
moss. Maybe he took a turn that I missed, or broke into the
clearing for some reason. I came up short. Then, I remembered a trick I saw in a movie. I found a long, sturdy stick

and went back to the two tracks in the moss. Placing one end of the stick on the front end of the toe print, I measured the distance to the back of the heel and made a notch with my knife—I now had a stride unit of the shooter.

I found the toe of the heel print at the edge of the moss—just a few broken pine needles. I measured out the stride and put my face right down on the pine straw where his footprint should have been—nothing. I wasn't discouraged. I measured again but found nothing. Third time's a charm, I thought to myself, and I measured another stride in the forest floor. I got down low and peered at the spot where the notch indicated, and there it was. Not even a snapped twig or crushed evergreen needles, just a slight depression in the spongy pine straw, moon-shaped—a heel. I blinked my eyes, clearing the image from my retinas, and looked again. It was still there. Was I Daniel Boone, or what?

I used my stride stick until the forest thickened again, leaving a nice canvas for me to follow the sniper's sprint. He moved south, keeping the edge of the clearing on his right, about twenty meters into the trees. He wasn't sneaking, trying to cover his progress. He moved quickly, almost in a panic. I wondered if he knew how close we were behind him, how close we'd come to confronting the shooter. The track continued to the south end of the open area, then crossed the main gravel road about thirty meters down from the southern edge of the clearing, turning west. The sniper's prints were only scuffmarks in the hard-packed gravel, but they clearly indicated his change of direction. On the opposite side of the road, I found a clear, unmistakable boot print from a military-issue field boot. Who the hell were we dealing with, here? Former military? Certainly fit the profile. Of course, you could buy army-issue boots just about anywhere.

I looked up into the thick forest on the west side of the

road. My vision couldn't penetrate the dense wall of pine boughs and ferns, then I froze in my own tracks and realized how stupid we were. We'd assumed the sniper was gone, picked up by his partner and escaped north toward the divide. Yet, here I was, tracking him south, his progress like that of a panicked animal, one that might turn on you if trapped. For all I knew, he could be waiting for me to step into the dark woods and take me out silently.

"Marty, this is Tatum," I said over my radio. "The tracks turn west here at the road, toward your position. I can't see one foot into the forest. Can you reposition?"

"You think he's still here?"

"I think he's still here."

"Gimme a second."

I waited while she pointed her rifle in my direction.

"Okay, Tatum, I'm about fifty meters west of you. I'm already in the trees, so I can see a little farther. There's nothing between the road and me. You're clear to enter."

This was a little dicey. If the shooter were between us, Marty would have to shoot toward me to take him out. I pulled my service pistol and stepped into the trees.

The tracks led into an enclosed clearing about the size of a department store changing room. Young spruce trees grew close together, clustered near the road, seeking the sunlight denied them by their older cousins deeper in the forest. Their low branches created a maze of evergreen— perfect for a hide. Their fallen needles silenced my steps. The only noise was the soft whoosh of the pine bows across my clothing. Of course, if the shooter were here, he would also hear my heartbeat, pounding in my ears. That's all I could hear.

Instead of walking straight down the sniper's line of movement, I wheeled around it to the south, keeping his track off my right shoulder. I sidestepped through the trees, my pistol at a low angle in front of me, ready to bring it up and fire at the ghost we were tracking. The low branches alternately obscured and opened my line of sight into the dense grove of young pines. I stooped to get under them and clear my field of fire. I broke through the evergreen grove on the west side and into the more open mature forest.

"There you are, Tatum," said Marty, over the radio.

"I think he's gone, Marty," I answered.

"Yup, you'd probably be dead by now if he wasn't," she said flatly.

I retraced my steps to the road and picked up his track, following it to the small clearing. The sniper had definitely entered the clearing, churning the thick bed of evergreen needles, but I saw no exit, no indication that he ever left the protection of the juvenile fir. What was this? I pulled out my stride stick and measured from the last print that entered the trees. The stride stopped smack in the middle of the clearing, right where the needles had been disturbed. I measured three more strides in the same direction, exiting the clearing and moving into the open forest—nothing. He must have changed direction again upon entering the trees. I returned to the young evergreens, feeling a little out of my lane. Without a track heading out, I wouldn't know which direction to place the stick. Not to be discouraged, I began circling my last known track, working my way out. I found nothing—not one bent branch or trampled fern. It was as if he'd been picked up by aliens.

I heard crunching footsteps on the gravel road and left the woods to meet the sheriff.

"Well, Tatum?"

"Sir, it looks like the shooter left his bike, tore off through the woods, heading south, crossed the main road here, and ducked into the pine trees right there." I gestured toward the thick spruce grove. "From there, I lose all sign. I could've followed his other track in the dark with a book of matches, but once he entered those pines, his tracks vanish. I circled out for twenty meters, found some mule deer sign, but that's it."

The sheriff absorbed this, looking up in the direction of the dirt bike, following the line of the clearing with his eyes. He peered at the tracks across the road, squatting down to get a good close look at the military boot print in the sand, then stared into the wall of pine branches where the shooter disappeared.

"Maybe he left the clearing the same way he went in," he said. "Hard to tell if anyone drove through here on top of his tracks, the gravel's packed so tight. He must've circled around to the south, backtracked on you, and left the dirt bike as a decoy. Maybe someone picked him up off the main road, and they took off together up north, toward the divide."

"Did you see anyone ahead of you on the road?"

"Nope, but there are plenty of side roads out of this area. His buddy could've been waiting up here already. That's how they got away from Deep Creek when he shot Jerry."

"But why would he move south? He was closer to the north side of the open area. It was a shorter walk for him."

"Probably because that's what we'd expect him to do, Tatum. Think about it. He knows you're chasing him and will enter the clearing from the southwest. He drops the bike where he knows you'll see it. Then, instead of running north like you'd expect him, he runs south toward a linkup point with his partner, in the opposite direction you're likely to search."

"But I never saw his buddy's truck drive through here."

"Look, his heading south was an insurance policy, just in case you were closer to him than planned. If his linkup was on the north side, his partner would have to drive through the open to pick him up, right in front of you. If the linkup was on the south side, he could hop in the vehicle out of your line of sight and take off in another direction."

"There's only one other trail out of this area, Sheriff, that's the La Garita pack trail, the one you drove in on yesterday to where Mayor Jeff was shot. The one that leads straight to the Halfmoon Ranch."

"Yup. All roads lead to Rome, it seems."

I thought about that. It was at least five miles to the ranch, not close by most standards, but we were in the mountains. Distance had its own relativity out here. Still, it was a long way.

I hoped my loyalty to Orville wasn't clouding my judgment, but his involvement just didn't feel right. Why would he shoot his own stable master? Now that we'd totally failed in our counter-sniper operation, it was time to refocus on the investigation. I shrugged off the looming despondency and cleared my head.

"I think we're clear, Sheriff. Let's bring Marty out of position and get Jerry down here."

Sheriff Dale called them in.

Marty came out of the woods, the bulging assault pack still on her back. I had left mine down in the canyon. I mentioned it to her.

"In all the excitement, I guess I just forgot to drop it," she said, a little embarrassed. "I never really noticed it after getting shot at."

She took off her boony hat and showed me the ragged hole in the crown, powder burns still fresh on the edges.

"Damn," I said quietly. "That's even closer than mine."

I unshouldered my rifle and showed her the dent in the bipod leg where the sniper's bullet struck it.

"Very nice," said Sheriff Dale. "Now if you hardened warriors are done showing each other your battle scars, I would like to move forward with this investigation. It's all calm and quiet up here, but we're gonna fly into a shitstorm when we go back down the mountain. I don't think Councilman Pitcher will be as impressed with your cuts and scrapes than with a dead cowboy in the middle of his Independence Day parade. I'll be surprised if we all have jobs when we get back."

We shut our mouths. The sheriff was pissed.

"Okay, girls, we have three big problems on our hands." He held up a big index finger and looked straight at me, "One—we still aren't one cunt-hair closer to finding this shooter, Tatum. I don't hold you responsible for the failure of our operation at the parade today. I approved it, and our chances were long, anyway. I do, however, hold you accountable to the investigation. I've given you a long rope, son, and you can either crawl out of the quicksand or hang yourself with it."

"Two." He held up a second finger. "We have a crystal meth problem in our happy town. Marty, this is your bag of shit. The kid under the slide today had no connection to the OD from yesterday. I want you to roust up all of their friends and shake them down hard. I want to find out who's buying, who's distributing, who's bringing it in, and who's making it. I want to nail this thing down at the source. Call in the state Meth Task Force if you have to. We can use all the help we can get."

"What about me, Sheriff?" asked Jerry, limping up to our huddle on his crutches.

"Son, let Tatum drive you back to town and get some rest. You're still on night watch." He looked down at Jerry's bleeding thigh. "Have Dr. Ed take a look at your wound, Jerry. I need you here, not back in the hospital in Pueblo." Jerry's display of courage and resourcefulness softened the sheriff's mood.

"Let's get the dirt bike in Tatum's truck and get out of

here. I'm certain the acting mayor will want some explanation for what happened today. That's number three."

I was actually happy with my own task. I'd rather track down the sniper than face Councilman Pitcher and the rest of the town fathers, and mothers for that matter. They were probably banging down the door of the station right now. The sheriff had the toughest job of all—keeping the hoards at bay in order to allow his deputies to investigate. Someone had to run interference, and Sheriff Dale was the best one for that. He was the public face of the department, anyway.

It was three in the afternoon by the time I dropped off Jerry and the dirt bike back in town. I ducked in the station to change out of my BDUs. Sure enough, the town council was waiting in Sheriff Dale's office when we pulled in— Thomas Pitcher, Becky Noonan, and Henry Earl Callahan. With this sour group was Cynthia Lange, looking like she'd aged ten years since yesterday. Her mother was still missing, and she had to arrange her own father's funeral. A lot for a daughter to handle without support. She blocked my exit, locking me with blue eyes, now rimmed in red, puffy, but still fierce.

"I bury my dad tomorrow, Deputy Bill," she said. "How close are you to catching his killer?"

"We're working on it, Miss Lange," I said. "I'm truly sorry you have to go through this alone. Any sign of your mother? We really need to talk to her."

She crossed her arms and looked away. She wore no makeup and had pulled her raven hair into a tight bun. Must have been in the way.

"I haven't heard from her." She paused, and I waited for her to continue. Something was struggling to get out. "But I think I know where you can find her." She turned back to me, and her eyes had lost their anger, revealing the scared little girl who just wanted her life back the way it was. I waited.

"She's with Dana Pratt. That's who she's been screwing around with all month."

"When did you find out?"

"One of his boys told me last night at the San Juan Tavern."

What was she doing at the San Juan Tavern with her father cooling off in Dr. Ed's locker? I didn't ask.

"Which one? There are five."

"The big one, Mack." The pony-tailed freak of nature. Wonderful.

"And you believed him?"

"I could tell she was fooling around. I told you this already." She was getting impatient. Well, she was never patient to begin with. "Why don't you get out of here and find her?"

"Why don't you go out and get her yourself?" I don't know why I asked that. I was getting defensive.

"You're the deputy, and I'm not going out to the Shallow Creek Ranch alone." I didn't blame her.

"Okay. I'll go get her." I put my hat back on and she let me pass.

"Better get that tire fixed first, Tatum." Marty Three Stones had overheard our conversation from the radio room where she was giving Jerry a thorough bout of training.

"Yes, Mother. Thank you." I left the office just as the screaming started from behind the sheriff's door.

Fifteen

Pᴇᴛᴇ & Zᴏᴏᴇʏ's Jᴇᴇᴘ Rᴇɴᴛᴀʟs ᴀɴᴅ Tɪʀᴇ Rᴇᴘᴀɪʀ was a couple miles west of town on Highway 149, on the way to the Shallow Creek Ranch. I turned into the circular gravel drive under the arching sign bearing the name of the establishment. Four main buildings made up the Mc-Claren's complex—the office attached to their small cabin where Pete filled out the rental forms, the garage with its sloping roof and mounds of tires, and two open-walled storage sheds, filled with a variety of the popular four-wheeled ATVs, two-wheeled dirt bikes, and about a dozen Jeeps and Toyota trucks. They spilled out of the sheds in neat rows, organized by vehicle type. It looked like business was good, judging from the number of empty spaces where grass grew long around the absent vehicles. A line of snowmobiles sat hibernating behind the larger shed, waiting for the first blanket of snow to awaken them. In addition to the functional machines, Zooey had many other hulks in different stages of inoperability scattered around the yard, giving the place a split personality of junkyard and rental shop. The character of each brother was laid out for all to see.

I parked the Bronco next to a teetering pile of truck tires, closer to the garage where Zooey would be working. Stepping out of the truck, I was greeted by the harsh smell of burning rubber and another chemical odor I couldn't identify. I dragged the ruined tire out of the back and rolled it as best I could into the garage. Inside, I found lots of tires and a jeep up on blocks, but no Zooey.

"Hey, Zooey!" I called out for him. I didn't want to step into the disarray of the garage, so I walked around the side. "Zooey! Yo! Got a tire for you!"

I rounded the corner and found, what else, more tires, weeds growing up around them. They surrounded a five-hundred-gallon propane tank like a black fortress. The unfamiliar chemical smell from before was stronger here, assaulting my nostrils. It didn't smell like a gas leak, but I checked the fittings on the propane tank anyway. They were severely corroded, looking dangerously close to rupture.

"Hey Zooey, where are you?"

I heard a rattling cough near the back corner of the garage, and Zooey's head popped up from behind the fortress of tires on the other side of the tank. He rose up out of the earth, carrying a big framing hammer in one hand. He walked right to me without a word, the hammer low at his side. He towered over me, stopping just inside my personal space. His black, stringy hair hung loosely around his lean face, which was covered with patches of growth. He peered down at me from cavernous eye sockets.

If I didn't know Zooey better, I'd be halfway to my truck by now. I know Zooey very well, so his approach and appearance didn't bother me in the slightest. This was Zooey. His social skills weren't very refined.

"What's up, man? Got a tire for me?" His voice was quiet, but light, with a tinge of surfer dude. Given a pair of glasses, he'd be a Tommy Chong look-a-like. He turned away and let out a spasm of coughing.

"Sure do, buddy. Check it out. I left it in the garage."

He abruptly wheeled around me and headed for the front, doubling over again with another coughing fit.

"Hey, Zooey, you should have someone check out this propane tank. The fitting's about to fall off from corrosion. Could be dangerous, my friend."

He stopped and turned his head, eyes shifting rapidly from me to the tank to the back of the garage.

"Yeah, man. I told Pete about that." He swiveled his head back around and kept moving. I guess that was that. I'd talk to Pete, too, and ask him about the smell while I was at it.

I followed Zooey's hunched gait to the front of the garage. He deftly picked up the ruined tire and dropped it on the workbench. I was astonished by the strength in his skinny arms. The iron bands of his forearms rippled with the effort, but he otherwise threw the tire around like it came off a Radio Flyer.

"Dude, this thing's really shredded," he said, whipping a tool around the bead, separating the tire from the wheel. "What'd you do?" This came out like "Whudjyadoo."

"Caught it on something on the way down the pack trail into town. Damn near ran right through Joe Bender's living room."

"Sweet."

"Can you fix it?"

"Sure." He wasn't looking at me. Instead, he was gazing around the garage, looking for something. I waited a couple seconds for a more detailed response, but I wasn't going to get one.

"When do you think I should come back for it?"

"Tomorrow." Still searching.

"Morning?"

"Sure." He turned away from the workbench and me and yanked a tire out of a stack, then another. I guess he was done with me.

"Great, Zooey, I'll be back tomorrow morning. Thanks." I went to talk to Pete. I knew I'd find him in the office.

Just like the dichotomy of the neat rows of clean rental vehicles next to scattered rust buckets, the confusion of Zooey's garage contrasted with the fanatic neatness of Pete's office. I walked through the door with the pleasant jingle of a customer bell. The reception area was paneled in light pine and smelled of the same wood. The simple tile floor shone with a fresh wax and buff, pretty odd for four o'clock in the afternoon. Pete had just cleaned up, no doubt. Photos of happy renters in identical frames lined the walls in straight ranks and files. I walked over to the counter and tapped the bell.

"Hey, Pete!" Where were these guys?

"I'm back here, Deputy Bill!" I heard Pete's voice from a room behind the small office area on the other side of the counter. How did he know it was me? I ducked under the hinged section of the counter and sought out the voice. The waxed floor continued through the inner office to the small room in the back, where I found Pete. The cramped space reminded me of the radio room at the sheriff's department, filled with racks of electronic equipment.

Pete stood on the first shelf of one of the racks, which climbed floor to ceiling, mounting a new gadget to an upper nook. There were no chairs in the room, which didn't surprise me. I never saw Pete sit down the three years I'd known him. He cropped his curly red hair close to his scalp—no doubt to keep it at bay and reduce preparation time after showering. He wore jeans and a blue polo shirt with "Pete & Zooey's" stitched on the left breast in yellow thread. Everything about Pete was thick—shoulders, forearms, legs. It was difficult to see the resemblance with his dark, lanky older brother. Pete McClaren was a short, tightly wound ball of energy. He never stopped moving.

"Hey, Bill." He hopped down and zipped over to me, grabbing my hand and shaking it vigorously. "Bet you're wondering how I knew it was you." He moved back over to the gadget he'd just mounted. It was a small monitor. On the black and white screen flashed different views of the rental complex, changing at regular intervals.

"See? I just installed a video surveillance system," he said proudly. "I have another feed running to my PC behind the front counter."

"Cool," I said, looking at the array of other gadgets. "What else do you have back here?" This was the first time I saw the back room.

Pete crossed the room again and ticked off each item rapidly, pointing to them as he passed. "Ham radio, routers and hubs for the local area network, the satellite dish controller, police scanner, power distribution cabinet, GPS tracker, CB radio, intercom system for the lot, UPS with battery backup, automatic transfer switch for the generator."

"Hold up, hold up," I said, laughing. He turned and scowled at me, unappreciative of the interruption. "Did you say local area network? Like a LAN?"

"Yes I did. I wired all the cabins with high-speed Internet access, tying them in to the satellite feed. You wouldn't believe how many guests want to surf the web and check e-mail on vacation."

Last year, Pete and Zooey built five small cabins on the south side of their lot, close to the Rio Grande. They were full all summer long. He was in the process of building ten more.

"Ham radio? Pretty last-century."

"WB0DMT, on-air for the last fifteen years. That was my first piece of gear. Can't part with it. Had it since I was a teenager. Never fails me—even when the satellite's down and the phones are dead."

"What's the GPS tracker for?"

"Every vehicle we rent has a GPS mounted on it. When folks get lost or don't return our stuff—I know where they are."

"Really? Isn't that pretty expensive?"

"Yes it is. But so's our vehicle fleet. I don't like getting ripped off."

"Can't they just remove the device?"

"We retrofit each fuel tank with the GPS tracker, attaching it to the inside at the bottom. They'd have a very hard time getting it out. We don't tell them it's there." He crossed his freckled forearms.

"Did you ever rent a jeep to a woman named Gayle Whippany?"

He blinked once, but didn't answer. He blinked again, still staring at me. I wondered if he heard my question. This was the first time he stood still for more than five seconds since I came in.

"Pete? Gayle Whippany? Ever rent to her?" I asked again.

"Yes, yes, yes. I heard you the first time." He started back up, brushing past me. He was scowling again.

He stood in front of his laptop tucked in the corner, mounted on, what else, a stand-up pedestal on wheels. It had its own battery pack at the base and no Ethernet cables attached to it. A fat, stubby antenna peeked out from behind the monitor, wireless. I could envision him wheeling it around the office, plugging into whatever piece of equipment needed work.

"It's a busy time of year. The busiest. I usually remember the names of everyone who rents, but that's just not possible during the high season." He banged out a few commands on the keyboard.

"Okay. Now I remember. She called in last week to extend her rent for another month. Verified her credit card."

"When last week? The end of the June was Wednesday."

"Thursday, one July. I was getting a bit concerned, but you know how folks are on vacation. The month ended in the middle of the week, most renters don't leave until the weekend."

The woman was already dead on 1 July. That's the day I found her on Deep Creek Trail.

"Can you tell me where she is, Pete?"

"Nope." He crossed his thick arms across his thicker chest.

"Nope, you can't, or nope, you won't?"

"Nope, I won't, Deputy Tatum." I was Deputy Tatum again. I was Bill when I came in. "I will not disclose the location of my customers to local law enforcement without some kind of court order." He sounded like he was reading off a prepared statement. He probably was.

"Look, Pete, it's kind of important I find the vehicle."

"Look, Deputy, it's kind of important that people keep renting from me. If folks found out that I not only track their movements, but I also provide that information to the sheriff's department as well, that whole fleet out there would look like Zooey's old beaters."

Having no other choice, I played my trump card. "Gayle Whippany is dead, Pete. I found her body on Thursday morning before the sun came up. Someone else made that call."

He did the blinking thing again, showing no other emotion. Then he did something I never saw him do—he sat down. Not all the way, but he perched on the edge of an equipment shelf, turning sideways to me, staring at the floor, still blinking.

"Holy shit." He rubbed his mouth with a beefy hand, then bounced back up and started working the keyboard on his laptop.

"I have my PC linked to the tracking system behind you. Every hour, the GPS systems in the vehicles wake up, get their position, then transmit the coordinates back to the box. I can bring up the track of any vehicle for the last thirty days."

I peered over his shoulder at the monitor. In a few keystrokes, a topographical image of Mineral County appeared on the screen, which was then immediately overlaid by a series of small red triangles.

"Each triangle represents a waypoint, a GPS coordinate reading," said Pete. "The program filters out repeats, when the vehicle is stationary for more than an hour."

"Do you have a date-time stamp for each waypoint?"

"You bet. The GPS satellites have cesium clocks onboard and broadcast time along with positioning data."

"When was the last record?"

"About thirty minutes ago. Looks like it's parked next to the Rio Grande Grocery." He clicked on the triangle in the center of town. A list of GPS events popped up. "It's been there since Thursday morning." The morning I found Whippany floating in the beaver pond. Someone moved her jeep after killing her and dumping the body.

I looked at the tangled web of waypoints; there were hundreds of them, trying to match the images to physical locations. I recognized a few right away—the Bristol Head, North Clear Creek Falls—tourist spots where she and Mayor Jeff visited. The screen didn't do justice to the true topography of the valley.

I just stared at the screen, the moment of discovery rising up like a good beer buzz. I was looking at an hour-by-hour record of Gayle Whippany's movements from early June to the day of her murder.

"Can you print these out for me, with the associated times to match?"

"I'll make you two copies. Do you want lat-long or MGRS?"

"Both, if you can." I was more comfortable with MGRS—Military Grid Reference System. I set up my own maps with the grid pattern I'd used for years as a paratrooper. Most civilians use standard latitude and longitude coordinates. A few minutes later, Pete handed me a short stack of paper filled with numbers and dates arranged in neat columns.

"Lots of data," he said. "Around three hundred waypoints or so. She moved around a lot."

"Thanks, Pete. I owe you one." I put on my hat and headed for the door.

"Just keep your sources to yourself, Bill," Pete called from behind me.

I remembered something and stopped.

"Hey, Pete," I said, "there's a strange smell back by the propane tank next to Zooey's garage. The tank itself is corroding like crazy. You should have it looked at before it all goes up on you."

"Oh, yeah? I never noticed. I'll have to check that out. Thanks."

Back in the truck, I leafed through the sheets. The coordinates were meaningless until I could get in front of the big map at the station and plot them out. That could take hours, a great job for Jerry tonight.

What was remarkable about this bit of evidence were the time entries associated with the coordinates. Until now, we knew nothing of Gayle Whippany's activities from when the mayor left her at the Equity Trailhead to when I found her floating in Deep Creek. The time stamps on the GPS tracker filled in those four missing days to the hour.

Sixteen

I GOT BACK ON HIGHWAY 149 AND WAS MAKING THE turn to the Shallow Creek Ranch when I finally identified the strange smell behind Zooey's garage.

"Ammonia!" I shouted out loud to myself. Weird.

Dana Pratt built his ranch across the small watershed where Shallow Creek flowed out of the San Juans and emptied into the Rio Grande River. From Highway 149, the ranch didn't look like much—just a cluster of low, green-roofed buildings, not indicative of the developer's showy character. I passed through the main gate and down the gradual slope that hid the subtle splendor of the Shallow Creek Ranch.

The dry, sparse vegetation of the valley floor ended at Pratt's fence in green pasture. Pratt diverted some of the creek into a small pond on the north side of the ranch. He pumped water out of the pond into big irrigation pipes to the top of the slope, then let the water flow downhill through a series of irrigation ditches. This system kept his grass lush and his longhorns fat. Fifteen head of the huge beasts munched and basked in the late afternoon sunshine, watching lazily as I drove by. At the far end of the pasture was a large training corral adjacent to the long horse stables. Pratt had transplanted a little piece of Texas to our valley.

I parked the Bronco in the tall Englemann spruce that lined the creek on the far side of the corral. The stable and other outbuildings were beautifully crafted of local stone and wood. Even the smallest shed received the greatest care and skilled workmanship. A real-live bunkhouse sat parallel to the creek, the evergreens surrounding it like sentries. The new, clean gravel was recently graded—no ruts or washouts for the Shallow Creek Ranch. Only Dana's black Duellie and a row of three 200cc dirt bikes accompanied my truck. I noted the motorcycles; they were very similar to the one the shooter used to escape. I wondered where the goons were. Probably in town, squeezing the last bit of pleasure out of the weekend.

I looked around for the main house. I noticed a path through the trees. I followed it and came upon a footbridge over Shallow Creek. On the opposite side was Dana's ranch house. The same skillful hands that made the utility buildings constructed the developer's single-story homestead. It was much smaller than I imagined, mistakenly thinking the Texan would be true to the stereotypes. A stone foundation supported the eighteen-inch logs and plate glass windows that formed the walls. He attached his wide plank deck to the front of the house. Not much of a sunset view, with the massive half-dome of Bristol Head rising in the west behind the cabin, but the sunrises must have been spectacular. On the deck sat a single rocking chair, occupied by the man himself.

Dana Pratt wore his uniform—a black twill shirt, black

jeans, and cowboy boots. His black Stetson rested next to him on the sanded decking. He had a drink in one hand and a cigarette in the other. He didn't stand up as I crossed the bridge and approached the house. I felt like I was crossing a moat and visiting the fortress-cottage of an alpine lord. Maybe that was the idea. I stopped at the edge of the deck, looking up at the man.

"Deputy Bill," he said, still rocking, "what brings you to the Shallow Creek Ranch on such a solemn Fourth of July?"

"I wanted to ask you a few questions about the sniper murders going on around the valley, Mr. Pratt."

"You're not going to arrest me, are you, Deputy Bill?"

"No, sir. Just had some questions. You're a hard man to find."

"I get found when I want to, Deputy. Why don't you go ahead and ask your questions?"

"Is Mandy Lange here? I wanted to talk to her, too."

That threw him off-balance. He didn't have a smart answer to that one. He took a final drag on his cigarette and squinted at me. He stubbed it out on his boot and tucked the butt in the breast pocket of his shirt.

"Why would she be here?" he asked. I loved it when people answered my questions with other questions. My radar went right up.

"One of your boys released that fact to the general public at the San Juan Tavern last night."

"Uh huh. And what makes you think he's telling the truth?"

"Good point. That is difficult for your crew, isn't it? Well, he has nothing to gain by lying and more to gain by telling the truth."

"Is that what you figure, Deputy Bill?"

He still hadn't answered my question. So that's how this was going to be. Fine. I had all night.

"Is Amanda Lange here, Mr. Pratt?" I repeated my question.

"No, she's not." Finally a straight answer.

"Do you know where she is?"

"Why should I?"

"Do you know where she is, sir?"

"No, I don't."

"Was she here earlier today, Mr. Pratt?"

"When earlier?"

"During the parade. Between noon and right now."

"You mean, when some nut job shot Jacob Stackhouse off his horse right in front of you and the rest of the department?"

"Yes, during the parade." I didn't rise to the bait, but my gut churned with failure. I would not let this prick manipulate me.

"She was with me, here, at the ranch, all day. Stayed the whole weekend, actually. Came here Friday night. She left not an hour ago. Has to get ready for her husband's funeral tomorrow."

In one statement, he verified Cynthia Lange's suspicions and provided Mandy an alibi for the murders of her husband and Jacob Stackhouse. How convenient.

"Can anyone else verify that?"

"I think they already have. Didn't you say one of my boys let it slip at the San Juan Tavern? Probably Mack, the big gorilla." He had me there.

"So, you admit to having an affair with the mayor's wife, Amanda Lange?"

"I admit she stayed the weekend. Nothing else."

"She didn't leave, even after her husband was killed yesterday?"

"She didn't find out he was dead until today. That's why she left. I told you this already."

"No one called?"

"I don't have a phone."

"You don't have a phone?" I asked. I sounded like an idiot, repeating him.

"Nope. I have e-mail and Internet, but no phone. Hate 'em. Don't need a phone to run my business. I either do things in person or by e-mail."

"How do you communicate with your ranch hands?"

"Motorolas. Probably better than yours." I didn't doubt it.

"When did you find out about the mayor's death?"

"The boys told me when they woke up this morning. I give them Sunday off, so they sleep in. They usually sleep 'til noon, burning off their hangovers."

"Then you told Mandy?"

"Yes, I did."

"We've been looking for her for two days. Her daughter had to deal with this alone."

"I'm sorry to hear that, but it couldn't be helped. They're together now, I imagine."

"Did you know a woman named Gayle Whippany?" I changed direction.

"Nope," he lied.

"Do you remember being interviewed by a woman from the *Rocky Mountain News* at the Belmont Hotel on ten June of this year?"

"Now, that I remember. She was a nice piece of work. A little feisty, though."

"When was the last time you saw the reporter?"

"That was the only time I saw her. I seem to recall she got out of line, and I excused her from my table. I don't appreciate an ambush."

"What was the interview about?"

"You seem to know we had a conversation. You tell me."

"I was asking if you recall."

"Well, then I don't recall. I'm an old man. That was almost a month ago."

I felt like Tom Cruise in *A Few Good Men*, asking Jack Nicholson questions and getting nowhere.

"I read the text of the interview," I admitted. "She seemed very interested in your relationship with the mayor and the town council. She suspected this relationship was key to your success here in Belmont. Why would she think that?"

"Beats me. Why don't you ask her?"

"I can't. She's dead."

Not one change of emotion rippled across his sunburnt face. He took a sip from his drink, keeping his squinty eyes on me.

"So that's why you're here," he said. "I'll ask you again. Are you here to arrest me, Deputy?"

"No, Mr. Pratt. I'm here investigating three murders—Gayle Whippany, Mayor Jeff Lange, and Jacob Stackhouse. I assumed you knew about the death of the Whippany woman."

"Only the mayor and Jacob."

"I found the body of Gayle Whippany three days ago. We believe the same person killed all three of them." I didn't believe he was unaware of this. "Is there any truth to Whippany's speculation that you paid off the municipal government to fast-track your projects?"

"Not at all. All my proposals are completely aboveboard."

"Neither the council nor the mayor has raised an objection to any of your developments. How do you explain that?"

"I don't know. Why don't you ask them? Maybe they share my vision. Maybe they know bringing in tourists is the only way this town will survive. I don't bribe them."

"What's the status on your latest project to build on the western slope overlooking town?"

"The council is set to vote on it this week."

"Do you expect an approval?"

"Yes."

"How are you so sure?"

"Well, I talked with Pitcher, Callahan, and Noonan. They all think it's a good idea."

"What about the mayor? What did he think?"

"Never got a chance to talk to him. Guess I won't, now."

"Doesn't the mayor have veto power over the council?"

"I guess so. He never used it."

"Maybe he never got a chance. How much is that development worth to you, Mr. Pratt?"

"Nothing. I'll probably net out once I'm done with it." Bullshit.

"In the interview last month, Whippany asked a few questions about Elk Hollow and its effect on the Rio Grande River." I started on a different track. "Have you read the reports on the declining fish population and the algae bloom downstream from your RV park?"

"No, I have not."

"Are you confident that the waste generated by the visitors to Elk Hollow isn't going directly into the river?"

"We follow every regulation in regards to waste management at all of my developments," he gave his stock answer.

"Why couldn't Ms. Whippany find the environmental impact statement for Elk Hollow at city hall?"

"I don't know. That's where I filed them," he said. "I thought you were investigating three murders, Deputy. Why are you questioning me about my projects? I've done nothing illegal. I think your line of questioning is inappropriate, so, unless you have anything more to ask about these terrible murders, get your ass off my ranch."

"I have only a few more questions, Mr. Pratt," I said.

"First, your ranch hand, I believe his name is Mack, does he have a black ponytail?"

"Yes."

"Where was he yesterday morning, between eight and nine?"

"He told me he was off looking for a stray longhorn," he said, without a pause. "Said he went up into Shallow Creek to get the bull before the mountain lion did. He left at sunrise."

"When did he return?"

"Lunch. Had the longhorn with him, too."

"He went alone?"

"Yes. He can take care of himself."

"Really. Is he a good shot with a rifle?"

"I wouldn't know."

"You said he could take care of himself. A man alone in mountain lion territory would have to be pretty handy with firearms, don't you think?"

"I guess."

"Does Mack own a rifle?"

"I think so."

"Is it here?"

"No, he keeps it with him. All my hands do."

"All your hands are armed?"

"You said it yourself, Deputy. You never know what you'll run into in mountain lion territory," he said. Then he smiled at me.

I felt a cold chill seize my spine. What if my implications were true? If they were, I was standing in the lion's den. If Mack were the sniper, he could have me in his scope right now.

"I guess I can find him in town?" I asked.

"Probably. Leaving so soon?" he taunted.

"That's all I had, Mr. Pratt. Please stay around town for the next few days. I may have some more questions for you."

"Come by any time, Deputy."

He was still grinning as he sipped his drink, rocking gently in the shade of Bristol Head. I managed to walk back to my Bronco with only a few upward glances at the ridge.

Seventeen

GAYLE WHIPPANY'S RENTED JEEP HAD BEEN parked behind the Rio Grande Grocery for four days, not three blocks from the station. I felt pretty stupid about that. I had envisioned tracking it down in the mountains somewhere, thinking it was the key to everything. Like Poe's purloined letter, it was hidden in plain sight. Red jeeps blend in like mountain bikes and dusty boots in downtown Belmont, so I guess I wasn't a complete idiot. The jeep sat a few dozen feet into the large public parking area downtown, just far enough away from the shops to keep anyone from complaining. I drove up to it, snapped on a pair of latex, and got out.

The jeep was no-frills, with a trailer hitch and tan bikini top. A "Pete & Zooey's Rental" stencil matching the embroidery on Pete's shirt decorated the rear bumper along with a phone number and Internet address. The standard layer of Colorado dust covered the outside of the jeep, understandable, given the reporter's recent travel around the valley. The interior of the car, however, was immaculate. Even the floor mats were shaken of the usual gunk picked up by lug-soled hiking boots. Someone had wiped the interior. This didn't surprise me. Our sniper had a habit of cleaning up after himself. He must have been the last person to drive the vehicle after dumping Whippany's body in Deep Creek.

I found nothing significant in the jeep. Actually, I found nothing at all in the jeep, just the keys in the glove compartment. Nothing like living in a small town. The placement of the vehicle itself was the significant point of this evidence. The shooter removed it from the scene after killing Whippany and parked it where it would go unnoticed for some time. This prevented us from having any clue as to where he murdered the young reporter. If he dumped it in the bush, someone would notice it and report the abandoned jeep. In town, it would vanish into the background. I drove it to the station.

The common office area was empty, but I heard stern voices behind the sheriff's door. The council was still in there, reading Sheriff Dale the riot act. It was after five o'clock. They'd been reaming him a new one for over two hours. I wasn't certain I wanted his job, anymore. Thomas Pitcher's deep, lecturing voice penetrated the cheap single-pane door without much dampening.

"Sheriff Boggett, as acting mayor and senior member of this council, I demand a swift and successful conclusion to this sniper situation. We are losing confidence in your department's ability to protect the citizens and visitors of Belmont."

What a windbag. It sounded like he was making a speech.

"In addition," he continued, "this terrible drug problem

is threatening the very lives of our young people, the future of this community. We do not understand how this wretched infection grew under your watch, but we expect you to root it out before any more youngsters die. I hope our position is clear, Sheriff."

"Crystal, Mayor Pitcher," came Sheriff Dale's voice, an order of magnitude quieter.

"Good, then we will leave you to what we expect is a late night of investigation. Please give us a daily report of your progress by eight o'clock, each morning."

I heard chairs scrape the floor. They were getting ready to leave. This was my cue to bug out. I didn't want to be in their slash-and-burn path. I slipped down the hallway to Dr. Ed's office.

I was surprised to find the old man at his desk. He was missing the evening hatch on the Rio.

"Evening, Dr. Ed. Not fishing?"

"My boy, even I must sacrifice the joys in life sometimes in the service of the good people of Belmont."

I sat down in the single chair in front of his desk. "Did you finish the autopsy of Jacob Stackhouse?"

"I did."

"Could you fill me in on the details?" I asked, "Hey, wait a sec. Isn't it getting a little crowded in your locker up there? You have them stacked up?"

"Very funny, Deputy." He smiled at my gallows humor. "As a matter of fact, the occupancy of my locker remains at one. A funeral director from Alamosa picked up the good mayor this afternoon, while I was examining poor Mr. Stackhouse. Jeff Lange's funeral is tomorrow."

"You were done with him, I hope."

"I was done with him, yes. I am still waiting on the toxicology report. I expect to have it by the noon post."

"Did you find anything interesting with Stackhouse?"

"No, other than these gunshot wounds all look terribly similar. Which, of course, is to be expected."

"Did you pull any fragments out of him?" I asked, hopefully.

"No, I did not. The bullet went through his head and exited below his left ear."

"So, it could still be at the scene?"

"I suppose it could. I did not stop to check. I was in the middle of a panicking crowd of tourists. You, I believe, and the rest of the sheriff's department, were off gallivanting after the perpetrator, leaving me, dressed in a clown suit, to handle body removal and crowd control."

I wasn't certain if Dr. Ed was joking with me or not. We really did leave him with a bag of shit.

"Sorry about that, Dr. Ed. We almost had him."

"That's not what I heard, but I appreciate your optimism," he said. "I'm fishing the bend below Emmett's place tomorrow morning. Care to join me?"

"I'd love to, but, by the sounds of the inquisition in Sheriff Dale's office, I think I'll be on the sniper case."

"A pity, but understandable."

"Well, I'm off." I stood up. "I think I'll go look for that bullet. Let me know when the tox screen comes back."

"Do you expect to find something?"

"I don't know. See you tomorrow."

"Not before noon."

I returned to the sheriff's office. Sheriff Dale was at his desk, staring at the blotter, looking deflated.

"Tough meeting, Boss?" I asked.

"Mr. Pitcher just needed to feel important. No skin off my nose," he said. "Did you find Mandy out at Dana Pratt's?"

"No, but she was there."

"How do you know?"

"Dana came right out and told me. Said she spent the weekend, Friday through Sunday. Didn't hear about the mayor until this afternoon, according to him."

"Yeah, right. He doesn't have a phone. I've heard it before. Where is she, now?"

"At home, I guess. The funeral's tomorrow. Dr. Ed said a mortician picked up the mayor earlier this afternoon," I said. Then I added, "I found the jeep."

"What jeep?"

I filled him in on Pete McClaren's tracking device leading to my discovery of the dead woman's vehicle.

"Son of a bitch," he said. "I probably walked by it three times."

"Me too, Sheriff. No big deal. We never expected to find anything important on the vehicle, anyway. The coordinates are the real find."

"When are you going to plot them?"

"I figured Jerry could do it tonight on his shift."

The sheriff looked at his watch. "He doesn't start for another three hours. Why don't you get on it?"

"I was kind of hoping I could check out the scene on the parade route and talk to Mandy."

"Yes, we do need to talk to her, don't we?" he asked. "Okay. Give me the coordinates, and I'll plot them on the big map."

"There's a lot of them, Sheriff Dale, are you sure?"

"Sure I'm sure. I got six Coors longnecks in the fridge and a tangle of nerves after that meeting with the town fathers. I could use a little menial work to get leveled out."

"Thanks, sir. Hey, where's Marty?"

"She's up at the Halfmoon Ranch, talking to everyone who knew Jacob Stackhouse. Turns out the two meth ODs came from there. You were right about the first victim—the missing cook. The kid from this morning was staying at the ranch with his folks. Marty made the connection and zipped up there."

"I think it's great that she's out of the radio shack," I said. "I'll be back in an hour to help you."

"I'll be done by then."

I left one copy of the coordinates on his desk and headed for Main Street.

Police tape and blood stains marked the street where Stackhouse died. He fell off his horse in front of Emmett Springer's sculpture gallery and was dead before he hit the pavement. A striking bronze sculpture of a cowboy breaking a frenzied bronco dominated the front panel, a strange coincidence with the dead cowboy just removed from the scene. I stood in front of Emmett's window and looked up into Windy Gulch where the shooter fired. It wasn't an easy shot. He had only a narrow lane to shoot through, and the distance was at least five hundred meters—no small feat for any sniper. I could've made the shot, but I was trained to do it. I stood sideways to the trajectory of the bullet, pointing up the gulch with one arm and into the street with the other. The imaginary arc of the bullet ended at the frame of Emmett's plate glass window, just below the bottom sill. I lowered my arms and squatted by the windowsill. Sure enough, a fresh trough of splintered wood marred the fresh sky blue paint of Emmett's gallery. With my Leatherman, I dug out the section of windowsill that held the chunk of lead and copper that ended Jacob Stackhouse's life.

The bullet didn't mushroom on impact. Usually, a bullet's copper jacket peels away from the lead, forming the shape of a mushroom. The sniper chose a fully jacketed bullet for this assassination, which is why it maintained its integrity. Only the lands and grooves of the barrel marked the bullet. He might have planned for the long shot and loaded his bullets to hold their shape and velocity on impact. I was uncertain of the type of bullet in the previous shootings because we only recovered fragments. This was the first intact bullet. I would send this one to the lab in Pueblo to be matched to the fragments.

I looked around the scene for anything else, but came up short. I knew the shooter had fired a second time, but that was at Marty, so I wasn't going to find another bullet here. I drove up to the eastern slope to her overwatch position.

I easily found my dead chemlite and the rocky outcrop of Marty's hide site. She covered her tracks well—I didn't see any disturbance in the dirt around the position. If I didn't know better, the spot looked completely unoccupied. She was good at this. The woman spent eight hours in this hide site, and the place looked pristine. She hardly fidgeted. I've heard women make better hunters and snipers because of their patience, ability to remain still, and higher tolerance for discomfort. Marty proved it up here.

I lay down in the hide and looked across the canyon at Windy Gulch. Now this was a long shot—almost nine hundred meters. The sniper must have gotten lucky and seen Marty on the eastern slope. He just slung a bullet her way to keep her head down and nicked her cap. She probably heard the snick of the bullet in the fabric before the gunshot. Both of them were lucky.

I turned my head, looking for the impact of the bullet in the dirt behind me. Chunks of loose granite mingled in the pale, dry soil of the eastern slope. The bullet could have easily ricocheted off a piece of rock instead of burying itself in the turf, which it probably did, because I didn't find it. I left the ridge empty-handed and went looking for Mandy Lange.

I found the less-than-bereaved widow at her house three blocks off Main Street. The Lange residence was a yellow and white three-quarter scale Victorian, complete with white picket fence and octagonal tower on the southeast corner. The Langes had done well in Belmont. No wonder they let Dr. Ed stay in the little mayor's residence. Now that their daughters had moved out, they must have rattled around in the big house with just the two of them. Maybe they needed their space. Cynthia answered my knock.

"Hello, Miss Lange," I said. "I heard your mother was here, and I would like to ask her a few questions."

"Can't it wait, Deputy Bill?" she asked. Her earlier defiance was gone. She was simply asking. "My father's funeral is tomorrow. Can you come back afterward?"

"Miss Lange, I wish I could, but with each passing hour, the likelihood of our catching your father's killer decreases. Please, I won't be long."

She reluctantly stood aside and let me in. She led me back to the bright kitchen, where an older version of herself sat at the breakfast bar, drinking a cup of tea, and reading the latest edition of the *Belmont Chronicle*.

"Good afternoon, Deputy." Amanda Lange greeted me as I entered, but she didn't stand up. "Or should I say good evening? I'm not certain."

She had the glazed-over look of the recently medicated. Dr. Ed must have paid her a visit. I doubted she could stand up without wobbling. I wondered how much I'd get out of her. Cynthia stood behind me, leaning on the kitchen sink, keeping an eye on both of us.

"Mrs. Lange, I am terribly sorry for your loss," I began, Resistol in hand. "The whole town will miss Mayor Jeff."

"Thank you, Deputy Bill. It's been quite a shock," she said, but her eyes told a different story. Absent were the web of capillaries and red rims of her daughter's grief. It looked as if the woman hadn't shed a tear. Maybe it was the drugs.

"Ma'am, if you don't mind, I had a few questions for you concerning your husband's murder."

Nice one. What else would I be here for, parking tickets?

"Fire away, Deputy," she said, "Whoops, that's not a very good choice of words, is it?"

"Mrs. Lange, I just came from Dana Pratt's ranch at Shallow Creek." No reaction. "He said you were there from Friday evening until this afternoon. Is this true?"

"I guess we can't have any secrets in this town," she said, flipping her loose black hair behind her shoulder and eyeing her daughter. "Yes, I was there."

"Then you confirm Mr. Pratt's story that neither of you left the ranch for the entire weekend, not until you found out about your husband."

"That is correct, Deputy. We hardly left his bedroom." Her eyes had a moment of clarity, their blue iciness telling me more than her few words. She was an angry, vengeful woman.

"So, the two of you were . . . intimate," I said.

Mandy Lange was my mother's age. I felt uncomfortable, and she knew it.

"Yes we were, young man. Might as well get it out in the open," she said, looking at her daughter again. "Oh, that's right, it's already out in the open. Do you have any other questions about my sex life? I fail to see the relevance with my husband's demise."

"A witness saw you, Jacob Stackhouse, and your father, Orville, up on Wason Park the morning your husband was killed. That's a long way from Shallow Creek, Mrs. Lange."

"Bullshit. I never left the ranch, and I'd never go out riding with that drugged-out prick."

"I never said anything about riding, Mrs. Lange."

She glared at me. "Well, what else would we be doing that far from the Halfmoon? My father doesn't leave the ranch unless it's on horseback."

We were going in circles. I couldn't tell if the woman was being deliberately evasive, or if she was simply whacked out.

"Okay. So you weren't up on Wason Park . . . east of the Ten-Miler turnaround . . . Saturday morning . . . between eight and nine?" I asked slowly.

"No . . . Deputy," she sighed, speaking just as slowly, mocking me. "Like I said . . . I was in bed with Mr. Dana Pratt most of the weekend . . . especially Saturday morning."

"Did you know a woman named Gayle Whippany?"

I was relieved to change the subject. Mandy turned away and uttered something unpleasant out the window.

"Yes, I knew that woman," she said, staring out at the street.

"Then you know she's dead?" I asked, picking up on the past tense of her answer.

"Yes. I know she's dead."

"What can you tell me about her?"

"Well, she was fucking my husband, for one thing," she snapped, whipping her head around to show me her anger. I got uncomfortable again.

"Yes, we know that. Do you know what she was doing here in Belmont?"

I immediately regretted my choice of words.

"Oh, besides my husband? Let me see." She stared up at the ceiling. "She was writing some story about how development is ruining the mountains. Bunch of crap."

"Your husband seemed to feel the same way, when I talked to him, yet he served as a guide, with your support," I said.

"Was there a question in there, somewhere, Deputy Bill?" she asked. "Whatever, yes, I let him go off into the mountains with that woman, hoping he could get our town a little publicity outside this rag." She held up the *Chronicle*. "Kind of backfired on me, didn't it?"

"When did you find out about his affair?"

"Wives just know," she said.

"Okay," I said, trying again. "When did you perceive that he was having an affair with Gayle Whippany?"

"When they spent a whole weekend together in the mountains, last weekend," she said, sad this time. "He just seemed different, like when we were first married. That's when I knew." She put her chin in her hand and stared out the window again.

"Did he tell you where they went, what part of the mountains they visited?"

"No, nothing more than they started at the Equity Trailhead and went from there. He was back by Sunday evening," she said, confirming the basics of her husband's story.

"Did he tell you anything else?"

"No," she said, "he did go on and on about how she was right, how he'd gotten so deep into business and commerce and politics that he forgot about the valley. He was like a born-again Greenie."

"So, she changed his mind?" I asked.

"I guess so," she said, her voice was drained of emotion. "Said he even changed his mind about Dana's new development up on the western slope. Said he was going to veto the proposal in favor of preserving it."

"Really? Doesn't the mayor's veto override the council?"

"Yes it does."

"Did he tell anyone else about his change of heart?"

"I don't know, maybe."

"Did you tell anyone?"

She looked back at me, eyes damp for the first time since I walked in.

"Yes, I did," she said. "I told Dana."

"When did you tell him?" I asked, not expecting this revelation.

"Thursday, when he came in for Eunice's steak special. I saw him at the Belmont."

"The two of you had dinner together?"

"That's right. Dana hates to eat alone. No one suspected anything. He has his Thursday steak with lots of people. I just happened to be his guest last week."

"What was his reaction to your husband's upcoming veto?"

"What do you expect? He was pissed," she said. "He stormed out of the restaurant and went looking for Jeff."

"Did he find him?"

"No, he came back after ten minutes or so. He hates a cold steak."

"What time was this?"

"Oh, around six, maybe a little after."

I thought back to Thursday evening. Six was when I met the mayor at the grandstand and gave him the initial report on the dead woman. No wonder Pratt didn't find him. Now, Pratt had reasons to kill both Mayor Jeff and Gayle Whippany.

"When was the last time you fired a rifle, Mrs. Lange?" I asked.

She had another moment of clarity, which gave her pause before answering. "Not in a long time, Deputy Tatum," she said carefully.

"How long, years?"

"Yes. I haven't hunted since I moved away, right after high school."

"You were a good shot, though," I said. "I saw the pictures on your father's mantel."

"I don't have time to hunt anymore," she said. "I'm too busy at the WWE."

"Where is your rifle? Orville said he doesn't keep it at the ranch."

"It's here."

"May I see it?"

She said nothing, but stood up and disappeared through a side door, which turned out to be the basement.

"You can't possibly think my mother murdered . . . " I heard Cynthia's voice behind me. "My mother is angry, but not vengeful."

"Miss Lange, I don't know, but I'll be honest with you. She is a suspect."

"But she couldn't have killed them," she said.

"Why not? Can you account for your mother at the time of the three murders? I know you can't. Just think about it, Miss Lange."

Mandy Lange ascended the basement steps with more stability than I expected and slammed a hard rifle case on the counter.

"Here you go, Deputy," she said, and sat back down, staring into her now-empty cup of tea.

"Please open it for me," I said.

Mandy scoffed, then opened the dusty case with a little difficulty. Inside lay the vintage Winchester 700 ADL .270 bolt-action rifle in mint condition. Attached to the top bracket was a large Nikon Tactical scope. A slender, plastic box of shells sat in a recessed cavity in the foam padding beneath the trigger guard. A hand-tooled leather sling lay folded parallel to the barrel. The faint smells of oil and gunpowder rose up out of the case. She not only took care of her rifle, she'd fired it recently as well. Or someone had.

"When did you upgrade the scope?" I asked, "Nikon didn't start making the Tactical scope until 1975."

Mandy looked up at me, surprised for the second time. She regained her composure more quickly.

"My father was so excited when I returned to Belmont. He thought I would take up hunting again. He bought me the Nikon for my birthday. Sighted it in himself up at his range. He picks it up before each season to keep it true, just in case I have time to hunt. Which I don't."

Whether she was telling the truth or just made up that story on the fly, I couldn't tell. The explanation covered the scope upgrade and the recent firing of the weapon.

"But your father said he didn't know where it was. What's the story?" I asked.

"I don't know, Deputy, you'll have to ask him," she said. "He was probably trying to protect me. Do you have any other questions? I have to bury my husband tomorrow."

"No, ma'am. I'll have to hold onto this for a while."

"Fine. Take it. You can let yourself out." She got up and left the room.

Cynthia walked me to the door and followed me out onto the front porch.

"Bill, I know how this looks, but you can't believe my mother would do these things," she pleaded. "She wouldn't hurt anybody."

"I understand how you feel, Miss Lange, but, like I said before, your mother is a suspect. No one but Dana Pratt can account for her whereabouts at the time of the three shootings. She is skillful with a rifle, and owns one that matches the caliber of the murder weapon. Finally, she has motive." Realizing I said too much, I turned and walked down the steps. Cynthia Lange had nothing more to say.

Eighteen

IT WAS GOOD TO GET OUT OF THE LANGE HOUSE and into the sunshine. The heavy mood permeated the atmosphere in the yellow Victorian and weighed heavily on my soul, but the mountain air cleared my head and quickened my step. By the time I hit Main Street, I was back to my old Wyatt Earp self. Fewer tourists than usual strolled along Main. They were still here, though. We weren't a ghost town, yet.

Marty Three Stones was at her desk writing when I walked into the station. Sheriff Dale was gone, but he left the completed map work. Red-tipped pins dotted the big 1/50,000 scale map of Mineral, Hinsdale, and Saguache Counties. White dental floss linked the pins in the sequence of Gayle Whippany's travel, and the sheriff labeled each date change with a little paper flag on the appropriate pin. I was impressed with the speed and accuracy of the sheriff's work.

"Where's Sheriff Dale?" I asked Marty. I walked over to the map and studied the pins, eager to see the results.

"Gone home for dinner," she said. It was already past seven. "He ran out of beer and was getting sleepy. He had a long day. Aren't you tired, too?"

I didn't answer her, engrossed in the dead reporter's final movements. I noted the pins for the Equity Mine Trailhead, North Clear Creek Falls, and other tourist spots.

"Hello? Tatum? Are you still with us?"

"Had a long day, yeah. We all did," I said. "How are you doing? Shakes go away?" I turned away from the map, seeing nothing. I could come back to it later.

"Yup." She leaned back in her chair and stretched her lower back. "Nice hot shower and a change back into school clothes does wonders for a girl after she gets shot at for the first time."

She nudged a duffel with her toe. "I washed your gear, too. Thanks for letting me borrow it. Sorry about the hole in your hat."

"It beats having a hole in your head, Marty," I said. "That stuff probably hasn't been that clean in years. Why don't you hold onto it? We might need it again before this thing's over."

"You're right. Thanks. Maybe we can start wearing BDUs every Friday, just to keep the rabble in line."

I laughed. Marty kept her sense of humor in the worst of times.

"Hey, what did you find out up the hill?" I asked, referring to her interviews at the Halfmoon Ranch.

"You wouldn't believe it."

"Try me."

"Okay, are you ready for this?" She built it up. "Half the summer staff up there are big-time crystal meth users. Jacob Stackhouse was their dealer."

"How did you find this out?"

"You know Wendy, the concierge? When I got up there, I found her in her office, bombed and sobbing. She spilled the whole thing. I guess she and Jacob were an item."

"Who was Stackhouse's supplier?"

"She said she didn't know. I believe her, poor girl. She was just trying to lose weight. I searched Jacob's room and found this." From under her desk, she withdrew a nylon case filled with flat plastic trays, the kind fishermen use for toting their lures or carpenters for small pieces of hardware. She pulled out one of the trays and snapped open the lid. Each of the individual compartments was filled with small packets of white crystalline powder.

"So, that's what crystal meth looks like," I said.

"You guessed it. Enough to throw one hell of a rave up there in the lodge."

"What are you going to do next?" I asked.

"Well, that's a good question," she said. "I tried calling in the state's meth task force, but they said a couple of ODs and a dead dealer aren't worth their time, the pricks. Stackhouse was my only link to the supply end, and he's dead. I'll have to interview everyone up there again and pry something out of them."

"Did you talk to Orville?"

"No, he was out with Darren Schmidt, the game manager. I'll hook up with him next time I'm up there. Where've you been? Who's rifle is that?" she asked, pointing to the case I still held in my hand.

"It's Mandy Lange's. I just came from there."

"Really? She finally came out of hiding, huh?"

"Right. Hey, you remember seeing her with Stackhouse and Orville yesterday, right about the time her husband was killed?"

"Yes."

"She says she was with Dana Pratt all weekend, from

Friday until this afternoon. Said she didn't even know her husband was dead until today."

"Did she now?" she asked, staring off into space.

"What are you thinking? She's lying, right?"

Marty looked sheepish and didn't meet my gaze.

"Well, Bill, I might've been mistaken about seeing her."

I just looked at her stupidly. "What?"

"In all the excitement, my initial report may have been incorrect."

"But you saw, her, right? Mandy Lange, her father, and Stackhouse."

"Well, I saw Stackhouse all right. He rode up to me, and we talked. That's when I had him turn around and head back to the Halfmoon, but . . . " She blew out a sigh. "I didn't get a close look at the other two riders. They kind of hung back a ways. I just assumed it was Mandy and Orville. It was definitely a man and a woman, though."

I just blinked at her.

"So . . . I can't be sure I saw her yesterday," she said.

I plunked the rifle case on my desk and slumped down in the chair.

"Shit. That changes a lot," I said. It meant that both Pratt's and Mandy's stories supported the other. It meant that Orville and Stackhouse told the truth about their activities on Saturday morning.

"I'm sorry, Bill. I hope this doesn't throw you off too badly," said Marty.

"Don't worry about it," I reassured her. "Everything I have against Mandy Lange is speculation, anyway."

"You don't think she could've done it?"

"Oh, I definitely think she could've done it," I said. "She has the skill and the patience, and plenty of vengeful anger over her husband's philandering. Of course, she did her part with Dana Pratt."

"She told you?"

"She told me," I said. "She told me a lot, actually. I think Dr. Ed gave her something to calm her down, so she was quite forthcoming." I briefed her on my interview with the mayor's wife.

"Sounds like she has more motive than jealous rage," said Marty.

"What do you mean?"

"Well, it looks like she's thrown her hat into another ring—Dana Pratt's. Upgraded her lot in life."

"I don't follow," I said.

"You men are so dense, sometimes." She leaned over her desk. "Mandy Lange is after more money, greater influence. She doesn't need a father to nurture her children anymore; they're all gone. She has control over the two most successful businesses in town—the WWE and the Halfmoon Ranch. She's looking to merge."

"But her father owns the ranch," I said, not catching up.

"Her father owns the ranch and runs the operation, but who makes the financial decisions?"

She was right. Mandy Lange saved the ranch from financial ruin when she moved back to Belmont years ago.

"Okay, I still don't see where this leads to murdering her husband and his lover," I said.

"What is Dana Pratt's motive for killing Gayle Whippany?"

"I think she was going to investigate heavily into political corruption and the environmental impact of his land developments."

"What is Dana Pratt's motive for killing Mayor Jeff?"

"He was going to veto the proposal to develop the western slope above town."

"How much is that worth to Dana?"

"He claims he'll break even."

"Do you believe that?" she asked.

"Nope. Nothing he builds doesn't turn a profit."

"So, it could be worth a lot. Millions, probably, by the looks of the man's success." She sat back in her chair and let me absorb that.

"So, Dana's motive—money and power—became Mandy's motive," I said slowly. "She was a willing conspirator because of both the money and her own jealousy."

"The two oldest reasons in the world—love and money," said Marty. "Dana and Mandy found each other just when they needed each other. There has to be at least two people in on this, you said so yourself."

"But where does Jacob Stackhouse fit in?" I asked.

"I have no idea," she admitted. "That's where my theory kind of falls apart, doesn't it?"

"Well, yeah. I don't see any link at all," I said. "Whoever killed him took an immense risk, but still got away with it. The sniper shootings get more hairy every time, and the shooter still manages to slip away. He must have a damn good reason for killing Stackhouse."

"You think it's tied into my case? The crystal meth?" she asked.

"I don't see how. Hell, I don't know." I got up and walked over to the map board, tracing the jeep's path with my eyes, looking for an answer I didn't think I'd find.

"You know, I can't see Dana Pratt doing the dirty work himself," I said. "He always uses his boys to do the heavy lifting, whether it's security or supervising a work line. Maybe they're in on this, too."

"You think they'd kill for him?" asked Marty.

"I don't think they'd hesitate. They're the kind of guys rednecks tell jokes about."

"I'll bet they're still in town. This is their only day off. They're probably making the most of it."

"Dana was alone at the ranch. I think I'll swing by the

San Juan Tavern. It's eight o'clock—not too early for them to be drinking," I said.

"Not too early for them to be drunk, either. Be careful, Bill."

"Aren't I always?" I grabbed my Resistol and stepped toward the door.

The last glow of twilight was slipping west, leaving the empty streets of downtown gray and quiet. Late guests at the Belmont ate and spoke in hushed tones, but no one walked on Main Street. Most of the shops closed at eight. Across the valley to the south, the fading orange light still illuminated Snowshoe Mountain's namesake—a patch of volcanic rock that hardened and cooled in the shape of a giant beavertail snowshoe. The thick evergreens around it were unable to penetrate its stubborn hide, leaving the round scar on the mountain for eons.

For some reason, this time of day always filled me with inexplicable apprehension, and today was no different. My civilized senses assessed the loss of the sun and the quick drop in temperature and injected an ounce of fear into my brain. Maybe it was ingrained in my DNA to fear the night, my reptilian brain alert to the new threat as the blue sky bled out to black. The fear was strong this night, pinching my chest. I could almost feel my pupils dilate with the fight-or-flight response. I remember feeling this way in Afghanistan, especially, hunkered down in a hide site, waiting for an al Qaeda terrorist leader to emerge from some mountain cave so I could blow him away.

Maybe I was just keyed up about confronting the Pratt goons. I handled them before but didn't look forward to it again. I was working on fumes already—up since three with little in the way of food, yet here I was, stepping into the ring with five rednecks itching to prove themselves. No wonder I was apprehensive.

"Hey, buddy, wait up," came a familiar voice from behind me. I whirled around. It was Marty.

"What are you doing?" I asked, trying to conceal my tension, not very well.

"Well, I asked myself why I'm letting you go out on your own, at night, to lock horns with five known troublemakers, while I'm sitting all safe at my desk. Figured you could use a partner."

"Thanks, Marty." I failed to hide my relief, and didn't want to. "I'm glad you're here. Which part do you want to play—good cop or bad cop?"

"I don't think it's going to make any difference to them—all cops are bad. We might as well give them a reason to believe it."

"I'm with you, Deputy Three Stones. Let's roll."

My fear didn't evaporate, but it did subside to a level I could use.

Nineteen

THE SAN JUAN TAVERN WAS HALF A BLOCK OFF
Main down a little dead-end side street that ended at
Willow Creek. It was the Belmont Hotel's seedy little
brother. The success of one depended on the other, like two
shoe stores on opposite sides of the street. The place was
always a tavern, ever since the recurring fires in the original town up the canyon forced the residents to move south
half a mile. The false front of the building bore many
names since then, but the essence of the establishment remained true to its origins—a bar where rough men could
drink and fight.

Unlike the movies, where the music stops and a hush
falls over the crowd when The Law walks through the door,
the patrons didn't miss a beat when Marty and I stepped in
and looked around. The bar was not yet half full. Two cou-
ples played pool, and three highway crewmen drank at the
bar, smelling of tar, sweat, and car exhaust. We left our

hats on, not knowing where to set them down, and not wanting to. They looked more imposing on, anyway, not that the clientele at the San Juan gave a rip.

Mack and the four other ranch hands from the Shallow Creek Ranch huddled around a corner table at the back of the bar. They didn't take their hats off, either. It looked like they were just getting warmed up, a pitcher of beer for each of them. Johnny Spotten, the owner and bartender at the San Juan, never served bottled beer, only tap in plastic cups. Bottles make great weapons and take longer to clean up. If you broke a pitcher at the San Juan, you never came back.

The place smelled of stale beer and locker rooms with just a hint of vomit—my kind of place. The chamber of commerce detested the San Juan Tavern, as did many of the other locals, but Johnny paid his taxes to the city and his dues to the chamber. He even donated the beer for their July 4th beer tent. As long as Johnny kept the rabble inside the tavern and prevented them from spilling out into the street, they tolerated him. The place was almost a landmark.

Marty and I noted the location of the Shallow Creek boys, then walked up to the bar. Johnny wasn't in, but his wife, Sheila, was tending. Johnny usually took the later shift and closed. Sheila was a pretty woman in her early forties, with big, frizzed-out hair and lots of makeup— classic biker chick. She and Johnny made the trip to Sturgis every year on their 1975 Softail Springer 1340, closing the bar for two weeks of the late season.

"Hiya, Deputies, the usual?" Sheila asked. Years of sucking in bar smoke and yelling at rowdy customers took a toll on her voice, giving it a rasp that made you want to clear your own throat.

"Not tonight, Sheila, we're still on duty," I said. Marty and I hung out at the San Juan more often then we came to break up fights.

Sheila set two cokes in front of us and leaned on the bar.

"It's about the shooting at the parade today, isn't it? You catch the guy, yet?"

"Not yet, Sheila, but we will," said Marty. "How long have the Shallow Creek boys been in here?"

"They just came in about an hour ago," said Sheila, trying not to look over at the crew. "They've been pretty quiet so far, but the night is young. Not enough people in here yet to start something."

"Well, we're probably going to get them riled up, Sheila, but we'll take them outside," I said, taking a sip of the coke.

"Be my guest. I got my bat back here, if you need reinforcements." She tucked her hand under the bar.

"Won't be necessary, Ms. Sheila. Thanks for the coke," I said, nudging Marty and turning around.

"Let me handle them," said Marty. "I have an idea."

I looked at her, a little surprised. "Okay, Deputy Three Stones. The floor is yours. I'll follow your lead."

We walked easily to the back corner. The five young men ignored our approach but were laughing too loudly to conceal their lack of indifference. I let Marty do the talking. Maybe it would throw them off.

"Hi fellas, enjoying your beer?" she asked. They all stopped and looked at us for the first time. None of them responded, eyeing us with contempt.

"Hey, Mack, you mind if we ask you a few questions about the parade today?" Marty said, directing her question to the big one in the middle.

"We weren't here," said the runt of the litter, sneering. "But we heard you all really fucked it up. I guess it's open season here in town." The others chuckled at this keen observation, all except Mack, stoic and staring at me.

This, of course, was a lie—four of their black pickups were parked near the beer tent hours before the parade. I wondered if Mack's was the absent truck.

"I think I was talking to Mack," said Marty, firm but casual, "How 'bout it, big guy? You got a minute to talk to us outside?"

"You talk to one of us, you talk to all of us," said the runt, who seemed to be the official spokesman.

"Suit yourself," said Marty, "Lead the way, gentlemen." She stepped back and gestured toward the door. With a loud scrape of chairs on gritty floor, they all stood up and shuffled outside.

Whatever light remained on our walk down to the San Juan Tavern had abandoned the valley, leaving Marty and I nothing but the neon glow of the Coors Light sign to illuminate the side street.

"Okay, gentlemen, if you all would stay with me while Deputy Tatum talks to Mack, that would be great. I have questions pertaining to the four of you." I didn't know what Marty was going to make up, but she was doing great, so I played along. The ranch crew seemed amused or surprised by her easy authority, and they obeyed her like sheep. I took ten backward steps toward Main Street while Mack pushed his way through his compadres. Marty had her back to me, and the other four formed a tall half-moon around her.

Mack was at least a whole head taller and outweighed me by fifty pounds. He was about my age but he looked ten years older. It was probably the thick black mustache. He squinted down at me, the contempt never leaving his face from the first time we walked in the door. He had his black hair pulled back in his signature ponytail, and three days' growth of black beard darkened his complexion even more. Mack and I had tussled in the past, with my getting the upper hand. I hoped he would remember that and keep his hands to himself. I pulled out a notebook and pen.

"Just a couple questions about your whereabouts the last few days," I began. He said nothing.

"Your employer, Mr. Dana Pratt, said you went off early yesterday morning after a stray longhorn and did not return until around lunchtime. Is this accurate?"

"Yes," his lips hardly moving.

"Did you find the steer?"

"Yes."

"Where did you go looking for it?"

"Up the creek." Very articulate.

"Shallow Creek?"

"Yes."

"About how far up did you travel?"

"About five miles."

"And you went alone?"

"Yes."

"Isn't that mountain lion territory?"

"Yes." This guy was a fountain of information. I could hardly keep up.

"Did you take a weapon?"

"Yes."

"What kind of weapon?"

"Rifle, shotgun, and my forty-five," he said, smiling for the first time. The guy liked guns.

"So, you were well armed. Do you always carry that much firepower?"

"I do when I'm up Shallow Creek alone."

"Fair enough. What kind of rifle do you have?"

"Winchester." Very forthcoming.

"And the caliber?"

"Two-seventy." My ears perked up, but I kept my head down in my notebook.

"Kind of a small rifle for mountain lion, isn't it? I'd expect a guy like you to have something with a little more stopping power," I baited him.

"Doesn't matter how big your gun is, it's where you put it," he said, giving me another scary grin.

"So, you're a pretty good shot?"

He stopped smiling, finally comprehending my line of questioning. Good for him.

"Not bad," he said.

"Do you have your rifle with you, maybe in your truck?"

"No," he was lying, "it's back at the ranch."

"You mind if I come out and look at it?"

"Are you gonna arrest me?"

"Do I have a reason to?"

"If you ain't gonna arrest me, you ain't seein' the rifle."

I was taken aback by such a long-winded answer.

"Where were you this morning, around nine o'clock?"

"I can't remember," he lied. "Probably working at the ranch." Nice and vague.

"Can any of your buddies verify your whereabouts?"

"I don't know. Ask them."

"I will. Can you ride a motorcycle, Mr., uh . . . " I didn't know the guy's last name. "How do you spell your last name?"

"S-M-I-T-H," he said. Nice one, Danno.

"Yes, thank you," I said, "Now, back to my question, can you ride a motorcycle?"

"Ride or drive? Bitches can ride." Good point.

"Drive."

"Yes, I can drive a motorcycle," he admitted. "We have some at the ranch."

"Yes, I noticed." I paused, short of a question.

"Are we done here, Deputy?" he asked, crossing his arms.

"You will be at the Shallow Creek Ranch all this week?"

"I guess."

"Please remain in Mineral County for a while. I may have more questions for you."

"Yeah, sure. Can I go now?"

"Yes, thank you for your time."

Despite the mild chill of the canyon after sunset, I was sweating. Marty finished up and walked over to me. The goons just stood in their semi-circle, staring at us.

"See ya later, boys!" Marty called out, then grabbed my elbow and pulled me back toward Main Street.

"How did it go with the others?" I asked, turning the corner on Main.

"Fine. Cut off the head, and the body goes limp. Without Mack, the other four are sheep."

"What did you talk to them about?"

"Drugs," she said. "It caught them off-guard. I think they expected me to ask about the shootings."

"Really? Did you find out anything new?"

"I think so. I know they're not in on the whole crystal meth thing," said Marty.

"Why's that?"

"First of all, they said Dana will kill them if they use drugs."

"You believe that?"

"Yes I do. These guys would be in jail or stuck in some dusty, flat town east of the mountains pumping gas if it weren't for Dana Pratt. Their loyalty and obedience to him is impressive."

"What was second-of-all?" I asked her.

"Well, just a feeling, I guess," she said. "They're pretty antisocial, no friends outside their circle, willing to bust heads at the slightest provocation. That really doesn't fit the profile of a dealer. Dealers are your buddy, your pal. To be honest, I don't think these guys are smart enough to run a garbage disposal, let along a drug ring."

"Maybe Pratt and Mack are the brains," I said, reaching.

"Do you really think that?" She looked over at me.

"No, just throwing ideas out there."

"What did you get from the head goon?" Marty asked.

"Not much, the guy's a rock." I said. "He admitted to

owning a two-seventy, though, and he can ride a motorcycle."

"He and half the town."

"Yeah, I know. Did you ask the other four about this
morning, where they were?

"Sure did. They claim they were at the ranch all day,
mending fence."

"Mack was with them?"

"Yup, all day. Nice alibi, huh?"

"Very convenient," I said. "They're lying, you know. I
saw their trucks parked at the post office, near the beer tent.
Only four of them, though."

"Really? Which one was missing?"

"Can't say, they all look alike."

We walked in silence.

"We're not far from where we started, are we?" I asked.
"Nope."

"Feel like we're both in over our heads?"

"Yup."

"Well, Deputy Three Stones, what do you think we
should do?"

"The only thing we can do—keep on it, keep asking
questions, following leads, and hope for the best."

I liked her attitude, but it wasn't very reassuring.

On the quiet walk through the dark and silent Belmont
downtown, I started feeling the day. Maybe it was my
dead-end interviews with Dana Pratt, Amanda Lange, and
Mack Smith. Maybe it was my failed plan to interdict the
sniper during the parade. Either way, I was smoked. We
stopped outside the station. I walked over to my truck and
opened the door.

"I need to go home and get some rest, Marty," I admitted, sitting down sideways in the driver's seat.

"Yeah, me too," she said. "I'm just waking up, though.
My body's still on the night shift."

"Reverse-cycle, we used to call it," I said. "Meet you back here in the morning?"

"You bet. What are your plans for tomorrow?"

"I think I'm done with interviews for the time being. I need to process the weapons I've collected, although none of the guns I got from the Halfmoon is the murder weapon, considering they were all locked up in the safe during the parade. I still have Mandy's weapon, though."

"Are you going to talk to Denver Petry?" she asked.

"Denver . . . " My withered brain tried to make the connection. "Oh, yeah, Denver—reloads. Yeah, you're right. I still need to talk to him about the spent shell I found up on the ridge. Damn, I completely forgot about that."

"If you plan on going anywhere tomorrow, you need to pick up your spare from Zooey," she reminded me.

"I'll go by there first thing. What would I do without you, Deputy Three Stones?"

"Just don't call me Friday."

"How about you? What's your agenda?"

"After the mayor's funeral, I'll head back up to the Halfmoon Ranch, see if I can shake something loose, maybe talk to Orville."

"I'm telling you, Marty, he has nothing to do with this meth problem."

"You're probably right, but I still need to talk to him. He might know something."

"Just go easy on him," I said.

"Sounds like you're protecting him, Bill," she admonished. "Don't lose your objectivity. We have no reason to clear him of any involvement with either the sniper or the meth case."

"I know, I know." I rubbed my eyes. "Can I go home, now?"

"Drive careful. See you in the morning."

Twenty

THE CHIRP OF MY RADIO PECKED AT MY EARDRUMS until I woke up. The tinny sound of Jerry Pitcher's voice did nothing to lessen my annoyance with being roused from much-needed slumber. Forcing myself out of bed, I wobbled over to the dresser—if I left the radio on the night table, I'd never get up. Snatching the object of my irritation, I continued to the bathroom.

"Tatum, here," I rasped through dry throat and chapped lips. I sounded like a wino.

"Hey, Deputy Bill, we got a problem," said Jerry, sounding chipper. He didn't have any reverse-cycle issues.

"It's two in the morning," I said.

"I know, sorry to wake you." He paused. "Are you peeing?"

"I like to call it multitasking," I said, approaching consciousness. "What's up, Deputy?"

"We have an abandoned vehicle out by Farmer's Creek," he said.

"You wake me up at two for that? I'll check it out in the morning," I said, flushing.

"There are dead people inside."

I was fully awake. "Meet me out there in fifteen minutes."

I was there in ten. Farmer's Creek was just north of the river on the east side of town, a runoff stream from the La Garita Mountains. Farmer's Creek Trail was very popular with rock hounds, who found calcite in abundance, the luckier ones finding geodes.

Jerry had parked his Bronco fifty meters from the abandoned vehicle—a red Nissan Xterra. He remained in the driver's seat, shining his high beams at the shattered windshield. I saw two shadowy forms slumped in the front seats. I got out and walked over to his window. Jerry reluctantly rolled it down. Heated air poured out into the cool night.

"Hey buddy," I said, leaning on the doorframe, hoping my relaxed posture would calm him down. I could see the entire whites of his eyes around the irises. "Whatcha got here?"

"Someone called in at around one to report it," he said, not taking his eyes off the truck. "Didn't give their name. Just said there was a truck parked out at the Farmer's Creek Trailhead with two dead people inside."

"Was it a man or woman?"

"It was a woman."

"Did you recognize her voice?" He shook his head.

"Did you get the plate number?" I asked, squinting across the parking area. He shook his head again. I was getting tired of this. It was too early in the morning to be camp counselor.

"Jerry, get your ass out of the truck and do your job. Just

because you're night dispatch, doesn't mean you can't get your hands dirty. Now, cowboy up, and let's go."

I opened his door and waited. He stared at me for a few seconds, realized I was serious, and slid out of the truck.

"Okay, Jerry, get out your notebook. I talk, and you chalk," I said, approaching the vehicle. I didn't know how he would manage with his crutches, but sympathy is hard to come by at two A.M.

"Red Nissan Xterra, looks like a 2002." We see a lot of them in Mineral County. "Minnesota plates . . . " I stopped talking and froze in my tracks, knowing the significance, but not quite there yet.

Then it came to me. "Andy and Heather Amundsen of St. Cloud, Minnesota," I said, finally.

"How the hell do you know that?" asked Jerry, peering at the front bumper, looking for their names.

"They checked out of the Halfmoon Ranch this weekend. They were with Jacob Stackhouse up at Wason Park yesterday morning when the mayor was killed."

"Holy shit, Bill. You think it's another sniper killing?"

"That's what it looks like." I turned and looked behind Jerry's Bronco. "The shooter followed them out here and shot them before they got out or after they back got in. He probably set up right there by the rifle range." I pointed to the small knoll to the west, still evident in the moonlight. "No one would think twice about hearing shots from there."

"Why do you think he'd want them dead?" asked Jerry.

"Same reason Jacob Stackhouse is dead," I said.

"What's that?"

"They must have seen the shooter, up on the ridge on Saturday when he shot the mayor."

"Why didn't he just kill them then?"

"It wasn't part of his plan. This guy doesn't take a shit

without a plan. That's why we haven't caught him. He does nothing spontaneously."

We inspected the vehicle. Both victims were in their early thirties, blond, like half of Minnesota. They were fit, young, and dead, each with a matching gunshot wound to the head. Neither had exit wounds, nor was the rear glass of the truck shattered. Dr. Ed would find the bullets still buried in their skulls. Their gear was packed up tight, and they wore street shoes, not fit for hiking. They did not come to Farmer's Creek to hunt geodes. Someone set them up to be assassinated.

Were they simply in the wrong place at the wrong time, or was there more to this than bad luck?

I leaned on the truck, staring up at the moon, sleep no longer a part of this night. I was many steps behind the sniper. I'd been on the case for four days, seen him kill twice, and he was still killing with impunity, right in my own backyard, literally. From the Farmer's Creek trailhead, I could see across the valley to my cabin.

Leaving Jerry at the scene, I returned to the station and called the sheriff. I roused Dr. Ed, too. He needed to take his coroner's vehicle out once in a while, just to make sure it ran. We met back at Farmer's Creek just as the night started burning away. Cold morning air, left alone all night by the sun to cool over the Rio, drifted across the valley to greet us. None said anything, falling in on the sheriff, letting the chill clear our heads. Jerry was coming around, having strung more yellow police tape than we used all of last year. He was busy snapping pictures and taking notes when we arrived. He crutched his way over to the sheriff.

Sheriff Dale had aged ten years since Thursday, the day we found Gayle Whippany in the beaver pond. Dark circles hovered over the suitcases under his eyes, but his uniform was pressed and clean, fresh creases lined his shirt and trousers. I wish I could say the same for mine, having grabbed it off the floor a few hours ago.

"Here we go again, Tatum," said the sheriff, not looking at me, but at the rising sun, just a promise of warmth and light. "Give me the details."

I let Jerry begin with the anonymous report.

"Do we have their identification?" asked the sheriff.

"Andy and Heather Amundsen of St. Cloud, Minnesota," said Jerry, handing Sheriff Dale their wallets. I was proud of Jerry—he pulled them out of their pockets while I was gone, all alone in the dark with two dead people.

"They were with Stackhouse yesterday on the La Garita Trail, the group that Marty saw about the time the Mayor was killed." I said. "They were guests at Orville's ranch, checked out on Friday."

"Why are they still here if they checked out two days ago?" asked Sheriff Dale. It was a fair question. We all stared at him, not having an answer.

"Maybe they never checked out," said Jerry.

"But Wendy at the Halfmoon said they checked out on Friday," I said, regretting the words as they came out.

"You mean Wendy, the crystal meth user? Girlfriend of the late Jacob Stackhouse, crystal meth dealer?"

Sheriff Dale needed a cup of coffee, but he was right; Wendy probably lied to me, covering for her boyfriend.

But if Wendy was covering for her boyfriend, why did her story conflict with Jacob's? In my first interview with Jacob, he told me the Amundsens were still at the ranch. Not thirty minutes later, he said they checked out. Then, Wendy contradicted him, saying they checked out the day before and never rode a horse once.

"Well, Deputies, are we done, here?" asked the Sheriff.

"I think so, Sheriff Dale," said Jerry, looking at me for support.

"Yes, sir, we've got everything we need," I said. "Not much of a mystery here, other than why. The shooter removed nothing from the vehicle—it's still packed up, ready for the trip home."

"All right, then. Doc, do what you need to do, then we'll help get them into your car," said Sheriff Dale. "Where you going to put them? Dead folks are stackin' up like cordwood in your locker."

"I'll have to see if Henry Earl will let me put two of them in his cold storage vault in the mine." Dr. Ed was referring to the old mine just north of town, used to house the fire department, mining museum, and underground storage facility.

We waited for Dr. Ed to complete his survey of the scene, then loaded the bodies into bags and into the coroner's vehicle.

"Jerry, go back to the station and help him off-load," ordered Sheriff Dale. Jerry wasn't pleased with this, but he obeyed without protest.

With Dr. Ed and Jerry gone, Sheriff Dale and I were left standing in the dark with our vehicles and the red Nissan. He gave no indication that he was leaving. He said nothing, just stared out to the east, where the sun would soon rise over Wagon Wheel Gap. He pulled a pack of Marlboro Reds out of his breast pocket and lit up. He offered me one, and I took it. After a few drags, he was ready to talk.

"This has gone beyond out of hand, Tatum," he said, the glowing ember illuminating his haggard face for a moment. "This thing has got to break open soon."

"Yes, sir, we're doing everything we can." I didn't know what else to tell him, so I briefed him on my interviews with Mandy Lange and Mack Smith.

"Not much to go on. Did you get a chance to see the map?" he asked.

"Yes, I did, but not to any detail. I figure I'll go out in

the field and follow her footsteps from last week. That should give me a clue as to where she was killed."

"Better get that spare back from Zooey's before you go very far. I don't want to have to come save your ass in the mountains somewhere."

"Yes sir," I said, "I'll do it this morning. Marty said the same thing."

We were silent for a while. The waning moon left the sky to the stars. The sheriff lit another cigarette with the butt of the first. I'd never seen him chain-smoke. I didn't blame him.

"Did you get any sleep?" he asked, blowing out.

"A little. That's all I'm getting today, though."

We watched the emerging dawn.

"Why don't you go home and get some rest?" asked the sheriff. "I'll get a hold of Henry Earl and have him tow this vehicle back to the maintenance lot."

"Are you sure, Sheriff Dale?" I asked. This was a dumb question. Sheriff Dale was sure about everything he said.

"I'll take care of this. I need you fresh today. Go on home. I don't care if you just lie in bed and stare at the ceiling."

He stubbed out his cigarette and got in his Bronco. I did the same. I had my orders.

I was wrong about getting back to sleep. I woke up well after sunrise, still in my rumpled uniform. It was Monday, the start of the week for most people. For me, it was just another day in the investigation. For others, it was a day to bury their husband and father. Jeff Lange's funeral was at 11:00 A.M. I pulled my clean uniform out of the dryer and plugged in the iron. The least I could do to honor the mayor was to have sharp creases and shined boots.

I left the cabin at nine, late for me, but feeling like a million bucks. I even applied some Brasso to my badge and cleaned the smudges off my Resistol. The sun shone in the big sky and the birds chirped in the blue spruce down by the creek. Whenever I looked at the mountains for the first time every day, my brain played a little fanfare. Today it was a symphony. I had no reason to think so, but I felt like the case could turn around on this clear, bluebird day.

I found Pete and Zooey together in the repair garage. Pete was saying something to Zooey in his usual manner, with his hands as much as his rapid-fire speech pattern. Zooey just stood there with his arms at his sides, looking down at his much shorter sibling. They stopped when I pulled up. How could these two be brothers? Both were dressed up in their own way for the funeral, too. Zooey was in the same clothes I saw him in two days ago, but had pulled his long, scraggly black hair back in a ponytail, and it even looked like he'd shaved. Pete had on a short-sleeved white shirt and tie. Pete scurried over to me as I approached.

"Good morning, Deputy Tatum. Come for your tire? Zooey's got it all ready for you."

I kept walking toward the garage. Pete walked beside me, still talking. Zooey reached up to a rack and swung down my spare with his casual strength. He bounced it to show me his work. I was struck by the same smell of ammonia as the day before. I made a mental note to mention it to Pete before I left.

"Dude, I found this in the rim," said Zooey, digging in the pocket of his jeans and pulling out a small, metal object. He handed it to me.

"It looks like a bullet, Bill," said Pete. "That's what it is, isn't it? I'm no hunter, but that looks like a bullet."

He was right. It was a fully jacketed rifle bullet, deformed from its impact with the steel rim. As far as I could tell, it was the same caliber as the bullet I dug out of Emmett's window sill, the same caliber that killed Jacob Stackhouse, Gayle Whippany, Mayor Jeff, and probably the couple from Minnesota—.270 Winchester. My slide into Joe Bender's backyard was no accident. Someone shot out my tire.

"How much do I owe you, Zooey?" I asked. Zooey just looked at Pete.

"No charge, Deputy Tatum. Anything to help," said Pete.

"No sir," I said. "No offense, but the sheriff is clear on ethics."

Pete frowned. "Five bucks, then, if you have to."

I slapped my back pocket for my wallet and came up empty.

"Shoot. I left my wallet in the truck. I'll be right back."

I walked back to the Bronco and opened the door. I hated carrying my wallet, so I usually put it in the glove compartment. The passenger side door was locked, so I went around to the driver's side, opposite the garage. This saved my life.

As I leaned across the bench seat to open the glove compartment, a monstrous explosion rocked the Bronco, skidding the vehicle a few feet across the gravel drive. The shock wave shattered the windshield and passenger side windows, raining safety glass down on me. Stunned and deaf, I slid backward out the door and crawled on my elbows around the front of the truck. The garage was a smoking hole. Pete and Zooey's charred bodies lay in the blackened mess, torched and burning tires strewn around and on top of them. I stood up and staggered over to where they lay. The contrasting smells of burning tires and human flesh overpowered me. I fell to my knees next to Pete McClaren's ruined form. There was nothing I could do for him or his brother. Shocked and bleeding out both ears, I collapsed in the gravel.

Twenty-one

I N THE MIST OF SEMI-CONSCIOUSNESS, I KNEW I wasn't doing what I should. My mind knew I should be working, investigating, up and about on the trail of a sniper, but I was on my back, not certain if I was awake or not. The confusion brought me around. I was back in my own bed, and my head felt like an elephant had stepped on it. I tried to sit up, but the room began to spin, and I flopped back down before nausea overcame me.

"Stay where you are, young Jedi." I heard a familiar voice from somewhere not here. The room kept spinning. "There is a bucket on your right if you need to vomit."

I leaned on my side and did, not feeling any better, but at least the room slowed to carousel speed. I set one foot on the floor to slow the rotation, without success.

"What happened?" I croaked, my voice echoing inside my splitting skull. I regretted saying anything and decided to refrain from doing so until the elephant removed his big foot.

"You were in an explosion, but, lucky for you, you survived. Pete and Zooey were not so lucky."

It was a man's voice, I could tell that much. I heard footsteps on the plank floor. I thought about turning my head to look, but then thought better of it.

Dr. Ed's face blurred into my vision. He shone a penlight in my eyes, damn him; it was like a tiny spear poked straight down my ocular nerve.

"Jesus, stop that," I said, whipping my head away from the needle of pain. The rest of the room followed with it, but a fraction of a second behind.

"Ornery, that's good," said the town doctor. "Can you hear me?"

"Yes, just don't poke at me, Dr. Ed," I begged him, "What time is it?"

"It's four o'clock in the afternoon. You've been out since nine or so. At least, that's when we figure the garage blew up. When we first found you, we thought you were dead, then you groaned a little. How did you not end up like the McClaren brothers? You don't have one burn on you."

"I was in my truck when it happened, below the dash, getting my wallet," I said. This sentence felt a little better.

"Ah, that explains things. You must have crawled around the truck on your elbows. They're torn to shreds."

I felt down along my arms and found matching bandages wrapped around my elbows.

"What else is wrong with me?" I asked.

"Well, as far as I can tell, the explosion didn't blow out your eardrums, but it probably feels like it. I don't think you have a concussion. The truck must have shielded you from most of the effects of the blast."

"Pete and Zooey are dead," I said.

"Quite so, they took the brunt of the explosion. Stood right in it. They died instantly."

I'd be dead with them, if it weren't for my own forgetfulness.

"The funeral," I said. "Mayor Jeff . . . "

"Most of us who work at the municipal building missed it. We were distracted by the mushroom cloud upriver. His wake is this evening, though, at the Belmont Hotel. Eunice has opened the bar. I intend to get thoroughly drunk remembering our beloved mayor. Here, take these."

Dr. Ed handed me two pills and a glass of water. I choked them down.

"They should clear your head a little. I think you'll survive, so I'm leaving. I don't make house calls, you know, and I don't want this getting around." He snapped shut his little black bag and walked out my bedroom door.

"You can go in and see him, now," he said to someone in the living room.

Marty Three Stones appeared in the doorway, hat in hand, leaning on the frame. I sat up quickly, not wanting to look like an invalid.

"How you doing?" she asked.

"Okay," I lied. "Head hurts like a bitch, but the room is slowing down a little. Feels mostly like a bad hangover now. I'll be up in an hour or so—missed a whole day."

"No need to rush, Bill, I think both of our cases are solved," she said.

I didn't think I heard her correctly. "What?"

"Pete and Zooey were the crystal meth suppliers. You know that propane tank corroding next to the garage? It was filled with anhydrous ammonia, a key ingredient to crystal meth. Zooey was cooking it in a lab under the garage. That's what caused the explosion. I guess that happens sometimes with meth cookers—occupational hazard.

Both were users of their own products and victims of their own carelessness."

"So what does that have to do with the sniper case?" I asked.

"Pete has a vault under the office. It was open when we searched the compound. In it, we found a two-seventy sniper rifle, reloading bench, and Gayle Whippany's laptop computer. It looks like Pete and Zooey were the sniper team, too."

I tried to process all that information. Connections snapped together as the scattered details of both cases organized themselves into a coherent picture. The first part was easy—Pete and Zooey supplied crystal meth to the Belmont Valley, using Jacob Stackhouse as their dealer. Zooey cooked it right in the valley, using the stinking mess of his tire repair shop to cover the distinctive smell of the lab. Pete was obviously the businessman of the enterprise, pushing product out to his own guests as well as the guests of the Halfmoon Ranch.

"But why did they start killing? Killing their own dealer?" I asked.

"Who knows? It could be simple witness elimination, like we originally thought. Maybe Stackhouse and the Amundsens saw Zooey take out the mayor on Saturday," said Marty. "You said yourself that Stackhouse acted pretty flaky when you interviewed him that afternoon. He could've been getting ready to rat out the McClarens. Dealing meth is one thing, murder is quite another."

"I'm still following up the connection to the couple from Minnesota," she continued. "Maybe Jacob was trying to branch out on his own. I can't find anything on the Amundsens, it's like they don't exist."

"How does the mayor fit in?" I asked.

"I think I know that one," said Marty. "Dr. Ed got the tox reports back on Mayor Jeff today. Meth user, no question. Probably a user for a long time, from the effects on his body. I searched his car and found a stash of meth. The Pueblo boys should match it to Jacob's supply I found yesterday and the meth stocks we pulled from Pete and Zooey's lab."

"So, you think the mayor was in on the drug ring?"

"Maybe. At least he knew about it. Maybe they paid for his silence with meth."

"All this is speculation, Marty," I said.

"Of course it is, dipshit," she sounded irritated. "Everyone involved is dead. Hard to do any interviews or determine motive when all your suspects are graveyard candidates. This thing just burned itself out, literally."

I stuck the heels of my hands in my eye sockets and rubbed vigorously, trying to clear my head and make sense of all the information.

"Why did they kill Gayle Whippany? What's she got to do with it?" I asked, blinking the stars from my vision.

"Ah, that one we know," said Marty, "We found her notes on the laptop computer. She started a new story, different from the original bullshit about 'mountain sprawl.' It was a piece on a little town in the San Juan Mountains with a big crystal meth problem. A town whose mayor happily participated in the drug ring, even covered for the dealers and suppliers. I'll give you three guesses on the name of the town, and the first two don't count."

"How did she find out?"

"My guess is she suspected the mayor was a user right away, then either stroked it out of him or just figured it out on her own. Either way, Pete and Zooey found out about it and started killing to protect their business."

"Looks like it got out of their control," she explained. "Killing Whippany led to killing the mayor, for reasons I don't quite understand. Stackhouse freaked out when he saw Zooey kill the mayor, which led to his demise. Then the Amundsens. They had to keep killing to tie up loose ends."

That made sense to me.

"You know, Bill, we could go round and round for hours, coming up with as many 'why' scenarios as fish in the river, but where will that get us?" she asked. "We have our suspects, charred, but in custody. They had the murder weapon, critical evidence from one of the victims, plenty of motive, and lots of opportunity. I say we count our blessings and close this case."

"What does the sheriff think?"

"He's happy as a clam. Took the whole town council out to the scene of the explosion, after we took the bodies away, of course. He walked them through it, and they were satisfied. They got it a little quicker than you did." She smiled at me.

I smiled back, suddenly relieved and exhausted. Ignoring the little prick in the back of my head, I reached out for the conclusion of the sniper case, of both cases, and took it, making it my own. I shooed Marty away, settled back in bed, and fell asleep.

My subconscious didn't let me off that easily. I slept poorly, wrestling with night terrors and dreams so vivid and colorful, I thought reality had reversed itself. I awoke sweating and panicky, the bed torn to shreds and soaking wet. Thankfully, the firehose of images churning through my skull began to dissipate, and I was struck by the quiet darkness that enveloped my cabin by Deep Creek. All was silent but the falling water of my little stream, which dampened the last echoes of my blaring dreams. I staggered, barefoot and shirtless, to the front porch and leaned on the railing. The dry, frigid air quickly evaporated the sweat on my skin and snapped shut my pores. It banished the surreal from my mind. I filled my lungs with the essence of the mountains. Reality once again in its rightful place, I came to grips with what my primitive mind already knew—Pete and Zooey didn't do it.

Despite all the evidence in their vault, despite their motive and opportunity, despite their knowledge of the people and terrain of Belmont, despite the year's supply of crystal meth smoldering under their flattened garage, I knew Pete and Zooey were not my snipers. Sure enough, they were meth dealers, and their demise was a happy day for Belmont's residents and guests, ridding our town of at least one of the modern problems of urban and rural America. But that was a separate issue. Pete and Zooey were drug dealers, not trained snipers.

They weren't even hunters or sportsmen. I'd never seen nor heard of either of the McClaren brothers firing a rifle, ever. Bench-loading rifle bullets required a place to test-fire them, and the only rifle ranges in the valley were the local range by Farmer's Creek and the Halfmoon Ranch. They'd have to travel to Alamosa or up in the mountains to test their loads without being seen. Pete and Zooey, however, rarely left their place by the river, except to stop in the grocery store or pick up mail in town. They provided a service to the outdoorsy types, but, unlike most other outfitters, they stayed home. Zooey permanently lost his license to drive years ago—his own drug use was well documented. Pete had to mind the store, close to his beloved electronics. These shootings took time and planning, time that would take Pete away from the rental shop during the high tourist season. Who would run the place? Zooey? I didn't believe Pete would relinquish control to his strung-out brother. Zooey, although probably capable of making the skillful shots, didn't have enough gray matter left to keep from blowing himself up in his own lab, let alone plan complicated assassinations and daring escapes. So what if he had long, black hair?

Finally, there was the list of GPS coordinates Pete gave

me, tracking Gayle Whippany's vehicle for the last few weeks. Why would he give them to me so freely? Well, not freely, it took some convincing. Unless he was an acting intern at the local repertory theater and set me up with a list of false coordinates, he gave me a crucial bit of evidence that would eventually lead to his capture. Maybe he had his brother shoot out my tire on the drive back from Orville's Saturday night, forcing me to have it fixed at his shop, giving him the opportunity to slip me the fake list, an electronic red herring, thus throwing me off his trail. How absurd was that? Why, then, would Zooey just hand me the bullet? Pete gave me the coordinates with the faith that he was helping me. Whoever shot my tire wanted me dead, or, at least, unable to complete the investigation.

That realization jolted me into complete clarity. Until now, I assumed I wasn't a target, not part of the sniper's plan. Maybe the timing of the explosion wasn't an accident at all. Maybe I was part of the objective, just like Jerry at the beaver pond. If that were true, it would clearly indicate the McClaren brothers weren't simply victims of their own corroding tank of ammonia. Someone planted the evidence and rigged their tank to explode when I was there picking up the tire. The late-night conspiracy theorist in me stretched this tenuous line of reasoning to its limits. Who knew I had blown a tire? Could be the whole town, once the Benders started talking. Zooey's repair shop was the logical place to have it fixed, being the only shop in the county. It wouldn't be too difficult to predict my behavior and set the stage for my demise along with Pete and Zooey. I shook these thoughts out of my head—too much speculation.

I was freezing on my front porch, so I went back in and threw on a flannel shirt and wool socks, but returned to the railing with a bottle of water and some more aspirin, this time pulling up the rocking chair. The night had saved me from my terrors, and I wasn't eager to go back to bed. It was nearly one A.M., and few lights remained in Belmont. The Winnebagoes down in Elk Hollow were silent, like sleeping cattle. Deep Creek still whispered off to my right, reminding me how simple life could be, how reliable the simple things were. It was hard to imagine the violence and death that had invaded our quiet valley, and I knew it wasn't over. My sniper was still out there.

Headlights appeared on the airport road. Then another pair appeared, turning the corner from eastbound Highway 149. Two more sets followed, one from Belmont. They passed through the Elk Hollow gate, parking outside the administration building, just a construction trailer left on-site when the park was complete. In the spare light, I recognized the signature Duellie headlights of Dana Pratt's black pickup. Two other trucks must have been his boys, just black shadows in the pre-moon darkness. One of the goons forgot to shut off his lights upon entering the RV park, flashing the fourth vehicle—Thomas Pitcher's white Ford F150. I wondered what the senior councilman and acting mayor was doing out so late on the day he buried his predecessor.

Recognizing their constitutional right to assemble, I applied my human right to be curious and threw on a pair of jeans, boots, and Resistol. I didn't intend on being detected, so I left my duty belt and uniform. One set was in the wash and the other covered with blood and auto glass, anyway. I would trade power for stealth. I went out to the barn and quietly whispered Pancho awake. He snickered and seemed genuinely happy to see me, but it could've been the apple I gave him. We saddled up and trotted down the hill toward the airport bridge.

Twenty-two

THE RIO WAS STILL HIGH, BUT COMING DOWN AS the dry season approached. Most of the winter snowmelt had drained out of the Rio Grande Reservoir, thirty miles upriver, and the outflow was a trickle. The Rio Grande went through a life cycle every year, starting as a tentative infant while the snow melted and the reservoir filled. It grew to boisterous youth, churning and high with the murky runoff from the feeder streams pouring into it. It matured by early summer, shedding the silt that clouded its beauty, but remained robust for the fish and insect hatches. By late summer, the river, tired from all the activity, slowed and receded from the highs of its youth. By late fall, the river seemed dormant again, waiting for the gift of life to fall from the sky and begin the cycle once more. The young river would cover my approach.

I did not intend to walk up on the late-night riders at Elk Hollow from an expected direction. The sniper in me threw out that course of action before I mounted Pancho. We were going to come in from the back side of the park, from the east, opposite the main gate. Crossing the airport road, I slowed him to an easy walk, stepped over the barricades near the bridge, and went down to the water. The air cooled as we descended to the bank, like moving through the thermocline under water. The white noise of rushing water echoed under the bridge and eliminated the sounds of our movement. The shadows beneath the bridge were a void.

Pancho didn't shy one step from the dark, loud river, plodding through it with the ease and confidence we had in each other. Once across, we turned east, staying below the steep bank and out of sight from the RV park. We followed the river downstream for two hundred meters on a bank getting wider by the day. The moon appeared, waning, but helpful still, lighting our way through the willows and smooth rocks along the Rio. From the airport bridge, the river traveled east a short distance, then took a bend to the north, placing me a few hundred meters behind the park. When I was confident of our unexpected avenue of approach, I nudged my horse up the bank, but not over it, just high enough for me to poke my head level with the valley floor. Pancho waited patiently on the incline while I surveyed the silent valley.

The headlights from before were gone, and darkness covered the nocturnal rendezvous. Men's voices carried across the flat terrain, but I couldn't make out the words or recognize the owners. They sounded urgent and serious. I coaxed Pancho up the remaining bank, and he mounted the rise without a slip or dislodged rock.

I closed the distance to Elk Hollow at a slow, lazy pace. Pancho was in no hurry, and I knew he wanted to sample the tufts of prairie grass along the way. He'd have his chance. I approached from the back side of the park, farthest away from the entrance and the headquarters where the men gathered. Wary of dogs that always accompanied motor tourists, I halted at the split-rail perimeter fence thirty meters from the nearest Winnebago. I spoke gently to Pancho, assuring him I'd return. I didn't need to tie him off; there were plenty of horse munchies growing around him, results of repeated afternoon showers from the last few days.

The urgent voices from the front of the park remained intense. Staying in the shadows of the modern bedouin shelters, I slipped toward the sounds, the only noise in the valley besides the river and the wind. I reached the last RV, took off my hat, and crawled underneath, scraping on my belly to the opposite side.

Two men huddled around a hole in the ground. At least, I thought it was a hole, because they were pouring something into it from what looked like a fuel can. I was only twenty feet away and downwind, and it didn't smell like fuel—it smelled like chlorine. Two others stood upwind of the can-wielding figures. They were doing the talking.

"Are you about done with that?" It was Dana Pratt, confirming the identification by sucking on his ever-present Camel. The red ember glowed and faded. A mumbled acknowledgement from his boys.

"Are you sure this will do it, Pratt?" Thomas Pitcher, too loudly for the dead of night, but just about right for Pitcher. He must've thought he was being quiet.

"Sure I'm sure," said Pratt. "Chlorine'll kill any bug you want, even E. Coli."

"Please don't use that word, even this late at night. We can't have a panic," said Pitcher.

"Now, don't you worry, Councilman. Whatever they find in the groundwater won't get traced back to here, I can guarantee that."

"Is this the only septic tank you have?" asked Pitcher.

"Yup, it's a big one, too." He flicked his butt into the gravel yard. It spun and shed sparks on its descent.

"Good. Now, what about your other developments? Are you going to visit them tonight as well?"

"Already have, Councilman. This is the last one. I still don't know why you're out here. I think I can handle this."

"It's my ass as well as yours, Mr. Pratt." I'd never heard Pitcher curse before.

"Well, you can rest easy tonight, Councilman. We just declared chemical war on the critters. We will prevail."

I heard my horse nicker and a dog bark behind me. The nickering stopped, but the little yipper kept at it. Three other dogs took up the chorus, and windows glowed in a few of the RVs. Compromised.

"What was that?" asked Pitcher.

"Sounded like a horse," said one of the boys. He took a few steps toward the trailer that sheltered me, looking around it in Pancho's direction. The barking continued.

"No one has any horses here," said Pratt. "Check it out." The pair said nothing, but obeyed. That was it. Time for a breakout drill.

Breakouts aren't about stealth; they're about hauling ass. I was unarmed and unofficial, trespassing on Pratt's property. Property rights are sacred to Coloradoans, and few were shy about physically protecting their own. I was sure to get a beating, or worse, if caught. Even if they recognized me, the darkness would give them an alibi for mistaken identity.

All this shot through my brain in a microsecond as I scooted backward like a lobster from under the trailer, not caring if the chuckleheads heard me or not, then sprinted back toward Pancho. The moon was bright enough for me to see the outline of the perimeter fence. Pancho could see it, too.

"Hey!" said one of Pratt's boys. It sounded like Mack Smith, or maybe I just thought so. Their boots dug into the gravel. A row of trailers separated us.

I let out a high, piercing whistle as I dashed toward my horse. Pancho heard it, nickered, and trotted toward me, hopping the fence. He closed the gap quickly, and I swung aboard, turning him back toward the split rail and coaxing him to a gallop. Pratt's boys weren't as fast. We jumped the fence at near-gallop, and I nearly lost it, but held on to the pommel for dear life. Pancho just kept right on going, heading east, parallel to the river.

"You fools, get in your trucks!" Pratt bellowed.

Less than thirty seconds later, I heard the roar of big V-eight engines behind me. I chanced a look back, not that I was guiding Pancho in his gleeful rush down the valley, and saw two pair of headlights bouncing crazily across the open plain. They would catch me in minutes. Finally coming up with an escape plan on the fly, I turned north before their beams found me. I hoped the moon wouldn't give me away.

Keeping my happy horse at full gallop, we intersected the east-west gravel road to the fish hatchery, which took me over the twin forks of Willow Creek before I dove headlong over their banks. The road followed the river east for a bit then angled north toward Highway 149. Keeping Pancho on his easterly heading, we left the gravel, zoomed past the hatchery buildings, and returned to the open pasture.

Confident my horse would continue churning through the field, I ventured another glance at my pursuers. The headlights were closer, but no longer directly behind me. Instead, they were following the hatchery road to the north, missing my departure from it at the bend. Good. I still had a long way to go, and they might figure out my plan.

A railroad embankment rose to our front, and Pancho stepped lightly over it, then clopped across Highway 149. I looked left and saw the sidelights of the trucks stopped at the highway, obviously wondering where I'd gone. To my dismay, they crossed the blacktop and took the road to the rifle range and my own destination—Farmer's Creek Trail. I goosed Pancho, and he gladly quickened his pace.

It was a race to sanctuary. The trucks were still behind me, but back on my direction of travel. They would see me and learn of their success. I galloped due east and came upon the no-name creek that trickled out of Dry Gulch. Working my way downstream, I found what I was looking for—a cattle crossing. We sloshed through the shallows of the ford and hit Farmer's Creek Trail. I looked back again and saw that Pratt's boys were nearing the trailhead. They would blow through the gate and keep right on going. We picked up the trail at a fast trot and moved east again.

They still had a chance of catching me if they were quick, only two hundred meters behind. This portion of the trail was wide open, plenty wide enough for their four-by-fours, but I'd already passed the decisive point of this chase, and I knew we'd make it. I hesitated to urge Pancho to a full gallop on a hiking trail in the dark. We pressed forward rapidly to the uphill turn in the trail where it climbed into the foothills of the La Garita Mountains, towering overhead. Pancho nimbly stepped up the steep trail, and we were safe. The trail narrowed to a footpath, and Pratt's boys would be out of luck.

We worked our way up the rocky path in the dark, and took our time doing it, not wanting to end up with a broken leg or pitched into the draw to my right. I heard the clowns in trucks roar by my turn, staying on the wider jeep trail that followed the base of the foothills. Soon they would realize they were no longer chasing me and backtrack, but I'd be gone, into the mountains and out of reach of their clumsy trucks.

I opened the map of the county in my head and thought of contingencies. I wasn't out of the woods, yet. They could still catch me if they paused to think. If they were tenacious and knew the trails, one of them could block my path behind, keeping me from backtracking. The other could go back to town, take the Wason Park Pack Trail into the mountains, and intercept me where it intersected Farmer's Creek Trail. If I kept going up the trail, I'd be trapped. I could wait until light and work my way cross-country, but so could they. My options were few, but I had the advantage of dark, intelligence, and patience. My back-track pathway was open, but the window would close shortly, once they figured out I was no longer in front of them. I quickly turned Pancho back down the trail, and used the pale light of the near-full moon to urge him down again as fast as he'd let me. I listened for the roar of internal combustion to my left. I had time, but little of it.

I made it to the wider trail, and turned west, toward town, but I didn't stay on it long. I found my cattle crossing again, and we splashed over, this time turning south toward the Rio Grande. I kept Pancho moving at a trot, but no faster, he had a hard run to Farmer's Creek. We crossed the flat pasture, found the Rio, and turned west again, upriver. Behind me, I heard the engines getting louder. They'd come back to look for me, but to them, I could be anywhere. Did I go up Farmer's Creek Trail, or did I back-track? I now had the additional advantage of having many options—would I stay in the valley, go back to town, or hightail it into the mountains? They were separated from their master, trying to sort things out on their own. I doubted they could track in the dark.

Then, I remembered their radios. They could easily contact Pratt and bring him into the pursuit. He might even be coordinating it himself. I reached the highway. Looking west, I saw headlights coming in my direction. I knew it was Pratt; his boys were still back at Farmer's Creek, trying to figure out where I'd gone. Pratt was running the roads to find me. We turned away from the blacktop and I dismounted. The bank to the Rio Grande was steeper here than at the airport bridge, and I led Pancho over the edge and into the darkness of the river. We waited for Pratt's Duellie to pass by, only a few dozen meters away. Not thirty seconds later, it thundered by. I counted another thirty, then climbed the cut. I saw Pratt's taillights to the south, then he turned west on Deep Creek Road. He was circling. I decided to follow him.

I whispered to Pancho, and he joined me at the top of the bank. I mounted, and we followed Pratt, not on the highway, but due south, toward Deep Creek Road. I was going to end this silliness. Pratt's taillights were still bright off to the west, and his boys were motionless at Farmer's Creek. We didn't have to hurry; I was heading back to my cabin, only a mile or so down Deep Creek Road. Pratt wouldn't return to search here for a while. I now had time to slink back to my cabin and let them drive around all night, looking for me.

Pancho picked up a trot after we crossed the bridge and entered the open field. We were back on Deep Creek Road in a few minutes, and I still had eyes on my pursuers. I knew my path was clear. I turned up my long drive at three A.M., but it seemed much later. I led Pancho to the barn, gave him a good brushing, and left him fresh water and an early breakfast. I changed out of my wet, dirty, and sweaty fugitive clothes and returned to my front porch with a cup of coffee, still interested in watching Pratt and his chuckle-heads drive around. Their truck lights circled the valley for another pointless hour, then they regrouped at Elk Hollow. They didn't bother to turn off their headlights, and I could see their dark forms gesturing in the circle of light. Pitcher wasn't among them. I guess he didn't have the stomach for night chases.

The light from my front window provided enough illumination for me to jot down my observations from the past two hours. Pratt was dumping lots of chlorine into his underground septic tank in the dead of night, not just at Elk Hollow, but at his other developments as well. Pratt mentioned E. Coli, which set off Thomas Pitcher. Pitcher had an interest in killing whatever was growing in Pratt's septic tank, not wanting a panic. He actually used that word. When they found someone spying on their little chemical warfare, they pursued with the dogged determination of the desperate and guilty. Maybe there was something more to Gayle Whippany's theory about political corruption and bad water. They certainly chased me intensely, but was it homicidal intent, would I be dead now if they'd caught me? I was glad they didn't have the chance. I would have to check with Dr. Ed in the morning, later this morning, to be more accurate. Not only was Dr. Ed the town physician, he was also in charge of public health. I went to bed after the three black pickup trucks drove away, returning to base at the Shallow Creek Ranch.

Twenty-three

I WOKE UP LATE FOR THE SECOND DAY IN A ROW. I guess I had a couple excuses, though. One I would share—being blown up the day before, and one I wouldn't share—being chased around the valley in the dark while out of uniform. I repeated my preparations from Monday, starching, ironing, buffing, and polishing. I even applied Kiwi to the brown leather of my duty belt. Creased and shiny, I went to the rack for my Resistol. I stood there, staring at the empty peg for a moment, hand frozen on the way to grab the missing cowboy hat. My stomach did a slow free-fall toward the plank floor. My mind raced backward. I remembered putting it on before going to Elk Hollow, but I didn't remember returning with it. My brain churned through the events of the wee hours, and then it came to me. I left the hat next to the Winnebago I crawled under while spying on Pratt and Pitcher. Well, I would just have to go get it.

That would be a challenge if they found it last night. It was also a challenge because I didn't have my Bronco, which I didn't remember until I walked out the door, bareheaded, keys in hand, and found the drive as empty as my hat rack. Seemed like everything was missing this morning. I turned to the barn. I could always rely on my horse.

We walked through the gate of Elk Hollow as nonchalantly as we could. At least Pancho would always act natural. He had no other style. A few guests were out, mostly older folks, walking the airport road or around the split-rail fence, drinking coffee under tiny awnings. I halted at the administration building, dismounted, and walked over the septic tank cover to the other side of the Winnebago that was my vantage point the night before. A nice older couple sat on folding chairs, chatting after watching the sun rise.

"Good morning, ma'am, sir," I said, almost tipping the brim of my absent Resistol. They looked at me quizzically while I stooped down and picked it up off the ground, just under the trailer, exactly where I left it. I screwed it on tight, touched the brim this time, and went back to my horse.

Dana Pratt was there, sitting in his black Duellie next to the admin building. I didn't even hear him pull up. Trying not to look shaken, I walked over to the driver's window to say hello.

"Morning, Mr. Pratt," I said as he powered down his window.

"What are you doing here, Deputy? You lose something?" he asked, blowing smoke toward me. I put on my best poker face while trying to see if he meant that literally. I couldn't tell. He must have been better at poker than I.

"Just stopping by to see our visitors. Can't leave them feeling unprotected," I offered lamely.

"You never stopped by here before. Don't bullshit me."

He looked tired and irritated. I knew why. I did my best Eddie Haskell.

"No bullshit, Mr. Pratt. Just your friendly neighborhood deputy. Well, I must be going. Takes me a little longer to get to work on Pancho."

"What happened to your truck, Deputy?" he asked, smiling for the first time.

"Blown up, sir," I said, realizing I sounded like Bill Murray from *Stripes*.

"Oh, yeah. I think I heard that yesterday from the ranch. You were there with Pete and Zooey when their place went up. Poor bastards. Not ashamed to say, serves 'em right, being drug pushers and all."

"I didn't think we released any part of the investigation, yet, Mr. Pratt," I said flatly. "Do you have a statement to make?"

"No," he said, and stepped out of his truck, crushed out his cigarette in the gravel, and walked off.

I hopped on Pancho and left Elk Hollow before Dana made the connection with this morning's visit to last night's chase across the valley. Even if he did, there was no way for him to prove that I was the object of his pursuit, now that I had my hat back. Unless, of course, he went around the park, asking what I was up to.

Pancho and I trotted past the softball field at the edge of town. I felt a little like Wyatt Earp again. The place seemed normal enough for ten o'clock on a Tuesday. Sunny and warm, the mountains playing their fanfare.

I was surprised to see Ralph Munger, our resident geologist, sitting on the front stoop of his rock shop. He rarely emerged from its depths this early in the day, and if he did, he was usually on his way to or from the field, collecting samples. Today, he was in running shoes and shorts, looking like he had just finished a run, and I felt a twinge of guilt. I hadn't run one step since I saw the mayor get blown away, three days ago. I needed to work out the kinks and clear my head with a hard run up Deep Creek. Ralph waved me over and let me set aside my guilt.

"So, you've been busy, Bill," he said, looking up at me through thick glasses held tight to his head by a strap; not the cool outdoor sunglasses keepers they sell at the WWE. This strap was plain brown elastic with the snaps that the optometrist gives you for free when you're eight and get your first pair of glasses. No slave to fashion, Ralph looked like he had had his that long.

I got off Pancho, so Ralph wouldn't have to look up at me, and sat down next to him on the porch.

"I heard you might have things wrapped up," he said.

"That's what I heard, too," I said. "I wasn't really involved with the culmination of the case."

"I'd say you were involved. I heard the explosion down in my shop while I was grinding away with my rock saw. I came out here and saw the black mushroom cloud down the valley. I thought the Air Force Academy was dropping bombs on us."

I laughed. He had an easy humor. He must have been a great teacher.

"You never came by to check on my analysis of your samples," said Ralph. "Guess you really don't need it, now."

"I was delayed, Ralph," I said, "but I'm still interested in what you found."

"Mine tailings," he said, reaching for his toes and stretching his hamstrings.

"What?"

"Mine tailings," he repeated. "Your samples were made of copper sulphate. You know, the piles of green stuff outside the old mines? It turns green as a result of oxidation, when it's exposed to the air.

"So, she was standing next to a mine shaft when she was shot," I said, as much to myself as to Ralph. I placed all the old mines in the Belmont Valley. A few of them were near the Equity Mine Trailhead, where Gayle Whippany was last seen, but none were on her reported direction of travel, along the Colorado Trail. She must have altered her itinerary after Mayor Jeff left her. I would check out the plots on the map.

"Ralph, if you went into the mountains with me and found a pile of tailings, could you match it to the sample?"

"Sure. I could do it with a field kit right there on the spot."

"Great. I'll be in touch. Need to do a map check." I stood up.

"But I thought the case was solved when Pete and Zooey blew themselves up."

"We'll see," I said, getting on my horse.

I stood in front of the map at the station, staring at each pin with its time and date. I was wrong—none of them were even close to any of the abandoned mines in the Belmont area, not even within reasonable walking distance. How the hell did she get the fragments in her face?

She was near the Equity Mine, however, on her final few days. Maybe that was the key.

"What are you doing, Deputy?" Sheriff Dale snuck up behind me again. I didn't jump this time.

"Oh, just going over her track. I didn't get much of a chance to do any real analysis on it."

"No need now, right? I'm closing this case. The snipers are dead, along with their drug trade. It all went up yesterday. You remember that, or are you still rattled?"

"I remember, sir," I paused, turning, "but they didn't do it."

"Say again?"

"Pete and Zooey weren't the snipers, Sheriff Dale."

He looked at me like I had a dick growing out of my forehead.

"Now, why in the hell would you think that?"

"It's more of a gut feeling, Sheriff. I was the last person to see them alive, and their actions just don't fit."

"They had the murder weapon, bullets, and reloader in their basement."

"I know, sir. We don't know for sure it's the murder weapon."

"The drugged-out one, Zooey, had long black hair, just like the suspect Ralph Munger saw on Saturday."

"Seems like lots of folks in town have long, black hair, and both McClarens were users. You should've seen Pete. He couldn't keep still."

"They were cooking meth and selling it to kids."

"I don't dispute that, Sheriff Dale. I think they got what they deserve. Punishment fit the crime. They didn't do the shooting, though."

"They killed their own dealer."

"Someone did, but why would they do that, and what about the couple from Minnesota? How do they fit in?"

He didn't answer my question; his face just got redder and redder.

"They killed the mayor," he said, his voice cranking up a notch, "and he was a meth user, too. Probably in on the whole thing."

"I agree, sir. I think the mayor was a tacit partner to the McClarens. Pete and Zooey just aren't the shooters."

He looked exasperated. "So, how do you figure?"

"They just don't fit the profile."

"Don't fit the profile? Who are you, Agent Starling?" He was mocking me. This was a new side of Sheriff Dale. I didn't like it.

"Sir, I know I'm not trained for this, but I have plenty of

common sense, and I know a thing or two about shooting."
I was getting belligerent, but I believed what I was saying.
"When was the last time you saw Pete or Zooey fire a rifle?
Do you know if they even owned one? Killing a man at
over four hundred meters takes training; it takes complete
understanding of your rifle and the ballistics of your loads.
When did the McClarens have the time to achieve that
level of proficiency with a rifle? They rarely left the shop."

I told him about how forthcoming the McClarens were
about the investigation and showed him the bullet Zooey
took out of my wheel. He was neither impressed nor convinced.

"They were probably jacking with you, throwing you
off the trail," he said. "How do you know Zooey pulled that
bullet out of the wheel? They probably had lots of bullets
lying around."

I didn't have any more answers for him, but he hadn't
convinced me either. I was silent.

"Look, Bill," he quieted down, "we found hard evidence
at their shop, unblemished and unmistakable. They had
motive. They had opportunity. Their victims all seemed to
have a connection with crystal meth, or at least had only
one degree of separation."

He stopped, waiting for me to nod or acknowledge his
line of reasoning. I did neither. He continued.

"I got the council on my back to close both cases. Not
that their heat bothers me, but all this just can't be coincidence. Why look hard for a conspiracy when the real solution blows up in front of you?"

He waited again for me to respond. I was pissed and
said nothing.

"Goddamn it, Tatum, say something. Give me a sign
that some of this is getting through your thick skull, because you're not going to work one more day on this case.
You'll close it today. Do you understand me?"

"Yes sir," I said, not meaning it.

I didn't expect this level of resistance from my superior. Needing to cool off, I let the sheriff return to his office, then I stepped outside into the late morning sunshine. I pulled out a pack of Marlboro Reds. They were old. I only smoked when I was drinking at the San Juan Tavern. Marty always gave me shit about that, calling me a casual smoker. I was smoking a lot more the last few days and running a whole lot less. Part of me longed for the normalcy of Belmont, wishing these troubles would vanish. Wishing would get me nowhere. I got even more pissed, knowing that a major drug operation had run completely under our radar. A shooter was blowing away people I had sworn to protect, seemingly with impunity. What the hell were we doing here at the sheriff's department, ineptly patrolling the county while real crimes went on? How could we be so blind?

Maybe we weren't.

That thought shot in from the back of my head and hit my frontal lobe like a line-drive baseball. Maybe we weren't so blind at all, maybe it was just me. Reality started to unhinge again like two tectonic plates sliding away from each other. This time, though, a little fresh air wasn't going to steady me. Jesus Christ, what was I saying? That the sheriff was in on this? That he covered for the drug ring, or even the snipers? My trust in the sheriff, Marty, and Jerry was absolute, like the rising sun and the flowing river. Now, in a moment, my world shifted and skewed as my mind traveled down the serpentine path of speculation and suspicion of my own colleagues, the people I trusted with my life, for whom I would risk my own. I was trained to believe in the team, to create a bond of implicit trust that would overcome lean odds and certain death.

All along, I'd made the assertion that no one could keep secrets in this small town, that the sniper was a local who

knew everything about us and everyone else in town. Our
quaint, small-town routines and naive complacency were
our weaknesses, allowing the shooter to plan his attacks
with precision and confidence. This small-town character,
however, should have worked both ways. No sheriff worth
his badge would miss a drug operation in a town this small,
especially if the mayor was part of it, for God's sake. Sheriff Dale was not incompetent. On the contrary, I'd probably
underestimated him.

I pushed off the wall of the municipal building and
strode quickly down Main Street, as if I were trying to
shove these thoughts away and leave them behind. How
far did I expect this conspiracy to go, to Marty Three
Stones and Jerry Pitcher? Jerry had a hole in his leg. If he
were part of a conspiracy, he was made of sterner stuff
than most of the Army paratroopers I fought with in
Afghanistan. What about Marty? How much did I really
know about her? In the last few days, I'd spent more official time with her than the last three years. She'd surprised me daily, with her performance at the
counter-sniper operation at the parade and handling the
goons at the San Juan Tavern. There was more to Marty
than I ever expected, but that could just be scratching the
surface. I thought about the rifle in her truck—a .270 with
a scope, just like the murder weapon. I wondered how
good she was with it.

These were dark suspicions of my own people. I looked
up from my stalk down Main Street, not knowing whom
I'd passed or how far I'd come. The small Vietnam Veteran's Memorial stood quietly in the placid garden of the
park to my right. I turned and gazed at the bronze monu-
ment, a dead soldier's marker: M16 rifle with a fixed bayo-
net, stuck in the earth, steel pot balanced on the stock, and
worn-out jungle boots on the ground, the long march finally over. I read the names of the young men of Belmont

who had died, wondering if they ever lost the trust in their buddies. Probably not.

What if the killings stopped? I believed they would stop, now that almost everyone involved was dead. That would certainly vindicate the sheriff's position and make me look like a fool. If the sniper were still alive, however, I was the only threat to his existence. The sheriff and Marty would close their cases, and Jerry would continue being Jerry. Regardless of who the sniper was, I was the only person in town who believed he was still breathing. I was the only loose end. I suddenly felt very much alone and tried hard not to look over my shoulder at the ridge behind me.

Now I was paranoid. How many more schemes was I going to dream up? There was only one way to find out if the sniper was blown up or not—make myself a target. I knew the whole mess started with Gayle Whippany, the reporter from the *Rocky Mountain News*. She was the catalyst. She stumbled upon something up in the mountains, and this discovery got her killed. Her demise was hidden somewhere in the map on the wall of the station. I went back to find it.

I stopped at the station door with my hand on the knob. The sheriff wouldn't look too kindly at me poring over the big map, looking for Gayle Whippany's last stand. I had my own maps, and they were better than the one in the station anyway. I could replot them on my kitchen table. The sheriff still had one copy of the coordinates with him, and I wasn't about to ask him for it, but where did I put the second copy? My mind picked through the tangled mess of the last two days. Getting blown up has a tendency to scramble your memory, but I soon remembered—desk drawer.

Feeling like an intruder in my own house, I quietly went inside the station and moved over to my desk. I could hear the sheriff talking loudly on the phone through his closed office door. Good for me. I found the copy of the coordinates, tucked them in my pocket, and turned to leave when the phone rang. I snatched it up reflexively.

"Mineral County Sheriff," I said.

"Yes, this is Agent Gallagher, SAIC of the DEA Field Division in Denver. May I speak with Sheriff Boggett?"

"He's in a meeting right now, Agent," I said, not quite whispering, "This is Deputy Tatum, can I help you?" What the heck was this about?

"Okay, Deputy, maybe you can help me. You probably know about the two agents we have working out there. It seems that we've lost contact. They haven't sent in a report in three days. Cell phones don't work at all, I hear. I was wondering if you could put me in touch with them."

I thought quickly, putting two and two together.

"Male and female, blond, posing as a couple from out-of-town?" I guessed.

"That's them. So you've seen them?"

"I think they're dead, Agent Gallagher."

Silence from the other end of the line.

"Hello? Are you still there?" I asked.

"What did you say?" came the response.

"I said, I think they're dead. We found two people matching that description early yesterday morning just outside of town, dead from gunshot wounds to the head."

"Jesus Christ, why didn't you tell us sooner? My agents have been working with your department for two weeks, and you wait for over twenty-four hours to tell us that they're dead! What kind of fucking podunk redneck operation do you run out there, Deputy? I'll have a team of agents in town by nightfall, and I'll be with them. You dickheads better have some answers for me when I get there." He hung up on me.

I set the phone down, stunned. The sheriff and Marty were keeping things from me. I was getting paranoid again.

If these agents were undercover, maybe the sheriff just limited their exposure. That made sense. I didn't need to know. It wasn't relevant to my sniper case.

I was just fooling myself. Of course it was relevant. The sheriff had plenty of opportunity to tell me yesterday morning when we found the agents' bodies at the rifle range, but he chose not to. I needed to get out of the station. I left the sheriff and Marty a note about the call from Agent Gallagher.

I bumped into Dr. Ed in the back parking lot, getting out of his green Ford station wagon. He had on his fishing hat—a brown fedora. From his step and whistle, he had a good morning casting flies and releasing trout. He patted Pancho's neck.

"Your mode of transportation is appealing, Deputy Tatum, but I prefer the old Bradymobile."

"How'd you do, Dr. Ed?"

"Same as always—came back empty-handed," he said, smiling.

"Hey, Dr. Ed, who does water testing around here?"

"That would be the Water Quality Officer."

"And who's that?"

"Yours truly," he said. "I hold many positions in the municipal government."

"Really?" I thought about Pratt's chlorine dumping last night. "What in the drinking water would scare the dickens out of a town councilman?"

"Fecal coliform bacteria," said Dr. Ed, without hesitation. He froze, making the connection. "You think that's what's causing the fish kills in the river and making the algae bloom?"

"I think it may be more than that, Dr. Ed." I told him the whole story about my escape and evasion the night before.

"Well, it would seem that I need to get my testing kit

and pay a visit to Elk Hollow, and maybe some of Pratt's other developments"

"Won't the chlorine destroy the evidence?"

"Maybe, but if Councilman Pitcher was worried about a panic, we might have a groundwater problem. If we have traces of fecal coliform in the groundwater or water supply, the bacteria will still be there."

I thought of my own well at the cabin and wondered about buying a filter.

"Do you want me to come along, just in case?" I asked.

"No, Deputy, I can take care of myself."

"I insist, Dr. Ed. Those clowns were deadly serious last night."

"Deputy, there will be many witnesses. It's not like I'm sneaking around in the middle of the night." He winked at me, "Anyway, the Pratt boys know I keep a rifle in the back of the station wagon."

Did everyone in this town have a rifle in their backseat?

"Okay, Dr. Ed, but why don't you take a radio with you, just in case. You can call in the cavalry whenever you need it."

"Quite literally, now that your other Bronco is out of commission. Very well." We parted company. I was worried about him, nosing around near Pratt's developments, testing the water, but I knew he could take care of himself.

Pancho and I were back at my cabin within the hour. I thoroughly enjoyed riding back and forth from town, rather than in the Bronco. I don't know why I hadn't thought of it sooner. He seemed to enjoy it, too. Beats walking around the corral all day. The valley seemed wider and the mountains loftier from the back of a horse. My sense of reality stopped shifting and set in its rightful place, but I was still troubled by the secrets in my own department. Why did the sheriff keep the information from me about the DEA agents? He had his reasons. It wasn't my place to question them.

I spread out the map on the kitchen table. It was a very new 1/50,000-scale topographical of the county, the same map I used to plan our failed counter-sniper operation for the parade two days before. I taped down the corners, erased the arrows and lines from the old plan, and started plotting, this time marking the map with my own fine-tip map pens rather than pins, numbering each in sequence. It didn't take me long using the Military Grid References that Pete printed for me. I was done in under an hour, plotting back two weeks before the reporter's death to the point where I found her jeep parked by the grocery store. I stood back and surveyed my work, shocked by what I saw.

Twenty-four

MY OWN PLOTS LOOKED NOTHING LIKE THE sheriff's on the wall of the station, especially around the time Whippany was last seen. No wonder nothing jumped out at me when I first looked at the sheriff's plots. Most of his were wrong. Had the sheriff misplotted to lead me astray, or was his use of longitude and latitude just rusty? He wasn't big on GPS, like computers. He got around just fine with a map and compass, and he knew the roads in the county like his own office, so why did he need to understand map coordinates or use a GPS system? Either way, my new plots told a story.

The mayor had lied to me. This didn't surprise me, but all along, I believed his story about leaving Whippany up on the Equity Mine Trailhead. Now, looking at the undeniable truth of the map grid, she was never near the place. I wouldn't have to go up and interview a bunch of tired Boy Scouts tomorrow. The plots matched some of the locations in her photos—North Clear Creek Falls, Bristol Head, the Reservoir, but the areas she visited in the days close to her death were missing from both her journal and the camera. They were revealed to me now.

She parked her vehicle on the afternoon of her murder, 30 June, at the trailhead of Shallow Creek, less than a mile from Dana Pratt's ranch. It remained there until well after dark. Someone then drove her jeep to the top of Deep Creek Trail in the middle of the night, then left it in town where I found it, four days later. There were two abandoned mines within easy walking distance of the Shallow Creek trailhead. I could be there in less than two hours, but first, I had to go back into town to see Denver Petry and pick up Ralph. I still had time; it wasn't quite noon.

I loaded a few items: Ruger Number One rifle with plenty of bullets, binoculars, Camelback, extra batteries for the radio, and a little chow. My desert BDUs were still in the pack, so I left them. The soldier in me always packed heavier than necessary. I strapped it to the back of the saddle. Pancho could handle it.

Denver Petry lived in a little shack on the west side of town. The block he lived in wasn't quite as nice as the trailer park next to the softball field. His wheelchair ramp leading to the front door had seen better days, leaning a bit to one side. I stepped around it and pounded on the screen door, noticing the bright orange "Beware of Dog" sign stapled to the frame. The inner door was open, but little sunlight penetrated the gloom within.

"Denver! Denver Petry! It's Deputy Tatum! Hello?"

"It's open!" came a voice from the interior. I couldn't quite tell from where. I opened the door on creaking hinges, and it banged shut behind me. I squinted into the dimly lit front room, and found Denver in the corner, but I saw the double barrels of his shotgun first, then heard the low growl.

"Now, hey, easy there, Denver, I'm just here to talk," I said, raising my hands slowly.

He put the shotgun down. "Just wanted to make sure it was you, Deputy Bill. It's okay, Larry." He wheeled over, coming into the faint light of the entryway, but Larry beat him to me. Before I knew it, two big paws landed on my chest, nearly toppling me over. Larry's hot tongue covered my face in a few wet licks. Larry was Denver's service dog, a big golden retriever with a massive head and gentle disposition, unless Denver said otherwise. I scratched both his ears then shoved him down playfully. He went over to Denver and sat next to his wheelchair.

Denver Petry was all chest and arms, his legs having withered away years ago, after the Marines let him go. He didn't look much like a marine: balding, spectacled, a little puny, pale from limited trips to the outside world, but he was Semper Fi, all the way, decorated for his sacrifice on a little island in the Caribbean called Grenada.

He wheeled away from me toward the back of the house; Larry led and I followed. We went through the swinging door, and I was blinded by the bright shop lights. Most of his kitchen was his workshop, low benches and no chairs. The windows were blacked out, and the room was spotless. He obviously spent most of his time here. Bullet presses, tumblers, shotgun reloaders, and powder measures covered the benches. Boxes of gunpowder, brass, primers, and shotgun shells were stacked neatly on two walls up to my chest, just high enough for Denver to reach up and pull them down.

"What can I do you for, Deputy?" he asked, then squinted at me. "You're sure you're not here to arrest me? I haven't done anything illegal in twenty years, except maybe a little tax evasion. Goddamn federal government doesn't deserve a penny. The only reason I let you in is 'cause your local. Local law enforcement, local government, local militia, that's all the authority I recognize, next to Jesus Christ our savior." He crossed his arms. I waited a couple moments, ensuring he was done.

"Do you recognize this work, Denver?" I got right to the point, handing him the shell casing I found in Deep Creek Valley on the first day of the case, a million years ago.

He took the shiny brass shell from me and looked at it for a full minute, turning it in his hands, checking the primer. Then he grabbed a jeweler's loupe from a little shelf, screwed it into his left eye, and did another inspection.

"This is my work," he said simply, setting the shell on the workbench.

"Are you sure?" I asked.

"No question."

"Do remember who you made it for?"

"Whom I made it for, Deputy Bill," he corrected me, "and yes, I do remember."

I was hit by a lightning bolt of adrenaline. "Can you tell me?"

"Well, I load two-seventy bullets for the members of the Halfmoon Gun Club, as you already know, but none of them are shooting their two-seventies this year, except one."

The guy was killing me. "And who is that?"

"Thomas Pitcher."

"Councilman Pitcher? Acting Mayor Thomas Pitcher?"

"The very same. He likes his two-seventy, brushed steel, fiber stock. Likes to shoot it real far too. He's not much into sneaking up on his deer. If he can see them, he wants to shoot them, so I load him up with some real nice maximum loads. The kind you can reach out to six hundred yards and drop a big, dumb mulie before he even hears the shot."

I couldn't believe what I was hearing. I could now tie Thomas Pitcher to the shootings at Deep Creek, where

Jerry . . . where his own son was shot. This brick wall ended my internal reverie. Could Thomas Pitcher have shot his own son? Was he that cold and ruthless? I didn't really know the man. The other killings were just as ruthless, but those victims were dead. Jerry was the only target to survive. Maybe Pitcher just couldn't bear to kill his own son, just wound him enough to hobble the sheriff department. What a bastard. I was going to pay the man a visit.

Getting Denver to promise his silence was like getting a nun to pray the rosary, which was not very hard at all. I didn't want to play Wyatt Earp today, so I left Pancho in Denver's tiny back yard, happily munching the unmown grass within a chain-link fence. I set off for Pitcher's house on foot. It was only a few blocks away on the "other" side of town. A stiff New Mexican wind blew up the canyon from the south, making dust devils in the dirt lot behind the grocery store.

I banged on the door of the senior councilman and acting mayor. He and his wife, Judy, lived in a neat yellow ranch next to the episcopal church, where he was a senior warden. Standing on the front stoop, you almost forgot you were in the mountains: manicured lawn, white iron fence, and white shutters.

I heard the door unlatch and open, and I turned to see Jerry Pitcher, my counterpart, in more ways than one. He wore a white T-shirt and baggy cutoff shorts and leaned on two crutches. His hair was a mess—he must've been resting up for his night shift. He stood there, blinking at me.

"Jerry, buddy, sorry to wake you. Is your dad home?" I fumbled. I forgot Jerry and his young wife, Julie, still lived with his parents.

"Bill . . . no he's not," he said, waking up. "What do you want Dad for?"

"I need to talk to him, Jerry. Can I come in?"

"Sure." He held open the screen door as best he could with a crutch in his hand.

"I got it, Jerry." I said. "Let's go in the kitchen and sit down."

"I'll put on some coffee, or do you want a Coke?" He was the eager host. It made me uncomfortable.

"Jerry, it's me, Bill. Just sit down, and I'll get it."

He plopped into a chair at the kitchen table and lifted his leg up on another, dropping the crutches beneath him. His left thigh was wrapped in a thick, white bandage. I grabbed a couple of cans of Coke out of the fridge, put one in front of him, and sat down.

I came right out with it. "Denver Petry says he loaded the rifle shell I found up on the ridge in Deep Creek Thursday," I said. "He says he loaded it for your father."

"What does that mean, Bill?" he asked.

"It means that you were shot with one of your father's bullets, Jerry."

He looked down at the can of soda on the table, then up at me, then back to the table, his night-shift mind trying to make sense of what I was saying.

"Are you saying my dad shot me, Bill? Are you saying my dad is the sniper?" He shook his head. "Pete and Zooey were the snipers, I thought. They blew up yesterday when you were there. I thought this was all over."

"I never said your father pulled the trigger, Jerry," I said. "On the contrary, I don't think he did." I said this as much to myself as to Jerry, still thinking this through. "His rifle is in the evidence locker at the station. I put it there on Saturday, but the sniper kept killing."

"So, why are you here, Bill? You said you wanted to talk to my father, but you're talking to me," he asked.

"I need to know how your father's bullets got into the sniper's rifle," I said.

Jerry absorbed this, then looked out the window. I couldn't tell if he was thinking of an answer or just spacing off. I waited.

"I might know how, Bill," he said finally, "I think I know."

"Okay . . . "

"I'm making a run for the gun club this year," he began.

"The Halfmoon Gun Club?" I asked.

"Yes. Dad's been a member forever, but I never took an interest. This year, I want in. I convinced Orville's game manager, Darren Schmidt, to take me out on the ranch and teach me the habits of deer and elk."

"On a horse?" I asked.

"Believe it or not, on a horse. Bucko and I came to an understanding." He smiled. "I'm okay in the woods and a fair rider, but I can't shoot worth a damn. Not even with a scope."

I jumped to a conclusion, wishing I was wrong. "So, you asked Orville to help with your shooting?"

"No, he said I'd have to learn to shoot on my own, or ask my dad," said Jerry, "I didn't even bother with Dad, so I went to someone else."

"Who?"

"Marty Three Stones."

"Marty? Why Marty?" I asked.

"You don't know it, but she's an amazing shot. She can drill dime-sized groups at three hundred yards with a stiff crosswind from a standing position. Says her grandfather taught her at the Ute Mountain Reservation."

"When did you shoot?"

"She and I went to the rifle range at the end of her shift, just after sunrise. We'd spend an hour or so shooting, two or three times a week."

"And you used your dad's two-seventy?"

"Hell, no. I don't even have the key to Dad's locker at the club. He'd never let me use it, anyway. I have my own, a Ruger M77," he said.

"But you used your dad's reloads that Denver Petry made for him?" I asked.

"Yup. Denver usually makes about ten times as many bullets as any of the club members need. I just pick them up at his house and only give Dad half of the boxes, keeping the rest for practice. He never pays much attention."

"Do you have any of the reloads here?"

"Sure. They're in the cabinet behind you. Bottom left drawer."

I opened the drawer of Mrs. Pitcher's china cabinet and saw a neat column of identical bullet boxes, each with twenty rounds apiece. I counted five boxes and pulled one out.

"That's only half of the reloads Denver made for my father," said Jerry. "The rest I gave to Dad. I imagine they're up in his locker at the ranch."

I opened the box; ten rounds were gone. I picked up the next one, again, ten rounds missing. The next one was full. The last two were empty.

"Did you fire sixty rounds?" I asked.

"Sixty? That's a lot of shooting." He stopped to think. "I don't know, maybe. That's a new batch of ammo. Denver loaded it for Dad two weeks ago, the week before this all started."

The wind blew strong and unrelenting against the thin pane of the kitchen window.

"Okay, Jerry. That's all I need. Try to get some sleep before your shift."

"What's going on, Bill? Are you still investigating the sniper case?"

"Maybe," I said. "It's supposed to be my last day on the case, though, so I'm just wrapping things up for the sheriff." I wanted to keep our conversation as casual as I could, but inside I was churning, needing to get out of town. I left Jerry with his leg propped up on the chair, staring at his Coke.

I walked the few blocks over to Ralph's shop, straight into the dry gusts from the valley. I found the dentist-turned-geologist in the front area. He had traded his running shoes for dusty hiking boots and was fiddling with an old Boy Scout pack. He still had on his thick glasses with the strap around his head.

"You ready to go?" he asked when I walked in. "I figured you'd be back soon, so I got my field gear together."

"Tell me about the mines up on Shallow Creek," I said. Ralph knew the history of every mine in the valley.

"There are two of them, one on the north side and one on the south, a few miles up from the trailhead. Morten & Sons held the claims from 1890 to 1895. They never did very well, so old Morten never improved them beyond the basic hole in the mountain with a few supporting timbers at the entrance. Are we heading up there?"

"I don't think it's such a good idea, Ralph."

"What do you mean?"

"Well, if I'm right, and the sniper is still out there, we'll make great targets. You don't need to risk your life."

"Bill, I'll take that chance. Who's going to collect and test the samples, you?" he asked, shouldering the pack. "Besides, I sat on a wheeled stool saying 'rinse and spit' for most of my adult life. Being bitten was my greatest threat. I can use a little excitement."

"I can't let you go, Ralph. I won't have your blood on my hands."

"Come off it, Deputy Tatum. Don't be so dramatic," he said, walking past me toward the door. "I'm going out there to collect samples, with or without you. You might as well come along and cover my butt."

He walked to his mountain bike, which was leaning up against the front porch. Ralph was very tall, and his bike matched his proportions. My feet wouldn't even touch the ground if I sat on it.

"I might as well ride, since you are, too," he said, straddling the bike, "Where's Pancho?"

"He's over at Denver Petry's," I said.

"Well, hop to it, Deputy. Go get him and let's roll." He pushed off. I shrugged and followed him.

We took Highway 149, the "Silver Thread," which ran west out of town then generally north all the way across the Continental Divide, through Lake City, and up to US 50 near Gunnison. As we rounded the corner near Fossil Hill, the whole Rio Grande Valley opened up to the west, Bristol Head and Seven Parks flanking the flat valley with the shining river running down the middle. The wind was a dry torrent, and I had to screw down my Resistol to keep it from blowing off. I glanced back at Ralph. He was pedaling away, drafting behind Pancho's generous hindquarters.

We passed the blackened remains of Pete and Zooey's garage. The volunteer firemen soaked everything down, so no more smoke rose from the hole that was once Zooey's repair shop. The wind blew away most of the burned rubber smell, but a residual odor reached my nostrils. I turned away from the charred ruins, faced the wind, and took a deep breath of high mountain air. Then we turned the corner and headed north toward Shallow Creek.

At the main gate of the Shallow Creek Ranch, I pulled out my binoculars and saw no activity down in the complex, but all six black trucks crouched in the lot next to the creek. Dana was having a huddle. I hoped we would have no trouble from him this afternoon. His property technically extended up Shallow Creek, including the trailhead. Years back, he swapped a chunk of land high in the mountains with the National Forest Service for the rights to

Shallow Creek, but part of the deal was that he would keep the trail open to the public. We would soon see how territorial the man was.

The dirt road leading to the trailhead had little traffic, so Ralph pedaled next to me. The mountains surrounded us on three sides, silencing the wind's roar, yet we kept our own silence, allowing the quiet to wash over us like a warm sunrise. A few cabins were tucked in on the north side of the little valley, toward the confluence of Rat Creek and Miner's Creek, Shallow Creek's older sisters. We took the left fork in the road toward the trailhead, keeping a watchful eye on the ranch to the south. Still no sign of Dana or his boys. As we approached the trailhead, we entered the deep draw of Shallow Creek, and the silence grew louder in our ears.

The trail up Shallow Creek started in the small grove of blue spruce where Gayle Whippany last parked her jeep, then entered a meadow of tall grass and river willows. A male willow flycatcher, pretending to ignore us, flitted and swooped in the thick, shrublike trees as we worked our way up the trail next to the creek. We barely heard the soft rush of the stream as we passed. I led the way, and Ralph spun in an easy gear behind me. The high sun baked us, taking its only opportunity to cast its summer heat down into the narrow valley. Soon the high ridge on the west side would block the sun and hide the draw in shadow. No aspen, only ponderosa pine crowded the steep western ridge in almost unnatural order, but the east ridge was rocky and barren with sharp outcroppings of crumbling granite and loose scree.

The trail left the quiet meadow and led us to a choke point through a narrow scree field. I had to watch Pancho's step for sunning rattlesnakes or wobbly rocks in the path. A little pica jumped up ahead and chattered at us angrily. I was surprised to see him at such a low altitude. A brave lit-

tle creature, he must have been, considering that this valley
was the legendary home of mountain lions.

I wondered if anyone had actually seen a mountain lion
in Shallow Creek. Since my tenure as deputy began three
years ago, our department had no reports of any, nor had I
read any previous reports. No hunter ever took a lion out of
the valley. I guess I couldn't call it an urban legend, but a
Belmont legend, certainly. This got me thinking—maybe
the legend was a convenient way to keep people out of the
canyon. Tourists shied away from the trail because of the
mountain lion stories. What a great place to hide something. What a great plot for a *Scooby Doo* cartoon.

What a great place to ambush a stupid deputy with his
gangly sidekick. I put myself back on alert, expecting a
shot to come at any moment. I didn't tell this to Ralph, but
rested my hand on the stock of my rifle, reassured knowing
it was still there.

We left the scree field and followed the trail as it traced
the creek. The dense willows were all around us. Even on
Pancho, I couldn't see over the top, only helplessly up at
the nearly vertical walls, which were getting closer as the
canyon narrowed.

Pancho abruptly stopped on the trail just as I heard
heavy, rapid footfalls and the crush of many branches in
front of us, like a giant was running through the trees.
Ralph halted a good distance back, in case Pancho bolted.
A bull moose crashed out of the willows and trotted down
the trail, right for us.

Pancho took five quick steps backward, holding his
head high. His eyes were wide with fear at seeing the creature. The moose was nearly as tall as my horse, and his
heavy antlers brushed the willows on either side of the
trail. He saw us with his beady little moose eyes, stopped,
and turned back into the brush, heading for the stream and

the opposite side. We watched him go with great relief. He never looked back.

We continued down the trail and happily climbed out of the low ground near the stream onto a scrubby, flat meadow. Aromatic sage and pin cushion cacti covered the sandy field. Shallow Creek must not share its water with the plants in this part of the valley, hoarding for its favorites down below.

"We're not far, now," said Ralph, speaking for the first time since we left town. "The first mine is just around the bend in the canyon up ahead." I nodded, checking the ridge to our front.

The valley took a sharp bend west-northwest out of the arid meadow and narrowed even further. At this point in the trail, the canyon walls were less than a quarter mile apart at the top of each ridge, an easy shot for anyone who could line up a crosshairs and pull a trigger without jerking. I began to question the wisdom of my endeavor.

The valley felt as dry and hot as a sauna; the super-heated air scorched my nostrils and roasted my lungs. The narrow canyon trapped the heat of the sun within its walls, and the rocks on either side soaked up the heat and reflected it down upon us. It seemed I could flick water on the rocks beside the trail and watch steam rise off them. I realized I hadn't taken a drink of water since leaving Belmont. No wonder it felt so hot. My dry skin didn't have one bead of sweat on it. I looked over my shoulder at Ralph. He already had his Camelback tube in his mouth and was sweating nicely. I took a long pull from my own tube and felt instantly better. The last thing Ralph needed was a dehydrated deputy. A few drinks later, I felt my pores slam open, and sweat started seeping out of them.

Heat exhaustion avoided, I checked my GPS for our location. Ralph knew where we were going, but I'd never been to the mines in Shallow Creek Canyon. We were two hundred meters from the first mine. I looked for it, seeing nothing.

"It's up and to the left, about halfway up the ridge," said Ralph, reading my thoughts. "See that big chunk of black granite overhang? The opening is right below that. When we get a little closer, you'll be able to see the timbers holding up the entrance." Ralph's voice was calm and steady, not even a huff to indicate he was winded at all from the ride up the trail.

I found the overhang, but couldn't see the opening. We picked our way along the rocky trail, devoid of plant life but for a little strip of sparse vegetation on either side of the path. Boulders and craggy embankments lined the canyon walls, with the occasional gnarled juniper growing impossibly out of solid rock.

We stopped just below the mine entrance, which, from the trail, looked like a mere nook in the jagged wall, about fifty feet up from where we stood, one third the distance to the top of the ridge. Piles of green-tinted tailings formed on either side of the mine, reminding me, absurdly, like toothpaste foam on the sides of a mouth. Ralph dismounted, set his bike on the ground just off the path, and, without ceremony or a spoken word, started climbing. He scrambled up the slope on all fours, his sinewy arms knotting and pulling his long body easily upward, like the creature Gollum in Tolkien's classic.

Pancho and I remained in place for a moment. I think we both felt a little exposed, still questioning our venture into a place where death's presence still lingered. I glassed along both ridges, looking for spots I'd set up to fire on a couple of easy targets like us. Seeing no one, I hung the binoculars around my neck and pulled my rifle out of its scabbard attached to the saddle. As I was doing this, the wind changed direction and rolled down the canyon. That's when I noticed the smell.

I jerked back in the saddle, rifle in hand. It was the same ammonia smell from the corroding propane tank that rendered Pete, Zooey, and most of their establishment black and charred. Anhydrous ammonia, Marty called it, a critical ingredient for the cooking of crystal meth. The wind carried it up the canyon during our ascent, away from us, but now the wind had shifted, bringing the telltale scent of drug manufacture down to my now-familiar nose. Pancho noticed it too, turning his head up the canyon, flexing his nostrils, and snorting a little. Such a good horse.

I looked back at Ralph, who was already at the mine entrance, pack laid open on the ground, obliviously taking samples.

"How far is the second mine, Ralph?" I called to him.

He looked up. "You see where the trail forks just up a way? That's the main trail. The south trail only goes about another hundred yards or so. Take the north fork. It'll run almost straight up that little draw on the north side over there. The mine sits right at the westward bend in the trail. It's only about twenty feet up. You can climb it easily." He returned to his work, not waiting for a response.

"I think I'll take a look," I said. "You okay?"

"Sure, fine. I'll be along shortly," he said, focused on the samples he was testing.

"Just holler if you need me," I said, not expecting an answer, but pretty sure he heard me.

I left Pancho untethered near the creek, sipping water and chewing on whatever grass he could find, and walked up the north fork of the trail, rifle in hand. I had my assault pack with me, too. One thing Sergeant Richter taught me as a paratrooper was never separate yourself from your ruck, because then you'd need it. I would be glad to have it later. The path led me up a narrow draw, barely a cut in the ridge, which might hold water during the runoff weeks of the year, but was now dry as the rest of the canyon. Farther

west, upstream, the canyon walls closed around Shallow
Creek, forcing the miners who made the trail to divert it up
the north side and run along a generally flat spot above the
little stream. The sun was unrelenting, finding the small
patch of blue sky over our heads and sending a day's worth
of heat into the canyon, making up for the time it was denied access by the steep walls. I had my Camelback with
me, however, and remembered to drink out of it as well.

Even though closer to the trail and an easier climb, the
other mine eluded me. As the trail turned westward, I left it
and continued climbing up the draw, rifle slung across my
back, thinking the entrance would open right up to me. Even
the ammonia smell increased in intensity. In the end, my
nose led me to the slit in the wall that was the mine entrance.
I passed it at first, climbing around the opening, which didn't
point straight down the draw like the other, but sideways, just
behind a vertical outcropping. I knew I'd missed it when the
ammonia odor diminished, replaced by light sage up the
slope. Retracing my steps, I saw the entrance easily, just a
cleft in the rock facing west, obscured from the approach below. Then I noticed the green tint in the rock on either side of
the mine—traces of tailings, but not the large piles of it like
the sister mine across the canyon. Runoff must have washed
most of the tailings down into the stream, but the residue
was evident in the rock, as was the fresh chunk of cliff missing from the wall outside the entrance.

It was at eye-level, a little crater about the size of a
baseball with an impact mark in the center, a beige pock-
mark in the light green face of the cliff. I stepped onto the
little platform of rock just outside the entrance to inspect
the bullet strike and nearly stepped on the bloodstain,
soaked deep into the pores of the rock. I'd found the spot
where the sniper shot Gayle Whippany.

Twenty-five

TWO MORE POCKMARKS EXPLODED ON THE WALL next to my face, stinging my cheek and eyes with tiny shards of rock, then a thunderous roar from the other side of the canyon. I dove blindly into the dark mine, jarring my wrists as the palms struck the end of the short entrance. Then I rolled to my side, stopping myself from crushing the precious rifle on my back. Three rapid-fire shots followed me into the mine, but could not turn the corner. I was out of reach, for now. Sitting up, I instinctively pulled my service pistol from its holster and aimed it back at the slit of light. I put the gun back and thought of Ralph on the other side of the canyon. If the shooter were firing from the south ridge, Ralph would be out of his direct line of fire, beneath the sniper. I hoped he made it inside his own mine. How long would he last, though? How long would the sniper wait before he came down from his perch and shot us like trapped animals? I wasn't worried about myself, fully armed and ready to put five bullets in anyone who dared poke his head into the opening, but what about Ralph? He had no weapon other than a rock hammer. I thought of my faithful steed, Pancho, hoping he was still alive and bugging out down the trail.

I took an inventory: two extra magazines for the Berretta 9mm, a leather bullet case filled with ten rounds of precision rifle ammo, radio, flashlight, a nearly full Camelback, and, of course, everything in my assault pack. Not bad. I could go for two days without resupply. I even had my hat, still tightly screwed down on my head.

Now that most of the adrenaline was pumped out of my system, I noticed the ammonia smell again, strong and acrid inside the dark place. Knowing that exit from the cave was out of the question for the moment, I stood up, snapped on my flashlight, and followed my nose.

The cave opened into a wide corridor running straight into the mountain. The ceiling was low, but not low enough for me to bump my head. No light turned the corner into the shaft, so my little mag-lite was all I had to illuminate the meth lab. It was enough to display the neat row of propane tanks lining one wall, undoubtedly filled with the anhydrous ammonia necessary for production. The opposite wall held two short folding tables running parallel to the corridor, a workbench with smaller containers of chemicals and bins of finished product. The whole operation looked as though it could be torn down in twenty minutes and packed out on two horses. Circling around, I found the horseboxes stacked in the corner for that exact purpose—easy mobility. Beyond the lab, the shaft narrowed quickly and yielded nothing, so I concluded the operation was limited to the front area of the mine, which was just as well. I wasn't interested in spelunking, anyway.

The ammonia was getting to me, so I returned to the short foyer of the mine shaft where I dove in, Berretta in hand. Fresh air circulated through the opening, and my head cleared, giving me a chance to think about escape. I was limited to the exit in front of me. I had no idea if the shaft that ran deep into the mountain had an alternate portal, and I wasn't about to test the limits of my flashlight batteries to find out. I didn't think my radio would do any good, but I tried anyway. No one responded to my call.

My watch read just after three o'clock—plenty of light remained for the sniper to nail me if I tried to make a fast break out of the cave. Where would I go, anyway? I was below the sniper in a little draw of a larger canyon. She knew I had one way out, and even if I got out, I would either have to climb the ridge or scramble down the slope, all the while avoiding her deadly accuracy with the .270. She had superior position, and I had a long wait until dark. Darkness was my ally, the great equalizer. Unless she had night vision attached to her scope, which I doubted, I had a chance to move out of the line of fire before the moon rose. I didn't think she'd come down and confront me at close range. She didn't need to; she had the advantage, and it wasn't her style anyway.

When did I start referring to the shooter as "she?" The question came clear and unsolicited. Could it be Mandy Lange, or, even worse, Marty Three Stones, up there on the ridge, waiting for me to poke out my head, so she could blow it off? My true self already knew the answer. It could only be Marty Three Stones, my friend, my teammate, waiting in her infinite patience to kill me.

The bullets she took from Jerry Pitcher I found at the scene of the shooting in Deep Creek. She shot him with his own reloads. She was probably using them on me right now with the scoped .270 she carried in her Bronco. How had she pulled off the Deep Creek shooting? She was in the radio room the whole time. Or was she? I recalled an exchange with the sheriff later that same day, when she said she would relay the dispatch radio to Sheriff Dale's handheld. She could have done the same with her own, receiving and sending calls from her radio while up on Deep Creek Ridge, waiting for me to run by. Her job as night dispatch gave her freedom of movement during the day as well as at night. It would only take Sheriff Dale to cover for her. She needed help placing Whippany's body in the creek above my cabin. I always assumed there was a sniper team, not a lone shooter. I just never thought it would be my own people.

Things started falling into place. I recalled snippets of conversation and observations that before meant nothing to my conscious mind, but somehow were stuck in my subconscious. No wonder I hadn't been sleeping well. When I spoke to Dr. Ed after finding the reporter's body on Thursday, he goaded me about coming into work late, being on "banker's hours," he'd said. He reported seeing Marty Three Stones drive through town at nine in the morning, before me. I didn't make the connection until now—Marty should've already been at the station, but she wasn't—she was returning from Deep Creek after shooting Jerry.

On the day of the Ten-Miler, when I got a bad feeling and sent Sheriff Dale up to the turnaround, he said he would get Marty and they would intercept, but Marty was already in position on the ridge, waiting for Mayor Jeff to hit the halfway point at East Willow Creek. It was Marty's long dark hair and drab sheriff's deputy uniform that Ralph saw on the ridge after Mayor Jeff went down. After the assassination, Sheriff Dale made it clear that Marty had already inspected the area for evidence, preventing me from going up there and finding another missing shell.

She chose her next victims—Jacob Stackhouse and the DEA agents posing as a vacationing couple—when they saw her coming up out of the draw after she killed the mayor. Her own report placed her at the scene at least twenty minutes after the shooting. The encounter seemed a coincidence, but she had no choice but to eliminate them.

Marty never set up in the spot I chose for her during the parade. No wonder it was so clean and undisturbed—she never occupied it. After dropping me off, Sheriff Dale must've deposited his sniper in Windy Gulch—exactly the worst place for us to interdict, which I'd so conveniently told them during the mission brief. She shot Jacob Stackhouse off his horse, then put a bullet through her own boony cap, which is why it had powder burns on it. A shot from across the canyon wouldn't have left burns, but one from two feet would. After taking a shot at me and zooming up the mountain on the stolen Kawasaki 250, she dropped the dirt bike in the clearing in the high country above Bulldog Mountain, skirted around to the south end, and waited for me to show up.

But the shooter who fired on me from Windy Gulch had on the same dark clothing as the sniper on the day of the race. During the antisniper operation, Marty wore my desert BDUs, which were light tan and brown. I would've easily identified her. Then I remembered her bulging pack and the military boot print in the sand in the clearing above Bulldog Mountain. After dropping the dirt bike, while I was dicking around on the north side of the clearing, she ducked into the thick trees on the south end and changed out of her uniform back into her BDUs, but she wore the desert boots the whole time, which left the prints I found in the sand at the side of the road. Her uniform was in the pack when she emerged from her position in the woods. Sheriff Dale acted like he was dropping her to overwatch from the south end of the clearing, but she was already there.

The DEA agents must have posed real trouble for the sheriff and Marty. No doubt, they pointed the agents toward the Halfmoon Ranch, chasing after the patsy Jacob

Stackhouse. When they saw Marty at the wrong place after killing the mayor, it would've been simple for Marty or the sheriff to set them up for disposal at the rifle range. Nothing as handy as trust in the law enforcement community to make your sniping easier. It was possible, though, that they were getting too close to the truth about the crystal meth operation in Belmont. Until the killing of the DEA agents, the sniper murders could be seen as vigilantism—a concerned citizen trying to rid the beautiful town of the scourge of drugs. All the victims, except Whippany, were somehow tied to the peddling of crystal meth. No one mourned too loudly at the demise of drug pushers.

Marty made up the story about identifying Mandy and Orville riding on Wason Park with Jacob Stackhouse the day she killed the mayor. It was convenient enough to throw me off the trail for a while, chasing the red herring of the mayor's wife and father-in-law. When their alibis held up to the light, Marty reneged, claiming that her first report was wrong. It didn't really matter at that point. She probably had her scapegoats lined up and ready to exploit—the McClaren brothers.

The final touch to the vigilante angle was the spectacular destruction of Pete and Zooey's lab, along with the brothers themselves. Rigging the unstable propane tank wouldn't have been difficult; it probably would have gone up on its own soon, anyway. The Internet was filled with How-to-Be-an-Anarchist websites featuring detailed instructions on building Radio Shack Specials—triggers, detonators, mercury fuses—all in the name of free speech. The McClarens had no neighbors nearby, minimizing collateral damage. The brothers rarely left their compound, so ensuring both targets were on site would not be a problem. Arriving at the scene, Sheriff Dale or Marty Three Stones placed the sniper rifle, reloading equipment, and the dead reporter's laptop in the vault. The explosion wrapped up the sniper case and the meth case quite nicely, too, ridding the town of both troubles and getting the council off the sheriff's back, allowing him to claim victory over the forces of evil and use it in his fall campaign for mayor.

The laptop in the vault, of course, was the same laptop Sheriff Dale was looking at the night of the storm. Now I knew why I surprised him that night, walking in on him, soaking wet and bleeding from the laceration in my forehead, fresh from my shortcut down the mountain after someone shot my tire. He didn't expect me to come off the mountain alive, or at least capable of continuing the investigation—just like they hamstrung Jerry.

The timing of the explosion with my arrival, therefore, was too much of a coincidence to be an accident. Both Marty and the sheriff asked me specifically if and when I was going to get my tire fixed. They seemed very concerned about such a simple errand. Now I knew why. They wanted to know when to set off their device at Pete and Zooey's.

All this meant nothing, however, if I couldn't get out of the mine. Maybe Marty was gone. Doubtful. If she were still up on the ridge, she would have her radio, and she could hear me.

"Marty, it's Tatum. I know it's you up there shooting at me. I know everything, now. Let's talk about this, huh?"

No response from the radio.

"Marty, this is Tatum. Are you out there?"

Nothing.

"Come on, Marty, let's end this now. You and the sheriff have killed a lot of folks, but most of them probably deserved it. I know how frustrated you are, the sheriff too. You guys were just trying to do what you thought was right, I can understand that."

I didn't believe a word of what I was saying, and she probably didn't either. I wasn't much of a negotiator, especially when I was the hostage.

"Okay, Marty, I'm going to poke my head out, please don't shoot it off. I just want to talk."

Now, I might be slow, but I wasn't stupid. I took off my hat and pushed it outside the mine entrance with my rifle. It was greeted by three rapid-fire shots from the ridge. I yanked it back before Marty put a hole in it. Okay, negotiations had failed.

I needed a plan, but I also needed a ghillie suit. A ghillie suit is a sniper's coverall, usually made of strips of cloth and other materials that hang off the suit and break up the human silhouette. No sniper left home without one, except me. I went back to the lab to make one.

I wanted to save my flash, so I first searched for an alternate light source and found it—a lantern, not kerosene, luckily, but battery-powered. I switched it on, illuminating the compact lab. I quickly stripped off my deputy uniform and changed into my BDUs. This change was probably the scariest minute of my life. I would die of embarrassment if Marty came in and caught me with my pants around my ankles.

I took out my knife and cut the uniform into strips, six to twelve inches long. It wasn't enough to cover me, so I scrounged around the lab. My luck continued when I discovered a supply of rock salt, neatly stacked in burlap sacks. Burlap—the material of choice for any sniper. I dumped out the salt and tore into the burlap sacks. In fifteen minutes, I had all the material I needed for a good ghillie.

The burlap material was loosely constructed, allowing me to pull out long strands of the course fiber. Using the strands as thread, I poked holes in the strips and roughly sewed them into my BDUs, first my shirt, then my pants, scattering the dark brown of the deputy shirt with the light tan of the burlap and trousers. I wrapped my rifle using the same technique, leaving free the trigger guard and scope.

Last came my boony hat, rolled neatly in the bottom of the pack. I piled it high with thin strips that hung down in front of my face and around my neck, merging the head-shape with the bulk of the suit. Up close, I would look like a pile of brush. From a distance, I would disappear completely.

I lost track of time during the construction of my suit, and when I looked up toward the entrance, no outside light entered the mine. I checked my watch. It was well after sundown. Time to move, slowly.

My plan was dangerous, but simple. I would crawl right through the opening, directly in Marty's line of fire, work my way up the ridge, and wait for daylight. When the sun came up, if she were still in position, I would identify and kill her. I was tired of being a somewhat incompetent deputy. I was an Army sniper again, and I was better at this than she was.

Twenty-six

THE KEY TO BEING INVISIBLE IS LIMITING MOVE-
ment. The human eye doesn't see things, it notices
changes, alterations in the background. Movement triggers
the eye. Humans are predators, and the slightest movement
on the very edge of peripheral vision will draw the eye's
attention like a shooting star. When hunting from a deer
stand, you look for movement and signs—the shape of an
antler through the trees, the flick of an ear in a nest of
mountain mahogany. If you present small changes in the
background, changes that seem innocuous, the mind will
tell the eye that maybe there is no change—that rock was
there the whole time.

Twilight was the best time to fool the eye. The changes
in light and shadow enhance the confusion in the background. In addition, the handoff from the color-detecting
cones in the center of the eye to the rods responsible for
black and white makes a watcher vulnerable to missing

things. That's what I was betting my life on. I was about to see who was more patient—Marty or me.

I left the lantern on in the lab. This would give Marty the impression that I was still there, comforted by the artificial light. I put on my assault pack under my shirt, which added a nice hump to my altered human form, put on the heavy shirt, and slung my rifle over my back. I stuck the tube from the Camelback in my mouth, not wanting to reach for it later. Sage-colored nomex flight gloves and boony hat completed the transformation, and I was ready to leave.

I eased up to the edge of the entrance, stealing myself for the long move into the field of fire. I got down on my belly and took a series of deep breaths, easing down my heart rate and working the tension out of my muscles. I would have to flow like a seeping spring down the mountain.

I took one last look upward toward the outside. It was gray and dull orange with the fading day. Twilight was in full. I put my face in the dirt, rested my hands under the brim of the cap, and pulled myself an inch through the opening, waiting for the shot.

It never came. I counted five sets of sixty seconds, breathing easily and thinking of nothing but being part of the rocks. I moved another inch, slowly, not jerking, taking a full thirty seconds to drag myself a fraction of the distance I would need to cover, but I had all night. I tried not to calculate the time it would take me at this pace to move out of danger and focused on the next count to five minutes.

In one hour, I moved one foot out of the mine. My head and shoulders were exposed to Marty's deadly accurate fire, but she didn't fire. I would feel very foolish if she were gone or watching me from above the mine entrance. That thought drilled a bolt through my core. Jesus. What if she was up there, letting me think I was safe, like a cat waiting for a mouse to emerge from its hole? Too late now. I was committed.

After two hours, I lost all feeling in my hands and arms, but I could still will them to pull me, inch by inch, down the trail leading to the mine. It was fully dark, and the most dangerous part of the escape was behind me, but I didn't allow myself to relax. The moon would rise soon, and that would present its own problems. Now, with no moon or moon shadow, I took the risk and stretched each move a little farther, counting only two minutes between pulls. In another hour, I was out of the cone of light outside the entrance to the mine. I was completely in shadow on a night lit only by the stars that found their way into the narrow canyon.

I pushed up on hands and toes and crabbed sideways off the trail, taking a full minute. Now, if Marty looked toward the mine, I would be in her lower periphery. The terrain took shape: boulders, sage, and small washes varied the landscape enough for me to further disappear in the folds of the earth. I abandoned my glacial movement for a low-crawl, dragging my body facedown, using one leg and one arm, but making gargantuan progress. Every five drags I stopped and listened to the night. After three hours in the dark, I knew what sounds belonged and which did not. I heard the soft scramble of rodents risking a meal, the patter of Shallow Creek down below, and, every once in a while, a jingle of harness or snort from my only loyal and fully functional partner on the force—Pancho. I prayed that he would still be alive in the morning and that he wouldn't smell his master and walk over to me, looking for a carrot.

An hour of low-crawling felt like a sprint, and I noticed the slope gradually turning upward. I was heading generally east, toward the opposite side of the draw. As dangerous as it was, I intended to climb the rocky wall in the dark. I dared to look up, just a tilt of my head toward my goal, and I saw the white glow of the moon, still behind the ridge, but coming nonetheless. Now, the moonlight was my ally. It would help me find the handholds I needed to scale the cliff. Not a cliff, really, but steep. A misplaced foot or crumbling hold would send me tumbling noisily down and give me away. I had six hours of darkness before nautical twilight. I would be in position in half that time.

I hoped Marty, as good as she was with a rifle, didn't understand the first rule of sniper tactics—relocate. Fire and move, Sergeant Richter taught me; no matter how well concealed you were in the hide, always plan your next move. If Marty understood that rule, I'd be in trouble. I would soon find out.

The waxing moon peaked over the eastern ridge of the canyon when I started my climb. If Marty looked in my direction, her eyes would be drawn to the nearly full satellite, and its light would illuminate the opposite side, not me. That was the theory, at least. I banished fatigue and discomfort, focusing on reaching for the next step, testing it, and easing up the wall. I stopped every few minutes to listen and ease the lactic acid from my forearms, trying to make my legs do the climbing. I glanced upward again, and could see the top of the ridge. Discipline and self-preservation kept me from scrambling up the last few meters. The last thing I wanted was to hoist myself up and give Marty a nice silhouette to shoot at.

Three moves from the top, I heard small animals racing around. One furry creature dropped down over the lip and froze, less than a foot from my nose. I could feel his panic. He smelled my hot breath and kept going, traversing the slope. He wasn't looking for a snack; he was running away from something. Then I heard a larger animal moving right above me, and I began to question my earlier assumption that the Shallow Creek mountain lion was only a Belmont legend.

Pancho must've detected it, too, because I heard him whinny and snort down below.

A low growl completely eliminated the legend status of the lion, and I, too, became the hunted. Jesus. I tried to remember if mountain lions were territorial. Probably. I did what any other self-respecting prey would do—I froze in my tracks and made like a hole in the earth.

The lion was now a dark shape, moving easily with the familiar fluidity I'd seen while watching Roger stalk mice outside Emmett's studio. Roger was the beat-up old alley cat that the sculptor adopted. He had only one eye, half a tail, and most of an ear chewed off by the local dogs, but he was still a predator. I hoped I wouldn't end up like all the mice in the studio, presented to Emmett every morning, slightly chewed and quite dead.

By now, the lion smelled me, my scent wafting out of the canyon. He stopped and debated his next move, deciding if I was worth his precious energy. My heart thumped against the earth, and I wondered if he could feel the vibration. I did my best to seem unthreatening, which wasn't very difficult, clinging to the side of the canyon in the cat's backyard. After a long moment of feline consideration, the big cat moved on, choosing to hunt smaller prey and leave the stupid human to himself.

I watched his ghostly form fade into the night and breathed again. A cool breeze found its way under the cloth strips of my ghillie suit and chilled the cold sweat on my back. I rested my cheek against the rough surface of the cliff and relaxed. After a few minutes, I slowly crawled up the last few meters and slid over the lip of the ridge, staying low and flat.

I looked around the flat step, a lunar landscape in the moonlight. Less than a hundred meters away, the slope rose again, toward McKenzie and Table Mountains at over eleven thousand feet. The ridge ran along a lower spur of these twin peaks, bordered by Shallow and Miner's Creeks farther north. Vegetation was sparse here, like the valley below, limited to clumps of sage and juniper, but enough for me to find a concealed path to a good shooting position down-ridge. I saw a gray hump of rock overlooking the canyon to my right. From there, I could look down into the canyon where the old mines opened up, and I could see the spot on the opposite ridge where I thought Marty would be waiting for me to emerge.

I high-crawled my way toward the perch, using my elbows and legs, a faster method than the low-crawl, but it still kept me close to the ground. I couldn't risk a crouch and run. There was no need to risk the extra movement and catch Marty's eye from across the canyon. I wasn't in a hurry. I crawled slowly and deliberately to each of my stopping points, pausing to listen and watch. My eyes had completely adjusted to the night, and, although the ability to see enhanced my confidence, I felt very exposed, even more than my initial departure from the mine. I made it to my shooting position without incident. My watch read two A.M.

I fought sleep for four hours, which wasn't difficult, considering I had a furry predator nearby and another one just as deadly on the opposite ridge. I didn't want to awaken to an open mouth or gun barrel. At six, the sun broke through the glow of dawn, and the sniper duel began.

I had all the advantages. First, and most important, I had the element of surprise. If Marty saw me moving out of the mine, she would have killed me by now. She would have risked a night shot rather than allow me to get away. Second, I was east of her position. If she looked in my direction, the sun would be in her eyes and her scope would send its telltale glare and give her away. Third, I was in my element. I might not have been the best deputy sheriff, but I was damn good military sniper. In the 82nd Airborne, I'd sat in many a mountain hide site, waiting for the sun to come up and my quarry to reveal himself.

Now that the light was up, I looked at my current hide

and decided I needed a new one. Big rocks are good for hiding behind, but you really can't shoot from them and stay concealed. A thin clump of Bristlecone pine grew defiantly on the north side of the granite outcropping, so I eased off the rock and worked my way into the evergreen, keeping the end of my barrel within its branches. I extended the bipod legs on the rifle, one of them dented, thanks to Marty's bullet, and rested the Ruger on its stock. I got out my binoculars and glassed the opposite ridge, now bright with the yellow-white of the new dawn.

The light penetrated the ponderosas on the western ridge, allowing me to see into the forest and identify likely areas where Marty might be hiding and waiting. I tried to project the source of the shooting from the muzzle blast and the placement of the eight rounds near the mine when she shot at me yesterday, but I was too busy dodging bullets to remember with any clarity. Instead, I pulled out my topographical and did a map reconnaissance. Putting myself behind Marty's scope, I would want a perch within three hundred meters of the opening of the mine, which was a challenge because the mine was in a little draw heading north. She would have to choose a position farther down the slope. In addition, she needed a spot that had easy ingress and egress in case things went badly and she had to bug out. Based on this criteria, I narrowed my area of observation down to a fifty-meter circle on the far ridge. I tucked the map back in my pocket and returned the binoculars to my eyes, focusing on the area I pinpointed on the map, only 250 meters across the canyon.

I glassed the ridge for an hour, methodically inspecting every potential shooting position in my search area, but I didn't see any sign of Marty, not one glint of metal or shift of foot. I knew she was good and finding her wouldn't be easy. I put down the binoculars to ease my eyestrain.

I took a few deep breaths of the frosty morning air. The

sun was barely up long enough to heat the alpine desert
and bring out the daytime fauna. Only the constant patter
of Shallow Creek reached my ears. I just noticed the cold,
along with the various aches and pains from diving into the
mine and crawling like a snake for five hours. Still, I felt
alive, more alive than ever before. I guess escaping death
does that for you.

The bottom of the canyon remained in shadow, but I
could see Ralph's mountain bike lying where he dropped
it, and Pancho had worked his way down the trail to a
wider part of the stream, in the river willows where we saw
the bull moose the day before. I was glad he would be out
of the crossfire. I saw no sign of Ralph, however, which
was good. I was relieved not to see him lying in front of the
south mine with a bullet hole in his temple.

Movement outside the south mine. My heart pounded
my chest, as if reminding me it was there. Jesus Christ, it
was Ralph. It was good to see him alive, but he wouldn't be
for long, if Marty saw him as well.

He carefully picked his way down toward the streambed,
stopping behind the occasional rock or ledge, thinking it
would provide him cover. I knew it wouldn't. Taking my
eyes off Ralph, I used his foolishness to identify Marty, but
I would have to be faster than she. Forsaking the wide-angle
binoculars for speed, I brought up the rifle, clicked off the
safety, and started a slow pan of my search area through the
Leupold scope. I hoped I would see Marty before she got a
chance to put a bullet into Ralph.

My hammering heart counted the seconds, each one
bringing Ralph closer to death. I willed it to slow, restoring
the calm necessary to make the critical shot and save
Ralph's life. I would not fail again.

There she was. A black head bobbed in the green and
gray of the trees and rock on the far side. She was adjusting
her point of aim downward, away from the mine with the

lab and toward the geologist climbing down the mountain. I saw the glint of blued metal in the sunlight as she took aim at my friend. She would never get the chance to fire.

The Ruger .30-06 rocked me back like a living thing, an extension of myself, as I squeezed off the single shot that ended Marty's life. I saw her black head turn red and slump against the gray granite, her rifle clattering down the slope, unfired.

Twenty-seven

KEEPING HER INERT FORM IN MY CROSSHAIRS, I rejected the spent shell from the breach and inserted another, smooth and easy. I narrowed my field of view and zoomed in on Marty. Her ruined head rested against her right shoulder, hand dangling down the slope where she dropped her weapon. If she moved again, I would shoot her again. I was no longer a sheriff's deputy.

"Bill? Is that you?" came Ralph's horse shout from down below. I didn't answer, focused on Marty. I would not give up my position until I was certain of my target's status. Not getting a response, Ralph wisely climbed back up and hid inside the mine.

After a full minute, I chose to relocate. I already had the spot picked out as well as the concealed route to it. I backed out of the Bristlecone and used the granite knob to cover my move to the next position—a clump of sage twenty yards back but to the right, closer to the mines down below.

I set up in the sage, its strong scent assaulting my nostrils, and looked for Marty in the scope, returning it to a wide-angle view. She hadn't moved. Her rifle remained fifty feet down the slope, her own scope broken off one mounting and hung uselessly from the other. It was a Ruger Mini-14—an excellent saddle gun, semiautomatic. Odd. This wasn't the rifle that Marty kept in her Bronco. That one was a bolt-action Sako. This made sense, actually. In the event further testing was done on a larger sample of rifles, she would never use her own to do the killing.

I watched Marty's dead body for half an hour, waiting for the slightest notion of life, which I would end quickly with my next bullet. She didn't move. She was dead. I'd killed one of my own. I thrust that thought deep into the recess of my mind. She would have killed me. I would mourn my dead friend another time.

It was time to move again. I closed the bipod legs on my rifle, slung it across my back, and eased back out of the sage.

The sun was high and happy, and a nice summer wind licked across the top of the ridge, conflicting with my own dark feelings. I drowned them in concentration. What if Sheriff Dale were nearby, waiting for me to emerge? I'd waited long enough. Putting my big rock between me and Marty's lifeless form, I crouched away from the edge then turned south, back down the canyon. I found a little draw that was easy enough for me to climb down without danger of falling, traversed the canyon, using the willow grove for cover, and went up the other side of the ridge, intending to come in behind Marty's firing position.

The opposite ridge was forested and less steep than its rocky partner, and I was level with Marty quickly, about a quarter mile downstream. I stalked my target, stopping

every twenty meters to listen and look, waiting for her partner to ambush me. The ponderosa pines that dominated the
western slope of the canyon denied any other real growth,
and the forest floor was as open as a city park. The trees
kept out the wind as well, and the stillness of the surroundings forced me to slow my approach. Even the birds kept
their mountain calls to themselves, like they were waiting
for something to happen.

After one hundred meters of careful movement, I could
see the rock and tree formation where Marty set up her final sniper perch, another hundred meters through the tall
trees. I squatted down by a huge ponderosa and watched
the spot for activity, first with my naked eye, then aided by
binoculars. No movement. I got up and circled around the
hide site to the north, then stopped again and watched. Still
no movement. I pulled out my service pistol and crept toward the hide.

At first, I could only see her scuffed boots, poking out
from behind the granite outcropping. She was in the prone,
the rest of her body obscured by the rock and ground-level
scrub. She was on a small ledge, the rock formation falling
away a few feet to the forest floor. I eased around the rock,
keeping her inert form at chest height and arm's length.
Then I froze. The dead body was over six feet tall, broad-
shouldered and masculine, the face still hidden by bloody
locks of long black hair. I took off my glove felt for the
carotid artery. Three days' growth of beard scraped my
hand, but no pulse. I lifted the chin, stunned at what I saw.
I'd killed Mack Smith, Dana Pratt's head goon.

I dropped the man's head and staggered back a few
steps. How did this happen? Well, I knew how it happened,
but why was my target Smith and not Marty? I turned and
leaned against the rock, trying to comprehend it all. I'd
been so sure of Marty and the sheriff's conspiracy. All
night long, I'd pictured Marty on the ridge, ready to kill

me. It all fit together, or so I thought. Yet here was Smith, graveyard dead, from my own bullet.

I felt no guilt from the act. He would have killed me without hesitation. Once I got over the shock, I actually felt a little better, knowing I hadn't killed my friend. Still, I had to put the pieces together.

How did Mack Smith fit into all this? What was his interest? That was obvious—he was involved in the pedaling of crystal meth in Mineral County. He must have seen Ralph and I going into Shallow Creek, then followed us along the western ridge on horseback. We would've heard an engine in the silent canyon. When I found his lab in the old mine, he was ready for me, just like he was ready for Gayle Whippany. I'd almost suffered the same fate.

Who was Smith's partner? I guess he could take his pick from the other enforcers on Pratt's staff. They all might be involved, but what about Pratt himself? I doubted the developer needed a small-time crystal meth operation to supplement his obvious wealth, but his boys could use their boss's standing in the community as cover, and Dana's extensive operations throughout the county allowed them to move their product around without generating much suspicion. Obviously no suspicion, because it happened right under my nose.

Nothing else, however, made sense. If Mack and the boys were teamed up with Pete, Zooey, and Stackhouse, why was there a second lab? The McClarens had good cover for their production site. Zooey worked on tires all day, generating odors that could explain away the various fumes created by the cooking of the crystal meth. They had no neighbors nearby to snoop or complain, and their customers didn't seem to mind, either. Why would they risk operating a lab so near a public access trail?

The bigger question was why Mack killed his partners.

They seemed to have a good thing going, why blow it by killing them so publicly? Something was missing.

I don't know how many times Sergeant Richter and I were on an operation, and things didn't work out as expected, or the way our military intelligence shop briefed us. We were usually deep in-country with little support and a long way from extraction, and the target wouldn't appear, or worse, the target would appear with five times the number of armed men as planned. When this happened, we still had our mission and were forced to plan on the fly. At that point, Sergeant Richter always said to question the assumptions, and the solution would present itself.

My assumption in this case was that Mack and the McClarens were working together, but their actions didn't support this speculation. What if they weren't partners, but competitors?

Two operations. A drug war in quiet, alpine Belmont? I guess it was possible. Smith and the boys weren't the type to share and play nice. The crystal meth market in the county couldn't be a big one, certainly not enough to support two suppliers. If Smith and company thought killing off their competition would guarantee a monopoly on the trade, they would do it, without hesitation. They obviously did, executing their own version of cutthroat capitalism.

Two things, however, conflicted with my gut. First was Smith's choice of weapon. The Ruger Mini-14 is not a sniper rifle, unlike its cousin the M14, used by Army snipers until replaced by the Remington model 700 ADL, or M24. Its short barrel and compact design make it an ideal pack rifle, but not a good weapon for killing targets at ranges of four hundred meters or more.

The second conflict was his accuracy from the day before, or lack of it. He fired eight rounds at less than three hundred meters at the mine entrance, but failed to connect on any of them. His previous shooting was deadly accurate, needing only one or two rounds to eliminate his target at much greater range. His rapid firing and poor shooting were inconsistent with his previously displayed skill with a rifle. I had a hunch that maybe Smith wasn't the real sniper, either.

Turns out I was right.

I didn't have time to think more on it, because as I stood there, rifle slung across by back, pistol dangling limply from my hand, completely letting my guard down, I felt a hard slap against the back of my neck. A rifle shot followed, then a burning flash of pain.

I dropped to the ground and crawled quickly away from the kill zone. No shots followed me. The bullet had ripped across the back of my neck, jerking the bushy boony hat askew. I was blinded by the strips hanging down from the brim and the pain-induced dots in front of my eyes. My brain told me the wound was superficial, but that didn't do my heart any good. I did my best to hold down the panic. After crawling ten meters to the nearest tree, I got small, lining up with the probable direction of the shot, across the canyon, about the same place from where I shot Smith. The irony interrupted my thoughts of escape and retaliation.

I decided moving was a bad idea for now. I was still in my ghillie suit, which blended nicely with the surrounding rock and vegetation. I probably looked like nothing at all, until I moved, so I didn't move. Of course, it would be hard to shoot back without moving, especially with my Ruger still strapped on my back. The big ponderosa provided necessary cover for the moment, but it was temporary. The sniper would probably relocate and try to find me. I changed my mind—I needed to move again.

Keeping the tree between me and the opposite ridge, I scooted backward, staying on my belly. This proved difficult, as the terrain was broken and uphill, but I had no choice. I was out in the open, pinned down by a highly skilled marksman. My choices were to stay and hide or escape and evade. The latter was riskier, but the former had only one inevitable conclusion—certain death. I chose the latter. I had to trust my ghillie suit. It had kept me alive so far. The suit obscured my profile enough to keep the shooter from pinpointing my skull, or I would have ended up just like Smith. As I scooted, I pictured the terrain from my earlier map reconnaissance. Sergeant Richter had me study the map of our objective area for at least an hour before a mission, so we would memorize every contour, stream, and fold of the terrain. I had done the same for this mission. An intermittent stream flowed into Shallow Creek not three hundred meters to the west, creating a deep draw that would not only provide defilade from the sniper's scope, it would give me a covered and concealed route to move out of the target area as well. It led to the top of the spur overlooking Shallow Creek.

After crab-crawling an agonizing fifty meters backward up the ridge, I could no longer see the opposite side of the canyon, which meant the sniper probably couldn't see me, either. Time to turn and burn. I pushed myself slowly up into a squat, pivoted ninety degrees to the left, and launched across the slope. I ran for twenty-five meters, waiting for the impact of the sniper's bullet, then flopped down, catching my breath. I didn't wait long, hurling myself up and churning my legs for the next twenty-five meters. Each bound seemed to take minutes, like I was running around a four-hundred-meter track, and I felt exposed and vulnerable. In the past, I'd performed this breakout drill with a partner, the other member of my sniper team, usually Sergeant Richter. As one man bounded away, the other would cover, and the team would peel away from the threat. This one-man break-contact drill was lacking, but I made up for it in speed. The ground fell away on my final bound and I half-stepped, half-slid down to the bottom of the draw. I was out of the line of fire, but I had to keep moving. It was a race for superior position.

As I climbed the steep draw south toward the top of the spur, I tried to predict my opponent's next move. He didn't shoot me, which meant he didn't know where I was, so he would stay on the north ridge, not wanting to risk crossing the canyon in the open. He would reposition and wait for me to make a mistake. I wouldn't. He would assume I'd stay on my side of the canyon. I wouldn't. The initiative was now mine. I wouldn't lose it this time.

He knew there were two of us—Ralph was still trapped in the larger mine. The sniper would remain fixed to his target area, not wanting Ralph to get on his bike and escape back down the trail. If I were the shooter, I'd move up the canyon along the north ridge and set up just above the other mine. From that location, he could keep Ralph pinned down and shoot anyone else coming up the trail. He could also cover his escape route, if necessary, but I didn't think he was looking to escape. He thought he still had the upper hand, and his targets were still breathing. I wanted him to maintain that illusion.

I couldn't get behind him to the west—the terrain upstream was much too extreme and open. He'd pick me off as I climbed the slope. This plan called for a bold flanking maneuver to the east, downstream. There was another feeder stream on the north side of the creek, only five hundred meters from his original perch. It emptied into Shallow Creek at the willow stand where we saw the moose. The draw would lead me to the north spur above the sniper, allowing me to get close enough to engage but out of his line of fire. All together, the maneuver encompassed over two miles of rugged alpine terrain. It would take me at least two hours to cover the distance in stealth and daylight, but I had all day. My only gamble, besides moving around in an area occupied by a sniper, was that my target would bug out, but I didn't think he was going to do that. He wanted me dead. He'd tried three times already and failed, but I had to be sure.

When did the shooter become a "he" again? After I shot Smith, I suppose, blowing away my Marty–Sheriff Dale conspiracy theory. But was that theory truly rendered unfeasible? Not really. Smith might have been the first one on the scene simply because he was closer, living at Pratt's Ranch. When he saw Ralph and I enter Shallow Creek, he could have contacted Marty, who would have instructed him to fix us in position until she arrived with her deadly skills. Of course, knowing Smith, he probably took offense to that and wanted to prove he could shoot just as well as any girl, which got him killed.

Or, the sniper could be another one of Pratt's boys, or Pratt himself, a late arrival to the canyon, there to support Smith in case things went poorly and to preserve their assets hidden in the mine. Either way, I knew how I could keep the other shooter in my target area—I held it in my hand.

The radio. Both organizations, the sheriff's department, and Pratt Development, used the same radio network to communicate. Smith and company probably monitored our frequency to track our movements and stay a few steps ahead. If Marty were the sniper, she'd already used the radio system against me. I was about to do the same, employing a little tactical deception.

I was on top of the south spur above Shallow Creek. The evergreens were tallest here, and I couldn't see down into the canyon, over one thousand meters down the slope. I was in a perfect place to rest after my climb out of the draw. It was also a perfect place for a radio broadcast.

"Marty, this is Tatum, come in," I said in low tones into the handset. I waited for a response I knew I wouldn't receive.

"Marty, if you can hear me, listen closely. I'm pinned down on the south side of Shallow Creek, about two and a half miles from the trailhead, above the two abandoned Morten & Sons mines. The sniper is on the opposite ridge. He already tagged me, so I can't move, over."

I waited another minute or so. "Marty, this is Tatum, over."

That was all the rest I needed, and all the deception necessary for the moment.

I hustled across the saddle on the top of the spur, picking up a faint trail that ran east-southeast toward the Shallow Creek Ranch. This must have been Smith's avenue of approach. I checked my pace a bit, wary of the other goons from below who could have listened to my false report just as easily, coming up out of the valley like the Sioux on the Little Bighorn.

My hyperalert senses noticed the distinct smell of horse drifting across the ridge, and I walked right up on Smith's horse, saddled and tied off to a tree, patiently eating tufts of mountain grass, waiting for a master who wouldn't return. Not missing the opportunity, I spoke quietly to him, jammed my burlap-wrapped rifle in the empty saddle case, and mounted the big black stallion.

After trotting down the trail for a bit, just to let him get used to me, I urged him to the left, into the open forest, traversing the steep slope down into the canyon toward the willow grove. We were over a mile from the sniper and around the southern bend in the stream, well out of range and observation. The stallion had a full night's rest, and he took to the challenge without hesitation, his treelike legs controlling the decent easily. Maybe he liked having a rider who weighed fifty pounds less than his previous owner. Either way, we moved down the slope with alacrity. I held him up at the tree line and dismounted, not wanting to break out into the open like the charge of the Light

Brigade. I whispered my thanks in his ear and gave him a swift slap on his hindquarters, toward his corral at the ranch. He just turned his head and looked at me. I guess he liked it up here. He would find his way home in his own good time.

I got down in the prone at the edge of the tree line and set up my rifle, glad to have it in firing position rather than on my back. I was high enough to see over the willows and into the draw on the other side of the canyon. Through my binoculars, I found my route across the open area, but waited. I wanted to know everything about this hazard before placing one foot into it. I scanned the opposite ridge for movement or presence of human activity. After twenty minutes of careful observation, I shifted my focus toward the downstream approach, listening and looking for someone coming up the trail. Only the occasional flycatcher or cliff swallow caught my eye and danced across my field of view. The morning breeze had left for the day, leaving the early afternoon sun to bake the narrow, arid valley. The quiet hush of Shallow Creek was the only sound that reached my ears. Nature ignored the violent human activity that interrupted its perpetual march toward eternity.

I watched the willows to my direct front for a bit, not looking for signs of men, but for the bull moose from yesterday. Neither of us needed another surprise like that. The stillness of the willow thicket ensured that he'd left the area, but I'd have to be careful.

After thirty minutes, I was convinced the passage before me was safe to traverse, but I wanted one last assurance. I made another plea to Marty on the radio, hoping to draw the sniper's eye to the ridge I'd abandoned hours before. That done, I folded the bipod legs and prepared to move.

Speed was my security. I held my breath and rushed down the slope, across the trail, and into the safety of the willows, crouched low and cradling my rifle, hoping the fall of Shallow Creek would drown out my heavy footfalls. I could afford slower movement within the thick branches. I wound my way through the thicket, working in and out of the dense clumps of river growth, stopping and listening occasionally for voices or a crashing moose. Hearing neither, I intersected the creek, shrouded from all sides by green, and turned west. After only twenty steps, I found the feeder stream, only a trickle of runoff from the slopes to the north. I followed it.

Reaching the edge of the willow grove, I hesitated, getting low and watching the path in front of me. I was about to leave the concealment of the thicket, and the rest of my maneuver would be out in the open, although out of sight from the sniper up the canyon. The runoff stream eroded a deep cut in the canyon on my left, blocking any view of me to the north and west, but my right flank would be exposed to the high ridge of the draw. This would be the riskiest part of the move. There was no vegetation to conceal me from above, only bare rock. I would prefer to make the climb in the dark, like the night before, but I didn't have that luxury today. I glassed along both sides of the draw, seeing nothing, but looking all the same.

Ignoring my screaming instincts to hide until dusk, I moved swiftly and deliberately out in the open, hoping that I hadn't missed another shooter on the ridge above, hoping that the sniper hadn't repositioned to the south, anticipating my flanking maneuver, hoping my radio transmissions kept him locked in place up the canyon. Hope is not a method, but it's all I had. We would soon see who was the better sniper.

The draw closed around me as I entered its embrace, and I felt a little better, but just a little, then it turned slightly west, bending around the narrow spur that formed the ridge. I was forced to use my hands to climb the western slope, and I regretfully returned my rifle to my back as

I scrambled upward. The climb wasn't demanding, just hot, and I reached the top of the ridge unvented by a rifle bullet, catching my breath in the relative safety of a clump of sage. I was now within eight hundred meters of my target and would soon have superior position.

Staying low, I worked my way north and west, keeping the top of the spur between me and the sniper. I moved with the easy pace of knowing he couldn't see me, and if he couldn't see me, he couldn't shoot me. When I thought I was high enough above him, I edged up to the crest and looked down into the canyon. I could see the larger mine on the other side and the narrow gulch that hid the entrance to the lab. The sniper was out of sight, but I would find him soon enough. I studied every inch of rock and vegetation through my scope, but failed to pinpoint his location. I needed to get closer. I was still out of range.

Finding a crease in the ridge, I crawled down the slope for one hundred meters, then stopped, poking my eyes over the lip. I was in position, just over three hundred meters east of the little outcropping where I thought the sniper repositioned, just to the right of the lab. I was still high enough to have the advantage. I set my rifle on the top of the crease, leaving all but my head behind it in a well-covered firing position. Not wanting to take my hands off the rifle, I used the scope to search the area for my target. I was exposed to my six o'clock, which kept me from feeling very comfortable. I didn't have long to take this guy out before his reinforcements came and put a bullet in my back. I widened the view of the Leupold scope, locked it on the spot I knew he'd be, and waited for him to move.

I waited, taking deep breaths, slowing my heart to a level that wouldn't affect the trajectory of the one bullet I had to drive home. The sun warmed the burlap and cloth on my back, soaking it with sweat that didn't evaporate. I took a sip from my Camelback, its tube still fixed in my mouth.

I was about out of water, but dehydration was the least of my worries. At least I wouldn't have to pee.

My heart thumped alive again with a jolt of adrenaline as the stillness of the scene in my scope shifted slightly—a few pebbles tumbled down the slope over the lab. I blinked over my dry eyeballs and looked again. The scene had definitely changed. There was a new, green patch standing out in the gray and brown terrain where no vegetation was before. I zoomed in on the green patch and saw a black zipper tab—like the tabs on my own assault pack. I was looking at the twin of the pack on my back, the one I gave Marty before the parade.

I stared at the pack, blinking, letting my brain fill in the details, and Marty's prone form materialized in my scope. I could see the shoulder and arm of my desert BDUs, then a gloved hand on the stock of her rifle. She was lying motionless, quartering slightly toward me, rifle pointed to my left, to the other side of the canyon, where she'd shot at me two hours earlier. She was in a depression in the slope, a natural foxhole that kept most of her body out of sight, except from above, from me. I had her.

I placed the crosshairs on her ear, partially covered by my own desert boony cap. At least she used the gear I lent her. Then I reached for my radio with my left hand.

"Marty, this is Tatum. I have you in my scope. Remove your hands from the rifle, stand up, and take ten steps back, keeping your hands where I can see them."

My transmission jerked her whole body. Her head twisted left and right, looking for me, then behind her. She never looked up, and she never took her hands off her rifle.

"Marty, this is Tatum," I repeated. "Leave your rifle on the ground, stand up, and back away."

Her left hand disappeared for a moment, then I heard a squelch from the speaker on my radio.

"Bullshit, Tatum, you're pinned down. I see you over there. Move once, and you're dead."

It was Marty's voice, but it wasn't the Marty I knew. It was Marty the sniper, the enforcer for a crystal meth operation that she'd killed to protect. How did she keep this side from me?

"Marty, this is Tatum. Step away from the rifle, or I will be forced to shoot."

Silence. She didn't move this time. I could feel the conflict and confusion down below.

Thirty seconds later, she came back.

"Hey, Tatum, take a look down in the canyon. See your buddy down there?"

I didn't want to, but I couldn't stop myself before glancing over at the larger mine. Ralph was standing at the entrance, looking around nervously at the ridge both shooters occupied, not seeing either of us.

"I know you see him. Want to see him die?" The transmission of radio waves failed to filter out her inhuman cruelty.

"Marty, let's end this here. Let there be no more killing."

"Why, Bill, what have I got to lose? It's not the first time, and it won't be the last."

"Yes it will, Marty. You'll be dead before you hear me fire."

"Take your best shot, Deputy Bill."

I did. She was dead before she even thought about pulling the trigger on Ralph.

I kept her still form in my scope, waiting for the slightest motion as I chambered another round. None came. She was dead.

I stood up and worked my way around the ridge, staying above her body and keeping an eye on my six. When I was directly above her, I descended to her level. I kicked the rifle away. It rattled down the slope and came to rest in front of the lab. I removed the bloody boony hat. Now it had two holes in it. Her mangled skull flopped to the side, and her open, lifeless eyes gazed up at me, but I felt no guilt, looking at my partner who betrayed me, who betrayed the whole town. She would've killed me, killed Ralph, killed anyone else who got in her way. I was glad she was dead. I did my job.

I lifted her onto my shoulder and carried her down to the creek, grabbing her rifle on the way and calling for Ralph. He poked his head out of the mine and joined me at his bike. Neither of us said a word.

I whistled for Pancho, hoping my trusty mount would still be nearby. He was. He came trotting up the trail out of the willows, happy to see me. He wasn't happy about having a dead body strapped to his saddle. I would have to go back up the spur and get Smith later.

Ralph and I rode back down the trail. I asked him if he was okay. He was, just a little sore from sleeping in the mine all night. He finally asked what happened, and I explained it all to him, every detail, barely having sorted it out in my head. This would help me write the report when I got back to the station.

Marty's Bronco was parked at the trailhead in the grove of tall blue spruce. I stopped and thought about what to do with it: leave it, or drive it back.

As I sat on my horse, assuming all was well, Sheriff Dale stepped out from behind the truck with a rifle at his hip, pointed straight at me.

"Hello, Deputy Bill," he said, smirking. "I see you've killed my trusted deputy, Marty Three Stones. I always knew you were the sniper. I never figured you to cover for a drug ring, but I guess you never know people."

"Now, Sheriff, take it easy, you've got it all wrong," I stammered, unprepared for this new ambush.

"Get down off the horse and put your hands where I can see them," he said, but I knew he wasn't going to arrest me. This charade was to confuse Ralph. He was going to kill me—Ralph, too. I put my hands on my head, but stayed on the horse, close to my rifle. Ralph just stood there, straddling his bike, jaw open, staring at the sheriff, then back at me.

"Sheriff Dale, Marty shot me. The blood is dried on the back of my neck. I can show you. She was going to shoot Ralph, too, if I hadn't stopped her."

"You have the right to remain silent. . . . " said Sheriff Dale, shouldering the rifle.

He didn't have a chance to finish the Miranda warning. A rifle shot echoed through the canyon, muted by the thick branches of the evergreens. A red stain burst on the front of the sheriff's uniform. He looked down at it, back at me, and fell to the ground on his face.

I jumped off Pancho and tore the rifle from his dead hands, then looked down the dirt road where the shot came from. There was another Mineral County Sheriff's Bronco, and Jerry Pitcher stood behind it, his rifle resting across the hood.

Agent Gallagher and his DEA team were with him, and we went straight to the Shallow Creek Ranch and arrested the remaining goons from Dana's bunch. As expected, Pratt was more than happy to give them up, and they came quietly, now that their leadership and protection were dead. The DEA also brought along a meth lab cleanup team, who went to work collecting evidence and sanitizing the toxic waste site that the lab created in the mountains.

After the DEA and everyone else were gone from the ranch, I stayed to talk with Pratt. We sat on his large deck on matching rocking chairs, each holding a bottle of Coors, smoking Camels from Dana's pack, and watching the setting sun paint the eastern mountains orange.

"Mr. Pratt, what are you going to do about your coliform problem?" I said, after gulping down half the beer and drawing heavily on the cigarette. I promised myself it would be the last one for a long time.

He looked at me, squinting. I must have been quite a sight, sitting there in my homemade ghillie suit, straps of burlap and sheriff's uniform dangling over the edge of the rocking chair.

"So that was you two nights ago over at Elk Hollow. You were trespassing, you know."

"Yup, I know," I said, squinting back. "What are you going to do about it, Mr. Pratt?"

"I'm going to clean it up and fix the problem before it gets out of hand and people start getting sick, just like Dr. Ed told me. What are you going to do about it, Sheriff Tatum?"

I didn't correct him. I'd been the sheriff for over a week already. I just didn't know it until now.

"I think I'll go fishing."

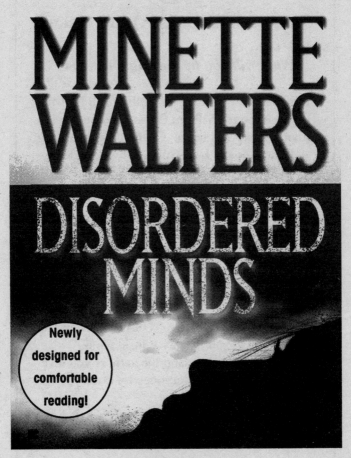

NEW YORK TIMES BESTSELLING
AUTHOR OF *FOX EVIL*

MINETTE WALTERS

DISORDERED MINDS

Newly
designed for
comfortable
reading!

0-425-19935-5